Startled, Cameron look

He was standing b
sunset. He'd changed i
and he looked more a
wore on Wall Street. H
earlier age, when men
managed to civilize his primal nature to accept the confines
of city life seemed to her a miracle – a triumph of the will
over the demands of the blood. At the sight of him, Cameron's whole body began to throb with a soft longing. She had
known this feeling only once before, and then she'd been
barely more than a child. Now that she was a woman, she
understood . . .

This was the man she'd been searching for in all those
other beds.

DAVIDYNE SAXON MAYLEAS

The Woman Who Had Everything

GRAFTON BOOKS

A Division of the Collins Publishing Group

LONDON GLASGOW
TORONTO SYDNEY AUCKLAND

Grafton Books
A Division of the Collins Publishing Group
8 Grafton Street, London W1X 3LA

A Grafton UK Paperback Original 1989

ISBN 0-586-20421-0

Printed and bound in Great Britain by
Collins, Glasgow

Set in Ehrhardt

To the 140 million Americans – myself included – who seek GOLCONDA, that legendary city in India of which it was said that anyone who passed through became rich. In America, GOLCONDA is known by another name – WALL STREET.

Prelude

Sunday was a hard day for someone like Adam Miller who was really only interested in 'killings'. Financial killings, that is. On Sunday, potential investors were with their families, or making love, or sleeping off Saturday night. On Sunday Adam Miller often had to postpone his efforts to sell shares in Olympus, which was a sports arena in Tampa, Florida; or in Hercules, a company that manufactured a salve which was guaranteed to prolong erections and which was wrapped in a plain brown paper carton. Or American Student Marketing, which had just been formed and as yet had no products. There was little for Adam to do on a typical Sunday except to play with his son, Byron Miller.

So, on Sunday, if the weather was good, Byron's father often took him to Central Park in Manhattan to feed the pigeons. While they tossed peanuts, Adam delivered his endless lecture on money, in firm, reverent tones. His entire life was dedicated to money. Years later, Byron realized that money gave his father his only satisfying insight into the meaning of life. It spoke of safety, of fulfilment, of joy. It gave Adam Miller a feeling of completeness.

There was much Byron chose to forget about his father but not the Sunday excursions to and from Central Park. On the way back to Brooklyn, they usually got off the subway at the Wall Street stop. There they passed through the heavy iron turnstile and trudged up the narrow, dirty steps of the IRT station to the street. They stood on the sidewalk, Byron's small hand clasped in his father's larger one, with their backs to Trinity Church – Trinity Church was not a place where money was made – and lingered for a moment to take in the view. It always gave them an overwhelming feeling of arrival as though this place were truly home. Walking through the silent, nearly deserted streets was a time of dreams for Byron. He listened, rapt, while Adam held forth on how fortunes had been made and lost in the stock market. When they stopped before the locked entrance to the New York Stock Exchange at 11 Wall Street, they smiled with both pleasure and amazement. This was really the place. Every time they saw it it was like the first time.

'Byron, behind those doors is the greatest gambling house in the world,' Adam Miller said. An old, wise child, Byron waited for his father to continue his standard litany. 'Believe me, there's more betting done in there than at every racetrack and casino in the world.' After a pause, he would declare, more to himself than Byron, 'Someday I'll get lucky and beat the odds.' Adam Miller's view of the stock market was hardly conventional wisdom. Looking back, Byron had concluded that it was one of the few astute perceptions his father ever had.

Then they would walk slowly back to the IRT station opposite Trinity Church, pause for a last look at the long shadows along Wall Street cast by the setting sun, and marvel at the golden glow on the windows of the buildings facing west. Reluctantly, they would retrace their steps down the narrow, dirty stairs to the subway and make the rest of the trip back to Brooklyn, where Sara Miller, Byron's mother, had dinner waiting. Sometimes Bryon wondered what his life might have been like if his father had been another kind of man. Would he have made all his millions? Would he have known Cameron Hightower?

PART ONE
The Street
1987

1

Wall Street, the short, narrow street in lower Manhattan running east from Broadway to the East River, is a place where stocks and bonds worth billions of dollars change hands daily. The neighbourhood is distinguished by glittering skyscrapers set back on handsome plazas and by other smaller office buildings, vintage 1920 or earlier. It is known to insiders as the Street. By and large, there is nothing exceptional about the look of the Street or the people who work on the Street. Nothing to suggest its concentration of wealth and power that make it the financial capital of the United States and therefore of the world. But the Street is more than a small geographic area. It is a state of mind. A dream street to the hundred million Americans who have a stake in a pension plan or a mutual fund which they count on to help them when they retire. It is the place where 'the public' – more than 47 million Americans who buy and sell stocks in their own name – express their hopes, fears, greed, and all too often their naïveté. It is this naïveté that is responsible for the Wall street axiom 'The public is always wrong.'

Herbert Coz watched the bulbs that make up the dot matrices of the four huge digital clocks overlooking the main trading floor of the New York Stock Exchange. The numbers changed: 3:59 became 4:00. A bell sounded. The trading day was over. Within a single heartbeat, everyone on the floor turned to look at their video screens. The words they were waiting for appeared. THE DOW JONES 30 INDUSTRIAL AVERAGE CLOSING PRICE – 2405. The Dow had closed over 2,400;

11

a Himalayan peak! April 6, 1987, was an historic day on the New York Stock Exchange.

The response was electrifying. Streamers of ticker tape were hurled across the floor. Flights of paper aeroplanes arched through the air. A few enterprising floor traders had stored rolls of toilet paper just for the occasion. They now threw them towards the ceiling. As they sailed skyward they unrolled, leaving ghostlike trails in their wake. Bald men with swollen stomachs threatening to burst their trading jackets capered about, each dancing to his own personal rhythm, slapping one another on the back, congratulating everyone in sight. No distinctions were made. Senior partners in charge of floor trading shook hands with page boys. Or girls. Specialists kissed one another like French diplomats. Five floor traders did a commendable buck-and-wing. A page girl stood on her hands. Somewhere, someone played a bugle. Someone else pounded a drum. Suddenly, a second cheer, as loud as the first, echoed through the high-ceilinged room. New words and numbers had appeared on the trading-post screens. NUMBER OF SHARES TRADED – 302,469,000. A second flurry of ticker tape, more toilet paper, and another round of paper planes were launched. The applause and stamping grew louder. Bravo for 300 million!

Long before the celebration had even started to wind down, word flashed around the world. Television and radio financial writers were churning out copy to be read by local network anchormen. It had been a memorable day on the Street. For the first time since 1792 – the year twenty-four merchants and brokers set up their first trading booth under an elm tree at 68 Wall Street – the Dow Jones Industrial Average had closed at over two thousand. And there was another first. More than 300 million shares traded. Computer-programmed buying triggered massive purchases of stock by the funds. The excitable public, galvanized into action by the morning surge in the Dow, then went on a wild buying spree in the afternoon. They were buying for their future. For their children's future. Their grandchildren's. The public cherished the myth of investment. Insiders like Herbert Coz did not. To Coz the stock market was the oldest permanent crap game in the world. Like any professional gambler, he counted his profits minute by minute: and when the market turned against him, he cut his losses and ran.

Coz was standing alone amid the riot that swirled around him, quietly clapping his hands, when he was joined by another floor trader. Both men were unknown to TV and radio commentators. They would never be mentioned in news reports. The public would never know they existed. But exist they certainly did; and in the world of Wall Street, each was a force to be reckoned with. The impact of their meeting could be awesome.

'Big day, Coz,' Tom Ucciarde commented in a carefully neutral voice. They'd been standing side by side for several minutes, and this was his first remark. Herbert Coz did not appear to hear it, but his silence was not offensive. He was known to be a quiet man. Besides, there is a comradeship between men who have had a hand in making history and are now contemplating the results of their actions. Tom Ucciarde was a big man – taller than Coz by a head – and had the confident gentleness of a big man. His face was heavy, with a fleshy nose and slightly sagging jowls. His dark hair was slicked back to cover a growing bald spot. Despite the surgeon general's warnings, he remained a heavy smoker. One could only wonder what the cost of maintaining a tightly controlled voice and careful movements was to this natural type A. His voice always sounded like a breathy whisper coming from somewhere deep in his chest. 'A very big day,' he repeated pleasantly.

'Yes,' Herbert Coz agreed. He was a little hobgoblin of a man with thick, light eyebrows, a deeply lined face, and flicked-up horns of sandy hair mixed with grey that seemed to want to fly off his head and made his ears appear pointed. 'A lot of action.' He glanced at Ucciarde and then away.

'Six to seven billion dollars' worth of action.'

'Yes,' Coz agreed again. He had placed himself strategically where he was confident the big man would find him; having been found, he intended to cooperate fully. 'Could be a new platform for the bull market.'

Ucciarde gazed down at the small man, his head cocked to one side, and for an instant he appeared to be a child studying an insect under a microscope. 'My theory exactly.' He smiled, trying to indicate that he shared Coz's conclusions. 'Of course, if someone assassinates the President? Or IBM goes belly-up?'

Coz had his answer ready. 'I wouldn't place any bets on the President. But IBM?' He shook his head. 'Nothing to worry about at IBM.' He fussed with the knot of his tie while Ucciarde watched. 'Could be another three-hundred-million-share day tomorrow. Full steam ahead.'

'Then why were you selling?'

'Getting rid of the dogs. Low beta stocks.' Coz sighed. 'The market goes through the roof, and those stocks move up a snappy eighth. They act like they're frozen.'

Ucciarde gave Coz a funny look. Coz was not a man ever to own a low beta stock. Who was he kidding? 'So you were dumping the low betas?'

'Yeah. This is a market to rake in the chips on the high betas.'

'My kind of stocks, too. High betas. Like a great woman. Responsive. Goes along with a man's mood. Never keeps you waiting.'

'Right. When the market flies, they fly higher.'

'So it's full steam ahead with the high betas. Of course, if bad news breaks, high betas can kill you. High beta stocks are the first to drop through the floor.'

'What bad news? The sun will rise in the east.' Coz's voice

14

came as close as it ever did to sounding cheerful. He enjoyed the disbelief in Ucciarde's eyes.

'No recommendations from your analysts to eliminate certain holdings? Unforeseen new development, as they like to say.'

Just the low beta stocks. You worry too much. God's in his heaven and looking out for us.'

Ucciarde ducked his head to hide his dismay. Coz was such a poor liar. Too fast when he had no ready answer. Too positive when he had one prepared. And that crap about dumping low beta stocks. What low betas?

'Well, you know the old saying,' Ucciarde muttered. 'Buy on Rosh Hashanah. Sell on Yom Kippur. But it's not Yom Kippur.'

'No, it isn't,' Coz agreed with absolute confidence. Then he had nothing more to say. He knew his signal had been picked up. 'Guess it's time to rest my oars.'

'Guess so.' Ucciarde drew in a breath to say good night, but Coz was gone. Tom Ucciarde had never seen a man who could disappear so fast in a crowd.

On his way to his office, Herbert Coz thought about his sister, Doris. He always thought about Doris after he'd pulled off one of his bigger stock manipulations. When her husband died and left Doris with a small portfolio of stocks, Coz had begged her to let him manage it for her. But Doris was adamant. Her husband, Harold, had been a psychotherapist – a college man – and always used a particular broker, Eric Hefflin, who had gone to college with him. Doris didn't hesitate to point out that Coz had never gone to college. How could he know more than Eric Hefflin? Hefflin read detailed reports on the market. He told Doris about giant computers wired to CRTs and high-speed printers which produced, at breathtaking speed, research reports on every listed stock. These reports were prepared by sophisticated analysts, then reinterpreted by the knowledgeable Hefflin, who gave Doris his expert opinions on what to buy and when to buy or sell. How could Coz argue with statistics, tables, fundamentals? Coz was only a floor trader. An 'executor,' as they called him. He just executed orders. What did he know?

What the hell do brokers know? Coz asked himself. Or stock analysts, for that matter? Half the time what little the analysts did know they couldn't say. It depended on how the brokerage house they worked for felt about a particular corporation. If the house was pushing Horse Manure, Inc., the analysts were bullish on Horse Manure, Inc. If not, they weren't. To Coz, the only truth was on the tape. And the TV screens. How a stock actually performed from minute to minute. The upticks. Downticks. And more important, who was buying and who was selling. For an instant he was tempted to call Doris and tell her that if she'd bought any stock today, she should not sell. No matter what Hefflin said. Not even if the bottom dropped out of the Dow. The market would come back by the close. But he knew it was useless. She wouldn't listen to him. Doris was lucky if she made 8 per cent on her money, including dividends. That figured. Eight per cent was for widows and orphans. Like Doris. Making eight times your money – 800 per cent – was for professionals. Like his boss. Cameron Hightower.

The windows of Cameron Hightower's office on the Street overlooked Brooklyn to the east, the Statue of Liberty in New York Harbor to the south, and west across the Hudson River to the Watchung Mountain range. The office did not conform to traditional standards; it was a mix of contemporary and antique furniture and lacked the variety of electronic devices often found in Wall Street offices. The office had a strong personal flair that impressed corporate clients, men who regarded the freedom to express one's personality in one's office furniture as a sign of status and power. The huge twin sofas were covered in shades of casual brown tweed and were complemented by modern Italian easy chairs with brown leather cushions and chrome frames. The floor was covered by a large Oriental rug. One wall had floor-to-ceiling cantil-evered shelves which were filled with leather-bound books and small art objects. The only concession to the Street was an IBM personal computer with a nineteen-inch monitor which was programmed to give Cameron Hightower neces-sary stock market information. Her desk was eighteenth-century English, a huge piece of mahogany furniture covered on top with green leather that had originally been designed as a partner's desk.

When Herbert Coz entered the office, Cameron High-tower was seated at the desk poring over computer printouts covering the trading Coz had done that day. She looked up and said, 'Very neat, Herbert.' As the managing partner of FitzGerald Associates, she also personally managed the trad-ing desk.

'Thank you,' Coz said.

'You played it perfectly from start to finish.' Her woman's instinct told her, as it always did with Herbert Coz, that she was feeding a passion in him; not love but an urgent, deep-rooted need to have her appreciate the fact that he could outfox the other pros. 'I see we netted just over four hundred fifty thousand dollars for the firm and our discretionary accounts.'

Smiling played very little part in Herbert Coz's repertoire of expressions, but now he smiled. 'It went like clockwork. I passed Tom Ucciarde the word that we were buying, but he didn't believe me. He's convinced we have some inside information that there will be bad news tomorrow.'

'He thinks we know something he doesn't.'

'He certainly does. Why else was I selling?'

Cameron was pleased. 'He took the bait. He's even more jittery than I'd hoped. What else did you say?'

17

Coz sounded thoroughly virtuous as he described how he had told Tom not to worry. 'God's in his heaven and so forth. All the truth.'

'But since he doesn't believe either in you or God or heaven, he should try to sell fast into the opening market rise.'

For an instant, the naturally flat eyes of Coz seemed to glitter with mischief. 'Before the bad news breaks. Bad news that I know and he doesn't.'

'Does anyone else know you were selling?'

'Sure. But Ucciarde's the linchpin. He's the floor trader for Mason, Adams, and Fenwick. And as John Mason goes, so goes the Street. When he starts dumping, the lemmings on the floor will follow. All those boys ever do is play follow the leader.'

'It's almost funny,' Cameron said without laughing. 'They sell because they think he knows something they don't. And he's selling because he thinks we know something he doesn't. And the reality is that nobody knows anything because there's nothing to know.' She paused for a moment. 'This should start a first-class market sell-off early tomorrow. The snowball effect.'

'The snowball could become an avalanche.'

'An avalanche they made themselves.' Cameron shook her head as though momentarily engrossed in some inner conflict. After that her words were swift and precise. 'The market is one big old-fashioned party line connected to hundreds of major institutional traders. They're supposed to be the pros. The pension and mutual fund managers, foundations, insurance companies, and so forth. The insiders who trade in hundreds of thousands of shares, the block traders. They can whipsaw a market anytime they bolt, either to buy or to sell.'

'That isn't the way most people see the Street.'

'I know. The public still lives in bygone days when one bought a stock on the so-called intrinsic value of the stock, the price at book value. But those days are gone. It isn't the way the market works anymore.' She said this with something akin to genuine regret.

'I like the way it is,' Coz said.

Cameron neither liked it nor disliked it. There was no sense being sentimental. Her aim had always been to make money for the firm and for the firm's clients. What was different was the method. 'That's why we play the games we play. The pros listen to one another's rumours, tips, heart-beats, burps. At the same time, they try to outguess each other. They try to get a jump on good or bad news. To get in on the ground floor of a hot issue. To get the inside dope never found in an analyst's report.' She smiled and shook her head. 'Their greed for inside information is insatiable. They're paranoid about what they might not know. That's why occasionally we can spook them, stampede them like cattle and make our own market.'

'I do my best,' Coz responded.

'And you do it very well.'

Coz silently agreed that he must be doing something right. Each month when he totalled his net worth – his stock holdings, bank statements, and IRA – he was always amazed that he was worth several million dollars and that his net worth was growing. Doris had no idea of this, and he certainly had no intention of telling her. Not with her Mr Hefflin and his college education handling her stocks.

'Anyway,' Cameron continued, 'the old order passes and, like it or not, I'm the new.' She looked at her printouts. 'The selling should dry up by noon – when there's no bad news. Then the pension and trust money that jumped off the wagon will climb right back on again. With megabucks flying.' The idea tickled her sense of the absurd. 'They'll have decided that the market is sound after all. They guessed wrong. And no bad news will be translated into good news.'

'The Dow Jones average could hit a new high. And if the public hangs in through the morning . . .'

'For once the public will be right.'

'And we'll have mousetrapped them all.'

'Yes.' Cameron gave Coz a questioning look. 'Which reminds me, how short are we?'

Coz had been waiting for that question. He respected Cameron as he did no other woman, and again she'd proven worthy of his trust. Her strategies were sound, her instincts accurate, and her nerves as good as his. She hadn't tried to duck at the last moment on selling short. Selling a market short was a dangerous game; one of the most dangerous games in the stock market. 'We're short a total of two hundred forty-eight thousand shares in six stocks, as per your instructions. With the selling I think we triggered, the Dow should drop about forty points, dragging the rest of the market with it.'

'We'll start covering our shorts one hour after the market opens and ride it all the way down.'

'Right!' Coz's eyes never left Cameron. 'We'll be liquid before noon and back in before the market starts to turn.'

They both knew the risk they'd taken. If the market didn't crack, under other circumstances, they might not buy back in. Or they might, at even higher prices. But once they sold short – sold stock they didn't own – they had no choice; they had to buy back in. If the market didn't break, they could lose millions scrambling to cover their shorts. They were both familiar with the old Wall Street doggerel: 'He who sells what isn't his'n. Buys it back or goes to pris'n.'

'Oh, Coz! It's a beautiful triple play. We made it on the way up. Tomorrow we'll make it on the way down. And tomorrow afternoon, on the way up again.'

'That's the plan, all right.' Coz's voice was flat. He'd seen big men crack under the strain of just this kind of triple play. But Cameron Hightower wasn't one to crack. Though she

20

was young enough to be his daughter, he was certain she was not one to break down. But he was wise enough to suspect a deeper truth. Once she'd been so afraid that almost all fear had been burned out of her.

'Something could stop Ucciarde from selling.' Even that possibility failed to alter the delight in Cameron's voice.

'You mean something like John Mason? That's true. Tom won't sell a hundred shares without Mason's okay.'

'I know. I'm counting on Mason. He'll go to ground.'

Coz had seen this happen. The pressure of tens of millions of dollars gyrating back and forth sometimes made even a major broker and investment banker like John Mason take cover. 'I think so,' he said finally, more to reassure himself than Cameron. He started to leave, paused and asked, 'You're seeing Mason tomorrow morning about that Byron Miller thing?' For an instant Coz studied the floor. 'That's a big deal, isn't it?'

'It's big enough.' Cameron said it without any flourish, wanting Coz to feel that nothing was more important than his performance on the floor of the Stock Exchange today.

A more thick-skinned man would have settled for that. But Coz knew there were worlds he didn't really understand. His face clouded fleetingly, then he shrugged. He understood his world where he was the consummate insider, and that was enough. He was through the door and out of sight in a blink.

Cameron stared at the empty air that had been filled with Herbert Coz's presence. Despite what she said, today was not yet a triumph. She was well aware of the risk she had taken. But risk was one of the truths she lived with daily; it went with the territory. What she had avoided saying to Coz was that in the final analysis, the meeting tomorrow with John Mason could make more money for both firms than Coz's best week of trading.

She opened the centre drawer of her desk and took out the signed letter of intent from Mason, Adams, and Fenwick.

This was a big fish; fifty million dollars' worth of fish, and the letter was only the beginning. Cameron clasped her hands together, resting them on her desk – a characteristic gesture when she was weighing many possibilities.

She knew Jake Stern would call tonight and tell her how the Thermoscan clinical tests had checked out. He'd left town five days ago convinced he'd find proof that Byron Miller had tried to pull something with the tests. 'That kid's a fast-talking, cheap con man on the make,' Jake had said. Cameron winced, remembering how they'd argued over Byron. Some very strong language had been exchanged. They'd finally agreed that since a final 'due diligence' investigation had to be done, Jake should be the one to do it. And he was doing it with a vengeance. Instead of writing or telephoning the doctors, he'd insisted on visiting the hospitals all around the country where the clinical tests were being conducted. And talking to the doctors personally. Reluctantly, he'd agreed that Cameron could go forward with the underwriting while he conducted his investigation; and nothing need be said to John Mason. Cameron refused to raise doubts that she was convinced had no basis in fact.

For the past week she had been living on the surface of every day, postponing or burying all thoughts as to what might result from Jake's investigation. Now her time of waiting was coming to an end. She glanced at the clock on her desk and then out the window at the red glow in the western sky. Beyond the red of the setting sun she would see a gathering of grey. They were thin, high streamers of cirrostratus clouds. She remembered her father's warning. During the night those clouds would thicken and drop, forecasting the rain to come. The unseasonably warm March weather would change by tomorrow morning.

The coming storm made her think of Tim. Her life with Tim FitzGerald had been like living on a huge ocean-going yacht. A boat able to meet the fiercest storm head-on and fight its way through the roughest water with minimum anxiety for those on board. Being on her own was another thing entirely. That was like living on a slim, graceful, thirty-metre sloop that was quick to the helm and could tack close to the wind. But it wasn't safe and it wasn't comfortable. The only way to describe it was thrilling. Cameron learned again something she'd known as a child – what it meant to be a 'wet-assed sailor'.

2

The telephone by Cameron's bed rang the next morning at five forty-five, fifteen minutes before the alarm was set to go off. Immediately wide awake, she had the impression she hadn't slept at all. The last time she remembered looking at the sky through her lacy bedroom curtains, it had been pitch-black outside. Now it was dawn. The clouds were dark and heavy, and the wind was driving the rain sideways across the window. She picked up the phone and said, 'Hello, Jake. Where are you?'

'At Kennedy. I've just spent seven days living on aeroplane food. And sleeping in uncomfortable beds. It's lucky I don't need much sleep and have a cast-iron stomach.'

'You have true grit.' She refused to let his irritation reach her. 'Why didn't you call last night before you got on the plane?'

'I was busy with a nurse before I caught the plane. Calling you from her bed seemed in poor taste.'

'But you're a happily married man, Jake.'

'This was pure business.'

'I'll tell that to Mrs Stern.'

'With partners like you, who needs enemies?'

'What happened, Jake?'

'You want lies or the truth?'

'The truth, damn it!'

'You're right. Byron Miller does enough lying for every-body.' He was suddenly angry. 'Did you think for one nano-second that I'd trust anything a doctor told me? With that promoter on the prowl?' His voice became slightly louder, as if he'd lost his hold on it. 'Your dear Byron, the clown you've been trying to housebreak for Wall Street, was in LA last week. Did you know that?'

'Of course.' Cameron could remember a time when Jake's description of Byron would have been a lot more colourful. And more obscene.

'Didn't it occur to you that that operator might have pulled a few stunts? Like offering the doctors money or stock options?' The anger left his voice. 'But nurses are harder to buy. I went to six hospitals and talked to six doctors publicly. And to six nurses privately. Fortunately two of the nurses were over sixty and more interested in booze than in me. But I take my work seriously. When I undertake a due diligence, I am truly diligent. I turn over every rock. If, here and there, I find a nurse under a rock – ?'

'I'm about to scream. What's the bottom line?'

'I hope you can stand it.' Jake's voice became carefully neutral. 'Anyway, I'm now satisfied I know everything that's going on.'

There was a full five-second pause while Cameron waited for him to continue. Finally, struggling to keep her voice calm, she asked, 'And exactly what is going on with the clinicals? What did you find out?'

'Enough to convince me. You'll thank me before this is over. But what kind of a partner are you, anyway? Are you worried about my exhausted body, my cramped legs from taking the red-eye from LA? Are you? No! All you're worrying about are your precious clinicals.'

'I'm not worried. I just want to know. Jake, I have a meeting with John Mason at nine-thirty. Sharp!'

'Is that a fact?'

'You know damn well it's a fact.' Cameron had had enough, and her voice became icy. 'Jake Stern, what are the results of the clinicals? I can do without the comedy routine.'

'All in good time. I have to go home. Take a shower. Change into some decent clothes. Have my usual breakfast of two poached eggs with bacon and toast. After that I'll go to the office.'

'Jake! I must know about the clinicals before my meeting.'

'You'll know when I see you. Ciao, partner.'

Cameron fell back on the bed and stared at the dead receiver. If Jake weren't Jake, she'd kill him. He could make her so mad. Then she replaced the receiver and began to laugh half hysterically. Of course! How stupid could she be? The reports he got must have been sensational; even better than Byron had claimed. Or Jake wouldn't have tried to irritate her with all that kidding around. It was his way of not having to admit he'd been wrong. It seemed she'd known Jake Stern almost forever; a very shrewd man who liked to keep his thoughts concealed behind wisecracks and obscenities.

The ringing of her alarm clock brought her back to the here and now. She shut it off and slid out of bed. If she dressed in a hurry, she'd be ready and waiting at the office when Jake showed up. He'd better show up. Mason would insist on a complete report about the clinicals before closing.

Standing naked on the thickly carpeted floor, she glanced around her shamelessly romantic, feminine bedroom. Given that her workday was full of investment decisions, financial reports, underwriting prospectuses, and a seemingly endless stream of numbers, she had wanted her bedroom to express the other side of her nature. So her bed was a copy of a fifteenth-century oak-frame four-poster, frothily draped and canopied with a delicate white-on-white silk print. Ivory silk upholstered walls and Regency-styled valanced drapes continued the mood of feminine seductiveness. On either side antique tile-topped nineteenth-century French tables that held an assortment of Fabergé animals, as well as a Fabergé cigarette box and more practical items such as a pencil case, a scribbling block for predawn jottings, the telephone, and a radio-alarm clock. Silk scatter cushions in a bright floral pattern were tossed on a chaise longue that was covered with an ivory silk that matched the walls. Two vivid Gauguin paintings hung on the wall facing her bed, adding to the sensuous mood. Lamps were scattered here and there, but for reading in bed, there were several baby spotlights that her decorator had hidden in the canopy over the bed. Finally, a life-size fibreglass statue of a nude young woman, posed for by Cameron, stood near the bed. It was especially seductive when silhouetted by moonlight.

Unconsciously caressing her breasts, Cameron decided that the bedroom was too feminine to make a man feel comfortable. When the right time came, she would make some changes. She glanced at the clock. If she was going to be in the office before Jake, she had to hurry. She crossed the room to what looked like a closet door. The door led to a small room that was a combination clothes closet and dressing room. One wall was lined with sliding mirrored doors. Behind the doors were racks of clothes for day and evening wear, as well as riding habits, tennis and golf dresses, ski wear, bathing suits and rough-weather sailing gear. Fine couturiers and smart boutiques in Paris, Rome, London, and New York had contributed their expert designs and workmanship to the collection.

Cameron glanced wistfully at the door, thinking about herself, about her past, about the years when she used to stand and stare at things she could not afford to buy. With her first pay cheque, she had bought a dress at Henri Bendel's that all these years later, though out of fashion, still hung at the far end of her closet. It was the first dress she owned that she paid for with her own money, and it cost a great deal more than she could afford. But it was worth every penny to her. It stood for her ability to survive against relentless odds and marked her independence in a world that had once almost forgotten that she existed. She remembered how she had combed the stores for just the right dress. And after she had found the dress there came the high drama of shopping for the right shoes, and debating the pros and cons of adding a scarf, of risking more dollars on a bottle of Mitsouko, once her favourite perfume.

Today she had a wardrobe full of clothes, clothes that were as well organized as a balance sheet. In recent years, stifling regret, she'd permitted herself none of the natural female fun of shopping, of selecting a dress, a suit, an ensemble. Instead she employed a lady who shopped for women like herself, women with high-pressure jobs and little time to spare. The shopper had Cameron's sizes neatly listed and catalogued, along with her most becoming colours. She knew which designers had Cameron's kind of body in mind when they prepared their line. Cameron and her shopper had quarterly meetings prior to the start of each new season. Then Cameron cleared her closets of the also-rans, and the women settled down to discuss what was needed to fill the gaps.

In due time boxes of clothes would arrive at the apartment, and Cameron would indulge herself by taking an entire Saturday to make the final choices. An appointment was then made for her fitter to come, to pin and repin every seam of every garment so that each selection hung with perfection. It was after these rituals that Cameron would sit on the terrace, sipping a martini, and sometimes think of her clothes as a disguise. She would occasionally yearn to experience what it would be like to devote a day to shopping. But now that she had the money to spend, she no longer had the time. Everything had its price, especially success on the Street. And the price was time.

She opened the closet, flipped through dozens of weekday possibilities and found the grey wool double-breasted coat dress designed by Ralph Lauren that she intended to wear. She took it out and hung it on a short rod which was used to hold whatever garment she chose for the day. The rod was next to a three-sided cheval miror such as one usually finds in a dressmaker's shop, so Cameron could stand between the wings of the mirror and see herself from all sides.

The far wall consisted of a series of Lucite shelves especially designed to hold shoes, riding boots, ski boots, and still more boots. Quickly, she chose a pair of gunmetal leather pumps that she would take with her to the office, and black rain boots to wear to and from the car.

Cameron moved to the other half of the wall, which was devoted to accessories and contained drawers for her lingerie, panty hose, stockings, and socks. She selected her lingerie and then opened the unlocked velvet-lined drawer that contained her jewellery. The only truly valuable items in the jewellery drawer were an enamelled emerald pendant and a star sapphire ring Tim had given her. She'd always made a point of not accepting many expensive gifts from Tim. Someday she might treat herself to an expensive bracelet. The firm was doing well; and when it was further down the road, she'd feel she could afford it. Although her income was now sizable, it had not been easy, building the business from the ground up again. Paying $200,000 for a bracelet was not her idea of a reasonable purchase for anyone who was not a millionaire many times over. Today she chose the star sapphire for the little finger of her left hand and added a heavy silver chain with a hand of Fatima dangling from it, and her usual liquid crystal chronometer with its black metal case and black leather band.

Her selection of clothing and jewellery completed, Cameron showered, then dressed quickly. Ready to leave, Cameron hurried to the kitchen. She had to deliver the menu for tonight's dinner to Alda, her cook.

'Hmm,' was Alda's comment as she studied the menu. 'Caviar. Oysters.' She placed the menu on the kitchen counter and raised her round blue eyes to stare at Cameron. 'Do you know the last time Mr Miller was here he ate a whole tin of beluga caviar? That was three hundred dollars, and I don't think he even likes caviar!'

Cameron had heard all this before. 'I'll try to be home by six-thirty,' she said. 'The guests will arrive about seven-thirty. You work out the appropriate hors d'oeuvres. Ice three bottles of champagne. Dom Pérignon, 1969. For dinner the wine will be Nuits-St-Georges, 1971. We'll dine by candlelight. Have Andrew place fresh candles in the chandelier and use the candelabras from the service. Also the Egrement crest silver.'

Alda watched her disappear through the double swinging doors that led to the dining room. Andrew and she had been with Mr FitzGerald for almost fifteen years before they began to work for Miss Hightower. She was a congenial employer. Besides the weekly $600 pay cheque, plus free room and board, working for Miss Hightower gave them considerable freedom. These days, she only had to prepare breakfast, occasional lunches, and sometimes dinner for Miss High-tower and her guests.

Once in the foyer, Cameron dropped her briefcase on a side chair and took her mink-lined raincoat from the hall closet. She tried not to think of Jake and the clinicals. Why the hell hadn't he told her the results? She tossed her raincoat over her shoulders like a cape and paused on her way out to glance at the Modigliani nude hanging next to the door. She did that every morning for luck. When Tim had bought the painting for her, he'd insisted it reminded him of her. Looking at it, Cameron thought that it took a man in love to see a resemblance. The only similarity was the elongated legs and torso and the black hair. Cameron's face was neither mystic nor poetic. She had an androgynous look. Her features were almost boyish in their clean precision, softened only by her slightly too wide, sensuous mouth and distinctly female figure.

Tim! How she still missed him! She supposed that no

matter what happened in the future, she always would. She wished they could have married, but she never regretted a minute of it. Tim would have been in complete agreement with today's business. A small company was about to be given a big helping hand, and some day it wouldn't be small. Tim felt that this was what America was all about. It was the Street at its best – and the best was for FitzGerald Associates to make money.

Standing under the canopy just outside her apartment at 975 Fifth Avenue, she glanced up the block. It was pouring with rain. But this was not the warm, tropical rain she had always loved. This was a semi-sleet that whipped round the corners of buildings and threatened to strip the trees in Central Park of their first buds. The doorman was helping a man into a cab. He'd be back in a moment to escort her to her car, a Mercedes 300 cabriolet that Tim had bought in 1956. He'd explained to Cameron that the cabriolet was a hybrid; a touring car crossed with a sports car. It was one of the Mercedes Company's few postwar mistakes. Though Tim FitzGerald had had a Bentley for daily use as well as formal occasions like Monday night at the opera, an Aston Martin for tootling around, and a Ford station wagon for country visits, the cabriolet had been his favourite. Instead of taxis, Cameron used it on special days, and this was one of those days.

When the doorman returned for Cameron, Andrew slid out of his seat behind the wheel to hold the door open for her. Andrew was a short, powerful man with a red face, brown hair sprinkled with grey, and a stomach that was beginning to bulge. Still agile with his hands and body, he made an excellent combination chauffeur, butler, houseman, and – on nights when Cameron needed to walk to clear her head – bodyguard. Standing at attention by the car, he felt a glow of pride as his employer approached. Andrew was a

31

natural vassal; Tim had been his liege lord and Cameron his lady. Now he was as loyal to Cameron as he had been to Tim. He was proud to be in her service. It was not simply her beauty, her breeding, her wealth that inspired his admiration. Andrew had worked for other such women, and none of this conveyed Cameron's rare quality. What made Cameron Hightower unique in Andrew's eyes was that she was treated as an equal by Wall Street professionals. He'd listened to their respectful talk at the dinners he'd served. Grey-haired men exchanging opinions with a child. This beautiful, tomboyish, black-haired young woman with her fresh face and easy smile – this child who was not yet a mother – had taken over FitzGerald Associates. This fact belied Andrew's sense of the natural order of things and made Cameron unique.

'Good morning, Miss Hightower,' he said as she was about to step into the car.

'Good morning, Andrew. Head for the FDR Drive, and let's make a run for it.' She entered the car and burst out laughing. 'I should have known. Oh, Andrew! What kind of a bodyguard are you?'

Andrew shifted uncomfortably from one foot to the other. 'He said you expected him. That you were giving him a lift to the office, ma'am.'

'I suppose I am.' Cameron leaned back in the seat and glared at the rumpled, poker-faced man sitting in the car. 'Jake! The clinicals!'

'Here.' He handed her a large manila envelope stuffed with papers. 'The clinicals are fine.'

'You louse!' She grinned and pecked him on a chubby cheek. 'I told you they would be.'

'I'm cautious. But Byron is clean.' The small, stocky man slumped down in the seat. 'The only thing that worries me now is Elmer Hansen.'

Cameron was silent for a long moment thinking about the

past and how the name Hansen had affected her life. 'Why? The Hansen Company has a fine reputation.'

'Yeah.'

'Then why are you worried?'

Jake's eyes were unreadable behind his thick bifocal glasses. 'I guess I like lying awake nights.'

'Were you aware that the photographic process on which the Eastman Kodak Company was founded was invented by two musicians in a barn?' John Mason asked. He was an average-size man whose once sharp features were blurred by an overlay of flesh, the result of too many gourmet meals and too many bottles of vintage wine. His hair, now snow-white and carefully parted in the middle, was as thick and low on his forehead as when he had been a teenager. His stocky, large-boned body was still full of natural strength that enabled him to withstand the stress his decades of work as an investment banker demanded.

'I've heard the story,' Cameron answered.

'It's always amazed me. The billions that one invention led to.'

They were seated in Cameron's office. John Mason had permitted himself the gallantry of agreeing to meet there rather than have Cameron meet him at his office because Life Sciences was Cameron's find. As managing partner of Mason, Adams, and Fenwick, he considered himself the heavyweight on the team and could have insisted on meeting in his own office. In fact, he could have chosen any meeting place. Even Trinity Church would have been a reasonable choice from John Mason's viewpoint. After all, wasn't God on the side of those with the biggest bank accounts?

While watching Mason, Cameron found herself glancing at the wall to her left where pictures of Tim FitzGerald and of Tim and her were framed and hung with care. Tim had taught her so much. Mason followed her eyes and thought about money. The multimillions Tim had made as one of the few first-class Wall Street investment bankers who would risk underwriting small companies with unproven products. He said, 'Tim would have backed the toothpick if it could have been patented.'

Cameron laughed. 'Or the safety pin.'

'What an instinct he had.'

'Yes, he did.' She said it with pride. 'Tim backed Halloid when it was selling for fifty cents a share.'

'Did he? I didn't know that.' Mason did some fast mental arithmetic. 'I'd estimate he made one hundred times his money.' His smile had a coating of envy. 'At the very least.'

'He did quite well.'

'I had the same opportunity, but I was gun-shy. It was a hard lesson.' He shrugged in his custom-made, dark grey suit with handmade buttonholes in the sleeves. He shot his cuffs and two large gold cufflinks in the shape of bulls appeared. 'I just didn't believe in it. Too many big companies had turned down the idea of a dry office copy machine. How long did he hold the stock?'

Cameron picked up a cheap red metal ashtray from her desk. Written on it in white letters was the word 'Halloid'. She showed it to Mason. 'I never use it for cigarettes. It's a keepsake.' She paused. 'Let's see. He held the stock until it became Halloid Xerox. Then Xerox. It kept going up and splitting and going up again. I believe he finally sold it in 1968 at about $132 a share.'

Mason made a sour face and laughed. 'I up my estimate. He made about one thousand times his investment.'

'You're closer.'

John Mason had been rich for a long time, not rich the way Tim had been rich, but rich enough; and he still regretted every opportunity he'd missed out on. Under the custom-made shirt and suit there still beat the heart of that brash, young trader from Omaha who had landed on the Street in the late thirties and then clawed, climbed, and married his way up. Now he wondered where Byron was. 'I have high hopes for our Mr Miller. And for his company, Life Sciences, and his remarkable home tumour test.'

'I'm as enthusiastic as you are,' Cameron said. 'And we have good reason. Not only is the potential market for the product enormous, but think of the good it will do.'

'Oh, I do. I do all the time,' Mason answered. 'And with the Hansen Company contract, it will get national distribution.' But Cameron understood that he was really thinking about the huge fees his firm would make from the underwriting and the millions he expected to earn later from the stock they would receive at only ten cents a share. That was where the real money would be made. When that 10-cent stock rose to $85 a share in the public market, you stopped counting the money.

Cameron thought of Byron. It troubled her that he was not all of a piece, but a peculiar mix of the bogus and the genial. He was unorthodox and charming. His mind could make dazzling leaps, but he was frequently outrageously childish. While she'd listened to his heroic dreams and often believed them, in her moments of objectivity every instinct told her that although the clinical tests had turned out to be everything Byron had claimed for them, Jake wasn't totally wrong. Byron must be carefully watched. He refused to take his time, and in his rush he sometimes blurred the line between truth and deception. Perhaps it was this very lack of scruples that gave him an intuitive grasp of how to deal with the professionals in the stock market. How to play off their greed against their sound judgement. Witness John Mason talking about Life Sciences in the same breath as Xerox. Byron had convinced him.

Mason interrupted her musing. 'There are money managers all over the Street sitting on their chequebooks. This could be another International Tabulator – which became IBM.'

Dreams of glory again, Cameron thought. Make no small plans. 'That was probably the greatest growth stock of them all,' she said.

'I did have that one, you know. Tim had it, too.'

'Tim never sold IBM.'

'Sometimes I wonder what Tim didn't have.'

Cameron looked away. There was too much in her face. Then she said, with a straightforwardness that was like admitting defeat, 'He had a lot.' She might have added, everything except time.

'Where do you suppose our young genius is?' Mason asked.

'Right here.' Byron Miller sauntered through the door with his arm around Cameron's secretary.

'I couldn't stop him, Miss Hightower. You know how he is,' Della said resignedly. 'He never waits to be announced.'

'I know exactly how he is.' Cameron smiled at Byron. 'Glad you could make it.'

'Make it!' Byron was properly indignant. 'In my mind this ranks second only to the launching of the first man in space.' He glanced at Cameron's desk. 'Where are the letters? I was up all night thinking about my signature. It's really a scrawl. Very difficult to forge.'

He grinned, his impish eyebrows went straight up, and his face suddenly became handsome and absurdly young. He seemed to Cameron the same teenager she'd first met years ago. If you were up all night, she thought, it wasn't because you were thinking about your signature. She pushed three copies each of two letters of intent towards him. One was from FitzGerald Associates, the other from Mason, Adams, and Fenwick. Byron took his horn-rimmed glasses from his jacket pocket and scanned the documents. That he was a natural speed reader had little to do with the few seconds it took him to read both letters. He'd seen many similar before.

Except for the specific terms when it came to the numbers – the money to be raised, for what share of the company, the time by which the money had to be raised, and the fees, both in cash and stock, the brokerage houses were to be paid – the letters were boilerplate.

Byron looked up and grinned at Cameron, then at Mason. 'Do you know this is a historic moment?'

'I agree,' Mason remarked, preening himself. 'Letters of intent from two firms like ours are important. I'm glad you appreciate their value.'

'I do, John. I truly do. And I'm grateful for the trust you put in me. In fact, I regard it as a kind of posting of the financial marriage banns.'

Mason smiled amiably. 'That's a romantic view, but in a way one could say there's a parallel.'

Cameron was familiar with Byron's quixotic nature and grew impatient. 'Will you please sign the documents, Byron?'

'With my heart's blood.' Byron drew out his Mont Blanc pen. 'But in truth, Cameron, and you too, Mason, we are entering into a hallowed agreement. These letters state the honourable intentions of your brokerage houses to use your best efforts to raise a specific amount of money for a company. In this case, it's my company, Life Sciences. And you're going to raise fifty million dollars.'

'Sign the documents, Byron,' Cameron said.

'I will. I will.' Byron's face was all earnestness. 'But I want you to know that you will never be sorry you made this commitment. It may well prove to be your finest hour. Your most important business venture. The products that the liquid crystal technology can create will prove a boon to mankind.'

'I'm very impressed with the Thermoscan,' Mason said firmly. 'It's easily a multihundred-million-dollar business.'

'Multihundred millions and a blessing,' Byron said

fervently. 'An early-warning test for the detection of breast tumours. A home test.'

'Byron, sign the letters!'

'Of course,' Byron said, his eyes still fastened to John Mason. 'And to think that the Thermoscan is only the beginning. There's a disposable thermometer to replace the old-fashioned glass one. A reusable patch for the detection of circulatory abnormalities. A urine test for – '

'Byron!'

'Sorry.' Byron sounded genuinely contrite. 'I get carried away. But they're not just another product like toothpaste or shoes. They're blessings.'

'And good business,' Mason said happily.

'That's true,' Bryon said. 'And business is what makes the world go round.' He removed the cap from his pen and began to sign the documents. As he did, a rapid series of emotions played across his mobile face. First wonder, then exultation, then something close to fear, and finally buoyancy again.

'Okay, Sarge. I did the drill.' He grinned at Cameron. 'What happens now?'

Cameron's exasperation with Byron passed as it always did, and she sat back, relieved and happy. Her pleasure acted as a signal to the two men. There was a shifting of bodies and a clearing of throats.

'We're about to enter the red-herring country, young man,' Mason answered.

'Ah, yes. "Red herring." What a quaint phrase. Wall Street is full of quaint phrases. Bull. Bear. Buy long. Sell short. Upticks. Downticks.'

'Do you know what a red herring is?' Mason interrupted, mildly irritated that his native language was being treated so irreverently.

'Of course I know.' Byron sighed with satisfaction. 'It's Wall Street shorthand for an offering prospectus before it gets final SEC approval. You can always tell by the red printing on the front of the document.'

Cameron turned to Mason. 'It's a little early, John, but would you like a glass of champagne? To toast the signing?'

'I suppose I could have one quick glass. This is a big day.'

Cameron asked her secretary to bring in the bottle of Taittinger Blanc de Blancs and three rock-crystal glasses. She looked at Byron. 'You've come a long way, Byron. With the speed of light. Do you realize we'll be offering two million shares of Life Sciences at twenty-five dollars a share? Which will establish the price for the stock. As chairman of LSI, you own three hundred fifty thousand shares. You'll be worth almost nine million dollars.'

'I do that arithmetic every morning. It makes shaving less of a pain.'

'You understand it's only on paper,' Mason added. 'You can't sell the stock. That is, not yet.'

'I know. But there is paper, and there is paper. This is gilt-edged vellum.'

Della's arrival interrupted them. She left a tray with the champagne and glasses on Cameron's desk. Mason uncorked the bottle, and Byron yelled 'Hallelujah!' when the cork popped and flew across the room. Cameron, Byron, and Mason toasted each other, toasted Life Sciences, and toasted the stock placement.

When the bottle was half empty, Cameron called a halt. 'Okay. That's it. There'll be more tonight. My place at seven-thirty.' She glanced at Mason. 'Are you sure you can't make it?'

'No, my dear. I'm dining with Guy de Rothschild. He's in New York for the week. I'll be doing a little pump priming.'

'I admire your style.'

'Thank you. I try to plan ahead, and I am a workaholic. But nothing compares with the natural instincts of a good truffle hound.' He said it with reverence. 'Tim had it. You

39

have it. Imagine – Halloid Xerox, IBM, and now Life Sciences!'

'I like the comparison,' Byron said, gratified.

'So will the Street,' Cameron predicted.

'It will, indeed. We've only begun.' Mason placed his arm around Byron's shoulders with possessive pride, dazzled by the millions he expected to make from this odd young man. 'You have a rare gift. And I predict a brilliant future.'

'Thank you, John. I think my present isn't too bad, either.' He reached for the champagne. 'I'll take what's left. See you tonight, Cameron.'

She watched him leave, then glanced at the television monitor next to her desk. 'Looks like there's some selling going on.' She pressed a button and the Dow Jones averages appeared. 'Interesting. It's way off yesterday's high. Dropped over thirty-four points in just the time we've been in this meeting.'

'Interesting,' Mason said. 'More sellers than buyers, I guess. Ucciarde made us a few million yesterday and sold us out at the opening. A good thing, too. Or we'd have given part of it back in this morning's drop.'

'Don't you think the selling pressure should ease by noon?' Cameron maintained a straight face.

'You think it will?' Mason's eyes were guileless.

Cameron nodded.

'After the bad news breaks?'

'What bad news.'

Mason took several moments to take this in. He stared at Cameron and finally asked, 'Why was Coz selling?'

'Because I told him to.'

It was so quiet she could hear the rain beating against her office windows. 'Aaaah!' Mason said, taking a deep breath. 'I think I understand. Coz and you started a selling wave.'

'You think we did?'

Mason raised his eyes to the ceiling. 'I know you did. And I helped you.' He looked straight at Cameron. 'You shorted all the way down, of course.'

'Of course.'

Mason was beside himself with admiration. 'What made you think you could pull it off?'

'Everyone was too optimistic. The Dow was heading for two thousand all afternoon. And there's a natural resistance at any number with a lot of zeros, so someone had to get jittery. Also computer-programmed selling, once the market starts to slip. I could feel it and I felt jittery, too. Twitchy. My twitch said "Sell." If anyone is going to break ranks, it might as well be me. The Dow should drop to 1,940 in another hour. A good technical support point. We'll have covered all our shorts by then and go long again.'

'A two-trillion-dollar industry wired to your twitch. Beautiful!' Mason was more amused than upset. 'You trapped us all – Ucciarde, me, and all the damn fools who followed us.'

'It does look that way.'

'If I weren't already married, I'd ask you to marry me.'

'Thank you for the compliment.'

'Since we can't get married' – Mason smiled at her – 'now that we're associates, I hope you'll keep me better informed as to your twitches.' He rose to leave. There were hundreds of brokerage houses on the Street and hundreds of managing partners. But there had been only one Tim FitzGerald. Now there was only one Cameron Hightower, the managing partner of FitzGerald Associates. What an extraordinary woman she was.

Cameron watched John Mason leave and paused to think about the day. It was a nice piece of business and it marked a change. It was the first time they'd done business with Mason, Adams, and Fenwick. The first time since she had managed the firm that FitzGerald Associates would be at the top of the tombstone – the framed announcement of stock offering printed in the newspapers – the way it had always been when Tim managed the firm. They were moving up, slowly but surely. Aside from the money, in the eyes of the Street the firm was regaining the prestige that had once belonged to the FitzGerald name. Yes, today marked a change.

Cameron glanced at the rain splattering against the windows. This was a northeaster – a driving rain that meant trouble for small boats at sea. But at least a northeaster was predictable. It wasn't a high, wild hurricane that might move erratically first in one direction, then suddenly swerve in another, then double back on itself. Her face grew very still. A wild wind and rain had marked the first great change in her life. Now, these years later, she thought again about that hurricane and the many things which had happened to her since that storm.

PART TWO

The Island
1966–1969

3

For fifteen glorious years, Gary and Lisa Hightower ran a charter boat service in the Caribbean. They were in love with the sun, the sea, and each other. The birth of Cameron only added to their happiness, and the death of Lisa's parents was their only pain. Then one afternoon in late August, out of nowhere, a sharp, hot wind came up from the sea. The first hurricane of the 1966 season was supposed to pass well to the east of the Hightower boat, but it made a sudden right-angle turn. Cameron guessed that the storm was upon her parents before they could make port at Coral Bay on St John. She could picture her father peering through his binoculars, unable to make out the outline of the mountainous island through the dark clouds and the heavy water thrown up by the huge waves breaking violently on the reefs. The sudden storm was a tragic reminder of how the arbitrary gods could swoop down on a paradise at will. The Hightower ketch, *True Love*, with all its crew and passengers, vanished in the turbulence.

Cameron had remained on St Croix playing with Myra, the lively daughter of the black postmaster and her first friend on the island. The day after the storm, and each day after that for a week, Cameron stood on the dock near the Old Town Square, under a cloudless, brilliant blue sky, waiting patiently for the familiar silhouette of the two-masted boat to appear. When she could eat, Myra's mother, Victoria, fed her, but most of the time she couldn't eat. Each night she slept fitfully in the small, empty house in Christiansted that her parents had rented for the season. Each morning at dawn she began her vigil again. Even as she waited, she knew what had happened. She had lived so much of her life at sea, had heard so many stories of boats being torn apart by the force of a sudden storm, that long before she knew it as a fact, she understood that she was alone in the world. She would never see the *True Love* again. Motionless, staring out to sea, she was like a memorial to the drowned.

By the end of the week, one mast and a few planks from the helm of the *True Love* were discovered washed up on the beautiful beach at Mayo Bay. But there was no sign of either the crew or the passengers. It was left to the postmaster, Harold Marvin Evans, to tell Cameron of the tragedy. At thirteen she was an orphan. He wished there was someone else he could turn to for advice, but the Hightowers had only recently returned to the island. His young daughter had met Cameron and her parents when they had stopped in the post office to fill out the residence forms. The youngsters had become friends, ignoring the island barrier that separated white children from black.

'Cameron,' he said, approaching her on the dock with his daughter beside him just in case he needed help. 'I have to talk to you.'

Cameron's face was calm, as if his words confirmed some knowledge deep within her heart. 'I know.'

'Who told you?'

'No one.' She stood looking out to sea where a small sloop could be seen dancing on the waves some three miles out. She spoke quietly as if not to disturb the distant boat. 'They'll never come back.' The young girl's thin face, with her short, straight hair, large deep-set grey eyes, and wide mouth, showed no emotion beyond an acceptance of reality. There were no tears and no hysteria. The hysteria had been out there in the empty sea. That her head rang with her parents' cries, that her heart seemed about to drown in tears, was nobody's business but hers.

'Come home now, Cam?' Myra asked.

'All right.'

Harold Evans walked between the girls. He was not deceived by the quiet acceptance in Cameron's face or manner. He understood suffering so deep that it cannot be expressed.

Cameron stayed with the Evans family for a week. This was the only familiar experience in the frightening new world in which she found herself. Since most of her life had been spent moving from island to island, she was accustomed to visiting strange families. Each year the *True Love* had anchored in a different marina on a different island. Her father and mother liked the change. Each September, Cameron had gone to a different school, made friends with different boys and girls, visited many different homes. This September was supposed to be no different. Gary Hightower had chosen Christiansted, the capital of St Croix and the town where Lisa had grown up. But they had died before they had a chance to reintroduce themselves and Cameron to any of the old families on the island who might have remembered Lisa and her parents. They had also made no school arrangements for Cameron. She was truly a child adrift.

During her week with the Evans family, she listened to Victoria and Harold Evans arguing over the supper table about her future. What should they do with her? A white child could not be raised by a Negro family, even if they wanted to, even if she wished to stay. The American authorities in Charlotte Amalie on St Thomas would have their own ideas. They'd probably place the thirteen-year-old child in an orphanage, unless relatives could be found.

'Don't you have family in the States, Cameron?'

'I think so. Daddy didn't talk about them very much.'

'Hightower is not a common name. We'll see what we can do to find them.'

Whether or not she had relatives made no difference to

Cameron. She had no intention of being placed in an orphanage. She'd read about orphanages in books, and they sounded like prisons. If she couldn't go on living with the Evans family, which she would have preferred, she would have to live by herself. One day, instead of going to the beach to play, she took Myra on an 'explore', as she called it. They walked down a two-lane, blacktop road leading out of Christiansted. They walked hand in hand and did not talk much. Myra was a sweet-tempered child and accepted the silence as appropriate to her new friend's loss. Actually, Cameron's mind was a kaleidoscope of ideas. She was searching for a place she barely remembered from early childhood, from another year when the *True Love* had anchored in Christiansted, and her mother had taken her on a picnic adventure.

The road was shaded by overhanging trees, and everywhere was the scent of ripeness and the buzzing of insects. Flowers and fruit grew so close together they appeared to be the same bush. Cameron, tall for her age, found it easy to reach up for soursops and pull down the most succulent fruit, and pass it on to Myra's outstretched hands. As the girls munched away, Cameron realized that at least she wouldn't starve. They came at last to a spot she remembered from years ago. There on the right was a barely perceptible path leading off into the forest. With an air of purpose, Cameron followed the path; Myra tiptoed almost furtively behind her. Soon the jungle seemed to close in. The air was heavy and the creepers dropped their tendrils like the rigging of a foundered ship. Tree trunks bore unexpected flowers all the way up to the canopy above. Cottonwood and tamarind trees were hung with emerald necklaces that dropped to the mossy forest floor. Hummingbirds, gleaming like red and green stars, darted across the path. There were pink begonias, purple orchids, and huge green ferns growing wild, as well as many other species of flowers and plants that Cameron couldn't name. The filtered light flickered through the lush roof of leaves. Everything gave off the sweet, humid breath of wild growth.

Finally they arrived at a place where more sunshine fell. In the middle of an open space in the jungle was a bowl of heat and light and a splendid mansion now in ruins. It had once been the estate of an early nineteenth-century sugar planter and had reverted to wilderness. But it was an old friend to Cameron. Stories her mother had told her about the great houses outside Christiansted came back in a rush. The houses had wonderful names like High Love and Jealousy and Whim. This one was High Love.

'It must have been beautiful,' Myra whispered in an awed voice. Although she was born and raised on St Croix, it had never occurred to Myra to look at the remains of the island's only period of prosperity.

'It still is,' Cameron answered.

A huge tree had fallen across the path directly in front of the house. It leaned against the trees which were still standing and guarded the door. A rapid climber flaunted its red and yellow sprays right to the top.

'I don't want to climb over that tree.' Myra hung back.

'You don't have to.'

'Then how will we see what's inside?'

'I don't need to go inside. I already have.' Cameron explained how she and her mother used to come here for picnics. She had only wanted to make certain the house was still there. 'I used to hide here when we played hide-and-seek.' She continued to stare at the house, lost in memory. A pair of gaudy butterflies danced around each other in the hot air. The sounds, the scents, the unalloyed wildness of growth lifted Cameron's heart. She recalled a tar-paper shack in the rear where her mother had told her tools used to be stored. She'd live there. It wouldn't be such a bad place, and no one would find her.

That evening, after the whole house had gone to sleep,

Cameron rose quietly from the cot she slept on in Myra's room and quickly put on her ragged shorts, T-shirt, and sandals. Then she picked up her bag, which contained about two dollars in change – all that remained of the money her mother had left with her. She understood that she couldn't stay with the Evans family because she was white and they weren't. While her mother had taught her that skin colour made no difference, Cameron knew Mr Evans was right. Skin colour made all the difference in the world to most people on the island. And she refused to be sent to an orphanage.

Darkness had dropped on the land. The stars seemed very close. Cameron hurried along the deserted street. Although she wanted to run, she made herself walk. She had several miles to go before she reached High Love. Two or three miles in broad daylight was only a longish walk, but the same distance in the dark seemed menacing. The muscles in her neck stiffened with tension. She edged silently through the arcades created by stone buildings with overhanging second-floor balconies. At one point she had to sit down. It was more fright than fatigue that paralyzed her. She stumbled over to an eighteenth-century cannon that had been inverted and embedded in the street corner as a marker and sat down on the axle. She dropped her bag to the ground and clasped her hands in her lap, trying to stop herself from shaking.

'Hey, girlie?'

Cameron held her breath. The voice of a man who was slightly drunk came from behind her.

'How 'bout a drink?' Cameron didn't move. 'You look like you need a drink.'

A man's hand touched her shoulder, and as she stood up, she drew her fist back to hit him. When she faced him, she saw a tall, young sailor. He caught her fist in midair, stared at her long, skinny body, her flat chest, short hair, and started to laugh. 'Sorry, kid. I thought you were a girl. But you're a boy, aren't you?'

'Yeah.' Cameron lowered the pitch of her voice.

'Okay, kid. Sorry I bothered you.' The sailor staggered away.

When he was out of sight, Cameron started to run towards the dark road leading out of town. Everything blurred. The road and the jungle were full of mysteries, shadows, dangers. Dimly, she knew there were crevices, ditches, where a fall could be disastrous. Places where a person with a broken leg could shout for hours and not be heard. When she reached the tar-paper shack in back of High Love, she was so exhausted she lay down on a wooden bench and passed out. She dreamed she was with her mother and father fishing off the stern of the *True Love*.

Someone was shaking her arm, and she heard a voice. 'Cameron, wake up.' The voice wasn't her mother's. 'Wake up,' the voice persisted. It was Myra.

She opened her eyes. Myra was shaking her, and Myra's father was standing beside her. 'You found me.'

'When you weren't in your bed this morning, Myra told me about this place. We looked around for an hour before we found the shack.'

'I won't go to an orphanage.' Cameron was on her feet.

'This place has no door, and the floorboards are soft with dry rot. It's not a fit place to live.'

'I'll fix it up. My father taught me how to use my hands. I can lay planks.'

'I'll help,' volunteered Myra.

'You're a girl. A girl shouldn't be living alone,' Harold Evans protested.

'I'm not a girl. I'm a boy.' Cameron told them the story of meeting the sailor the previous night and ended by asking, 'Mr Evans, please look at me. Couldn't I pass for a boy? Couldn't I?'

51

The postmaster stared at Cameron. 'Turn around. Again.' He started to smile. 'Hmm. Why not? You could be a boy. You've not started to become a woman yet.' He looked up at the ceiling. 'It might be the best thing until we find your family. As a boy, you could get a job.' He went on thinking aloud. 'I could fix the door and do a repair job on the roof. We'd have to get you a hammock to sleep in so the bugs wouldn't eat you alive.'

'You'll help me?'

'We'll help,' he said. Myra nodded and grinned.

A wave of relief surged through Cameron, and she hurled her thin body at the big black man. She hugged him as tightly as she could.

He patted her head awkwardly. 'Come on, now. Is that the way for a brave young boy to behave? Why, you're acting like a scared little girl.'

'Yes, sir.' Cameron stood back and swallowed. 'Can you help me get a job?'

'Maybe, son. Maybe.'

Although there were many times when the life she led terrified her, Cameron hung on. Harold Evans helped her to make the shack almost livable. And he kept his word. He got her a part-time job as a bellboy in a small inn on the outskirts of Christiansted, well off the tourist path. Every morning she walked the three miles to the inn, and every evening the three miles back to her shack. Sometimes, but not too often because they didn't want to start any talk, she would stop at the Evans's house for dinner. In addition to carrying luggage, when there was any luggage to be carried, she scrubbed the floors, helped make the beds, and did the laundry in an old tub behind the inn. Her luck held; she had no difficulty passing as a teenage boy.

The tar-paper shack was her home. Though Harold Evans did his best to repair the roof and floor, the roof still leaked when it rained and the moisture seemed to rise off it when the sun shone. Her bed was the hammock that they'd put up together, and her toilet a lime-filled hole in the ground. Although the Evans family certainly would have helped, Cameron did not want to impose on them any more than was absolutely necessary, so her toilet paper was carefully hoarded copies of the local newspaper. The ocean was her bathtub, the sand her soap. Her meagre income was barely enough to buy a pair of jeans and a new shirt. She needed the rest of her money to buy fish and canned food in the local market. The day she was able to purchase a roll of toilet paper and a cake of soap was a celebration.

Despite the hardship and fear that ran like an undercurrent through all her days, living as close to the land as she did provided moments of extraordinary beauty and hope. The brilliant, beautiful flowers and the hot yellow sun, the white sand and the blue-green sea, even the occasional rainfall which she caught in tin cans and saved for drinking water, were things she learned to cherish. Nature became mother and father to her.

As the days became weeks and the weeks turned into months and the seasons changed, Cameron gave up all attempts at keeping track of time. Although at first her biggest single fear was being discovered and sent to an orphanage, when she began to menstruate six months later, the fear of being recognized as a girl became her most pressing anxiety. Fortunately, her mother had told her about menstruation, so the blood didn't frighten her. What did scare her was the knowledge that she was growing up. Every day she would look at her naked body in a cracked mirror she'd taken from the great house; she would search for those physical changes that would give her away as a girl. She knew it was only a matter of time before her breasts would begin to bud and everyone would know she was a girl. Working at the inn and listening to the talk of the young women who used the hotel and bar as a place to conduct their business gave her a sordid glimpse of what might happen to her. She was aware of the wretched life that awaited an untrained, uneducated young girl with no family to turn to.

But Harold Evans proved to be a good friend. He delicately prodded the St Croix authorities – without telling them why they were being prodded – to notify the kin of Gary and Lisa Hightower of their deaths. Finally, with the sluggish aid of the officials on St Thomas, the Hightower relatives were located. Only when that had been accomplished did Harold Evans inform the authorities of the existence of Cameron Hightower.

After that, things happened quickly. Cameron was literally hustled out of her tar-paper shack by a tall woman with a formal smile and an imperious manner. She was taken, first by plane, to New York and then, by limousine, to Princeton, New Jersey. There she became the centre of a family council. A council composed of relatives whom she had never met and only dimly remembered existed.

The Hightower family council was held at Hightower Farm, the estate of Geraldine Hightower, in Princeton. Cameron's first sight of the house filled her with dismay, because it seemed confining, almost cramped. Growing up as she had on a variety of Caribbean islands, she was accustomed to another kind of architecture. This house was not white, it wasn't pink, it wasn't open to the sky and the trade winds. It had no colonnades, and it wasn't Spanish with a gay red tile roof. But, she had to admit, it wasn't a leaky tar-paper shack, either. Only the rear of the house looked vaguely familiar. Not the world Cameron remembered, but not totally strange. She saw a landscaped terrace overlooking tennis courts, and just a short distance away a swimming pool and pool house set against groves of well-pruned trees. Cameron was familiar with tennis courts and swimming pools. These people did some of the same things her mother and father had done. But nowhere were there long stretches of white beaches and deep aqua water shimmering with light. How she longed for her parents to come back so she could go home. But there was no home anymore, anywhere. She'd learned that all too well during the year it took for the officials to find her relatives.

The Hightower family council held to discuss Cameron's future took place in the library. Geraldine Hightower presided over the council from the thronelike chair at her desk. Cameron found her new cousin regal and intimidating. Geraldine's face reminded her a little of the strong, weatherbeaten face of her father. Her smile, when it unexpectedly occurred and fixed on Cameron, was surprisingly familiar and affectionate. But the eyes belonged to Geraldine alone; they were keen, cool, and appraising and made Cameron wish that in some magical way she might become invisible. So those penetrating eyes would stop looking at her, seeming to see inside her and to read her very thoughts.

Before the discussion started, it was suggested that Cameron wander about the estate: they'd send for her when they were ready. Cameron did as she was told for as long as she could, but finally she was drawn back to the anteroom of the library. She pulled a small footstool from behind a chair and sat quietly, listening like a stowaway to the voices that came from the slightly ajar door. She'd become an attentive listener and watcher while learning how to survive on St Croix.

'She's a biggish child.' That was her fat cousin. 'Much too big for piggyback rides. She didn't open her mouth once at lunch. I had to worm every word out of her.'

'She was frightened. We're strangers,' Geraldine answered.

'She frightened me. I think she's retarded.'

'How can she be retarded? She's a Hightower,' said Geraldine.

Cameron's tongue crept between her lips. She bit down on it to make herself stay quiet. She must not speak. Only listen. And remember who she was and where she was.

'Tobias was a Hightower. So was Gary. How do you explain them?'

Cameron caught the implication, and it made her even more angry. How dare that creepy man who sat opposite her at lunch talk that way about her father and grandfather? Her father had had a picture of Grandfather Tobias in his cabin in the *True Love*: Grandfather had a big moustache.

'Tobias was not retarded.' Geraldine sounded irritated. 'He was brilliant.'

'And what was Gary's excuse? Certainly not brilliance!'

'Gary was very intelligent. He simply wasn't interested in money.'

Visions of her parents mingled in Cameron's mind with the faces she attached to the voices coming from the library. It was hard to believe that her parents wouldn't be coming for her at any moment, to take her home, away from these unkind strangers who didn't know them, had never known them, but seemed to enjoy saying nasty things about them.

'My dear Raymond,' Geraldine said, 'there is quite enough money in this family to take excellent care of one young girl. So let's not make money an issue. And Cameron is not retarded.'

'Her mother was the daughter of the owner of a bar. Good heavens!' That was her cousin with the yellow hair and cold eyes who told Cameron she didn't consider her to be an equal.

Cameron stared at the door in wonderment, without hope, like someone at a railroad station watching the express trains roar by. She thought about the long journey that had brought her here and about how she would have to find a way to leave. But where would she go?

'Roselind, I'd like to remind you that, distasteful as it may

56

seem to you, a large part of the Hightower fortune comes from the distillation of alcohol. And alcohol is sold in bars, praise be.' Geraldine grew more stern. As everyone present knew, she wasn't the family matriarch by accident. Neither was she by far the richest of a very rich family by chance. She'd inherited most of the family's quotient of brains and single-handedly managed the Hightower Trust. 'We have two alternatives. We can set up a trust to support the child, with a companion to raise her until she graduates from college and can take care of herself. Or one of us can take her under our wing, foot the bills and responsibilities. Any of us can easily afford it. A Hightower does not become a public charge merely because her father happened to like the sun, beaches, and boats better than making money.'

Cameron listened as there was a shuffling of legs and people changed positions. It was true, she thought. Her father had not been very interested in money. But it hadn't mattered. They were so happy – her mother, her father, and she – that they never thought about money.

'I suppose it is the proper thing to do,' she heard her fat cousin say resignedly.

'How much of a trust?' asked the creepy one.

'Half a million. We contribute equally.'

'Are you sure she's a Hightower?'

A look of disgust passed over Cameron's face. Given what her cousins were like – except maybe for Geraldine – she had the strong feeling that being a Hightower was not that much to be proud of. The Evans family on St Croix were better people.

'Yes, Leo, she's a Hightower. I had my attorney check all the available records while Jenny and I packed her things. Though there was precious little to pack. She'd been living like a waif and working as a slavey in a fleabag hotel.'

'Do you have a record of the marriage?'

This was too much. Cameron found it hard to breathe.

'Yes, Raymond, I have photocopies of their marriage certificate and also Cameron's birth certificate.'

It struck Cameron with chilling force that she would have to stay here. Forever! If the past year had not taught her all about terror – that she was alone and there was no place to go – this was the final proof. And with that recognition, all her fears and her attempts to behave in a manner she assumed was expected of her were swept away in an explosive fury at what had happened to her life. Mom's and Daddy's marriage certificate! Her birth certificate! Who were these people? What gave them the right? She burst into the library like some desperate, wild animal.

'You give me those certificates! Give them to me!' She hurled herself across the room at Geraldine, who had just taken the papers from a drawer in her desk. 'They're mine. They belong to me! To my mother and father! Give them to me!'

'They are yours, my dear.' Geraldine calmly handed the certificates to the irate child. 'Sit down, George. You too, Leo.' She gestured at the two Hightower men who had risen, ready to remove Cameron bodily from the library.

Cameron clutched the papers to her breast. 'I'm not going to stay here. I'll find someplace to live.' She turned to run from the library.

At which point Geraldine did something she had never done before in her life. She responded physically to another human being's cry for help. This wasn't an arm's-length donation, like one of her many charity contributions. Nor was it the committee she chaired that dealt with problems of people she never knew and had no desire to meet. Geraldine knelt and caught the child in her arms, embracing her in the timeless way of a mother comforting her young. She patted Cameron's head and made soothing noises. 'There, there. Don't cry. It's all right now.'

'I'm not crying, and it isn't all right. It will never be all right again. I won't stay here.'

'Darling, this is your home.'

'No it isn't.'

'It is. Don't you see you belong with me?' Geraldine was almost pleading. Without releasing Cameron, she lifted her eyes to the stunned faces of her relatives. She was as surprised at herself as they were. 'I think that settles the matter of Cameron. This is her home. She will live with me.'

The men and their wives looked at each other in bewilderment. Then, one by one, several with their faces showing immense relief, they gathered themselves and left. Once Geraldine and Cameron were alone, Geraldine's face took on a sad, odd expression. She, like Cameron, would have a lot to learn; probably more. After all, Cameron had had a mother, and she had never had a child.

Stroking the young girl's hair absentmindedly, Geraldine thought of the daughter she never had; a girl with the Hightower brains and stamina. The kind this child must have had to survive under the most difficult circumstances. She visualized Cameron growing up: her education; her tennis, horseback riding, and dancing lessons; the parties to come at The Farm and the Pretty Brook Club; the boys she would meet; the new world she would give her. Cameron was worth her best efforts. Geraldine's heart lifted. Her instinctive acceptance of Cameron was right. It was almost as good as being young again, to have this second chance.

Cameron looked up at Geraldine's glowing face. She looked so happy that for a moment Cameron felt relieved. But the relief was mixed with anger at whatever there was in life that had robbed her of her real world, of those she loved. The lonely, watchful girl, her senses sharpened by too much experience, tried to understand the older woman. What kind of a person was she? What did Geraldine Hightower expect from her? She knew she would have to wait to find out. Meanwhile . . .

'Thank you for accepting me,' Cameron said quietly.

'You're very welcome. And thank you for being what you are. The blood hasn't thinned in you.'

Cameron didn't understand the meaning of Geraldine's words, but she realized it was a compliment of some sort. She said, 'I'm glad I'm a Hightower.'

'So am I. You will be a strong new branch on the family tree.'

It was exactly as though they were courting each other.

As part of Cameron's education, Geraldine gave the young girl a brief history of the Hightower family and how it became so wealthy. The huge farmhouse had been begun in 1801 and was finally completed in 1850 by Hezekial Hightower and later lived in by Hezekial's son Moses and his daughter-in-law Meggie. Moses and Meggie Hightower were Geraldine's great-grandparents. She explained that the family fortune had been founded during Colonial times in the rich farmlands surrounding Princeton. But the three original Hightower brothers were not simply farmers. To them, farming was a means, not an end – a means to make money. Inevitably, in the early nineteenth century, they developed a devotion to apples, not for eating but for drinking. At that time there was a widespread belief that spirits were healthier and safer to drink than water. But while water was free, applejack, apple cider, and apple brandy were not. It was this national intoxication with apples that put the Hightowers in the distillery business. Their customers were distributors and shopkeepers up and down the East Coast, from Boston to Richmond.

Liquor was only the beginning. Geraldine told how succeeding generations of Hightowers had expanded the business into rubber, coal, steel, and glass making, all the while adding to their real estate holdings. Geraldine concluded her history with a discreet reference to Cameron's grandfather, Tobias. Tobias Hightower preferred travelling to exotic locations to do on-site work in ancient religions over the financial rewards of business. He spent huge sums of money on research and published many important papers before his death. With his son's blessing, his will left most of his fortune to the Museum of Natural History in New York.

One winter day in early January neither of the two tutors Geraldine had hired to prepare Cameron for entering the Paddington School in the fall – the same school Geraldine had attended forty years earlier – were able to make it through the first snowstorm of the year. Cameron waited patiently until the afternoon, but when the second call came in from Mrs Bell saying she was stuck in the snow outside her driveway, Cameron knew she was free for the rest of the day. She let out a yell of glee as she pressed her nose against the cold windowpane and stared across the broad lawns of The Farm, dazzled by the change in the scenery. It had been snowing all day. Cameron had never seen real snow. She'd only read about it in books, and her father had described snowstorms and skiing. But neither his words nor the pictures could equal the sight of the white snow resting on the bare brown limbs of the elm and oak trees, on the evergreens – spruce and pine – close to the house, bent at odd angles, heavy with the weight of the snow. The driveway lay under a carpet of white. The privet hedges no longer separated one part of the lawn from another but were part of a continuous white sweep. The red clay of the tennis court was replaced by a monochromatic coating of white. Everything was different.

Cameron kicked off her loafers and pulled on a pair of calf-high, fur-lined waterproof boots, tucking her brown corduroy jeans into them before zipping them up. Then she put on a heavy cable-knit Irish wool sweater and over that a white ski parka. Mittens and a white wool hat completed her outfit. She took the stairs two at a time, running out the front door. There was no traffic on Route 206, and she slipped and slid along the snow- and ice-covered road. A clear, grey light filled the air. The snow on the side of the road gleamed as though bathed in moonlight. As she stared at the houses and trees and fields, which looked like a Currier and Ives print – all that was missing was a horse-drawn sleigh – Cameron asked herself a question. Is this world real or make-believe? This world that appears to be so perfect, so calm, so at peace?

4

The long drive leading to Hansen Hall had been regularly cleared of snow during the day by the handyman and gardener, and the black Cadillac limousine bringing Elmer Hansen, Sr, home from work was able to pull up in front of the gracious English manor house. Usually the sight of the house pleased Elmer. The handsome façade of cut stone and half-timbered stucco, the air of tradition, all gave him a sense of his achievement. Although too new to be on the Princeton historic tour, it was one of the finest residences in the town. But today the house gave him no pleasure. After handing his coat to the maid, he went in search of his son.

As expected, he found Elmer junior in the library. The library was Elmer senior's favourite room in the twenty-nine-room house. It had triple bay windows, a huge fieldstone fireplace, and it was panelled in old English pine. There was a large Oriental rug over the stone floor and numerous leather couches and chairs. Next to the window was a gaming table with a chess set ready for players. Two of the couches were back-to-back with only a narrow refectory table between them. The arrangement was similar to one Elmer had seen and admired in a magazine. The only thing missing in the library was books. Other than books on business which he kept in his office, Elmer had little interest in reading. Today, as it often did, the sight of his son in the room offended him. The Hansen Company was his life, and years of watching his son fail at even the simplest of business problems brought back unpleasant memories of his useless, wild brother, Butler Hansen. He'd given Butler 10 per cent of his company in the hope that Butler would grow up, but neither the stock nor the company had meant anything to Butler. He'd got himself killed long ago in a stupid barroom brawl. This constant reminder had helped change Elmer's natural love for his son to a feeling of contempt. He struggled constantly – and not always successfully – not to show his contempt. Totally engrossed in their conversation, neither his son nor his grandson, Cyrus Hansen, were aware of his presence. Elmer slid into a chair next to the door and listened.

Ellie, as most people called Elmer junior, was gesturing wildly as he spoke to Cyrus. He held a glass of Scotch in one hand that occasionally slopped over the rug. Elmer gazed with growing dismay at his only son's performance.

'It's a fine idea,' Ellie was saying. 'Glass breaks when you drop it. In a bathtub or shower that's murder.'

'It sounds sensible, Dad.' In spite of his support, Cyrus knew his father had made another bad mistake. 'Did you say you ordered a million bottles?'

'That's right. One million. To test-market in Albany.'

It got worse and worse. Cyrus felt his heart sink.

Elmer decided it was time to interrupt. His voice was matter-of-fact. 'By the way, did you ask my permission to order those plastic bottles?'

Ellie turned quickly and saw his father. All at once his legs felt weak. He half sat and half fell into the chair behind him and placed his glass on the table so as to ready himself for what he knew was coming. Ellie was a man in his early forties, built like a Coca-Cola bottle – big and heavy below the waist and small above. His legs, covered by grey flannel pants, were large and fleshy, his ankles thick, his feet broad. His body above the waist did not belong to his legs and feet but to a smaller, slimmer man – as though his maker had made a mistake and had matched a 36 jacket with a 44 trouser. Ellie's once almost pretty face had prematurely aged. His small, delicate features – the thin straight nose, the well-shaped mouth, the large brown eyes half hidden by long thick lashes

– were blurred by an overlay of unhealthy-looking fat. Now his body was braced, testifying to the fear of the always persecuted. He was a man dancing one step ahead of his personal devil.

'As I said, did you ask my permission to order those bottles?'

'No.'

'I thought not. I have no record of your asking in my diary. Did you ask my permission to set up a test market for Caress, our leading shampoo?'

The answer came after a slight hesitation. 'No.'

'I see. Do you think that I'd have agreed to either decision?'

'Plastic bottles are a marvellous idea.' Ellie's voice was muffled.

'What did you say?'

Ellie forced himself to speak up. 'I said, plastic bottles are a fine idea.'

'Are they really?' Elmer asked with the air of a man who really wanted to know. He ran his hand thoughtfully over his immaculate white hair. For all his sixty-six years, there was an enormous vitality about the man. He was an absolute ruler in the world in which he lived. 'I gather you believe in those bottles?'

'I do. Plastic bottles are better than glass. The whole industry is switching to plastic.'

'How do you know what the whole industry is doing?'

'I read it in the magazine *Packaging*.'

Elmer took the time to digest this answer. 'So you read it in *Packaging*? A splendid source of information.'

Ellie nodded. 'The article was written by John Galway, vice president in charge of marketing for Bristol-Myers.' He waited, hoping for his father's approval.

'Bristol-Myers? Our closest competitors in the shampoo field?'

'Yes. It's worth keeping an eye on them.'

'You think so?' Elmer's eyes rolled upward.

'Of course. Don't you?'

There was a long silence during which Elmer reached a decision. When he spoke, his tone was somewhat weary. 'Junior, we have the largest share of the market. They have to keep an eye on us. We do not do anything because Bristol-Myers does it. Or Warner-Lambert, or J and J. They follow our lead. At the Hansen Company, we do not act on a whim, or out of panic. Nor do we run with the pack.'

'But we want to remain the leader. And to do that, our shampoos belong in plastic bottles.'

'The wave of the future,' Elmer remarked.

'You're against it because you didn't think of it yourself,' Ellie exploded. Then he cringed, shocked at his own words.

'I learn something new every day,' Elmer's voice was still reasonable. 'My son, the psychologist.'

Ellie felt like a river trying to run in two directions at the same time. He was terrified of his father, but he wanted to hit out at him. 'It's true. Plastic bottles are a fine idea.'

'What is true, Junior, is true when I say it is true. Do you understand that?'

Ellie didn't answer.

'You will never learn.' Ellie remained silent. 'For the sake of appearances, I gave you the title of marketing director of the Beauty Care Division. A division for which, as you well know, I personally make all the marketing decisions. And you have managed to make a hash of even that meaningless assignment. Please remember your title is *pro forma*. The reality is, you are my yes-man when I want a yes, and my no-man when I want a no. You have no other duties.'

'I thought you'd be interested in plastic bottles. They don't break.' Ellie desperately wanted some show of respect from his father.

'Junior, you're a fool. Do you want to know why you're a fool? No, of course you don't. You'd rather go on being a fool, but I'm going to tell you. I'm going to give you a short marketing course designed for children.' The level of his son's ignorance never ceased to dismay him. 'Plastic bottles are a good idea. But you don't select a bottle simply by ordering a million assembly-line bottles from a passing supplier. You select a bottle by having one specially designed for a product. Or five bottles, even twelve bottles. Then you research those bottles, panel-test each of them to hell and back. Until you're sure you have the perfect bottle – the right size, shape, and feel. To please the men, women, and children of this great country. In the regular size, giant size, travel size. When you have the perfect bottle, you prepare an advertising campaign. Print, television, radio, billboards. To announce to the world that a great new bottle is coming.' Elmer leaned forward to contemplate the still figure in the chair. Ellie's head had dropped forward. Deep crevices appeared around his nose and mouth.

'I'm sorry,' he muttered. 'I didn't know.'

Elmer ignored the apology. He walked to a teakwood cabinet. When he opened the door, a light went on. Inside the cabinet were bottles of liquor, liqueurs, and mixes as well as glasses of all sizes and shapes. Elmer poured himself a shot of gin, swallowed it neat, and poured a second. In all the years Junior had worked for the company, he had never volunteered so much information. Information was valuable to him. He never threw it away, and to talk to Junior was throwing it away. He glanced at Cyrus, who was watching him from in front of the fireplace. Should he stop now or go on? Elmer decided to go on. For better or worse, he would at least give Cyrus a lesson. Someday Cyrus might be his heir.

'Now, Junior,' he said, looking at his son but addressing his words to Cyrus. 'I'll tell you what else you don't know. While all this designing is going on, you call in bids from proven suppliers and compare them against the numbers our production people tell us it will cost to manufacture the bottle ourselves. And when all that's done, there are still a few thousand more things to do. And after you do those few thousand things, then and only then – and all too often not even then – do you test-market. In Syracuse, or Omaha. Not in Albany. We have spent millions of dollars researching the country, picking twelve locations in the United States that are good test markets. Albany is not one of them, neither is New York or San Francisco. We test-market in Syracuse because it is a nice cross-section of country. Syracuse or Omaha. Which is exactly what we are doing, Junior. If you'd kept your eyes and ears open and looked around a little, you'd have discovered that the Hansen Company has been developing a plastic bottle for the past two years. We'll have the bottle ready for test-marketing in about six months. Which is one of the reasons why I cancelled your order for a million plastic bottles.'

Ellie had lapsed into bitterness and confusion. 'But I never get memos,' he muttered. Bewilderment and hurt still echoed in his voice when he added that he didn't know anything because he was never invited to meetings, research reports were kept from him, and no matter what position he occupied in the company, business was always routed around him.

'Nobody ever sent me memos on how to build a business, Junior. Or how to get rich. As a matter of fact, they kicked my ass around pretty good before I learned. But I did learn. Go away, Junior,' Elmer said as calmly as he was able. He knew that if his son didn't get out of his sight immediately, his control of his temper would slip, and he'd say even more things he'd bitterly regret. As had happened too often in the past and would probably happen in the future. 'I want to have a quiet drink before dinner. I'll eat alone or with Cyrus tonight. Phyllis and you can have dinner in your rooms.'

Ellie stumbled out of the library, his hands shaking, his mouth open, his face turned away from his son in shame. Cyrus watched his father leave and felt his shame as his own.

There was no way to help him, and knowing this made Cyrus furious.

When his son had closed the door behind him, Elmer turned to his grandson and said in a wry, half-mocking voice, 'So much for this evening's entertainment.'

Cyrus looked straight at his grandfather, not past him but at him; as if he was measuring Elmer for when the time came.

'Want to join me in a drink, Cyrus?' Elmer asked.

'No, thank you.'

'Going out?'

'Yes.'

Cyrus's long, strong body – so similar to his grandfather's – had an unusual tensile strength. He was sweating, but he maintained his poise. The angrier he became, the tighter he held himself in check. That scene between his father and grandfather had been played many times before, and he knew he must not rise to the bait. For he understood that if he fought with his grandfather's weapons, he would become like his grandfather. His rage at and hatred of his grandfather would destroy him; even as Elmer's scorn of his son had warped the old man's life. Cyrus stood still for a moment, his blue eyes ice-cold, then he turned and left the room.

Cyrus disengaged the clutch and slammed the gear stick into reverse. He gunned the motor and released the clutch. The T Bird shot out of the garage into the partially cleared driveway area. He threw the gear into first and stepped on the gas. The car sped down the driveway spraying snow behind. By the time he reached the road, he was in third gear and still accelerating. The town maintenance man running the snowplough had been careful not to pile snow in front of Hansen Hall's driveway – if he had the town council would have heard from Elmer Hansen in the morning – so Cyrus crashed through the low snow pile and turned left to head down Route 206. The car went into a wide, controlled skid which Cyrus deftly corrected. He was a natural, instinctive driver who gave little thought to the mechanics of driving but relied on the feel of the car, the road, and what his machine would and would not do. Often, the only way he knew to rid himself of the rage he felt at his grandfather was to drive hell-bent for nowhere. The faster he drove, the less he felt.

He hurtled south on the empty road, hitting sixty miles per hour and downshifting to fifty on the curves. Cyrus knew every bump, every rise and fall, every turn in the road. Despite the ice and snow, there was nothing he couldn't easily handle. He shot past Lawrence Academy where he'd prepped for Princeton. The road dipped into a long slope which he knew would bottom out two miles farther on and turn into a gentle rise. Cyrus let the car run full out. Sixty-five. Seventy. Seventy-five. Eighty miles per hour. Suddenly his muscles tensed. Some idiot was running and sliding in the middle of the street. As he looked for the best way to pass the fool, the kid slipped, fell, and slid sideways across the road. There was no way around the sprawled body. Cyrus barely had time to shift into neutral, kill the engine, hit the brakes, and turn the wheel. Maybe he could use the piled-up snow at the side of the road as a cushion, ride the bank on two wheels, and come down on the other side of the kid. Instead, the T Bird slewed too sharply to the right, hit the snowbank, almost turned over, then bounced across the road, slowly revolving. The car crossed the road sliding backwards, still turning, and smashed into a tree broadside. The only reason Cyrus wasn't killed was because the passenger side, not the driver's, happened to crash into the tree.

He was knocked out cold. After a few minutes, when he opened his eyes, his head ached where it had hit the window. His nose and his mouth were bleeding, and his hands, still locked on the wheel, were rigid.

'Are you all right?' Staring at him through the window were two big eyes and a young, scared face.

70

Cyrus made a grimace of pain and disgust. 'No. I'm not all right.' He tried the door and, surprisingly, it had not jammed. But it took all his strength to open the door and crawl out of the wreck. He found himself standing in snow up to his knees.

'Excuse me, but you're bleeding. Can I help?' the kid asked.

Cyrus fished a handkerchief from his pocket. 'Thanks for telling me.'

'I'm sorry.'

'Not as sorry as I am.' He dabbed his nose automatically. 'You scared the hell out of me. I could have killed you.'

'I know. I was scared, too.' Cameron watched him dab at his nose. 'Your head is bleeding.'

Cyrus touched the aching part of his forehead and winced. 'Ouch! What a knot!' He turned to the kid. 'Christ, my nose and mouth are a mess. I probably have a concussion, and my car's a wreck. What the hell were you doing on your ass in the middle of a main road?'

'I was running and sliding, like ice skating. Then I slipped and fell.'

'Ice skating on Route 206? Are you nuts?'

Cameron swallowed. 'Yes. At least, I think so now.'

Cyrus wavered and fell back against the car. He closed his eyes, trying to shake off the sudden dizziness. Then he asked, 'How old are you?'

'Right this minute, a hundred and one.'

'Quit it. I'm not in the mood for jokes. How old?'

'Fifteen.'

'Fifteen! Jesus! At fifteen you should have more sense.' Cameron nodded, biting her lips. 'Do you live near here? I've got to get to a telephone, and this car isn't going anywhere for a while.'

'No. I don't live near here. But there's a house just up the hill. They'll have a telephone. You want to go there?'

71

'Yeah, before I give out. I feel lousy.'

'I know.' All of a sudden Cameron started to cry. She couldn't help herself.

'Hey, kid.' Cyrus put a hand on her shaking shoulders. 'Stop crying. Boys don't cry.'

'You almost got killed because of me.'

'I'll be all right. I'm just banged up and a little dizzy. Quit crying. Fifteen is too old to cry.'

'You have a concussion and . . .'

Cyrus became conscious of the cold. He felt nauseous and the sight of the kid crying wasn't helping any. It reminded him of his father. Cyrus had seen his father cry too often. Unable to stand up any longer, he collapsed into the car and closed his eyes.

As suddenly as she'd started to cry, Cameron stopped. For the first time she really looked at the young man. His hair seemed brighter than any gold she'd ever seen. He had a strong, square chin, and his closed eyes had thick, blond lashes. His forehead, now creased with pain and oozing blood, was high and broad. She reached out and touched it.

'What the hell are you doing?' Cyrus opened his eyes.

'Feeling your forehead. Does your head hurt?'

'And then some.'

'Okay. You sit there, I'll go up to the house and call Cousin Geraldine. She should be home by now, and she'll know exactly what to do.'

'Who's Cousin Geraldine?' The world was spinning around for Cyrus.

'My cousin. Geraldine Hightower.'

Cyrus considered this while he still held on to consciousness. 'Geraldine Hightower? You're the Hightower kid?'

'I suppose I am.'

'What's your name?'

'Cameron Hightower.'

'That's the right name. But aren't you a girl?'

'Yes.'

'I see. The boy turns out to be a girl.' That was the last thought Cyrus had before he lost consciousness.

Cameron stood for a moment staring at the beautiful young man. She had to help him. Nothing was as important as that. She turned and ran through the snow towards the house.

Geraldine was home. She listened to Cameron's story and talked to Mabel Mitchell, the owner of the house. Mrs Mitchell grabbed two blankets and hurried down to the wrecked car with Cameron following her. They covered Cyrus with the blankets and waited for Geraldine. She arrived a few minutes before the ambulance from the Princeton medical centre. With Cameron riding in the ambulance and holding Cyrus's hand, the ambulance, followed by Geraldine, made its way to hospital.

While waiting for the doctor to report on the extent of Cyrus Hansen's injuries, Geraldine called Hansen Hall. Elmer Hansen said he'd be right over. He arrived just as the doctor finished with Cyrus.

'How is he?' Elmer demanded.

'He'll be all right. He's in shock and suffering from a deep concussion. But there are no fractures. He must have a skull like iron. We'll have to see how he reacts to a series of tests we'll be giving him.'

Elmer understood. 'Like depth perception and coordination?'

The doctor nodded.

'Do you know who I am?'

'Yes, Mr Hansen.'

'You have my grandson in there.' He might have added, the heir to the Hansen Company – the only heir. 'I want him to have the best care. Anything he needs.'

'Of course, Mr Hansen.'

'And you call me the minute he comes to. I want to see him.'

73

'It'll be at least a day before I can permit visitors.'

'Listen to me, young man, I am not a visitor. I'm his grandfather, and if I wish to see him I will see him.' Elmer turned to Geraldine, who had been watching and listening. Even a casual observer couldn't miss the change in his attitude. 'Geraldine.' He held out his hand.

'Elmer.' Geraldine acknowledged the greeting and shook hands.

'And you're Cameron Hightower?'

'That's right, Elmer.' Geraldine answered for Cameron.

'I gather if you hadn't come by, Cyrus might have died in the cold.'

'But I –'

'Yes, he might have.' Geraldine did not like the way Hansen had spoken to the doctor, and she had no intention of allowing Cameron to take any blame for the accident.

'You have my deepest thanks. I'll see to it that Cyrus thanks you himself. Just as soon as he's up and about. Good night, ladies.' With that he was gone.

5

Cameron waited for Cyrus in a fever of hope and doubt. Suppose he'd forgotten that today was their day to go ice skating? What would she do? Shrivel up and die. The possibility that he might have forgotten made her stomach feel queasy. She swallowed hard. She knew that she put too much stock into his every word, every glance, every casual opinion. They branded themselves on her heart like eternal truths. But she couldn't stop herself from feeling the way she did. No matter what the poets said about love – if this was love – it was terrible to feel so intensely about anyone. She looked up and down Rockefeller Plaza. Where was he? The temperature seemed to have dropped while she waited. She was chilled to the bone, and the dissonant sounds of the traffic and the jangle of people's voices grated on her nerves. The skating rink was full of strange people whirling and whizzing about. The wonderful way they skated made her feel even more miserable. In most teenaged girls, tears are very near the surface and can come at the first sign of an emotional crisis, but Cameron only cried in empathy for others' suffering, never her own. She'd come to understand all too well during her year on the island that crying for oneself did little good. She would simply have to wait. But where was he?

Cyrus parked the T Bird in the garage under Radio City and hurried to the street. He was late. He asked himself again why he had offered to take Cameron ice skating. After he'd recovered from the accident, he'd got in touch with Cameron and began seeing her occasionally. They went hiking, watched football games on television, or went to the movies together. In Princeton. But this was New York, and she was still a kid. This was going to be a bore. Sure, she was unusually bright and fun to be with, but there was a grown-up young woman – they'd done a spread of her in *Playboy* – waiting for his call. Ready to go with him to Renata's gallery and afterwards to bed. What the hell was he doing with Cameron? Maybe the old Chinese proverb was true. If you saved someone's life, you were responsible for the person forever. Damn it!

When he arrived at the rink, he couldn't spot Cameron in the crowd, and he wondered whether today was the day they'd arranged. Maybe Geraldine's limousine was stuck in the Lincoln Tunnel. Or suppose the kid had been picked up by some jerk? She was smart, but was she smart enough to take care of herself in New York City? He'd bet his shirt that idiot of a chauffeur hadn't the sense to wait with Cameron until he showed up. Then he felt a pair of gloved hands clasped over his eyes.

'Guess who.'

Cyrus was surprised at the extent of his relief at hearing the familiar voice. 'Greta Garbo,' he responded.

'Who? Guess again.'

'Ava Gardner.'

'Closer. Try again.'

She started to whistle. First the serenade from Mozart's *Don Giovanni*. Then segueing into *Georgia On My Mind*, done with a sweet, sad jazz beat, sensitive to the shadings of the foolish and lovely old tune.

'I know. Leon's ghost.'

The hands dropped from his eyes, and Cameron ran around in front of him. She was dressed in blue jeans, her Irish wool sweater, clothes very much like his own, whistling with fluent ease, 'After you've gone, babe. After you've gone away.'

76

'Cameron Hightower! I'd have sworn it was Bix Beider-becke.' He'd given her Mozart operas and Bach cantatas. Music and more music. And to round off her musical education, he'd loaned her some rare records of the great jazz master, including that incredible young man from the corn belt, Leon 'Bix' Beiderbecke. Cameron had proven equal to his efforts. She was a remarkable student, listening for hours to the flow of the music. She had absolute pitch and an instinctive ear. She could whistle a complex melody, carry it with the ease of an instrument. Cyrus was pleased. With someone who could whistle like that, maybe the day wouldn't be such a bore. 'Come on, let's skate.' He didn't bother to ask what she had in the small carryall that dangled from her shoulder. All women brought some kind of costume for ice skating.

'I've been practising everything you told me.'

'Good. I'll get the tickets.'

'I'm not as good as I wish I were.'

'It takes time.'

Cyrus laced up his skates and waited for Cameron to return from the ladies' room. When she appeared, he was startled. She had on a skin-tight powder-blue body stocking with a thigh-high ass twitcher of a skirt that showed off her long, straight legs in their white stockings. He watched her walk ahead of him, her butt moving neatly, and he had to admit that she looked surprisingly mature for one so young.

'You look pretty whippy,' he said.

'Thank you,' she replied, almost primly.

Cameron waited at the entrance of the rink while Cyrus took a few turns about the ice, his arms locked behind his back, his weight forward and perfectly balanced as he went into a cross-step turn. She followed him with her eyes, her face glowing with happiness. The chilly air seemed warm, and there was a festiveness about the skaters that she had not noticed earlier. Before, all she could think of was how much

77

better everyone skated than she did. But now she was sure they wouldn't mind her lack of skill; they were kind and tolerant and enjoying themselves. As she was, now that Cyrus was here. When he skidded to a stop in front of her, the razor-sharp blades of his hockey skates shaved a spray of fine ice before him. He took her arm and guided her onto the ice. For a rapturous moment, she saw herself as someone else. She was an ice sprite, a figure of grace and beauty, doing figures and spins and leaps. And all the time Cyrus watched her, his eyes shining with admiration. Then, as he released her arm, reality flooded over her. She stood still, trembling and unsteady. Taking a deep breath to clear her head, she started to skate. But she leaned too far back. Her skates flew out from under her, and before Cyrus could reach her, she sat down hard on the ice. It was a swift, unwelcome anticlimax to all her dreams of impressing him. Laughing, Cyrus helped her up, while Cameron, extremely self-conscious and her face aflame, held on to his arm tightly. She was full of apologies and promises to do better.

But the moment she let go of his arm, she made the same mistake. She leaned back. Her skates slipped out from under her, and she was flat on her rear. Cameron tried not to sound as wretched as she felt. She made herself laugh, get up, and try again. An hour passed and, with each minute, she only managed to get worse. Sitting on the ice and watching the skaters glide past her, around her – one had to leap over her so as not to trip over her body – she wished Geraldine had not insisted on buying her such a fancy skating costume. It only made her constant falling down much more conspicuous. Feeling clumsy and forlorn, Cameron struggled to her feet for the umpteenth time. This time she had fallen near the railing so she was able to hang on and watch Cyrus skate. When he stopped next to her, somehow she lost her grip on the rail and sat down on the ice.

'Aren't you hungry?' he asked, helping her to her feet.

'Yes.' She wasn't hungry. She was too miserable to be hungry. It was awful to be such a disappointment to Cyrus. She'd practised, but ice skating at Radio City was different from skating on Lake Carnegie in Princeton. There were so many fantastic skaters at Radio City that she felt inadequate. This feeling made her forget everything she'd practised.

'What would you like to eat?' Cyrus asked, guiding her to the exit.

'Anything you would like.'

'We could eat at the café and watch the skaters. Or . . .'

'Anything.' The art of flirting was unknown to Cameron. She was young enough to be happy just being with Cyrus, agreeing with him.

'Let's go down to the Village. We can eat there, and it will give us something to do. Geraldine won't expect your call much before five.'

Cameron gulped at his words. The day that had been so full of promise was empty. Skating had been horrible. Now Cyrus was filling in time before he could courteously get rid of her. She felt in the way, an unwanted responsibility to be packed off as quickly as possible.

'I'd love to go to Greenwich Village,' she replied quietly.

'Good! It'll be fun. I like the Village, and it will be even more fun for you.' Cyrus bent over and kissed the top of her head, seeming to want to reassure her. 'Now move your rump and get in there and change. We'll leave the skating outfit in the Bird. While you change, there's a call I have to make.'

'Sure. I'll be right back.' Cameron felt the strain lifting. She had misjudged him. There was nothing wrong between them. It was simply that he had other plans. Her friend was back with his kindness and caring. He had kissed her, too. It was brotherly, but he had kissed her. The day, for all its awful moments, wasn't so bad after all.

* * *

Cameron and Cyrus wandered through the Village, Cyrus finding his way like a native. The air was full of autumn sunlight that fell like a blessing on the old bricks of the small buildings. Cameron walked beside him, the wind blowing her hair, happy in his silence, yet eager to hear anything he chose to say. Whether or not he talked made little difference to her as long as she was with him. Her only enemy was time. The minutes kept passing and precious time slipped away. They drifted with the seemingly endless variety of people; the narrow, crooked streets swarmed with a swift, electric life. Cameron watched men loading crates onto a truck. Despite the coolness in the air, their arms were bare, reminding her of other men loading crates onto a boat on a wharf somewhere else. That scene was so vivid in her mind she might have seen it yesterday. She desperately wanted to remember this one too, and she shut her eyes for an instant to file it in her memory forever. They strolled through Washington Square. Children with shiny black Latin hair were playing soccer. They dodged among the heavy flow of adults, shouting loudly to one another between the slow-moving buses. Old men, bundled up in heavy coats, some wearing round skullcaps, sat on benches in a quiet corner of the park and played chess on stone tables.

They ate lunch at John's on Bleecker Street between Sixth and Seventh avenues. There were no cloths on the tables, the napkins were paper, and the white tiled floor was covered with sawdust. But Cyrus insisted, 'They make the best pizza in New York.'

Cameron, her mouth full, agreed. 'It's nothing like the pizza in Princeton.'

They put away eight wedges of pizza. And as was every place Cameron visited with Cyrus, the small pizzeria was invested forever with a heady glamour.

After John's, they poked into antique shops before visiting Peter's Bookstore on Fourth Street. The store was a beehive of activity, crowded with customers looking for books and getting little help. Peter, a gnome of a man, was seated on a high stool behind an old-fashioned cash register. He was reading a book with the help of a large magnifying glass.

'Hi, Peter.'

'Hello, Cyrus,' Peter replied without looking up.

'Peter, this is Cameron Hightower.'

'Hello, Peter,' Cameron said.

'Hello, Cameron Hightower,' Peter said, still reading.

'Did you find my books, Peter?'

Peter looked up. 'Sure.'

'What do I owe you?'

'Ask Effie. She wrapped them.'

'What books, Cyrus?' Cameron was interested.

'*The Cream of the Jest* and *Nightwood*. Hard to find.'

'Very hard,' Effie corrected him. 'I've been offered double what I agreed while I waited for you to collect them.'

Cyrus paid Effie $25, and Cameron and he left the store. They wandered down Cornelia Street where there was a stable still smelling of horses, but there were no horses. Only a bakery. In the bakery they bought a bag of anise sticks and munched them as they walked. They moved like swimmers floating with the tide, and discovered a grocery which was full of great bread and cheese and salamis hanging from the ceiling. Cyrus bought some cheese and a salami.

'We'll bring a present.'

'To whom?'

'You'll see.'

They strolled back from Bleecker Street and stopped in front of a long, narrow two-storey loft building on the corner of Bleecker and Sixth Avenue. Cameron followed Cyrus through a small door into a dark, dingy hall that smelled of urine and up a flight of stairs that had a definite slant away from the wall. She wondered if the stairs might give way under them at any moment.

81

'Sam has the second floor,' Cyrus explained.

'Who's Sam?'

'A friend of mine. He needs cheap space for his work.'

At the top of the stairs, Cyrus knocked on a surprisingly solid wooden door and waited. Before he could knock again, the door was opened by a young man in his early twenties. He wore brown corduroy jeans that were splattered with paint, hand-tooled boots, and a T-shirt; a man perfectly cast by nature to fill the requirements of what romantics believe a painter should look like. He was lean, above average in height, and nicely built. Not muscular but not skinny. His head was well shaped and he had curly black hair, a pointed beard, a full sensuous mouth with astonishing red lips and large white teeth. His dark eyes were alert and mischievous under amazingly thick eyebrows.

'Cyrus! Welcome! My friend and patron.' He spoke with a faint accent Cameron couldn't identify. 'I thought you said she had blonde hair.'

'That's someone else. I've brought my friend Cameron Hightower.' He handed Sam the salami and cheese and grinned at Cameron. 'Cameron, this is Saddam Chamoun. Known to his many friends as Sam. There are three things in the world that matter to Sam. His painting. Blondes. And the sun. I'm not sure in which order.'

'Hello, Saddam.'

'How do you do, Cameron. Any friend of Cyrus's must call me Sam. You have good cheekbones.'

'Sam looks like a painter. Dresses like a painter. Talks like a painter. And when he paints, he paints like a painter. That is between blondes. Fortunately, you're not a blonde. Or he'd insist on your posing.'

'Oh?' Cameron was flustered. A tiny quiver ran through her stomach as she wondered about posing for Sam. Then Sam stood aside and waved them into his loft.

The long, open area Cameron found herself in had been

something else before it became a studio. The windows were washed and the floor was a clean, light hardwood. The only furniture was a sofa with broken springs and a collection of worn chairs. In the middle of the room, under a large skylight, an easel was set up along with a table full of paints and brushes. At the far end of the room, unpainted plasterboard had been nailed to exposed two-by-four studs. Cameron guessed that the crude walls separated the several rooms necessary to serve human needs other than painting. Probably a kitchen of sorts, a bathroom, and a bedroom. In a way, the studio reminded her of her tar-paper shack. It made her feel a kinship with Sam.

Sam had been watching her. 'During the day, the light is ideal.'

Cameron nodded. The old brick wall had been painted white and canvases were stacked, one on top of the other, along the wall. Splendid paintings. Flashing, brilliant pinks and oranges, pulsating greens and blues, so deep one felt like diving into them. She hadn't seen this much colour since leaving her island.

'Do you like them?' Sam asked.

'They're beautiful!'

'He's very good,' Cyrus agreed, giving Sam an approving smile. 'But I gather they didn't suit Renata. You won't be showing them at the gallery later?'

'Oh, no!' Sam laughed. 'That's an entirely different grouping.'

Cameron stared at Cyrus, her face full of questions.

He explained. 'I'm the heretic member of the Hansen family who collects art. As well as annual reports. I buy Sam's paintings. It helps him pay the rent and buy wine.'

'Painting is not as financially rewarding as selling disposable diapers.'

'Maybe after today it will be more rewarding,' Cyrus said.

He looked around the studio. 'Did Renata take everything else? I've more taste for her leftovers than her main courses.'

'Since I believe there should be no secrets between an artist and his patron, I'll show you something I did recently, B.R. Before Renata. A labour of love.' He went to a corner and returned with a canvas, being careful to face it away from Cyrus. When he turned it around, it was with a great flourish. 'There! What do you think?'

It was a beautifully detailed painting of a full-size guitar overpainted with a translucent image of Harry Belafonte's face.

'It's pop art. The guitar is very good, but I don't care for pop art.'

'I find it interesting. And it sells. Maybe not as well as the paintings I did for today's showing, but I can't complain.'

'I suppose you have to do what you have to do. But why use your guitar and Belafonte?'

'Why not? Marilyn Monroe doesn't interest me. And I have no feelings for flags. Or numbers. Or soup cans. Or comic strips. But guitars are beautiful, so I painted my guitar.'

Cameron started to whistle the tune to 'Come back Lisa, come back girl. Wipe the tears from me eye . . .' Then she stopped. 'I like the painting very much,' she said softly, her eyes roving around the room. 'Where is the guitar?'

'Wait a minute.' Sam disappeared behind one of the partitions and returned carrying a black case. He opened it and showed Cameron the guitar in the painting.

Cameron stared at the guitar. It was a beautiful classic instrument with three spun-silk strings and three nylon ones. The wood was almost black but the grain was clearly evident. The tuning pegs were white ivory while the neck of the guitar was inlaid with white and black ivory.

'You want to play it?'

'How do you know she can?'

'She can. You heard her.' Sam turned to Cameron. 'This

guitar is over eighty years old. It was made in Seville by Antonio Torres, the man most responsible for the modern guitar.' He handed the instrument to Cameron. 'The master gave this guitar to my grandfather in 1909.'

'Wonders never cease. Sam never allows anyone to touch his paints or his guitar.'

Cameron began to strum the instrument. Hesitatingly at first and then with more authority. She stopped to tune the E string. An odd, far-off expression came over her face as the sound filled the studio. In a clear, natural soprano, she began to sing. 'Day O. Day-ay-ay O. Daylight come and I wan'na go home . . .'

Cyrus listened, fascinated, while Sam moved about the room dancing to the rhythm. When the song ended, they clapped and shouted, 'More! More!'

She sang for a half hour, both men entranced by the purity of her voice and the ease with which she handled the calypso rhythms. Then she stopped. 'No more.' She handed the guitar to Sam.

'My God! She's another Joan Baez,' Sam enthused.

'Where did you learn calypso?' Cyrus asked.

'On the islands. You know I grew up there.'

Cyrus glanced at his young friend, and for an instant saw memories reflected in her face that told of more than grief for her parents. How did someone so innocent know how to sing those songs the way she did?

'Do you like Princeton?' Sam asked.

'I like it.'

'But not much,' Cyrus added.

'I like it,' Cameron insisted. She returned Cyrus's look, her eyes pleading not to be questioned. He knew almost everything about her except The Year. He believed what everybody in Princeton believed. That she'd been found and adopted immediately after her parents drowned. According to Cousin Geraldine, The Year was nobody's business. And what Cousin Geraldine said was law in the Hightower family. Privately, Cameron felt that all the rest of her cousins were glad to forget The Year. And Cyrus might not like knowing about it, either.

'It's getting late,' she said. 'I ought to call Cousin Geraldine and have her send the car.'

'No way!' Cyrus insisted. 'We're going to Renata's gallery and take in Sam's show. After that it's Bertolotti's for dinner. Where everybody sings and I can show you off.'

'I thought you had a date for dinner.'

'I did. I'll cancel it. Call Geraldine and tell her I'll drive you home.'

'Okay.' Cameron glowed.

The three left the loft together. Sam hurried to get to his exhibition in time for the five-o'clock opening while Cameron and Cyrus dawdled, walking slowly up Sixth Avenue.

Eventually they entered the lobby of a five-storey building on Greenwich Street. The building was about as far west as one could walk, almost at the Hudson River. There was an elevator with the door standing open and a hand-painted sign on it that said, 'Out of Order. Use the Stairs.' An arrow pointed to a staircase behind the elevator. At the foot of the staircase was another, more colourful sign. It said, 'Renata's Gallery – Fifth Floor.' Below were the words, 'Walking up stairs is good exercise. Try it. You'll like it.' Cameron and Cyrus started to climb. They were followed by a couple who had entered the lobby just after them.

'Boris discovered him. I think Boris found Lichtenstein.' The bearded man in the black turtleneck sweater and tweed jacket directed his words as much at Cameron as he did at his companion. He assumed everyone knew who Boris was and was interested in what he had to say.

'No,' the lady disagreed. 'Renata found him. She's one of the smartest dealers around. She's tiresome, but she has a certain Armenian cunning.' The woman was dressed in a tight black lace gown and an ermine wrap, and she wore black shoes with stiletto heels.

'Personally, I'm not crazy about erotica. I'm not sure sex has any significance.'

Cameron wondered how the woman managed to climb the stairs in her skin-tight dress and her impossible shoes. After sixty-five steps – Cameron counted them – they reached the fifth floor and arrived at the gallery. The large room was lit by bare fluorescent bulbs that perfectly simulated daylight. The paintings were mounted on display racks that extended out from aluminium poles like spokes from the hub of a wheel. There were six floor-to-ceiling poles, each holding eight paintings.

Cameron gaped, shocked by the paintings. They were what the man said. Erotic! Highly erotic! Full of explicit, graphically detailed sex. There were single figures, mostly girls, touching themselves. There were couples wound around each other. And more complex groupings. Two men and a girl. Two girls and a man. Two men. Two girls. And more. All enjoying some form of sex. The colours were enough to excite an emotional response apart from the subject matter. Cameron felt a warmth in her body, a confusion of the senses, and saw Cyrus staring at her.

'I think I made a mistake,' he said, glancing around. 'I didn't realize what the exhibition would be. Maybe we ought to go?'

'No!' Cameron said vehemently. It was important not to allow Cyrus to see how affected she was. 'In Art Appreciation, we study all kinds of paintings. You know Titian did nudes. So did Picasso.'

'All right,' Cyrus said. 'As long as you understand that this is only another form of art.'

'Of course.' Cameron tried to sound casual.

'I'm going to find Sam. Why don't you wander around?'

Cameron's heart pounded so hard she was glad it was noisy so that no one could hear it. Everyone was talking at the top of their voices; laughing, shrieking, for no reason that she could tell. The studio was packed with an astonishing collection of people. Some, Cameron guessed, were Village artists. Others might be art dealers or critics. Geraldine had told her that they were the powers in the art world. There were also what looked like uptown people dressed in outrageous clothes, ogling each other and only occasionally looking at the paintings. There seemed to be a lot of kissing going on: kissing on the cheek, on the lips, on the forehead, on the hands. Wine was being passed around by two young women – their hair in pigtails, with beaded headdresses and peasant skirts. One was wearing red eye shadow and the other green. Each girl was followed by a young man, stripped to the waist, wearing scruffy jeans – the men could have been twins – and carrying a tray loaded with canapés of Italian salami, sardines, pickled artichokes, crackers. The guests were up on their hind legs, sniffing and snorting like mares in heat.

'Did you see . . .'

'Do you like . . .'

'They say he sleeps with his collectors.'

'Before or after they buy a painting?'

A young woman with a small dog nestling in her arm drifted over to Cameron. She was wearing white satin knickers, a white satin halter, and a red feather jacket. 'What's your name?' she asked in a soft, childlike voice.

'Cameron. Cameron Hightower.'

'I'm Princess. You can call me Princess.'

'Hello, Princess.'

'Hello, Cameron.' Princess glanced at the paintings. 'Aren't they succulent? They remind me of the Black Pagoda. A Western version of the temple sensuality of India.' She tilted her head sideways. 'Have you slept with Saddam yet?'

'No!' Cameron was nonplussed.

'Neither have I. But I will soon.' Princess drifted away.

Cameron felt completely out of place. Then she glimpsed Cyrus at the far end of the gallery talking to a woman wearing a see-through blouse and very tight velvet pants who she recognized as one of the models. The one being made love to by two men. Cameron felt a wave of pure female jealousy. Cyrus should be with *her*. No! That was silly. She didn't own him. Nevertheless, she felt forlorn and forgotten. Cyrus seemed to fit in. He looked as thought he belonged at the showing. Not like her. She was always an outsider.

'I love parties like this,' said a man on her right dressed in a conventional three-piece business suit. 'I really believe in supporting the arts. How do you feel about environmental art? Minimal art? American realism?' Cameron kept shrugging in puzzlement. 'Don't you like anything?' The man sounded exasperated.

'I go to school. I got an A in Art Appreciation.' Cameron extracted herself from the conversation. 'Excuse me. I have to see a friend.'

Somehow she managed to work her way through the crowd and approach Saddam. Saddam was speaking to a short, stocky woman with outlandishly dyed, fire-engine red hair. When he paused to catch his breath, he noticed Cameron had joined them. 'Our calypso singer. Welcome, Cameron Hightower, this is – '

He was interrupted by the woman, 'Hightower? Cameron Hightower?' The woman wore a plain beige dress that was a bit too short, showing off a good pair of legs beneath a barrel-shaped body. 'Are you related to the Princeton Hightowers? To Geraldine Hightower?'

'Yes,' Cameron said slowly. 'I'm Geraldine's cousin.'

'Saddam, shame on you. You never told me you knew Cameron Hightower.' The woman sounded petulant.

'I only met her this afternoon.' Saddam glanced at Cameron. 'This is Renata Parsons. My dealer.'

'How do you do, Mrs Parsons.'

'It's Ms Parsons. But you can call me Renata. Everyone does. How do you do, Cameron Hightower. It's a pleasure to have you with us. You be sure to give Geraldine my regards. A pity she couldn't come.' Her voice had become a purr.

'Who is Geraldine?' Saddam asked, seemingly offhand.

'Geraldine Hightower, my boy, is a collector of impeccable taste.'

Saddam gave Cameron an appraising look. 'Aaah, Cameron.'

'She's a sweet child, Saddam. Show her around.' Renata smiled at Cameron but spoke to Saddam. 'I must say hello to Benjamin. And you must speak to our dear friend Charles.' Still smiling at Cameron, she edged away.

Saddam gestured to a very young man seated on the floor nearby, his back resting against the wall. 'Byron, get up. Come and meet a new friend of mine. Amuse her.'

The very young man, younger even than Cameron, unwound his body and stood up. A long, string bean of a boy. Lank black hair hung over his eyes. He had a high forehead, hollow cheeks, and his eyes gleamed with a mournful keenness. His most striking characteristic was his immaturity. It seemed to be fuzzed all over him like the beginnings of a beard. He reminded Cameron of herself only a few years ago. He grinned cheerfully at her. 'Hi. I'm Byron Miller.'

Cameron thought he looked like a boy who might like to leap from peak to peak as though there were no valleys in between. 'Hello, Byron.'

'You must excuse me for one moment only,' Saddam said. 'Do you see the man leaning on his cane? He's the publisher of *Art Vision*.'

'A good review from him could double the price of Sam's paintings,' remarked Byron, half smiling. 'Give him a painting now, Sam.'

'You can't give an art critic a painting.' Cameron was wide-eyed. 'He wouldn't accept it. It's like a ... well ...' She swallowed. 'It's like a bribe.'

'Believe me, Cameron,' Byron said quietly as Saddam approached the publisher, 'he will accept it. In fact, he expects Sam to give him a painting. The only question is which one does he want? That's what Sam has to find out.'

'But it's bribery!' Cameron insisted.

'It's also the way of the art world.'

'It doesn't sound very businesslike.'

'It's extremely businesslike. It's all about making money. Except there are none of the usual rules.'

Byron's enjoyment of Cameron's naïveté was blatant. He explained to her, with the relish of a boy lecturing an older person who should have known better, how art critics became art dealers and then sold the paintings they'd collected from the painters for giving them good reviews. And how art editors became curators and bought their own collections for museums. It all struck him as funny. Particularly when painters became critics and hated everyone's work but their own.

'You mean the critics' reviews are biased? I mean, biased in favour of the paintings that they already own? Or expect to receive as a gift?' Cameron was deeply shocked.

'Sure. When a critic likes a painter's work, he always gives the painter a good review. And that increases the value of the critic's paintings.'

'It sounds dishonest.'

'It happens to be very profitable. If you're a critic.'

'You sound as if you'd like to be a critic.'

Byron pursed his lips thoughtfully and said that being a critic had its merits. To become an art critic one didn't need any training. Or a degree like a Ph.D. All one needed was a magazine or a newspaper to publish one's opinions. And then, with the right collection, a critic could make a fortune. The look of a wise child came into his eyes. 'The only thing

I ever learned from my father was to be an insider. It makes no difference if you're on the inside of Wall Street or of the art world. You make money.'

Cameron had an impulse to ask Byron what his father did, then changed her mind. 'You're very interested in money, aren't you?'

'The only people who aren't interested in money are people who have too much of it. I don't. Besides,' Byron added rather wistfully, 'money can be very rewarding. But I've settled for chemistry. Even though I like paintings, I'd never make it in the art world. I don't have the knack for discovering undiscovered painters. And then convincing myself that they should be discovered. Too often, they all look alike to me.'

Saddam rejoined them full of cheer. 'He thinks my colours are dominant. Sensuously tonic. Byron, what the hell is he talking about?'

'Don't you remember? He used to be the music critic for the San Mateo *Mercury*.' Byron explained that the critic was probably referring to the chords in music. The tonic chord and the dominant chord. 'Classical composers like Mozart and Haydn used them as the basis for a lot of their music. I'm sure he loves your work.'

Cameron found she liked the strange boy, despite his teasing. 'Byron, what don't you know?' she asked, smiling.

'I know a lot.' He nodded, satisfied. 'I have a broad-gauge mind.'

Saddam rubbed his hands together with pleasure.

'So you're Geraldine Hightower's cousin?' Renata had rejoined them. 'What do you do, child?'

'I go to the Paddington School.'

'Ahah! The Paddington School in Princeton. They have a fine art collection. Who brought you here?'

'Cyrus Hansen.'

'Cyrus Hansen!' She glared at Saddam, who grinned and nodded. 'Is Cyrus Hansen here, too?'

'Yes.' Cameron pointed to Cyrus, who was deep in conversation with a beautiful blonde. A different girl from the one he'd been talking to earlier. They nodded and smiled as though they'd just agreed on something pleasant. Then Cyrus kissed the girl lightly on the forehead – as earlier in the day he had kissed Cameron – and broke away to work his way through the gawkers and join them. Once again Cameron tried to hide the sting of jealousy within her.

'Well.' Cyrus was full of the good humour a man feels after arranging matters to his liking with a beautiful woman. 'Are you enjoying yourself, Cameron?' He glanced carelessly at the lanky boy shuffling from one foot to the other. 'Hello,' he said. 'I'm Cyrus Hansen.'

'Hi.' Byron stuck out his hand. 'Byron Miller.' They shook hands.

'Have you had enough, Cameron? I don't know about you, but I'm ready to go.'

Cameron felt all the helpless despondency of a child whose treat is over. And Cyrus had doubly spoiled the day by his interest in other girls.

The look on Cameron's face made Cyrus conscious of his desertion of her – how he'd left her alone almost as soon as they'd entered the gallery. The temptation of so many available women wandering around, just waiting for him, had been too great. He had hurt her and now he wished to make amends. 'Did you forget?' he asked. 'We're going to Bertolotti's, Cameron, where all the waiters sing. You and I. Wait until they hear you.'

The words passed slowly into Cameron's brain. Cyrus said them so casually as though the matter was of little consequence. He wasn't going with one of the other girls. He was still taking her to dinner.

'I guess I'll be going,' Byron said.

Cameron heard Byron, and he sounded like an echo of her

dejection moments ago. She recognized her own loneliness in his expression. He felt like an outsider, too.

'Could Byron come with us, Cyrus?' she asked.

Cyrus still wanted to make amends, and if Byron's coming along pleased Cameron, then Byron must come along. 'Sure.' He waved at Byron. 'Want to join us? My treat.'

Byron did not hesitate. 'I make it a point of honour never to turn down a free meal.'

'Okay. Good luck with the porn, Sam.' Cyrus linked his arm through Cameron's right arm while Byron slipped his much thinner arm under her left. Cameron glanced at him, pleased with the world. Byron was nice, and she had a hunch they would become friends. The three of them marched across the floor, out of the door, and down the sixty-five steps to the street. Cameron started to whistle. She was still young enough to consider going to dinner with Cyrus to be a triumph. Cyrus had chosen her over the beautiful, more adult women in the gallery, in the city. This was the happiest day in her life.

6

One Saturday afternoon when Cyrus was ten, in what seemed like a rare display of grandfatherly affection, Elmer Hansen took his grandson to the Bronx Zoo. As it turned out, the visit was intended to be an object lesson rather than an outing. The very young Cyrus stared at the animals with wide eyes. He watched the lion pace up and down and listened to his roar and heard the answering roars of other animals. Elmer watched him curiously.

'He's very big.'

'He comes from Africa, and when he roars, the other animals are frightened,' Elmer explained.

Cyrus nodded. 'Look at his teeth. He's strong.'

'He is strong,' Elmer agreed. 'He could kill a guard with one blow of his paw.'

'Wow!' Cyrus gasped.

'He's called the king of the jungle.'

'He looks like a king.'

'He doesn't to me.'

A silence followed as Cyrus waited for his grandfather to explain.

'One day hunters caught the king of the jungle in a simple trap. Then they locked him up in that cage behind iron bars.'

'If he got out, he would eat people.'

'He can't get out. And if he did, the guards would shoot him.'

'Listen to him roar.'

'I hear him. He's roaring because he's angry. Look at that cage, Cyrus. It's not much larger than your room.'

'Is he unhappy?'

'Yes. He's unhappy and angry because he wants to get out of the cage.' Elmer paused. 'In a way, he reminds me of your father.'

Cyrus looked up at his tall grandfather and saw something he'd seen many times before; something in his handsome grandfather's eyes.

'You know your father lives in a cage. Most men live in a cage. They live there because they don't know how to escape.'

Cyrus huddled in his jacket and pretended not to hear.

'I don't live in a cage. I'm freer than that lion. Wouldn't you agree, Cyrus, that makes me a king?'

'No!' Cyrus screamed. He punched his grandfather. 'My father doesn't live in a cage. He doesn't!'

Elmer laughed. 'Punch harder! Harder!'

Cyrus started to cry in frustration.

'You're starting to learn, Cyrus. Punch! Hit the enemy. But you must learn to hit harder or you'll live in a cage, too.'

'No I won't,' Cyrus muttered through his tears.

That night Cyrus had a bad dream. He dreamed of his father imprisoned in a cage and his grandfather walking around the cage shouting. 'You're in a cage, you fool. You'll never get out!'

The truth was, Ellie Hansen could have got out long ago. Since his uncle, Butler Hansen, had left him his shares in Hansen and Hansen, Ellie was a multimillionaire in his own right. It was Butler's joke on Elmer because he'd always insisted that Ellie might have been his son. There were times when Elmer wondered if maybe Butler wasn't right, given that Junior had no brains and Louise had been a beautiful, sensual woman. The only thing that made him think otherwise was Cyrus. Cyrus not only looked like him, he had his brains, not Butler's.

But despite his huge personal fortune, Ellie could not get out of his cage, because Elmer so dominated his spirit. And on this Sunday in October, his life depended on his getting out.

'You didn't keep that appointment with Hardy, did you, Junior? I'd like to know why.'

As usual, Ellie was unable to answer a direct question from his father.

'I'll ask you again. Why didn't you keep the appointment?'

Ellie's gaze moved from the library window to fix on his father. Elmer was a fine figure of a man in his tweed jacket, riding breeches, and polished brown boots.

'As I remember, I gave you three months.'

Ellie cleared his throat and tried to make his lips move.

'The time ended Wednesday.'

'I don't want to do it,' Ellie gasped.

Elmer looked into his son's eyes. He liked looking into people's eyes. When he did that, he felt he controlled them. 'It is sad but true. You are useless.'

'I don't want to do it,' Ellie insisted.

'You misunderstand. What you want to do doesn't matter. Only what I want you to do matters.'

Ellie went to the liquor cabinet and poured himself a shot of brandy. 'There are no grounds,' he said at last.

'She's an alcoholic.'

'She drinks a bit too much Scotch before dinner.'

'And vodka in her orange juice at breakfast. And a flask of brandy when she rides. She'd probably be better off in an institution, and if you make it necessary, I'll see to it that she's placed in one.'

Ellie put down the brandy snifter and pressed his arms against his sides, clenching and unclenching his hands. They were sweating. 'I love her.'

'You love her. That's nice.' Elmer took no pleasure in the pain in his son's face. He hated Ellie's dumb, helpless, dark eyes that never seemed to mirror a thought, that accepted life

97

like an animal. 'There is an alternative. If you refuse to speak to Hardy, you'll force me to speak to Phyllis.'

'Please don't speak to Phyllis.'

'You give me no choice.'

'I'll see Hardy. Just don't say anything to Phyllis.'

'Why don't you get dressed?'

'Ellie! You're not ready?' Phyllis Quincey Hanson entered the room wearing jodhpurs, boots, and a brown hacking jacket.

'I forgot we're riding today.'

'You know we practise on Sundays, Ellie.' Phyllis was a tall woman with a robust body that was only at ease outdoors. Over the years, her skin, weathered by sun and wind, had become grooved with a thousand tiny lines. Once she'd been considered handsome, but time had changed her expression. Now her face had a haunted look.

'As I suggested, Junior, will you please change into your riding clothes?'

'Ellie . . .' Phyllis gave her husband a pleading look, and he hurried from the library. She made herself smile at Elmer. 'I telephoned the stable, Dad, and told them to saddle Rainwater, Changeling, and Dancer.' She never permitted her hatred of Elmer to show. Often her feelings were so strong they frightened her, and she drank too much in an attempt to dull them. If she weren't careful, she could bring disaster down on Ellie and herself. She flattered Elmer constantly. 'I always believed your buying that acreage and clearing your own trails was a wonderful idea, but it's worked out even better than I expected.'

'We needed a place where you could help me work on my jumping technique.' Elmer sounded almost friendly. 'My tailor tells me my scarlet jacket will be ready Wednesday. I'll wear it to the Saturday hunt.'

'You'll cut a handsome figure in it, Dad.'

'Thank you, Phyllis. And thank you for your efforts over

the years. I don't believe I'd have been awarded the colours if it hadn't been for you.'

'No, Dad. You did it yourself. You've become a fine horseman. Everyone in the club admires you.'

'I'm glad.' Elmer accepted her compliment. 'Things have been on schedule, more or less. And you've been an asset to the Hansen family.'

Instinctively, Phyllis shrank from his praise. Something more was coming. She had worked long and hard and tactfully to have Elmer invited to join the Essex Hunt Club. Her family, going back many generations, had been among the founding members. She understood only too well that it was her family's social position that had persuaded Elmer to permit his son to marry her. As it was the Hansen money that had persuaded her father to allow her to marry Ellie. Raymond Quincey was a snob who looked down on the Hansens as though the Hansens, not the Quinceys, were on their uppers. Her father could spend hours talking about Somerset Quincey, the ancestor who gave his name to a New Jersey county, as if Somerset were alive and well and his dearest friend. But in the end, Raymond Quincey was not above getting some mileage out of his ancestry. After a private conversation with Elmer Hansen, he'd agreed that Phyllis, his only child, could marry Elmer Hansen, Jr, even though the Hansens were nobodies. Considering the extensive financial arrangements involved, Phyllis thought the marriage might well have taken place in an accountant's office instead of a church. The fact that Ellie and she loved each other was of no significance to either parent. There were times when Phyllis couldn't decide who she detested more, her father or her father-in-law.

'I'm glad you're pleased, Dad.'

'I'm quite satisfied. So now we move on the next phase.'

'The next phase?' Phyllis was puzzled.

'The question of heirs to the Hansen name.'

'What about Cyrus?'

'He was almost killed last year in a car accident. Things have a way of happening. I want more than one heir. Two at least, maybe three.'

With great effort Phyllis maintained her composure. 'Ellie and I have been trying to have another child.'

'You've been trying for years without success. Having tested Ellie, we know that, for once, he's not at fault.'

'There's a new drug that – '

'There are always new drugs that don't work. The fact is, you're getting ... shall we say, older?' There was a dead silence in the room. 'Therefore I think it best for you to divorce Junior so he'll be free to marry someone more suitable.'

In spite of herself, Phyllis was shaking. She knew Elmer wanted many male heirs. He never allowed her to forget it. Every time she missed a period only to have it come a month later, she fought off the knowledge of his rage. Then Cyrus had had the accident, and she could think of little else.

'Does Ellie want a divorce?'

'Don't pretend naïveté, Phyllis. You know me quite well. Have I ever asked Junior what he wants or doesn't want?' Elmer's mouth turned up in the most agreeable of smiles. 'You will divorce him.'

'On what grounds?'

'No grounds. It won't be contested.'

'I won't do it.'

Elmer stopped smiling. 'You will!'

A scream rose in Phyllis's throat; she stifled it. 'No! I refuse.'

Elmer's anger showed openly. 'You will call a lawyer and start divorce proceedings. Or I will cut off the allowance I pay your drunken father.'

The impulse that had been jerking at Phyllis's wrists

suddenly broke free. She lunged at Elmer, her hands flying. 'You bastard!'

Elmer caught her wrists. He held them for an instant in front of him. Then he quickly shifted his grip to her shoulders. He shook her violently. Phyllis's head snapped back and forth with each shake. Abruptly, Elmer was sickened by his loss of temper, a trait he despised in others and would not tolerate in himself. He released his daughter-in-law, and she fell into a chair. He leaned down and spoke softly in her ear.

'I'm sorry, Phyllis, but your obstinacy is very trying. Since you cannot give me any more heirs, another woman will. Please listen and listen hard. If you give me any trouble, I shall be forced to see to it that your family loses the house in Palm Beach and the house in Princeton. And the box at Churchill Downs and the membership in the Hunt Club and the Pretty Brook Club. Must I go on?'

Phyllis burst into low, hoarse sobs. 'I don't want to leave Ellie.'

'You failed to give my son another child. The Hansen Company must have the security of more than one heir.'

Phyllis's sobs grew louder.

'I will make my point as clear as possible. As long as you cooperate, you and your family will live in complete comfort, in luxury. Your alimony will be sizable enough for your father to drink himself to death, while your mother continues with her endless needlepoint. And you can live anywhere in the world you like, do anything you please. I will even agree that if you marry again, your alimony will continue. You'll be a wealthy woman. There are women who would sell their souls for the freedom I'm offering you. You see, Phyllis, I have nothing against you. I actually like you. But I must have another heir. The future of the Hansen Company must be secure.'

Phyllis slumped in her chair. She'd had too much to drink

101

earlier. Her neck ached horribly, and there seemed to be two Elmers crouching in front of her, swimming in and out of focus. Elmer reached for the flask she always kept in her jacket pocket. He unscrewed the cap and handed the flask to her. 'Take a drink. You need it.'

Phyllis accepted the flask and managed to get several sips down. Now there was only one Elmer.

'Would you like another drink?'

She answered his question by all but draining the flask.

'Good! That should hold you for now.' Elmer took the flask from her unresisting hand, walked to the liquor cabinet, and refilled it with brandy. Then he handed it back to her. 'Screw the cap and put the flask back in your pocket.'

Phyllis did as she was told, all the while avoiding looking at Elmer.

'Take your car and drive to the stables. Junior and I will meet you there. And please drive carefully.'

Phyllis blinked and nodded. The shaking and the alcohol made her head swim.

'You will say nothing to Junior about our talk. Not a word. Is that clear?'

Phyllis's chest heaved as she made an effort to speak. 'I hate you.'

'That's unfortunate. It would be easier on both of us if you understood.'

Phyllis left the library swaying slightly.

Fifteen years earlier, when Elmer had decided that he wanted to join the Essex Hunt Club, he'd bought the property he'd named The Meadows – 143 acres of open, rolling pastures and woodland in the heart of the New Jersey estate and hunt country. He had a stable built with stalls for eight horses as well as a two-storey barn in which feed was stored. There were two bedrooms and a bathroom attached to the red wooden barn where the stable boys lived. The only other building on the property was a small, comfortable white clapboard house near the stables for the stable master, Tom Freeman, and his wife.

There was land enough for numerous excellent riding trails. In addition, a large exercise ring was laid out where horses could walk, trot, canter, and gallop at the same time. Beyond the exercise ring was a flat area where a jump course could be set up with brush spreads, Toronto fences, rustic oxers, post and rails, simulated stone walls, spreads, a water jump – man-made replicas of almost anything one might encounter when fox hunting. Elmer had used a number of different layouts while learning how to jump. He'd practised rigorously under Phyllis's excellent instruction. She was a superb horsewoman. Today they were going to try a new arrangement of jumps. Tom and the stable boys had put together a course identical to the one used in the 1966 World Championship in Buenos Aires. The course represented a taxing challenge for any rider who was not world-class.

Although she'd sipped liberally from the flask of brandy while waiting for Elmer and Ellie, Phyllis could still walk steadily when the two Hansens arrived. She was leading her seven-year-old gelding, Dancer, out of the stables. The horse nuzzled her shoulder, asking for his usual sugar cube. 'Later, boy.' She rubbed her hand against his velvety nose. 'Hi, Ellie,' she called out as the men got out of the station wagon.

It took only one glimpse of her white face for Ellie to realize that his father had said something. A shudder passed through his heavy body. 'Hi, Phyl.' He took one step towards her, then stopped. He wanted to comfort her, to reassure her, but he had no comfort to give. Not with his father watching them.

Elmer remained in the car. 'Saddle Beaut,' he shouted to Jimmy, one of the stable boys sitting on the fence. 'And Galahad for Junior.'

Jimmy blinked and looked to Tom Freeman for direction.

103

Freeman wadded the end of his chewing tobacco and spat into the dirt. He'd already saddled Rainwater. That was the horse Mrs Hansen had chosen for her father-in-law, and Changeling for her husband. But since Old Man Hansen wanted Beaut. Beaut he would get. And Galahad for his son. As usual, something unpleasant was going on in the family; and he didn't like it. But a job was a job, and Elmer Hansen aside, this was a damn good job.

'Move, Jimmy,' he ordered the stable boy. 'You heard the man.' Jimmy moved.

Phyllis flushed as she listened to Elmer's instructions. It was as though he were shaking her again. She reached for her flask and took a deep swallow. Her hands felt clumsy as she adjusted the stirrups to the proper length for jumping. Once they were set, she motioned for Tim Freeman to give her a leg up. She could smell the earth around her, smell the stables, the manure, the saddle soap. She walked her horse around the ring, then took him into a trot, then a canter, and finally a short gallop. By lengthening and shortening Dancer's stride, she warmed him up before trying the new set of jumps.

'Phyllis,' Elmer called from the car, 'you're holding the reins too tight.'

Phyllis ignored him.

'You're pulling too hard.'

Phyllis clamped her jaw shut, a chaos of sensations loose in her. She left the exercise ring and started down the course. First the brush spread – coil and over, engagement, release. Hold him. The Toronto fence – up and over. So far so good. Now the rustic oxer – maximum height and length; up, forward on his neck. She heard a tick. Damn you, Elmer Hansen. She mustn't look back. But she looked back.

Ellie closed his eyes.

Phyllis jerked her head forward and wheeled her horse about. Here was the post and rails – over. Next the wall with poles – shorten stride, gather him up; engagement, forward, balance. Maybe she could make it. She took the spread breathing hard. With each jump her dizziness increased. The second post and rails was coming up. She saw double; there were two jumps. Dancer took the jump but he was moving too fast. Phyllis realized she had lost engagement. Everything was spinning around, and all she could do was try to hang on. They approached the final oxer.

It happened. Dancer refused the jump. Phyllis pitched over the horse, bouncing off the side rails. Dancer reared, the sun glinting off his steel shoes. Phyllis was unable to move and the horse's hooves pawed the air above her. The folly of her mistakes overcame her, and she saw with pitiless clarity the years that had been lost. She gave out a strange, small cry as the hooves descended. Ellie's face flashed before her; trusting and loving and needing her. Then, as twelve hundred pounds of horse crushed her face and neck, all connections to her brain were smashed. Phyllis fell into blackness, returning to the pattern of things.

The morning of the funeral, Ellie could barely open his eyes. But the dull pounding in his chest, the dryness in his throat, the heavy feeling of misery forced him awake.

After a while, he was able to heave himself out of bed. Every movement required a special act of will. A command his brain gave and his body obeyed. He thought about Phyllis. He thought about his father. Slowly, carefully, he shaved, showered, and dressed. Everything he touched was puzzling, even when he had his hands on it. But he managed to knot his tie properly, put on his jacket, and move towards the bedroom door. The worst yet remained. He must meet his father downstairs and drive to the church, sit next to him in church, then drive to the cemetery and stand beside his father while his wife's coffin was lowered into her grave. Cyrus was going in his own car. He refused to go in the limousine. Cyrus? Once he'd had a wife and son. Now it didn't matter. There were only two people in the world, his father and himself. Whatever happened next was between them.

The autumn air was warm over the half-mile lane that wound across fields and through mature woodland to that corner of The Meadows where Elmer Hansen had obtained permission to establish a private cemetery. It was bordered on one side by a meandering creek, and within the low iron fence was a half-acre pond. The landscaping of the cemetery, designed by a fine landscape architect, suggested far more understanding and compassion than Cyrus believed his grandfather capable of feeling.

The funeral was restricted to the immediate family. Phyllis's parents had flown up from Palm Beach. Raymond Quincey remained silent and sober throughout the services. Not so his wife, who wailed with such volume that it was difficult to hear the minister. Eventually, Raymond had to help her back to the waiting limousine. As the heavy mahogany coffin with thick solid brass handles was being lowered into the grave by experienced handlers Elmer had hired for the day, Cyrus found a measure of relief in the knowledge that this was the countryside his mother loved the best. Here were the meadows, the grass, the woods, and wide skies. A place where the hooves of horses could be heard by silent listeners. Once he'd thought his mother not very bright; but as he grew older, he realized that she took in information through her senses, not with her mind. He remembered her remarkable sense of smell, keen as a rare trained dog.

One afternoon of his childhood stood out with special clarity. They had wandered together over the fields when suddenly she stood still, sniffed the air, wrinkled her nose, and led him to her discovery of wild berries hidden in the undergrowth many yards away. The memory made the grief in his body rise and settle behind his eyes, pressing against the lids. He glanced at his father staring vacantly at the peaceful countryside. The land was too big a burden for a man who would never know peace again. In the brief time between his mother's death and the funeral, Cyrus had watched his father constantly, searching for clues. There had been no red eyes, no tortured features, no unshaven stubble of a beard or sloppy item of clothing to alarm him. His father had been like always, inarticulate and kind. Nevertheless, Cyrus was afraid.

The service finally ended. Ellie and Cyrus remained standing at the graveside after Raymond Quincey and Elmer Hansen returned to their cars. With the intensity of his caring, Cyrus was able to sense his father groping blindly for a place to rest. Suddenly Elmer was standing before them.

'Junior, it's time we were on our way.'

Cyrus watched his father slowly turn and look at Elmer.

'I accept the tradition that one mourns. So I give you this week to mourn,' Elmer said. 'But no longer. Be in my office Monday at two o'clock. We have plans to discuss.' He gestured to Cyrus. 'You bring him home.' Then Elmer left.

Ellie passed the week in a semistupor. He felt empty, as though he were nothing, no more than a shadow creeping under the sun. He let Cyrus take him on drives and let Cyrus do all the talking. He let Cyrus sit in silence in his study. He never mentioned Phyllis or how he felt. Cyrus wanted his father to move out of Hansen Hall and take an apartment with him. Ellie refused. He said he had something to do first. Occasionally, Ellie went for drives on his own. Sometimes he drove to the Hansen Company and sat in the parking lot staring at the buildings. Sometimes he drove to the grave site. If he happened to see his father in their home, he looked past him or avoided his eyes. If Elmer spoke to him, he stopped hearing. It was only the coming of Monday at two o'clock that mattered.

107

On Monday he drove to the Hansen Company. As usual, Elmer was in meetings, but there was a message waiting for him confirming that they would meet at Elmer's office at 2:00 P.M. Ellie left his office at noon, and drove to the Princeton airport. He parked his car at the small airport parking lot and left the key in the ignition. It was his last connection to the rest of things. His heart beat heavily, and he only wanted to lie down and not be disturbed. But there was something he had to do first.

His plane was waiting for him, and seeing it gave him a sense of relief. Flying had always been his favourite hobby, as riding had been Phyl's. Over the years he'd owned a number of light planes, often buying them from owners who – for one reason or another – had not maintained them properly. Ellie enjoyed restoring them with his own hands and then selling them. While he doubted his ability when it came to thinking through a business problem, he had no doubts about his ability to fix anything with his hands. Once he'd tried to explain to Phyllis how it was something like her being able to sense the movements of her horse through her legs, her fingers, and bottom. He could feel through his fingers how metal, wood, and fabric wanted to be worked. It was a genuine gift. Under different circumstances, it might have been a valuable gift, but to Ellie Hansen, it was merely the only thing he knew he could do better than his father.

As part of his love of fixing old planes, he'd joined a club whose membership was limited to people who owned and flew World War I planes. Ellie had a perfectly restored and maintained Spad fighter plane, exact to the point of having a camouflaged fuselage and the multicoloured circles on the wings and tail, as well as the single machine gun in the front of the open cockpit. The only changes from what had existed in 1917 were the FAA licence number on the tail and the modern radio under the instrument panel. As he'd requested the Spad had been wheeled near the takeoff runway. Ellie put on his leather helmet, donned a windbreaker he always kept in the trunk of his car, and pulled down his goggles. He climbed onto the wing and scrambled into the cockpit.

The waiting mechanic called out, 'Switch on?'

Ellie responded. 'Switch on.'

'Contact?'

'Contact,' Ellie called back.

Using his foot and hands, the mechanic pulled on the propeller. The engine coughed once – a puff of smoke shot from the exhaust – sputtered and caught. Ellie allowed the motor to warm up for a short time, then he taxied the plane to the runway. Slowly at first, gathering speed, he moved down the narrow asphalt strip and lifted the Spad into the air. When he glanced down, he saw the houses below him looking like toys. The meadows and woods glowed in the early afternoon sunlight; a world of dreams. And he was outside that dream. He was in the sky where each thing existed alone. The sun shone off his goggles, and he flew like a man possessed. Diving and pulling out, skimming the tops of trees, inside loops and and outside loops, wingover, heading straight up until the plane went into a dead stick stall and then spun towards earth – Immelmann turns. Nothing was impossible. Each manoeuvre took him closer to the Hansen Company headquarters. He circled the red brick buildings, flying low and fast; so close he could see the startled faces peering at him out of the windows. Then he began a long climb, rising in a straight line towards the sun. This was a classic tactic for World War I aces; to attack the enemy from out of the sun because one couldn't be seen until it was too late. He was high enough. Ellie glanced at his watch. It was 2:05. His father would be in his usual fury at being kept waiting. Ellie pictured his father at his desk. Sit still, Father. I'll be right there.

He put the Spad into a steep dive. Ellie raised one hand to the machine gun. The lack of bullets was meaningless. He saw the window of Elmer's office centred in the crossed hairs of the machine-gun sight. Heavy convulsions shook Ellie's body. A pulse beat rapidly in his temple. Could he actually do it? For an instant he believed he could. Then, no. At the last second, he pulled back on the stick, and the angle of the plane's dive changed slightly. Ellie shut his eyes to everything. The Spad hit, exploding. The few seconds of pain that Ellie felt seemed to belong to another self.

Elmer Hansen, Jr, died as he had lived – afraid of his father. He was glad his life as a coward was over.

The news of the double tragedy in the Hansen family swept through Princeton. People spoke of little else. In private they had curious opinions.

'I can't understand Phyllis Quincey – I mean Hansen – falling off a horse.'

'Everyone falls off once in a while.'

'I keep telling myself that.'

'But not to roll out from under the horse? Phyllis?'

'It's hard to believe, isn't it?'

'They shot Dancer.'

'Too bad. Fine horse. Not his fault.'

'Good way to keep the horse from talking.'

'Come on, Jess.'

'If he hadn't hit the roof, well, he might have crashed into Elmer Hansen's office. Makes one wonder.'

'It's a miracle no one else was hurt.'

'With all that open area, what was he doing stunting over the Hansen Company?'

'Dudley, you read too many murder mysteries.'

After Ellie's funeral, Elmer Hansen returned to his office to prepare for a business trip to the Coast that would take two weeks. Cyrus Hansen drove to Hansen Hall. He packed his toilet articles, a change of underwear, a pair of jeans, and several shirts into an airline bag. He added up the money he had in his chequebook, his bankbook, and his investment portfolio. At the moment, he was worth a little over $100,000. That would be more than enough to pay for his senior year when he transferred to Yale. But school was in the future. He couldn't think about that now. Or the fact that he was his father's sole heir, inheriting 10 per cent of the Hansen Company. All he knew was that the moment his grandfather returned home, he was in mortal danger – and the danger lay within himself. He'd seen his grandfather as they stood side by side at the grave site. Elmer looked like a huge white cat, crouching, ready to leap. Elmer wanted him as he had not wanted his son. He was waiting for Cyrus to act. Daring him to act. And if he did act and lost his nerve at the last moment – as he was certain his father had – he would be in Elmer's grip forever. And if he succeeded – if he actually killed his grandfather – he would lose the whole world. Cyrus had to get out, get away, run for his life; if his life was to be worth living.

The T Bird roared down Route 206 past Lawrence when Cyrus noticed some kids walking along the side of the road. All at once he remembered Cameron and braked the car to a screeching stop. He could call from a nearby house and say good-bye. He started to open the door and stopped. No! He was finished with everyone connected to Princeton. Even Cameron. Anyone who might remind him of his grandfather. He started the car again and was touching seventy within seconds as he ran from himself.

Every other week or so after Cameron and Byron met, she would take the train to New York to see him. They would wander the city together, visiting art galleries, museums, the Cloisters, the Planetarium, the Battery – everywhere. So they

111

became friends. For Byron, Manhattan was the universe. He loved the crowded pavements, the bumper-to-bumper traffic, the tall, looming buildings, the noisy, pushy subways. It grieved him that he did not live in Manhattan. She didn't know exactly where he did live except that it was in what he called 'no-human-land' while waving vaguely towards the horizon over the Queensboro Bridge. 'It's where all the people are dying to get into the cemeteries,' he said, smiling.

But during the year that her friendship with Byron grew, it was Cyrus Hansen who was really the centre of her life. She was always in danger of saying 'Cyrus says . . .' or 'Cyrus thinks . . .' or 'Cyrus does . . .' Sometimes she couldn't tell if he was serious or teasing. At bottom she didn't care. When they were apart, she could hear his voice in her ears, close her eyes and see his face. After her parents died, she'd thought very little about being happy. Happiness was something she remembered from the time she was a small, heedless child, before the wildness of the hurricane. But with Cyrus she again felt pure happiness. The sun seemed to burn more brightly, the air sparkled, every leaf of grass shimmered with its own interior light – a light that seemed to shine out from her as well. With Cyrus, time stopped. She felt contented, cocooned in a joyous peace.

When Cyrus's mother and father both died as the result of accidents, the golden time ended. All the brightness fled from her days. A familiar nausea gripped the pit of her stomach. She could feel the weight of the sky pressing on her head. The old pain of the past, the tightness in her throat and the deadly weariness she had known the first time returned. At night she would grow feverish, her body drenched with the cold sweat of fear. Memories rushed back as she thought of the things that had happened to her and the things she might say to Cyrus to console him, to comfort him, to show him how completely she understood and wanted to share his grief.

And with it all, she knew for the first time that in her own way she was stronger than Cyrus; strong enough for both of them. He could lean on her and give vent to his rage and bewilderment and sorrow. She knew all there was to know about that kind of anguish. But as time passed and Cyrus made no attempt to reach her, Cameron grew increasingly alarmed. She felt herself bound to him by a bond that made her ties to the rest of the world superficial. She had etched him so deep into her heart, felt so much a part of him, a part of his grief, that she couldn't understand his silence. Even without his being with her, she could feel his misery passing through her whole body. And as each bleak day passed and she heard nothing from him, she wondered if she dared to intrude, dared to make the first move. Should she write? Should she telephone? Or should she do nothing and wait? Her world was growing grey and dark. She went about The Farm in a daze. Geraldine, seeing her white, strained face, decided to ignore Cameron's neglected schoolwork. But Cameron's absent-minded conversation at breakfast and dinner eventually provoked her.

'Cameron, would you like to go to a matinee on Saturday? I'll get tickets to the Metropolitan Opera.'

'I don't think it's possible.'

'Getting tickets? Of course it's possible.'

'Tickets for what?' Cameron toyed with a lamb chop.

There was a moment of silence.

'The moon is made of cottage cheese, not green cheese,' Geraldine said.

'I think so, too.'

'Cyrus, Cyrus, strong and able, get your elbows off the table.'

'Cyrus?' Cameron raised her eyes from her plate. 'What did you say? Have you seen him?'

113

'No. And I think it's about time you stopped playing Ophelia because he hasn't telephoned.'

Cameron wiped the tears from her eyes. 'I want to help him, but I don't know what to do. I feel awful. The funeral was two weeks ago.'

'Dear, that young man is having a dreadful time right now. There is nothing you can do.'

'I could telephone.'

'Again? How many times have you telephoned already?'

'Three.'

'And what did the maid say?'

'He's not available.'

'Exactly. The same thing she told us when we paid a condolence call. He's not ready to talk to you. Or to anyone. Why not write him a letter?'

Cameron took a deep breath. 'Yes. That's what I'll do.' She stood up. 'I'm not very hungry. May I be excused?'

'You're excused. Go write your letter.'

Cameron sat at her desk rereading the letter she'd written three days ago. She'd tried to tell Cyrus that she understood his loss, that she wanted to reach out and comfort him. In her quirky, sprawling handwriting, she'd filled five pages. She read the letter again. Then, slowly, efficiently, she tore the letter into small pieces and dropped the scraps into her wastepaper basket. It was no use. She removed the two sealed envelopes from a special compartment in her desk. Both were addressed to Cyrus, and both had been returned unopened, stamped 'MOVED. NO FORWARDING ADDRESS.' She tore them up very slowly, very carefully and dropped them, one piece at a time, into the basket. Then she stood up and walked aimlessly around the room, finally sitting down at her desk again. She lowered her head, swallowed hard, but that had no effect. The tears came anyway. She had done what she could, and it hadn't been enough. Although the air in the room was warm, she shivered violently. Her hands and her feet were cold as four gravestones. She would never see Cyrus again.

PART THREE

The Decision Tree
1973–1974

7

At Byron's suggestion, Cameron and he were seated on a bench in Riverside Park between Seventy-second and Seventy-third streets overlooking the Hudson River. They were eating wedges of pizza and sharing a bottle of Chianti supplied by Cameron. Byron was still never one to turn down a free meal, and he waited until he'd chewed the last of the burnt crust on the last wedge of pizza and washed it down with the last of the wine. Only then did he consider the real reason why he'd asked Cameron to meet him. They'd been friends for over four years, and it was a friendship he wanted to keep. So, very gingerly, mentally poised to retreat and regroup should Cameron's reaction be too strong, he tiptoed his way around the subject.

'How did your final exams go?' he asked with elaborate casualness.

Cameron stretched out her long legs and looked at the sun, still high over the Palisades. Even though it was almost seven o'clock, this late in May there was still more than an hour of light remaining.

'A breeze,' she answered. 'The courses in business accounting and marketing at Columbia were a piece of cake. I should get an A in both. That'll help me get into Harvard Business School next year.'

'Harvard Business School.' Byron couldn't keep his disgust from showing. 'Where they teach you to run the corner grocery store like General Motors. Shit! If I see one more "decision tree," I'll throw up.'

'What do you mean? It's the best business school in the country.' A defensive edge crept into Cameron's voice.

119

'Right! It's the best business school in the country.'

Although Byron had agreed with her, the way he said 'business school' left no doubt as to what he thought of business schools and of Cameron's wanting an M.B.A. But after three years of battling the dean and her faculty adviser at Barnard to allow her to take business courses at Columbia. Cameron was in no mood to argue with Byron. She was determined to get an M.B.A. She needed that degree if she were to make any kind of a career in the corporate world. Byron had always known her goals, and his attitude was out of line.

'It seems to me that you telephoned and suggested a small celebration when my finals were over. This is it. I've wined you and dined you. Did you really suggest the celebration to make cracks about business schools?' She stood up. 'If that's the case, I'm going back to the dorm. As of now, I'm on vacation, and I still have to pack.'

'No!' Byron jumped up. 'Let's talk some more.'

'I haven't anything more to say.'

'I have.'

'About what?'

'About me,' Byron said after a moment's hesitation.

'Oh?' Cameron studied Byron. She sat down. 'What about you?'

'Me. And you.'

Cameron stood up again. She was in no mood for nonsense. 'There is no "me and you". I'm leaving.'

Byron stood up. 'I don't mean it that way. I mean we're both in the same boat.'

Cameron sat down again. 'What are you talking about?'

'I'll tell you if you promise to stop bouncing up and down like a yo-yo. It's exhausting.' He sat down.

'Okay. You have the floor.'

Byron began by explaining that as a chemistry major, he had long ago given up dreams of glory. He did not hope to discover a way to control the free radicals that damage DNA, lipids, synovial fluid, membranes, and other tissues. There was no Nobel Prize in his future.

'That's not the way the field of chemistry works for me.' He shot a sharp glance at Cameron. 'When I get out of college, I'll get a job with some chemical company, and with a little luck, I might reinvent nylon, or maybe Styrofoam. For which I'll get a raise and eventually make forty thou a year. I'll be a senior chemist for Dow Chemical, or Merck. And if I walk softly, wear a chain-mail vest to deflect back-stabbing, and do not scare the fishes, I may survive the corporate infighting. And become a division vice president in charge of animal droppings. Are you following me?' He did not wait for an answer. 'So I'll never be a big-game hunter in Africa. Or a spy in Hong Kong. I'm going to fall into the arms of some corporation and wear a white shirt and a nice, single-breasted suit. But you don't have to do that. You can jump ship.'

'I don't want to jump ship.'

'Yes you do. There isn't a pot of gold at the end of the corporate rainbow. Only a pot to piss in. I know a kid who is related to a once very good physicist. That physicist helped invent colour television for RCA. What happened? They gave him the David Sarnoff award. I think that was about forty grand. And at the age of fifty-odd, they fired him.'

'That doesn't tell me anything. There are always losers in business.'

'Sure. But why volunteer to be a loser?'

'I don't intend to be a loser.'

'You will be. Corporate men are a dime a dozen. And corporate women come cheaper. If the climb is the Himalayan peaks for me, it's a blind alley for you. You'll just keep climbing up and up the ladder. But for you the ladder has no top. You'll never be a chief executive. You might – just might – get as far as senior management. Make vice president, maybe.'

'I'll go as far as my brains take me.'

'Listen to me, please. I checked all the Fortune Five Hundred companies, and there's only one female chief executive officer on the list – Katherine Graham of *The Washington Post*. She inherited the stock from her father, Eugene Meyer, and the job from her husband, who died in the early sixties. She's a very smart lady, but the smarts alone didn't do it for her.'

'What are you talking about? What's this new hobbyhorse you're riding?' Cameron sounded as if she were accusing Byron of some crime.

'I've been waiting for the right time to talk to you. And the right time is now, before you walk over the edge of the cliff and end up at Harvard. Pure and simple, you're in the wrong ball game. If you take a job with a big corporation, it'll be the biggest waste of talent since Marc Antony dumped Rome to screw Cleopatra.'

'He enjoyed himself.'

'He came to a lousy end.'

'Look, Byron, maybe you're right for today. But I don't believe it will always be that way. By 1980 everything will be different.'

'It won't.'

'Why not?'

'I'll tell you why women won't be welcome in the executive suite for a long, long time. Because men don't feel comfortable with them in business. Can a man slap a woman on the back for pulling off a whippy deal? Or can he tell her a really crude, dirty joke? Or kick her ass around for fucking up? Suppose your boss kicked your ass?'

'I'd kick him back.'

'Wrong! You'd bend over to be kicked. And when he does, you'll say thank you.'

'I won't. I'll be the first in a new tradition in Fortune's Five Hundred.'

Byron was losing patience with Cameron. 'You have a chance to do something else. Even if you make it to senior management, the most you'll make is seventy-five grand. Maybe a hundred. And if by some miracle you become a chief executive officer, you know what you'll be worth at retirement? After, say, forty years? A snappy two or maybe three million dollars, if you're lucky. For which you've given your life.' He waited for a moment and then threw in everything. 'I have an obsessive interest in truth. Crap artists drive me crazy, no matter who the crap artist is. The truth is often rotten. But the trouble with lies is you end up lying to yourself. So here goes.' He took the plunge. 'Do you believe for one nano-second a lousy three million dollars is going to impress your Hightower relatives? They'll consider you as much of a failure as your grandfather Tobias. And your father, who, I understand, died in an accident – broke.'

Byron had touched a spot where touching hurt, and Cameron winced. Then she became furious. 'Who told you about my grandfather? And my father?'

'The Hightower family reminds people of the Mellons. And the Hightower Trust is loved by anyone who loves money. As a matter of fact, Renata told me. In an alcoholic, chatty moment, unsolicited by me, but she went on talking.'

'Renata Parsons? The art dealer who sells Geraldine paintings?'

'The very same barracuda. You remember. Renata owns the art gallery where we met. If you think about it, you must realize she deals with some of your close relatives other than Geraldine. And not all the Hightowers are as discreet as your cousin Geraldine. Or as nice. They think of you, to use Renata's words, as "Geraldine's waif" – her "charity child". And something less than equal.'

Cameron sat frozen in a position of tense resistance, her whole body poised, leaning forward in anger. But not a muscle stirred.

'I'm sorry.' Byron hurried to fill the gap of silence, regretting that he had found the chink in her brave front, the hurt behind her confident face and manner. He apologized profusely for listening to loose gossip and heard his voice sounding strained. Finally, he said he was pushing her so hard because, as he had said before, they were in the same boat. Weren't they both outsiders in their own way, and didn't both of them have great ambitions and great visions? But she had the advantage of being in a position to make her dream come true. She was a free agent. He wasn't. He had family complications that forced him into the corporate world. He said all this without pausing for breath, feeling frightened and slightly sick. 'It just doesn't make sense for you to trot down the tired, beaten corporate road,' he insisted.

Cameron remained still but her face encouraged him, and little by little her body relaxed.

'If you end up a division vice president, you'll be the toast of women's lib. But there are other worlds, Cameron. There really are. And the toasts will be larger.'

'I don't suppose you're suggesting I should become an actress? Or a model?' There was an amused glint in her eye.

Byron looked insulted. How could she think him such an idiot? Anyone who chose to earn their living with their body, such as models, ballet dancers, athletes, and prostitutes – even actresses – were begging for dynamic obsolescence. They wore out young. Only brains kept you in business into your nineties.

'Then what are you thinking?'

'The biggest game in town. And you're a natural for it. I know your background. Your interests.'

'What is it?' Cameron was finally curious.

'Meet me tomorrow morning at nine-thirty in front of the Kodak exhibition at Grand Central Station.'

'Where are we going?'

Once she asked the question, Byron knew he'd won. 'To

124

my home away from home.' He looked at her, but his eyes were fixed on some private memory. Nothing could conceal from Cameron the longing he felt. 'Or maybe it's my real home. And yours too, I think.'

Cameron was on her feet. She exhaled sharply. Whatever it was, it meant a lot to Byron, and she had nothing better to do. It really wasn't Byron's fault that Renata Parsons talked too much. The Hightowers were so rich that people who knew any of them liked to gossip about them. It was a kind of showing off. And at that, what difference did it make? Everything Byron had said was true. If her Hightower relatives chose to be rotten about her, let them. She smiled inwardly, thinking of the havoc Geraldine would spread among them if she ever mentioned what they'd said. But she wouldn't. She started to move away, saying that she'd see Byron tomorrow. Her adrenaline was still racing full-speed and needed an outlet. She'd walk back to Barnard. The walk would give her time to think about everything Byron had said.

Byron watched her stride up the path. Then he left the park, heading for the Seventy-second Street subway entrance. He was aware of a strange new feeling. In fact, if he were to put it into words, he might say that he was infatuated with Cameron. He had never felt like this about a girl before. What was worse, he recognized that he was totally out of line. It was like getting a fix on a movie star or a rock star – something he'd never done – and he considered it Jerksville. But that was how he felt. He could live with it and, eventually, outlive it. He looked forward to seeing Cameron tomorrow. At least he'd show her the way. Someday she'd thank him for it. A look of exasperation crossed his face. That sounded just like his father.

When Cameron entered her room in the Barnard College dormitory, her roommate, Lucia Manzone, was at her desk studying medieval history for her last final the next day. Lucia looked up at Cameron, startled. 'What are you doing here? I thought you had a date with Gil?'

'I did, but I broke it. I just finished splitting a pizza with Byron Miller.'

'Byron Miller?' Lucia swung her chair around to face Cameron. The two girls had been roommates for three years and were much closer than most college friends. Although Lucia came from the very large, very Catholic Manzone family, who had never been east of Interstate 5, bought their clothes from the Sears catalogue, and whose lives were devoted to their huge winery in the Napa Valley in California, Cameron found she had more in common with Lucia than she'd had with any of her schoolmates at Paddington. This permitted Lucia to take liberties she'd permit no one else to take.

'Byron Miller?' Lucia repeated. 'What's with that kid that you'd break a date with Gil Morrison for him?'

'Byron's a lot smarter and nicer than Gilbert Morrison,' Cameron said without a trace of embarrassment.

'You going to bed with him? You in love or something?'

'With Byron?' Cameron couldn't keep the surprise out of her voice. 'He's a kid! He just finished his freshman year at City College. I'm not in love with him. I like him. That's all.'

Lucia laughed softly. 'You don't have to be in love to go to bed with him. I'm not in love with Ralph.' She became reflective. 'In fact, the idea of love scares me. Unless I marry the man, I'll get hurt when it ends.'

'I suppose so.' Cameron blinked rapidly to keep the unexpected tears from flowing. Unwillingly, she remembered the first and only time she'd been in love and how badly she'd been hurt by the experience.

'You all right?' Lucia asked, picking up the sudden tension in Cameron's face and body.

'I'm fine.' With a conscious effort. Cameron slammed the door on her memories. She had never talked about Cyrus to

Lucia, and she wasn't going to start now. 'If you take a break for dinner, I'll eat with you,' she said. 'I'm going to work out in the gym for about an hour.'

Lucia returned to her books, and Cameron headed for the gym, still puzzling over what Byron had said.

Cameron glanced at the escalators leading to the Pan Am Building. Time was a contrarian. The more fun you were having, the faster it went. The more uncomfortable you were, the slower time passed. Only two minutes had passed since she last looked at her wristwatch. It was 9:20. Ten minutes to wait, if Byron was on time. What on earth was she doing in Grand Central Station waiting for Byron Miller? What kind of a lunatic stunt was in his mind? All that wise-ass talk about the corporate climb! What did he know? Maybe his father was some kind of a corporate executive? No. Byron never had any money, and he never mentioned his father. In the years she'd known Byron, she'd learned almost nothing about his personal life. Not his exact address or even his telephone number. He always called her. She didn't know if his father was dead. His mother wasn't, but she seemed to make no difference. Maybe that was why Byron lived an almost rootless existence. They always met in Greenwich Village or at the college, before they began their wanderings through the city. And after his vehement refusal of her first invitation to visit Geraldine and her at Hightower Farm, she'd never asked him again.

'I meant to be here by nine so you wouldn't have to wait. But the IRT did me in. Like it does everyone.' Byron was standing in front of her, bouncing up and down on his toes. He was so eager he had difficulty standing still, and his apology sounded like one continuous sentence.

'You're on the dot. But why the getup?' Byron was not wearing his usual jeans, sneakers, and work shirt. He had on a pair of polished loafers, pressed chino pants, and a white

127

shirt with a dark tie. His long black hair was slicked back. He wasn't exactly Brooks Brothers, but it was a definite change.

Byron gave her a sheepish grin. 'Well . . . I don't know. It seemed more appropriate. For where we're going . . .'

Cameron started for the Amtrack ticket booth. 'I've brought enough money for both of us. What time does the train leave? And where to?'

'We're not taking the railroad.' Byron turned Cameron about and directed her down a flight of stairs leading to the Lexington Avenue IRT. 'It's the subway.'

'Uptown or downtown?'

'There's nothing uptown besides Bloomingdale's.'

'Express or local?'

'Relax. Just follow me.'

When the subway doors opened, Byron hustled Cameron out of the train, shoving her towards the rear of the platform. He had her through the heavy iron turnstile before she saw the name of the station. He took the steps two at a time with Cameron hurrying to keep up. When they reached the sidewalk, Byron stood still, staring at a narrow street hemmed in by tall buildings.

Cameron was fascinated by what she saw. But she was looking in the opposite direction, at a very old cemetery and a beautiful church.

Byron came out of his reverie. 'Cameron, this way.'

'The church is beautiful.'

'Church? Oh! Trinity Church. Yeah, it's beautiful. And the cemetery is at least two hundred years old. But we're not here to take gravestone rubbings.' He turned her around. 'What do you see?'

'A street.' She read the sign. 'I didn't know Broadway ran this far downtown.'

'Cameron, we did not take a subway ride for you to discover lower Broadway. There!' He pointed his finger at the corner of a narrow, canyonlike street that ran at right angles to Broadway.

Cameron used his finger as a sight line. 'Wall Street?' Suddenly she realized where Byron had taken her. 'Wall Street? The stock market?'

'I knew if you tried hard you'd get it.'

'What's this all about?'

'Never mind. Let's get going.' They crossed Broadway and walked along the narrow sidewalk that bordered Wall Street. Byron acted as tour guide. He pointed out a two-storey, neoclassic structure with a flight of stone steps leading up to it and a statue of George Washington standing on a stone pedestal in front. 'That's the old subtreasury building. George Washington was inaugurated President there in 1789.' Byron checked his watch. 'Almost ten. Move!' They walked a short distance down Broad Street and entered a building.

Cameron read the words aloud. "New York Stock Exchange." What are we doing here?'

'We're going to watch the fun. There are few things in the world more inspiring than watching the privileged classes enjoy their privileges.'

'Don't you have to be a member of the Exchange to go in?'

'You have to be a member to get on the floor of the Exchange and place your bet. But if you want to watch the gambling, there's a visitors' gallery.'

'I'll buy the tickets.'

'No tickets. It's free. Do they charge admission at Monte Carlo? Or Las Vegas?' He answered his own question. 'No. The more watchers, the more gamblers.'

His cynicism irritated Cameron. 'Buying stock isn't like playing roulette. Or shooting craps. That's gambling. Buying stock is an investment.'

'Yes, indeedy. The New York Stock Exchange has been campaigning for years to change the idea that buying and selling stocks is a gamble. And they've succeeded with you. Okay. That's the way it ought to be. But it isn't. Step along. We want to catch the opening of the casino.'

As they walked along, Byron waved hello and hi to several of the uniformed guards.

'You're looking more and more like your father,' one said. 'How is he? Haven't seen him in a while.'

'He's just great.' Byron hurried on.

Cameron could tell this was something Byron did not want to talk about. But his father was still alive. And Byron was a familiar face in the visitors' gallery.

'How often do you come here?' she asked as they climbed the gallery stairs.

'Less than I'd like and more than I should.'

They joined a small crowd standing in a long glass-enclosed gallery overlooking the floor of the Exchange. Cameron stared down at the floor below in surprise. It looked like a political convention. The floor was crowded with men. Men in light grey coats, men in shirt sleeves, old men, young men, all milling about between numerous counters above which darkened television screens were stationed. Cameron glanced at Byron and saw him with his nose almost pressed against the glass. Here, she realized, was the passion of his life. She was hesitant to break into his private thoughts, but her curiosity was mounting.

'Who are those men? What are the television screens?' she asked softly.

'The men are floor traders, specialists, two-dollar brokers. They all own seats on the Exchange, or work for companies that own seats. It gives them the right to trade on the floor and not pay commissions. It's better than a lifetime movie pass, believe me.' His tone grew musing. '"Seats," what a quaint word. I've never seen anyone seated on the floor. They'd be trampled to death.'

'The Hightower family used to own a seat. I remember Geraldine telling me.'

Byron stared at Cameron with undisguised awe. 'They owned a seat and sold it?' He couldn't believe it. 'How much did they get for the seat?'

'I wasn't paying much attention. I think fifty thousand dollars.'

'Fifty thousand dollars! Honestly! They must have sold it in 1940. In 1968 a seat on the Exchange was worth about five hundred thousand. Now I think they sell for three hundred thousand dollars. It's off its high.' He shook his head despairingly and turned back to the window. 'What's a few hundred thousand more or less to a Hightower? Excuse the reference, Cameron. But it does illustrate my point.'

For the first time Cameron understood. 'What are the television screens for?'

'When trading opens, the screens give stock prices, number of shares traded, the Dow Jones averages – vital statistics like that. Now watch the clock.'

Cameron stared at the large, round clock mounted on the wall facing them. It was 9:59. The second hand moved around the white face in staccato jumps, one second at a time. It was 9:59 and 30 seconds. Cameron counted the seconds to herself. At 10:00 a bell rang. All hell broke loose on the floor. The network of screens lit up. Letters and numbers flashed on and off with lightning speed. A long, narrow board – like a scoreboard – came to life. Orange symbols and numbers crawled across the board: stocks, prices, number of shares traded with each transaction. Men, idly chatting seconds ago, were galvanized into action, rushing back and forth between the various specialists' trading posts. Paper was flying around. Although she had no idea what was happening, Cameron was riveted by the frenzied action.

Someone was pulling on her arm. Impatient at the

interruption, Cameron yanked her arm away. Then she realized it was Byron.

'They never go to the toilet,' he said. 'They don't dare.'

'What do they do for lunch?'

'A sandwich. They make up for it after four o'clock, when the market closes,' he said. 'Come on. It only gets worse. More frantic.'

Still dazed, Cameron allowed herself to be led away. 'That isn't how I pictured the New York Stock Exchange.'

'I know. It looks wild. Nobody stands still. No thoughtful discussion, or logical analysis. No debate – only action! Buy fast and sell fast. Sell and buy faster. Get your bid in first and hope you guessed right. We need a little peace and quiet. To map out your future.' He led her out of the visitors' gallery and down the steps, talking as he went.

'Byron! Stop horsing around. I'll map out my own future, thank you. You want me to change plans that I've had for years and do something or other on the New York Stock Exchange. Is that the scoop?'

'The floor is certainly a possibility.'

'The floor looks to me like a boys' club. Just as much as any executive suite.'

They ended up in a coffee shop on Broadway so immersed in their argument that when the waitress brought them coffee instead of the tea they had ordered, they never noticed.

'I'm not thinking of the floor, specifically,' Byron finally admitted. 'I'm actually thinking of Wall Street. The Street. The brokerage houses are already peppered with women. Even the investment banking houses. They have ladies' rooms now and not just for the customers. A sizable chunk of the female population would rather do business with women. The way they prefer women psychiatrists and marriage counsellors and gynaecologists. It's only the beginning.'

Listening to Byron's enthusiasm irritated Cameron. 'Byron Miller, if you're so crazy about Wall Street, why don't you forget corporate life and set your sights on the Dow Jones? Yes, I know you have responsibilities. I imagine that means you must have a steady pay cheque. But there must be jobs on Wall Street with regular pay cheques. Why not get one of those? Instead of punching a clock at Hoffmann-La Roche.' Cameron shook her head. 'I don't want to hear any more mammy palaver about my going to work on Wall Street.'

Byron lifted his hands in amazement. Looking out for Cameron's own good was no easy job. He was ready to give up – almost. 'Okay. I bruise easily. Would you do me a favour? Just one?'

'What is it?'

'What are you doing Monday evening?'

'Nothing. Unless Geraldine has arranged something.'

'I'd like you to meet me at the New School for Social Research at seven-thirty. It's on Eleventh Street between Fifth and Sixth Avenues.'

'Why?'

'There's a lecture I'd like you to hear.'

'Who's giving it? And what's it on?'

'It's *on* Wall Street. And Timothy FitzGerald is giving it.'

Cameron left a dollar for the untouched cups of coffee and slid out of the booth. She glared at Byron. 'You stop bugging me! I'll meet you. But that's it.'

'Are we still friends?'

'Friends? Sure we're friends. That's different.'

8

The school term had ended, and it was time for Cameron to return to Hightower Farm for the summer. Cousin Geraldine sent her chauffeur-handyman, Jack O'Toole, to help with the move. After Jack stowed her luggage in the rear of the station wagon, they drove down the bumpy West Side Highway, through the Lincoln Tunnel, and onto the New Jersey Turnpike. Cameron sat silently beside Jack and thought about her conversation with Byron and their visit to Wall Street. The New York Stock Exchange had shaken her. She had tried and failed to imagine what it would be like to work on the Street. Halfway to Princeton, Cameron realized that the perfect person to talk to was Cousin Geraldine. Geraldine spent each morning in her study, reading the financial news in *The Wall Street Journal, Forbes, Fortune.* She constantly reviewed a series of large ledgers which Cameron had been told contained the listings of stocks, bonds, and other holdings that made up the Hightower Trust. Although her cousin could easily pass for ten years younger, Geraldine was nearly sixty-seven years old, and she'd been managing the trust for at least the last twenty-five years. She did all her stock trading via a small, low-profile Princeton brokerage house whose entire clientele consisted of some forty multimillion-dollar portfolios. Geraldine sometimes exchanged views with a Mr Hubert who executed her orders. More often, she made her own decisions and Mr Hubert merely listened.

Yes, Cameron decided, that was what she would do. Geraldine would put her mind at ease. She would point out the flaws in Byron's thinking and explain why nothing he said applied to her. Cameron could almost hear Geraldine insisting she not muddle her future with Byron's foolish ideas about the corporate world, or his fantasies of Wall Street.

The station wagon wound up the circular gravel driveway, flanked with freshly painted white stones, and came to a stop in front of the steps leading to The Farm. Cameron stared for a moment with pleasure at the great old house. The sharply pointed brick glowed in the late afternoon sunlight, the windows reflecting the green lawns sloping down to the high, full privet hedges. This was her home and had been her home for the past seven years. She'd come to love it, to take the same pride in it that Geraldine took. She got out of the car and hurried towards the house. The century-old huge white wooden front door was slowly opened by Jane, one of the maids.

'Miss Cameron!' she said happily. 'How nice to have you back for the summer.'

'It's nice to be back, Jane.' Cameron's greeting was affectionate. 'Where is Miss Hightower?' She felt a twinge of disappointment that Geraldine had not been waiting to greet her as she often had in the past.

'In the library, Miss Cameron. With Mr Hansen.'

For an instant Cameron's heart stopped. 'Mr Hansen?'

'Mr Elmer Hansen, Miss Hightower.'

'Ah!' Cameron crossed the high-ceilinged entrance hall wondering what on earth Geraldine and Elmer Hansen had to talk about. She started up the stairs when Jane called after her.

'Miss Hightower said you were to go to the library when you arrive.'

Cameron retraced her steps and headed towards the library at the end of the corridor. As she approached, she heard their voices.

'Another school would jump at it.'

Elmer Hansen was speaking in a strong, low tone. Cameron was startled to realize how much he sounded like Cyrus.

'Another school is not the Institute for Advanced Studies.' Geraldine's voice was soft and equally firm.

'They won't accept two million dollars?'

'They won't accept the money for a chair in marketing. I won't even present it to my friends on the board. They'd think me ridiculous.'

'Your friends have a very limited and, I might add, a too academic view of the world. Marketing makes the world go round.'

'It used to be love.'

'Another form of marketing. All right. What will they accept?'

'I told you. The Elmer Hansen, Jr, Chair of Social Behaviour.'

'Marketing is the study of social behaviour.'

'You asked me what I think they'll accept. You do want to fund a chair in your son's name, don't you?'

'Yes. But social behaviour?'

Cameron stepped into the silence that followed Elmer's last remark. 'Hello, Geraldine.' She glanced at Elmer Hansen. 'Mr Hansen.'

'Cameron! You're home! I'm so glad.' Geraldine rose from her chair in front of the unlit fireplace and went quickly to Cameron. The women embraced fondly.

Elmer Hansen watched them with something like distaste, although neither saw his expression. After a moment, he said with grudging pleasantness, 'Hello, Cameron.' When Cameron turned to acknowledge him, he asked, 'Have you heard from my grandson?'

Cameron blinked. 'Cyrus? No, I haven't.'

'Neither have I. Though I must say he does manage to keep me informed via the newspapers.'

Despite his sarcasm, Cameron was pleased at the note of respect for Cyrus in Elmer's tone.

Geraldine remained impassive. 'Elmer, why don't you think over what I said and phone me in the morning. Tell me your decision then. Right now, I want to welcome Cameron home.'

'I'll tell you my decision now. It's the Elmer Hansen, Jr, Chair for Social Behaviour.' Somehow Elmer made what Cameron realized was his surrender sound like a victory; as if the Elmer Hansen, Jr, Chair for Social Behaviour was exactly what he'd meant to call the chair in the first place.

'A wise decision, Elmer. We'll go over the details in the morning.'

'In the morning,' Elmer said, rising and walking swiftly towards the door. 'Nice to see you again, Cameron. Good evening, Geraldine.'

Cameron watched him leave, noting his stride and posture. Seeing him again after so many years, she realized how much alike Cyrus and he were. Cyrus too would become an extremely distinguished-looking older man. When Elmer shut the door behind him, Cameron glanced at Geraldine, puzzled.

'Why did he ask me that?'

'Ask what? You mean about Cyrus?' Geraldine was peculiarly vague. 'Elmer Hansen is a very complicated man.'

'But why should I have heard from Cyrus if he hasn't?'

Cameron's questions confirmed Geraldine's instinct. Bright as the girl was, in some ways she was still new to the so-called civilized world. She didn't realize Elmer Hansen knew every move Cyrus made. There was no point in Cameron's learning this – certainly not now, maybe not ever.

But Cameron was a quick study. Something in Geraldine's voice prompted her to say, 'Then I'm glad he hasn't heard from Cyrus. If he really hasn't.'

'I agree,' said Geraldine. She seated herself in the chair she'd just left and indicated that Cameron join her. She waited just long enough for Cameron to fold her legs under her before asking, 'How did your exams go? And how is Lucia? I spoke to Lucia's parents several weeks ago. They're very optimistic about this year's grape crop, although it's a few months until harvesttime. I asked them to send me ten cases each of Manzone Cabernet Sauvignon and Chardonnay from 1970. We'll age them in our own cellar.'

Cameron listened with half a mind to Geraldine's talk. Grades? Lucia? Wine? They meant little to her, dwarfed for the moment by the many questions she had about Cyrus. Finally, she interrupted the older woman. 'Geraldine, tell me about Cyrus. I've read about him in the papers, but I'm not sure I understand. Exactly what does he do?'

Geraldine chuckled. 'It's a little hard to put a name to it. He's been called everything from a corporate raider and a pirate to a white knight. A saviour and the average shareholders' Robin Hood. What he is depends upon who is describing him.'

Geraldine's elliptical answer left Cameron almost as much in the dark as ever – which was what Geraldine had intended – but she was still too young and unsure of herself to expose her ignorance by asking more questions. She pretended she understood. After a few minutes, she excused herself to go upstairs to unpack and wash up for dinner. Once in her bedroom, she removed a carefully folded newspaper clipping from her purse, smoothed it out, and studied the headline: CYRUS HANSEN STRIKES AGAIN. Then she reread the first paragraph of the article.

Cyrus Hansen, the self-proclaimed corporate scourge, announced the acquisition of 22% of Pantronics. He stated that he has tendered for another 35% at $28 a share, $10 a share over the most recent quoted market price. Mr Hansen, 25, states that when he obtains control of Pantronics, his first act will be to get rid of the board of directors and the 'incompetent management'. They will be replaced by men of his own choice. Marvin Wilson, chairman of the board of Pantronics, has said, 'This corporation intends to resist the unwarranted and unwanted intrusion of this reckless and irresponsible young man with every means at our disposal, including the use of the courts.'

Cameron read the entire article and shook her head in dismay. She gave up trying to understand what it was all about, opened one of her suitcases, and fished out a large gold-embossed brown leather album – the kind usually reserved for pictures of loved ones. She added the article to her growing collection of clippings about Cyrus Hansen.

When Cameron awoke the next morning, it was almost nine o'clock. Geraldine had already finished breakfast and was at work in her study. Cameron settled for juice and coffee and went to find her. She tapped on the closed door of the study.

'Come in,' Geraldine called, looking up from her work. She was seated at her conference table of a desk where she'd been concentrating on a page in one of her many ledgers scattered about. 'It's wonderful to have you home, dear, but I still have three hours of work ahead. We can talk at lunch.' She stretched her arms to rid them of stiffness. She was wearing, as usual, a pair of impeccably fitted white pants and a white silk shirt, and a pair of horn-rimmed glasses dangled from a chain around her neck. Cameron thought of this as her 'executive look'.

'We can . . . but I thought this might be the place to begin. It has to do with that.' Cameron gestured towards the ledgers. 'How you spend your mornings.'

Geraldine raised her eyebrows. She couldn't imagine Cameron prying into the affairs of the Hightower Trust. What on earth was on Cameron's mind that she would interrupt her at work? Cameron had never done that before.

139

Did she need money for something? Did she want to make an investment? She put down her gold pen and swivelled her chair to gaze at Cameron. 'Sit down, Cameron.' She motioned towards a chair beside her at the desk.

Cameron entered the study slowly. She had only been inside it occasionally. Now she glanced around with curiosity. The study was like no other room in the house. Except for the floor, which was typical of the old house, the study was a creation of technology. One half of a wall contained built-in file cabinets that could be opened only by combination lock. The files were Geraldine's jewels. There was spare room on the other half of the wall for three microfiche readers. Geraldine had a library for all her financial records and any news items that she considered relevant to her work. The library was scrupulously updated by Geraldine's assistant, Miss Hampton, who had worked for her for years. Miss Hampton arrived at Hightower Farm every day at one o'clock, after Geraldine had left the study for the day. Against the opposite wall was a large TV monitor connected to a quotron. By pressing a few keys, Geraldine could be apprised of the price, volume, and movement of every stock traded on the New York Stock Exchange and the American Stock Exchange and of over-the-counter stocks as well. Cameron realized it was an expanded version of the screens she'd seen on the floor of the New York Stock Exchange. Next to Geraldine's chair was a Dow Jones ticker tape standing on its pedestal, reporting the financial news minute by minute.

'What is it, dear?'

Cameron had been thinking how best to open the conversation so that she would sound detached and objective – she didn't want to bias Geraldine's answers – so she settled for an opening that was close to home. 'Does the Hansen Company have stockholders?'

'About one hundred fifty thousand.'

'And its shares are traded on the New York Stock Exchange?'

'Yes, dear. It's a publicly held company and very profitable.' Geraldine was wondering where Cameron was leading and she tried to encourage her. 'Actually, the original seed monies the company needed to begin operation were provided by the Hightower Trust, and the trust still owns about four per cent of the company.' She watched as Cameron absorbed this information. 'Our position is worth several thousand times our original investment. Elmer Hansen is a brilliant executive. That's why the company has grown.'

'And selling stock publicly helped it grow. Wall Street is important to business?'

'Wall Street is the lifeblood of the business community. It's where companies raise money to expand their operations, to pay bank debt. Even to buy other companies. Why?'

'I'm thinking about my future. For instance, someday, when – oh, not now – in, say, twenty-five years or so when I get to be chief executive of, say . . .' She braced herself. 'Well, let's say RCA. Or Sears. How's that?' She smiled. 'I'll have to send my treasurer to Wall Street to raise money. To build new factories. Or add new product lines. Or pay off bank debt. Right?'

Cameron waited for Geraldine to say something. Anything. Finally, Geraldine spoke. 'Some material came for you from Stanford Business School. I expect Harvard will be sending theirs along shortly.'

'I expect.' Cameron persisted. 'But that's what will happen, isn't it? When I'm chief executive of RCA or Sears?'

'Yes. When you're chief executive of RCA or Sears.'

'You don't sound enthusiastic.'

'I have difficulty with self-delusion. I thought you did, too.'

'I do.'

'Then I don't understand what you're talking about.'

141

Now it was Cameron's turn to be quiet. 'You don't think I'm smart enough to be a chief executive officer?'

'I think in twenty-five years or so, when you have the experience, you'll be smart enough.'

'So? Why are you sounding so negative?'

'As I said, I don't like self-delusion. And if that's the kind of goal you've set for yourself, you're deluding yourself.'

'Why?'

'Because it will take several more generations before a woman will become a chief executive officer of a corporation like RCA or Sears. A woman can start and run her own business today, and build it into a sizeable enterprise. Look at Lauder cosmetics. But when we speak of corporations that gross billions of dollars, not tens or hundreds of millions, but billions? No. That's not yet in the cards.'

'You mean I can never hope to be chief executive officer of RCA or General Motors?'

Geraldine laughed. 'General Motors! Nothing less. That's as good an example as any. No, you can't.'

'That's what Byron said.'

'Byron – whoever he is – is right.'

'He's a very smart young man.' Cameron saw Geraldine raise her eyebrows and realized she had the same idea Lucia had had. 'No. It's not a romance. He's a friend. I met him in New York years ago.'

'You never mentioned him before.'

'There was nothing to say. Friday morning, we went downtown to the New York Stock Exchange.'

Geraldine gave this her full attention. 'Byron took you to Wall Street?' Cameron nodded. 'I should have done that, but I didn't think you'd be interested.' Even as she said it, she told herself that people only listen when they're ready to listen. Cameron must be ready. 'I gather he's interested in Wall Street.'

'More than anything, I think.' Cameron hesitated and then laid it out. 'He thinks I should get a job on Wall Street.'

'What kind of a job?'

'Byron loves the floor of the Exchange. But he says any job with a brokerage house on Wall Street would be the way to start. He thinks I could make a bigger success on Wall Street than in the corporate world.'

Geraldine collected her thoughts. 'I think he's right.'

'I won't make it in the corporate world?'

'You won't make it the way you're dreaming.'

Cameron felt unsure of her ground. 'You really think I should go to Wall Street?'

'Why not? It's in the Hightower tradition.'

'I don't give a damn for the Hightower tradition.' Cameron flared, just as Geraldine had expected. 'My grandfather didn't and my father didn't. Why should I?'

'I'm merely stating a fact. You're a Hightower. And though I think it's a good idea, there are drawbacks.'

'Like what?'

'Like the name. The name "Hightower" cuts both ways. It's a familiar name on the Street. As a result, it can work for you, or against you. It will cast doubts – both in your mind and in the minds of others – about the reasons for your success. At the same time, it can magnify any mistakes, any failures.'

'Are you suggesting that without the Hightower name, I might not succeed on Wall Street? And with it I might fail faster?' Cameron stood up and started to pace about the room. She had never thought of herself as a Hightower, not in the same sense Geraldine was. She sometimes thought she was an imposter and would remain one until she had succeeded on her own. Now it occurred to her that the Hightower name was the short end of the stick. It brought with it envy for wealth she didn't have and misguided expectations. 'I'll change my name,' she said softly.

'That's too absurd to comment on.'

Geraldine watched Cameron wrestle with her dilemma and deeply sympathized. But she never doubted Cameron's capacity to handle it. Although they were not mother and daughter, they had something equally viable. Within the wealthy, seemingly sheltered woman was a strong intelligence, a steadfastness of purpose, a toughness of mind, a will to succeed, that did credit to her industrious ancestors. To Geraldine, Cameron and she were of the same breed.

'As for having a career on Wall Street, all I can say is that I wish I were twenty again. With the opportunity available to me.'

'Being a woman wouldn't get in your way?'

'No. Outside of a few large houses, the Street is a collection of small firms. Each is in competition with the other. They live on their toes, not on their rumps. It takes talent, judgement, nerve, a willingness to put your money where your mouth is. Those qualities are always in short supply. A woman who has them can go far.'

'Even a Hightower?' Cameron was half serious.

'Yes. Even a Hightower can succeed on Wall Street on her own merit.'

'Have you ever heard of Timothy FitzGerald?'

Geraldine blinked. 'Of course. Brilliant Wall Streeter, absolutely brilliant. The Hightower Trust has invested in a number of his offerings.'

'Byron wants me to go to a lecture given by Fitzgerald Monday night.'

The telephone rang and Geraldine frowned. 'Elmer, on the nose.' She picked up the phone and listened. 'Jane, tell him I'm out but you'll give me the message. Wait. Better still, tell him to call back this time tomorrow. Thank you.' She hung up, slightly puzzled. 'What's Byron's last name?'

'Miller. Byron Miller. Why?'

'That wasn't Elmer Hansen. That was Adam Miller.'

144

'Adam Miller. Who's he?'

'Byron's father. I was planning to ask you about him.' Geraldine observed Cameron's confusion. 'He called earlier this week. Your Byron didn't mention that he would call?'

'No.' Cameron was flustered. 'We never talked about our families.'

'Byron must have mentioned you and your family to his father. He thought I would be an ideal investor.'

'For what?'

'Mr Miller is putting together a syndicate to finance a new kind of battery. It will power a car to go sixty miles an hour for over five hundred miles before it needs recharging.'

'That's some invention. How much money is he looking for? And for what percentage of the business?'

Geraldine was pleased. This was proof positive of the blood running true. 'Well done. You're a rank amateur and you've asked two of the key questions. How much for how much? Seventy thousand for a twenty-five per cent interest. The company is called Proto-Dynamics.'

Cameron drummed her fingers on the desk. 'That's not much for a twenty-five per cent ownership of such an important invention.' Why hadn't Byron mentioned this to her? Then she had another thought. 'How did Adam Miller get your number?'

'We *are* in the phone book. And I'm known to make investments in start-up situations. Very few, maybe one out of ten, are successful. That one pays for all the others, many times over. Remember, the Hansen Company once needed money to get started.'

'But you're a complete stranger to Adam Miller.'

'So was Elmer Hansen. Except that Mr Miller is not the businessman. He's the money raiser, the promoter.' Her tone became reflective. 'Promoters with good track records can raise millions over the telephone. Tim FitzGerald does it.

145

He's a top-grade promoter. At his level, they're called investment bankers.'

Cameron felt herself grow cold. What had her friendship with Byron got Geraldine into? 'Are you going to make the investment?'

'I need to see the entire financial package before I give it serious consideration.'

'Don't do anything until next week. I'll be seeing Byron at the seminar, and I'll ask him about it.'

'Dear, even if I were wildly enthusiastic, I would do nothing without seeing the financial package, management history, cashflow projections, patents, and the like. After all that arrives, it will take at least two weeks to check it out.'

Cameron felt foolish over her concern about Geraldine. After all, Geraldine was a professional. 'I'll let you get back to work. And since I'm on vacation, I'll go swimming.'

Cameron was relieved as she left Geraldine's study. She'd be glad to see Byron Monday evening. Byron was an acquired taste, and she'd acquired it. She liked him more and more, and worried about him more and more. His intensity, his longing for a world he'd never known. His own world wasn't good enough. She wondered if that came from his father. What was his father like? Perhaps they would have a real talk Monday after the lecture.

Monday evening, Cameron used the family Jeep to drive to New York. For once the traffic in the Lincoln Tunnel behaved in a rational fashion and she was on her way down Ninth Avenue in near record time. Finding a parking place took more time than the tunnel, but she arrived at the school entrance at seven-fifteen. Byron was waiting for her.

'Hi,' he called out. 'Glad you came.'

'Were your ears burning this weekend? We talked about you. About Wall Street. About the corporate world. Also about investments.' She watched Byron for some reaction. There was none.

'Does your cousin know much about Wall Street?'

That sounded like no more than natural curiosity. 'Yes. She manages the Hightower Trust.' There was still no reaction from Byron.

'Does she make her own decisions or use the idiots who work in the trust departments of banks?'

That question might have a purpose. Byron could be asking whether Geraldine would take her father's proposal to a banker for advice, or make her own decision. Cameron saw no reason not to tell the truth. 'Cousin Geraldine neither asks for nor needs advice on investments. She makes all her own decisions.'

'Good for her. No one can look out for your interests as well as you can yourself. If you have a minimum of brains, that is.' He noticed the people entering the building. 'Come on. Before the seats up front are gone.'

Byron led her into the modern-looking building. A sign announced that Timothy FitzGerald was speaking in the main auditorium and an arrow pointed out the direction they were to take.

As they walked down the aisle, Cameron asked casually, 'Did you know your father spoke to Geraldine last week? About an investment?' Was it her imagination or did Byron's face change?

'I didn't know. He doesn't always tell me what he's doing. Dad's a very busy guy.' There seemed to be something caught in Byron's throat. Cameron could barely hear him. 'What was the investment in?' Byron asked.

They found seats on the aisle in the third row from the stage.

'A battery fluid of some kind. Geraldine didn't give me the details.'

'That one.'

'Does your father put together a lot of groups? Investors, I mean.'

'That's his business. Getting people to invest in projects. He always has a number of things going.'

'Geraldine said she'd give the proposal serious consideration.'

Byron slumped in his seat. 'How large a commitment was my father talking about?'

'Not that large,' Cameron answered brightly. 'Seventy thousand.'

'That's large enough.'

Cameron glanced away from Byron and stared at the stage. He didn't seem to know about the phone calls and the proposal. That could be a pose, but why should he pretend? Geraldine said these promotions were done all the time. Cameron felt extremely uncomfortable with her suspicions. Why was she suspicious? And of what?

A tall man dressed in slacks and a sweater, with a shock of black hair, a full beard, and wearing glasses walked out of the wings and approached the lectern. He adjusted the microphone.

Was this Timothy FitzGerald? Cameron asked herself.

'Ladies and gentlemen,' the man said. 'As part of our regular Monday-night course on the American economic system, we are tonight going to hear a talk on Wall Street and its influence on American capitalism.'

Cameron felt relieved that this man was not Timothy FitzGerald.

'We've been fortunate to persuade Mr Timothy Fitz-Gerald, managing partner of the well-known Wall Street banking house FitzGerald Associates, to speak tonight. It's my honour and pleasure to present Mr Timothy FitzGerald. Fitz,' he called into the wings, 'they're ready for you.'

Cameron saw a man she guessed to be about fifty years old stroll on to the stage. Although 'stroll' was not the right word.

He moved in a perfectly straight line, neither too fast nor too slow. But one moment he was in the wings and the next he was at the podium. She had the immediate impression that he would be hard to stop once he got started. Anyone who was in his way put themselves at risk. Looking up at him, Cameron couldn't make up her mind if he was short or tall. She could, however, see that he was a heavy-boned, powerful man. Large hands and thick wrists extended below the shirt cuffs showing out of the sleeves of his single-breasted dark grey suit. In truth, Timothy FitzGerald was a man born with great physical strength, so much so that he took it for granted. His face was a set of conflicting planes, as though his creator was ambivalent about the type of person he wished this man to be. He had a fine, high forehead and sea-green eyes that scanned the audience with cool, almost scientific appraisal. But the intellectual quality of the features stopped there. His nose was high-bridged and thin, his mouth generous, and his jaw was square with a deeply cleft chin. A man of the mind, a man of action – both extremes combined in one face.

His hair was an unusual shade of red, like deeply burnished copper, thick and curly, with white sprinkled along the temples. He wore it cut short and combed straight back. His skin had high colour and was stretched tightly over his high cheekbones. There was something about Timothy FitzGerald that brought to Cameron's mind an older Ireland when Tara was the seat of the High King who ruled the five parts of the land. The sight of him made Cameron think of legendary heroes.

Cameron looked sidelong at Byron. His knees were pulled up to his chest, and his hands were locked under them. His eyes were closed. It was impossible for her to tell whether this was Byron's way of concentrating on the lecture, or whether his mind was somewhere else. When FitzGerald began to speak, Cameron forgot about Byron.

'Thank you, ladies and gentlemen, for being here tonight.

You could have gone to a baseball game, or a rock concert at Lincoln Center. Or done any number of things people do in the evening. But here you are, ready to listen to me talk about a subject I love . . .'

Tim FitzGerald was probably the worst public speaker Cameron had ever heard. His sentences did not roll forth in a rich, even cadence with the proper emphasis placed at precisely the right places, the way a good actor or politician tends to speak. FitzGerald had a light, Irish-tenor voice that varied from smoothly persuasive to low and breathy. Cameron had to listen with concentration in order to catch every word. And then there was his accent. In her years at Barnard she'd come to recognize typical New York speech patterns. And FitzGerald's was a classic. But it was mixed with a strange Irish lilt. One moment he was Hell's Kitchen, the next one could smell the peat bogs of County Kerry.

Yet with all these contradictions, Timothy FitzGerald was an effective speaker. Cameron was mesmerized. She, like the others, was caught by the intelligence and vitality of the man, by the conflict she sensed between his gentleness and strength, between his grace and power.

'I'm not going to give you the history of the New York Stock Exchange and Wall Street.' He smiled at the audience and Cameron felt herself warmed as though by the sun. 'That information is available in numerous books. I'll start,' Fitz-Gerald said, 'by asking how many of you here own stocks or bonds personally? Or via pensions, trusts, mutual funds, or insurance companies?'

About 60 per cent of the audience raised their hands. Cameron was surprised to see that Byron was one of them.

'Yes, that's about the right proportion. In this class, it's a little more than half. The Census Bureau says that in the United States one hundred twenty-five million people over the age of twenty-five, either directly or indirectly, own stocks in publicly held companies. That's a pretty wide ownership.'

'Do you think it's wide enough?' a birdlike woman in the back row called out.

'No. I think the more the better. But it's growing.'

'That's not what I meant.'

FitzGerald gave the woman a second look. 'I think I know what you mean, but hold it till later.' He surveyed the room. 'This widespread ownership in publicly held corporations is a made-in-America phenomenon. It's one of the best examples of the way a capitalist democracy works.' He raised his head slightly, and Cameron saw that he had the audience with him. 'Who here owns their own business? Alone or with partners?'

Three hands went up. FitzGerald called on a short, well-built man in his late forties who wore a rumpled suit. 'What's your business?'

'Vitamins. I specialize in the synthetic version. They're as good as the natural kind. A molecule is a molecule. And they're a lot cheaper.'

'Got it. Only this is not a vitamin discussion. This is about finance. How did you get started?'

'Like everybody. My father, my brother, cousins, friends put up some money. They all take vitamins. Then I borrowed some more money from the bank. I live in Hewlett, Long Island. My factory is in Islip. So I set up distribution all over Long Island. In supermarkets, groceries, drugstores, health food stores. All over.'

'Did your business grow?'

'Like crabgrass. In business there are only two basic problems. Too much production and not enough orders. Or too many orders and not enough production. I've had too many orders.'

Cameron didn't know where FitzGerald was going, but he'd certainly picked the right man to question.

'What are you doing to keep up with the orders?'

'My lawyer used his noggin. He contacted a small

151

brokerage house, Jones and Fine. We had a meeting, and they went over my books. They took my company public.'

'In other words, you sold stock in your company to people like these here tonight. How much did you raise?'

'One million three hundred thousand. Now we're opening a second warehouse. The company's going great guns.'

'Are you still selling stock?' a woman's voice called from across the room.

'You bet. It's traded over-the-counter. We're not big enough for either of the exchanges. But the stock is moving.'

'What's the name?'

'Vita-Plus. Call your broker.'

FitzGerald grinned and rubbed his hands together happily. 'The way Vita-Plus got started is much the way many major American corporations got started. With slight variations on who provided the seed money.'

Then, with the dispassionate ease of a surgeon describing a successful operation. FitzGerald went on to talk about a skinny kid who grew up on a farm in Wayne County, Michigan. 'He didn't like cows and chickens. But he loved anything mechanical. In his spare time he repaired clocks and watches just for the kick of it. What happened to the kid was inevitable. How could you keep him down on the farm when he was a grease-monkey genius?'

Although FitzGerald's words were flippant, Cameron heard something like reverence in his tone.

'At fifteen he went to work as a machinist's apprentice in Detroit.' FitzGerald then went on to describe how the kid spent the next twenty years in the field of engineering. 'Mostly working for other people,' Fitzgerald said, sounding pained. 'Until one day he decided to go out on his own and build racing cars. He did, and the cars set records. The publicity attracted people to him. A company was formed, and a few people bought stock in the company. It was this skinny kid's company that built the Model T. With the Model T, the car stopped being a rich man's toy. Everyone could afford to own a car. It took a while for the Ford Motor Company to go public, but today hundreds of thousands of people own stock in the company that first put America on wheels.'

Cameron decided that Timothy FitzGerald loved the idea of American capitalism as much as Henry Ford loved engines. She listened to the relish in his voice as he compared the way Willi Porsche, the brilliant car engineer, started the Porsche Company. When he needed money to expand he went to the banks, because in Germany the banks own most of the company stock that is not owned by families or friends of the original entrepreneurs. FitzGerald stated with some impatience, 'Since new stock issues are seldom offered to the average German citizen, banks dominate German industry.'

Cameron had a view of the American economic system that she'd never had before.

FitzGerald concluded his lecture. 'Both means of financing corporations work. You judge for yourselves which provides the general public with a greater share of the wealth of the nation.' He paused. 'Now for the questions.'

All over the room there was a buzzing, some applause, and then a multitude of hands went up. FitzGerald called on a man to the right of Cameron.

'Mr FitzGerald,' he said angrily, 'you may approve of the way the American stock market works, but I lost the money for my son's college education investing in a stock. And what kind of redress do I have?'

'Sir, what reasons did you have for buying stock?'

'My dentist told me the stock had gone up fifteen points since he'd bought it. But the stock collapsed two weeks after I bought it.'

'Did your dentist lose money, too?'

'No way. He got out in time.'

'Why don't you ask your dentist for redress?'

There was laughter mingled with a few catcalls that

FitzGerald ignored. He glanced around the room. 'You, madam.'

'I inherited a hundred thousand dollars from my father, and I gave it to my broker to invest. In three years he's lost almost all of it. There's only about ten thousand dollars left. It's lucky that I have a good job.'

'What do you do?'

'I'm a package designer.'

'That takes talent and intelligence. How did you find your job?'

'I researched the field and picked a firm that I knew was growing.'

'Did you research the brokerage field to find a broker smart enough to handle your hundred thousand dollars?'

'No.' The woman looked blank. 'I went to the firm with the most convenient office. I thought they were all alike.'

'They are not. Do the research and find another broker before you lose your last ten thousand.'

A woman from the other side of the room called out, 'I know a broker who's smart. He put me on to Texas Instruments twenty years ago. I still have the stock: and it's bought me a summer house.'

'How did you pick your broker?'

'I married him.'

Over loud laughter, Cameron heard FitzGerald say, 'My compliments to you on your judgement.'

A middle-aged man stood up and asked, 'Do you think new issues are a good thing?'

'I do. For the right investor,' FitzGerald said. 'New issues mean new companies starting up. It's the American way. Give a man a leg up and help him start his own company. This creates new jobs and new industries. And the public shares in the profits in the dividends they receive and the rise in the price of the stock.'

'I bought Dot Matrix. A new issue. And I lost my shirt.'

'I happen to know that stock. Did you read the red herring?'

'What's a "red herring"?'

'The stock prospectus. Did you read the caveats?'

'What caveats?'

'Did you study the financial statement? Did you see their earnings? I should say, their losses. Did you look at the debt? Their projected cash flow?'

'I'm a phys ed instructor. I don't read financial statements.'

'Sir, you are not a man who should invest in the new issue market. I suggest AAA bonds might be a better place for your money.'

'What kind of bonds are AAA?'

'If you don't know that a Triple A bond is about the safest investment in the world, how could you possibly risk buying Dot Matrix?'

'Mr FitzGerald.' Cameron stood up.

'Yes?' FitzGerald's smiling gaze made her feel awkward.

'I have a question about investment bankers.' It seemed to Cameron that his eyes narrowed. 'I believe they earn a commission when they sell stock to the public?'

'They do.'

'Are they large commissions?'

'Large is a relative term, young lady. The commission is proportionate to the risk.'

'You mean,' Cameron said, 'the higher the risk, the larger the commission?'

'That's correct.'

'The risk to whom?'

'The investors.'

'In other words, Mr FitzGerald, the more likely the public is to lose its money, the greater the profit Wall Street makes on the transaction.'

A chorus of laughter ran around the room. Cameron was chagrined. She had not really worked out where her questions would lead and had not meant to embarrass Timothy

FitzGerald. However, he wasn't embarrassed. He was laughing as hard as anyone.

The birdlike woman exploded. 'That's what I mean about the market.' Her voice was strident. 'It's rigged! Only the insiders make money! The bigger the market, the more money they make!'

'Madam, if that were true, then there are a lot of insiders in this room,' FitzGerald replied courteously. 'How do you account for the people here tonight who have done very well on their investment?'

'Flukes. Pure flukes. It's a mug's game.' She had had her say.

'I'm sorry you feel this way – '

Cameron interrupted. 'I didn't mean what the lady said.' She swallowed hard. 'I mean . . . I guess the arrangement struck me as . . . well, as unfair.'

'It may seem that way on the surface,' FitzGerald answered. 'But you've omitted a crucial factor. The reputation of the investment banker.'

'I don't understand.'

'A banker who continuously loses money for his investors will soon lose his investors. That's why we choose the companies we offer with such care. And while the public loses money if a company goes under – and that's serious enough – the banker will lose his business if he repeats his mistakes. That's also serious.' He added as an afterthought, 'You realize I'm speaking of reputable investment banking houses. Not what we call bucket shops. They don't care what they sell, so they lose clients quickly and are constantly scrambling for new customers.'

Cameron sat down. She had to think over FitzGerald's answer.

The question-and-answer session continued well beyond its allotted time. Timothy FitzGerald generously responded to every question, antagonistic or friendly. Then the lights blinked.

'Ladies and gentlemen,' FitzGerald called out. 'The janitor is telling us something. Let's call it a day and allow the man to sweep up the words we've strewn over the floor.'

After the audience filed out of the hall, Cameron hurried to catch FitzGerald before he left the stage. 'Mr FitzGerald, I didn't mean to imply that you would sell stock in a company knowing investors would lose their money,' she stammered. 'Just for the commission.'

'I understand. FitzGerald Associates would not.' Cameron could hear the pride in his voice. 'But as I said, I won't vouch for all houses. Like all businesses, we have our share of double-dealing.' He studied her face intently. 'What's your name?'

'Cameron Hightower.'

'Hightower? Are you related to Geraldine Hightower?'

'We're cousins. I live with her at Hightower Farm.'

'Give her my best. You have a very bright cousin.' He smiled. 'And from your questions, I suspect your cousin has an equally bright cousin.' Cameron felt the heat rising to her cheeks. 'Now if you'll excuse me, I have friends waiting.'

Cameron watched him disappear into the wings. She felt as if the windows of her mind had been blown open by a strong wind; and after she'd accepted it and stopped smoothing her hair, it had blown out again, leaving her wistfully behind, wondering where all the excitement had gone. She looked for Byron. At first she was afraid he'd left without saying good night. But she spotted him leaning against the door in the rear of the hall. She hurried towards him.

'Wasn't it worth listening to?' He gave her a thin smile.

'I wasn't sure you heard anything. Every time I looked at you, your eyes were closed.'

'That's the way I concentrate.'

Cameron didn't believe Byron, but there was no point in

157

making an issue over his closing his eyes. They left the building and walked with tentative steps to where her Jeep was parked. Byron was trying to say something, and Cameron was trying to be a good listener.

'I don't know why my father called your cousin. He talked to me about the battery-fluid deal, told me he's raised so much money he's going to have to parcel out the shares. Only a few to each member of his group.'

'Oh! I'm pleased it's going so well.' Cameron's spirits lifted. Whatever had been wrong was now all right.

'So tell your cousin to forget about the investment. Dad's oversold it. He won't call her again.' Byron rubbed his eyes with the back of his hand. 'Did Dad tell her the work on the battery fluid was going on in Texas?'

'I don't think so.'

'Umm.' Byron pursed his lips. 'Well, Dad asked me to fly to Dallas and spend the summer working there with the inventor. He thinks I know enough chemistry not to get in the way, and I might be useful. It'll be a great experience for me.'

'Sure!' Cameron tried to be enthusiastic. But Byron had not sounded as if he thought Dallas would be a great experience.

'It is! Great! I'm real lucky!' He was vehement. 'Look, Cameron, I've got to get moving.' He kissed her gently on the cheek.

'When are you leaving?'

'Tomorrow.'

'Oh! Will you call me when you get there? So I can give you my blueprint for my new career.' She smiled at him affectionately. 'You had a hand in it.'

'Sure I will.' He was shifting from foot to foot. 'I really gotta go, Cameron.' Even in the dim street light, she could see Byron's Adam's apple bobbing up and down. His voice

158

had a catch in it. 'Gotta run.' Without waiting, he loped down the block towards Sixth Avenue.

Cameron unlocked the door to the Jeep, hesitated for an instant, then slammed the door shut and started to run after Byron. She couldn't let him go like this. For some reason he was running away from her. Maybe he thought she was angry because his father wanted to sell Geraldine an investment. She wasn't. His father was oversold anyway. But what his father did had nothing to do with Byron and their friendship. She turned the corner and saw that Byron was so far away that she'd never be able to catch him. Suddenly he stopped and smashed his fist against a lamp post. Then he started running again, holding the knuckles of his hurt hand to his mouth, as though he were crying and didn't want anyone to know.

Cameron turned back. She'd try to reach him the first thing in the morning.

The next morning, Cameron spent two hours trying to locate Byron Miller's telephone number. He'd never given it to her because he said his mother objected to girls calling. There was no Byron or Adam Miller in the Queens or Brooklyn directory. Or any directory. Cameron waited all day in the hopes that Adam Miller would call Geraldine, and she rushed to answer each ring. She wanted to see Byron, to talk to him, to tell him how smart he was and how much she liked him. He had brightness and warmth and energy, and he was kind. These were important things. She wanted to tell him that he was much better than he thought he was. By nightfall she accepted the fact that, as Byron had said, his father was oversold and would not call Geraldine again. By the following week, she admitted that Byron Miller was no longer a part of her life.

But he'd left her something in his place, probably the only

gift he could give her. He'd shown her the direction she must take. One more year in college – she'd forget the Harvard Business School – and she'd be ready for Wall Street.

9

On Tuesday, June 2, 1974, Cameron Hightower and Lucia Manzone graduated from Barnard College, and then, with financial help from Geraldine and Lucia's parents, the two girls settled into a two-bedroom apartment Geraldine had found on Fifty-sixth Street and First Avenue.

Although Lucia had no qualms about accepting her parents' help, Cameron did. It seemed to her that she'd taken enough from Geraldine already, and it was only after her cousin agreed to treat the money as a loan to be repaid with interest that Cameron finally went along with the plan. She told herself that since she expected to get a job on Wall Street very quickly, the loan wouldn't amount to much and she'd soon be able to repay it.

Cameron reached for the pale blue Princess phone next to her bed and dialled the proper seven numbers: 235-1000. As soon as she heard the first ring, she started shaking and hung up. Disgusted with herself, she paced across the room and stared at the traffic streaming down the East River Drive. Everybody was going to work except her. And if she kept postponing interviews and evading callbacks, she'd never have a job.

She wandered into Lucia's room. Late for work as usual, Lucia had flown out of the apartment an hour ago leaving her usual mess of panties, bras, and jeans on the chair, the bed, and the floor. Eye shadow and mascara and tubes of skin cream were strewn on her dressing table.

In the month they'd shared the apartment, Lucia had changed from a reasonably neat roommate into a slob, but since she kept the mess confined to her bedroom, Cameron did not complain. Also Lucia adhered strictly to their one rule about men: no sex in the apartment. Cameron had no wish to wake up one morning, wander into Lucia's room, and find her getting laid. Optimistically, Lucia had purchased an answering machine in case one of them was spending the night out. So far, Lucia had made eight phone calls while she'd called in only twice. Cameron promised herself that once she got a job, she'd concentrate harder on men.

After all, sex was fun. It was even healthy. Still, it would be almost impossible to keep up with Lucia. It wasn't simply that Cameron was more naturally selective. In fact, she hadn't as yet turned anyone down. But Cameron was five feet ten inches in her bare feet and gave most men under six feet an instant inferiority complex. Lucia had no such limitations. She was five feet five inches, and if the man was short, she wore flat heels. But if the man was tall, she wore spiked heels and fitted comfortably under his arm. Cameron considered suggesting they divide the male world by height – under six feet was Lucia's territory, over six feet, hers. Then she met a man in the supermarket, an inch shorter than she, who was so gorgeous that she gasped. They hit it off immediately. After a lovely dinner, they spent a splendid night at his place, so she dropped the idea of dividing the men by height.

She finally located her reason for entering Lucia's bedroom. Lucia had forgotten her cigarettes. Cameron seldom smoked, but she needed a cigarette now. She returned to the living room to get a match. There was a brandy snifter – so large it couldn't be used for brandy – on a free-form glass cocktail table. There they had dumped the matches they had collected from the restaurants they'd been taken to. They'd collected an impressive variety – Veau d'Or, Maxwell's Plum, the Russian Tea Toom, Le Cirque, and more. Lucia's contribution to the collection more than doubled hers.

Cameron lit the cigarette and slumped on the tweed-covered couch. A telephone sat on the Spanish-style refectory table behind the sofa. She closed her eyes, picturing Timothy FitzGerald as he had appeared at the New School. During the year between that lecture and her graduation, she'd thought about him constantly. Although she knew it was foolish, she was unable to curb her fantasies about him. The realization that she was infatuated – that was the only word for it – with a complete stranger panicked her. She could not fend off her obsessive desires, which fluctuated between cool reason that told her FitzGerald Associates was an excellent place to begin her career and her absurdly vivid erotic fantasies that warned her to stay away from Timothy FitzGerald.

What was there to be afraid of? Only herself. The thought gave her pause. Unreasonably, she became angry at Timothy FitzGerald. In her overheated imagination, it was his fault. Who did he think he was – the only game in town? Not so. There were dozens of other games. Damn that man! If she couldn't get the job she wanted, she'd bloody well want the job she could get. She dialled the number. This time she would not hang up when the phone started to ring.

'FitzGerald Associates.' The telephone operator had a French accent. 'Who would you like to speak to, please?'

Cameron gulped. 'Uh ... Mr FitzGerald, please.' Her normally husky voice was squeaky.

Cameron waited, shivering. Then another woman's voice said, 'Mr FitzGerald's office. May I help you?' This woman had a British accent similiar to the kind Cameron had heard watching TV films about the English upper class. Was being born in Europe a job requirement at FitzGerald Associates?

'Yes. I would like to speak to Mr FitzGerald.'

'Who is calling, please?'

'Cameron FitzGerald. No! I mean Cameron Hightower,' she sputtered. 'I met Mr FitzGerald last year at a lecture.'

163

'I'm sorry but Mr FitzGerald is out of the city. He'll return at the end of the month.'

'I'll call back.'

'Is there anything I can do for you in the meantime?'

'No, thank you.' Abruptly Cameron changed her mind. 'Wait. Yes, there is . . .' The woman's voice sounded friendly. 'The fact is, Miss . . .?'

'Mrs Atherton.'

'Mrs Atherton. I'm sorry. The fact is, I would like to apply for a position at FitzGerald Associates. I've just graduated from Barnard and plan to make my career on Wall Street.'

Mrs Atherton did not show her amusement. Cameron was the fourth applicant this morning. 'What did you say your name was?'

'Hightower, Cameron Hightower.'

'Might I make a suggestion, Miss Hightower?'

'Please.' Cameron was eager and afraid.

'Mr FitzGerald doesn't involve himself in the hiring of entry-level personnel. He leaves that to an associate, Mr Jacob Stern. I suggest you speak to him. Besides,' she added in an intimate fashion, 'Mr Stern is available now.'

'Thank you. I'll call Mr Stern.'

'Why don't I switch you over?' Rosemary Atherton said.

Rosemary Atherton was not Timothy FitzGerald's private secretary because she had an impeccable British accent, an excellent figure, a beautiful English complexion, and natural dark blonde hair. Not only could she handle the telephone, she could take dictation flawlessly up to 120 words a minute and transcribe her dictation on her IBM typewriter at over 60 words a minute with no mistakes. But her most important asset to FitzGerald was her unique memory. While she kept a complete file on everyone who invested in FitzGerald Associates' many offerings, the file was only a backup for those times when she was out sick or on vacation and someone less familiar with the operation needed information.

Rosemary Atherton did not need a file. She knew the names and addresses and anything of importance pertaining to the investors. The Hightower name registered – Geraldine Hightower, Princeton, substantial investor, and more. To Geraldine's file entry, Fitzgerald had added in his own handwriting, 'Cameron Hightower – cousin.' This knowledge influenced her response to Cameron. Ordinarily, she would have said politely, 'May I have your address, so we can send you an application before setting up an appointment.' Instead she pushed the intercom button and tapped out Jake Stern's number. He picked up the telephone on the second ring.

'Jake, Rosemary here. I've got Cameron Hightower on the telephone. She's looking for a job – entry level – and she's scared silly. She's Geraldine Hightower's cousin.'

'Who?' Jake Stern's job at FitzGerald Associates was working with outside counsel on the preparation of private placement memoranda under SEC Rule 146. He was also responsible for overseeing all the prospectuses for the public offerings that FitzGerald managed. He was a Wall Street veteran who knew more about the legal requirements for those documents than most Wall Street lawyers. 'Who the hell is Geraldine Hightower?'

'An important client.'

'What the fuck do I care about important clients? I'm up to my ass in alligators trying to separate fact from fantasy in the pile of crap that Fitz laid on my desk. You should read what the National Bullshit Inc. put together.'

Rosemary Atherton knew her man too well to allow his language to irritate her. Jake Stern was fourth-generation Wall Street, a graduate of the Petty School and Williams College. He was crude because crudity was the trademark of a group of veterans on the Street. It helped them pretend that Wall Street was still a boys' club, full of tough, dirty street fighters, as it had been for their grandfathers. Besides, for all her artfully cultivated British accent, Rosemary had been born in Liverpool – christened Mary Mutt – and had worked from the time she was fourteen; which was twenty-two years ago. Although there never had been a Mr Atherton, she liked the Mrs before her name, and Atherton was an improvement over Mutt. As far as gutter talk was concerned, she could drown Jake in language any time she chose.

'Geraldine Hightower's cousin is looking for a job, Jake,' she repeated patiently. 'I think you should interview her since you've had an opening for an assistant for three months now.'

'Oh, shit!' Jake yelled. 'Okay. Put Miss Rich Bitch on. I'll put her through her paces.'

'Not on the phone, Jake. See her.'

'See her! That's all you fucking cunts can say. As if I've nothing better to do.'

'That's enough, Jake. Or I'll be forced to remind you of our recent weekend in Westhampton when you were hardly a swashbuckler. More the "gosh" and "golly" type. How many times did you get it up? And what were the excuses? Too much sun? Food? Drink? Too much everything. Couldn't I tell our mutual friends some lovely stories about the indomitable lover Jake Stern?'

'Crap! But she better be good. Or she can go fuck herself.'

'If she doesn't show promise, FitzGerald Associates doesn't want her. And, Jake, I was only teasing. You weren't that bad.'

'Shut up and put her on.'

'Miss Hightower?'

The sudden sound of a man's voice startled Cameron. 'Yes.'

'This is Jake Stern. Can you get yourself down here tomorrow morning at eight-thirty sharp?'

'Yes!'

'You know where the office is? At 65 Wall Street. Thirtieth floor. I'll expect you at eight-thirty. Good-bye.' He slammed down the phone.

166

Cameron slowly replaced the receiver. She had an appointment with FitzGerald Associates. And with a man named Jake Stein. Or was it Jake Stern? Cameron had the phone halfway off the hook to call back that nice Mrs Atherton and ask her. Then she stopped herself. It was unbusinesslike. His name was Stein. Jack Stein. And she'd be there at 8:30 sharp.

That evening Cameron waited on tenterhooks for Lucia to arrive. She was full of her news and wanted to share it. Yet, at the same time, a part of her wanted to say nothing. Superstitious, she was afraid that if she so much as mentioned the appointment, she might jinx her chances. She was only half surprised at how personal and possessive she felt about a job that she didn't as yet have. She longed for it the way she might have longed for a lover. She was convinced it was absolutely the right job for her, whatever the job was. She had mentioned briefly to Lucia her wish to work at FitzGerald Associates, pointing out that it was one of the most prestigious investment banking houses on the Street. But she had not said a word about Timothy FitzGerald. He was her secret and hers alone. She tried to put the whole thing out of her mind, to concentrate on the cooking since this was her night to prepare dinner. With a superficial glaze of calm, she cleaned the asparagus.

Lucia slunk into the apartment after six, looking frazzled and upset. She complained about a headache. Her shoulders sagged, and she hardly seemed the same Lucia who had left that morning in an exuberant burst of energy. The steak Cameron had bought was seasoned and prrepared for broiling and the asparagus were scraped and ready for the steamer. Lucia was on a weight-losing regime. High-protein steak and asparagus meant low calories. But watching her slump off to her bedroom made Cameron wonder if she were sick or had run into trouble at the job. Concerned, she fixed herself a martini and poured a glass of red wine for Lucia. Lucia drank wine before, with, and after dinner. Apparently she felt that there were no calories in wine.

'Cameron, look at me. Is there something wrong with me?' Lucia was standing in the kitchen doorway.

Cameron stopped measuring the vermouth to glance at Lucia. Then she spun around, almost dropping the bottle. Lucia was poised in the doorway, naked except for her bikini panties. Her hands were on her hips and her breasts jutted forward aggressively.

Cameron blinked. 'You haven't gained an ounce. If you have, I can't see where.'

'Skip my weight.' Lucia rolled her eyes in mock desperation. 'What about my boobs?'

'Your boobs?'

'My breasts, dopey. You know. Tits.'

'Are you all right? Should you see a doctor? Or have you seen one?' Cameron felt a stab of anxiety. Here she'd been thinking only about herself, and Lucia might have a serious problem.

'I'm as healthy as a horse. But my boobs are not haute couture.'

Cameron exhaled. 'Whew! Is that all?' Her relief was edged with irritation.

'Isn't that enough?'

'Phooey on haute couture! Who said so?'

'Lance said so. Lance, the rat with women.'

'Here,' Cameron said, offering Lucia her glass of wine. 'It will all go away after you drink this.' Relieved that it was only fashion, not health, that was bugging her friend, the evening seemed bright again as Cameron thought about her news. She just couldn't keep it in. She would risk the jinx. She slid past Lucia into the living room. 'Lucia, I have something marvellous to report.'

'Goody! Because I have something nonmarvellous to

report.' Lucia was disgusted. 'Do you know that I have pear-shaped boobs?'

'You do?' Cameron hesitated and then said, 'I made a job call today.'

'You do that every day.'

'This was special.' Cameron couldn't help smiling.

'Oh?' Lucia pursed her lips. 'You mean FitzPatrick and friends?'

'FitzGerald Associates.'

'That's what I said. FitzPatrick and – '

'FitzGerald!'

Lucia stared at her in exasperation. 'I'll bet you have bell-shaped breasts.'

'Bell-shaped? You mean like a statistical bell curve? That's a very useful concept.' Cameron grinned. 'I've got a super job lead.'

'And I've got a super headache. Take off your blouse. I want to make sure.'

Cameron frowned. 'I said I have a super job lead.'

'I heard you. Take off your blouse.'

'We've been roommates for over four years. You've seen my breasts hundreds of times. Will you please listen to me?'

'Don't argue. Take off your blouse. Then I'll listen.'

'If I didn't know you so well I'd worry.' Cameron placed her drink on the cocktail table and unbuttoned her blouse.

'I'm not going les. I want to prove a point.'

'The things one does in the name of friendship . . .'

Lucia glared at her, shaking her head. 'See! Just as I thought. Yours are bell-shaped.'

'And you are losing your mind,' Cameron said, buttoning her blouse. 'I have an interview tomorrow.'

'You told me. I had an interview today, and I was mortally insulted.' Lucia took another swallow of wine. 'When I think of the business I've thrown to Lance, he gets an Oscar for sheer ingratitude.'

169

'Will you listen to me, please?'

'No! You listen to me. Do you know what he did today?'

'There's no way I can stop you from telling me.' Cameron relaxed on the couch and sipped her martini. 'I thought he was your favourite photographer.'

'He was. I also liked him as a person. As a group, photographers are awful. They're riddled with insecurities. Now I don't even like him as a person. He actually refused to photograph me.'

'Why should he photograph you? You're not a model.'

'No, I'm not a model, I'm a fashion coordinator. A glorified "gofer". This time Lance required a nude model with warm skin.'

'A nude model? With warm skin? What for?'

'For a nude shot. What do you think?'

'A nude shot in a fashion magazine?' Cameron shook her head. 'Isn't that a bit much for the public to accept? In one sitting? Maybe a leg first? Then an arm – '

'Stop it! This is not a *Playboy* nude. This nude was to keep her legs clamped together. And her skin was to be painted.'

'Aaah. A new summer fashion. Painted-on bathing suits. Should I start shorting bathing suit companies? Will Cole of California go down the tubes?'

'It is not for a fashion article.'

'Of course. Forgive my ignorance. It's a health and/or beauty piece. How to stay naked and healthy. And you're the nude, warm-skinned health addict.'

'My moment of glory.' Lucia sighed.

'Can't *Bazaar* afford models?' Cameron smiled sweetly.

'With friends like you, who needs enemies? Lance was desperate. This is no ordinary health-beauty article. It's not the usual junk about body moulding, teeth capping, boob firming, or even ass raising. It's a real story. The paint is no ordinary paint. It's got something in it called liquid crystals.

170

And the paint changes colour depending on how warm your body is.'

'I'm beginning to get the idea. The article is on sex.'

'No, that's not what the paint is for. It's a medical breakthrough. The inventor says that when he works it out, a woman will be able to detect breast tumours years in advance. Because the heat of the tumour will cause the colours of the paint to change. It's better than feeling yourself up.'

'That's a big idea. What's the inventor's name? What's the company's name?'

'His name is Harry Horn. And he's nice. If you like shy, serious types about forty. He has the liquid crystals in the paint, but he has to figure out another way to use it. You can't expect a woman to go around painting herself every month.'

'What's the name of his company?'

'I don't remember. Therma something.'

'On the big board? No! I'd know about it. Not on the Amex, either. Is it over-the-counter?'

'Forget Wall Street for the moment.'

'You do your search for happiness, and I'll do mine. You may be on to something very important.'

'I was. I was immortalized. Like Venus on the half shell. Lance shaved the model until she was hairless in Gaza. But the gook wouldn't turn colours. Her skin wasn't warm enough. Horn says he has to work on the temperature range. So I volunteered because Mark and Harry say I have very warm skin.' Lucia smiled sheepishly and then her face fell. 'When I came out of the dressing room, naked as a jaybird, Lance yelped and refused to photograph me.'

'He respected you too much.'

'Respected me, my ass! My breasts are not the right shape. They're not like yours.'

'They're larger. What's wrong with that? Do you know how

171

much women spend each year on silicone implants just to make their breasts larger?'

Lucia was indignant. 'It's not the size that counts. It's the shape.'

'What shape? All breasts are round. Sort of.'

'I told you. Mine are pear-shaped.' Lucia held her breasts in her hands. 'Pear-shaped! Yours are bell-shaped. In the fashion world, bells are in. Pears are out.'

'Lucia, forget about bells and pears. The shape of your breasts makes no difference. I have an interview tomorrow with FitzGerald Associates. It's the beginning of my career on Wall Street.'

'What about *my* career? I'm a loser.' Lucia saw the look on Cameron's face and stopped. 'I see what you mean. I'm not a model. It doesn't matter if I'm a pear or a bell.'

'No, it doesn't,' Cameron said flatly. 'But it does matter where I work.'

'Yeah. And I'm glad for you. Well, well.' Lucia stared at the ceiling. 'FitzPatrick – Sorry. I mean FitzGerald Associates. The company you've been itching to work for. Timothy FitzGerald doing the interview?'

Cameron was flustered. 'How did you know his name?'

'You raved about him once. You said he was very smart.'

'I did?' Cameron felt acutely embarrassed.

Lucia raised an eyebrow and smiled. 'Maybe you had had too much beer that night. It was the day you turned down the job at E. F. Hutton. You said you wanted to work for Timothy FitzGerald. Or nobody.'

'I said that?'

'You said that.'

'Well, he is highly regarded,' Cameron said primly. 'But the man who is to interview me is named Jacob Stein. Or Stern.'

'Which is it?'

Cameron floundered. 'I'm not sure. But it's one of the two names. I'll ask the receptionist when I get there tomorrow.'

'You must have been pretty rattled not to remember the name of the man who's interviewing you. The idea of FitzGerald's company must have – ' Lucia's eyes sparkled.

'You stop that, Lucia Manzone. Go put some clothes on, because dinner is about to be served.' Cameron got up and strode into the kitchen.

Cameron stood on the Lexington Avenue subway on her way to her eight-thirty appointment with Jack Stein. Or was it Stern? Damn it! Get the name straight! She'd selected a light beige crepe suit – guaranteed not to wrinkle – and a slightly darker blouse with small ruffles down the front. Despite the fact that it was mid-July and her legs were tanned from sun bathing on her postage-size terrace, she wore pantyhose and beige snakeskin pumps. She carried a handsome, slim briefcase – feminine yet businesslike – and a small brown shoulder bag. This was the first full-scale New York subway rush Cameron had ever experienced. Hot, sweaty bodies were packed together like the proverbial sardines. One could have a heart attack and die and no one would know it until the car emptied and the body slumped to the floor. To make matters worse, the subway car was a cauldron. She could feel the perspiration dripping under her arms. Maybe her suit wouldn't wrinkle, but it could stain.

When the express train pulled into Fourteenth Street, men and women spurted out of the overstuffed car. There was a seat, and Cameron dove for it. She reached it just ahead of a short, bald man with a heavy black moustache. The man, in his brown seersucker suit, brown shirt with a button-down collar, and brown tie, looked as hot and uncomfortable as she felt. She settled herself and smiled somewhat smugly at the man. He grimaced and moved away. Cameron kept an eye on him. It wasn't until the train stopped at the Brooklyn Bridge

173

station that he beat a plump, middle-aged woman, dressed in much too tight pants, to a vacant seat. Once seated, he opened a copy of *The Wall Street Journal* and studied an item in the second section of the paper.

Cameron left the car at the Wall Street station. The man she'd beaten to the seat was just ahead of her, standing in a long line waiting to get through the revolving exit. It took several minutes for the crowd to work its way through. Cameron waited on the corner of Broadway and Wall Street for the light to change. The man in the seersucker suit was next to her. Although he had folded his paper, she could tell he had been looking at the page where the notices of new offerings were placed. The names of the investment-banking houses were normally too small for her to read, but by squinting she made out the name FitzGerald Associates on the top line of one of the notices.

The light changed and the crowd surged across Broadway and down Wall Street. The sidewalk was much too narrow for all the people, so a few, including Cameron's rival for the subway seat, stepped off the sidewalk into the street. Cameron glanced at her watch. 8:20. Hesitating at first, she joined the group on the street. Any car trying to use the street would have to commit mass murder to get through. When she came to the corner of Wall and Broad streets, she was again standing next to her fellow subway rider. They crossed Broad Street together and continued down Wall.

It got worse. They both entered the express elevator at 65 Wall Street and the man pressed 30, then glowered at her. He remembered that she was the reason he'd had to stand most of the subway ride. Cameron prayed, please let it be someone else! They left the elevator together. At the far end of the lobby Cameron saw the sign that said FitzGerald Associates in large brass letters over a heavy, double glass door. The man hurried in that direction, opened the door and was through by the time Cameron reached it. He did not

174

hold the door for her. As she entered, she heard the receptionist say, with a charming French accent, 'Good morning, Mr Stern.'

The temptation to cut and run was strong. She'd call in and say she was sick – the flu, pneumonia, measles, anything. So she'd see Mr Stern next week, wear different clothes, bleach her hair blonde, and slump so she'd look shorter than her five feet ten inches. He'd never recognize her. Yes he would; he would remember her as the girl who had taken his subway seat. The unfairness of the coincidence angered her. Of all the subway riders, she had to run into Jake Stern! The hell with it. She'd give Mr Stern five minutes of her time, then go home and collapse. Bell-shaped boobs were in. If she became a model, she'd take taxis wherever she went.

Cameron gave her name to the receptionist and was kept waiting for half an hour. Finally, a woman with dark blonde hair, wearing well-cut pants and a stylish blue blouse, beckoned to her. 'Miss Hightower?' She held out her hand. 'I'm Rosemary Atherton. We talked yesterday.'

Cameron shook hands. 'I hoped I'd get a chance to thank you for arranging the interview.'

Rosemary Atherton's appraisal of Cameron was so open and acute that Cameron felt uncomfortable. 'My, you are an attractive girl. Jake is in for a nice surprise.'

'Thank you.' Cameron silently footnoted that his surprise might not be so nice.

'He's ready for you now. You go down the hall, turn right at the end of the corridor, and his office is the second door on the left. Mr Stern's name is on the door.'

'Thank you,' Cameron said again. She strode briskly down the hall, the sound of her footsteps muffled by the thick carpet. When she arrived she saw a brass plate on the door. 'Jacob "Jake" Stern – Vice President.' Cameron stiffened her back and tapped on the door.

'Knock, damn it!' a rough voice called out. 'Knock loud! Like an adult. Don't scratch like a frightened child.'

Something snapped in Cameron. She was suddenly too angry to be afraid. She raised her fist and pounded on the wooden door. Bang! Her fist was about to crash against the door for a fourth time when it opened, and her fist stopped just short of Jake Stern's nose.

'I said knock. I didn't say to break the damn thing down.' He wheeled around and stalked behind his desk. 'Come in and sit down.' There was a leather chair facing his desk. 'Or do you only sit in subways? In other people's seats?'

The bastard had known all the time and had kept her waiting to let her stew before getting rid of her. 'That was not your seat. I got there first.'

'Okay, forget it. Sit down and let's talk.'

Cameron stood still, glaring at him. 'Do we really have anything to talk about?'

'We do if you want a job. Or is riding subways during the rush hour and wasting my time interviewing you the way you get your jollies?'

Cameron sidled into the office. More than anything in the world, she wanted to work for FitzGerald Associates – for Timothy FitzGerald – and she'd be damned if she was going to be put off by this miserable creature.

'Shut the door!'

Cameron slammed the door so hard the framed announcements of FitzGerald Associates' placements rattled. She sat on the edge of the leather chair. 'Mr Stern, did anyone ever tell you that you are rude? And impossible?'

'Frequently. I am rude. But I am not impossible. I'm quite possible.' He gave her a comedic leer and stroked his moustache. 'Wanna try me?'

A more mature Cameron would have seen immediately the sly teasing in Jake. But Cameron was young and inexperienced, and her indignation flared. 'Is that a proposition?' She could hardly believe it.

Jake Stern leaned back in his chair, lifting his feet onto his desk. The soles of his shoes were only a few feet from Cameron's face. 'If you think it is, it is. How about it?'

Cameron erupted. She knocked Stern's feet off his desk. In doing so, neat piles of paper were scattered over the desk and floor. 'Take your proposition and shove it!' She was halfway to the door before Stern reacted.

'Don't tell me a good looker like you has never been propositioned.'

Cameron whirled around. 'Not during a job interview.'

Jake Stern took offence. His accent changed from New York tough to Ivy League sophisticate. 'My dear child, did I in any way suggest that your working here had anything to do with sex?' He answered his own question. 'I did not. Women grow more and more erratic. They cling to the cliché that because a man is interested in the unique aperture between their legs, he is prepared to pay for all favours rendered. With money, or jewellery, or a job.' His accent reverted. 'Shit! Screwing you does not go with the job. For the job you have to qualify. Now, for God's sake, sit down! I'm getting a crick in my neck looking up at you. How the hell am I going to find out if you know anything if you keep standing there pawing the air like a filly in heat?'

'You really do work hard at being gross.' But Cameron's heart wasn't in her words. By some perverse chemistry, she found herself starting to like this crude little man. Then she recognized the ring on the pinky of his right hand. The Williams College graduation ri..g was a dead giveaway. Jake Stern knew better. His vulgarity was a performance that he put on for some crazy reason. Well, to each his own. She sat down, crossed her legs, and waited.

'Got a résumé?'

Cameron opened her briefcase. 'It's not a résumé. I just

177

graduated from Barnard.' She dropped a piece of white paper on the desk. 'My bio. With schools, grades, majors, special courses.'

Jake put on a pair of gold-wire-rimmed glasses and ran quickly through the biography. Although his face showed nothing, he was impressed. He'd graduated college with what were called gentlemen's grades – three C's and a D per semester. But he understood what it took to graduate summa cum laude. She had also taken extra courses in accounting and economics. Apparently the girl could add and subtract, despite the fact she was strikingly beautiful.

He grunted. 'No physical description. Age, height, weight, cup size.'

Cameron could give as good as she got. 'Twenty-one, five feet ten, one hundred thirty pounds, thirty-two twenty-three thirty-five. I never wear a bra. What else?'

'Can you type?'

'Some.'

'Hunt and peck? Two fingers?'

'Ten fingers and my nose.'

Jake made a scribble. 'Do you know what I do?'

'No.'

'Ever seen a prospectus? For a stock or bond placement? The kind the SEC has to approve?'

'I took two courses on Wall Street at Columbia. They included analysing public offerings.' She didn't mention that Geraldine had given her a collection of over twenty Fitz-Gerald offerings in which she'd bought stock.

'Do you know what risk factors are?'

'Some. They vary with each offering.' It was then that Cameron had a strong impression that Jake Stern liked her. He'd liked her from the moment he saw her on the subway. This gave her the confidence to ask, 'Would I be working for you?'

'Yes, you lucky girl.' He sniffed noisily. 'If I decide to lower the standards of the office and hire you.'

'You were going to tell me what you did.'

Jake searched through the mess that had been created when Cameron had knocked his feet away. At last he found what he'd been looking for. 'What do you see?' he asked, handing it to her.

'A prospectus.' Cameron studied the front page. 'US Electric. One million shares at sixty-two dollars a share. That's a sixty-two-million-dollar stock offering. Two and a half per cent commission. Nice piece of business. Over a million and a half dollars in commissions to be spread around. No red printing. It's been approved by the SEC.' Cameron glanced at Jake. 'When is this effective? The date is blank.'

'Yesterday.' He tossed her *The Wall Street Journal* he'd been reading on the subway. 'The tombstone is in today's *Journal.*'

Cameron found the tombstone. She counted the number of Wall Street firms participating in the underwriting. There were forty-eight banking houses listed. Then she thumbed through the prospectus looking for the page that gave the number of shares each house had circled. It was on the next to last page. FitzGerald Associates was the syndicate leader with three hundred thousand shares. Thirty per cent. 'Very nice, Mr Stern,' she said. 'That's almost five hundred thousand dollars for FitzGerald Associates alone.'

Jake Stern had been watching her closely. Cameron had done all the right things. There was much more to the prospectus than she'd picked up, but her instincts were good. He could teach her the rest.

She held up the prospectus. 'You put this together?'

'Yeah. Me and a nitwit lawyer over at Wilkie, Farr. They always need a lawyer's opinion. It's called a comfort letter. That jerk of a lawyer couldn't find his ass with two hands.

179

Let alone if anything wasn't kosher. But he's a lawyer, and Wilkie, Farr is lousy with comfort letters.'

Cameron shrugged. 'Stupid rules are stupid rules. You live with them. For a five-hundred-thousand-dollar fee it could be worse.'

'How much salary do you need to keep from whoring on the side?'

Cameron could feel the pulse throbbing in her neck. Her heart was somewhere in her throat. By some magic, she was being offered the job. For one of the few times in her life, her hands began to sweat.

'What's the job?'

'Christ! You just blew it. I'd begun to think maybe you were a smart broad. Then you ask a dumb question.' He imitated her. 'What's the job? Cleaning typewriters and windows!' he roared. 'You'll be my assistant, stupid!'

'How much did your former assistant get?'

'Thirty thou – ' He caught himself. 'No way. Becky was experienced, and she put out like a bunny.'

'I don't have experience and I don't put out. So how much will I get?'

Jake wanted to hire Cameron. She was smart and a pleasure to look at. Add to that, he thoroughly enjoyed making her mad. 'We might start you at fifteen thousand.'

From his tone, Cameron guessed she could do better. 'How about twenty-five thousand?'

Mentally Jake reviewed his department's budget. He could offer her $17,500 and settle for $20,000. That was high enough for an inexperienced assistant. Or he could offer her a take-it-or-leave-it $20,000. He recognized in Cameron the aura of money and breeding – he'd grown up with women who had the same air, like his mother before things fell apart. He wouldn't haggle.

'My top offer is twenty thousand. That's it. And three weeks a year vacation.'

Cameron sat up very straight. 'The vacation does make a difference.' In spite of herself she started to laugh. 'Also your charm and good manners. And the fact that this is FitzGerald Associates. I'll take it.'

Jake offered his hand across the desk. 'Shake.'

She accepted his hand. It was a surprisingly delicate hand, small boned with long, slim fingers. 'When do I start?'

'Right now. See that mess you made.' His thumb pointed to the papers scattered on the floor. 'Clean that up. If you're so smart, figure out what goes with what and stack 'em on my desk in neat piles.' He got up and started for the door.

'Where are you going?'

'To the men's room. I'm also going to pick up a W-2 form so we can put you on salary.'

Once Jake was out of the office, Cameron tossed her briefcase and purse in the air. She danced around the room singing. 'I did it. I said that I could do it and, by God, I did.'

PART FOUR

The Wall Streeter
1974–1980

10

Cameron had been working at FitzGerald Associates for almost a year and the most she'd seen of Timothy FitzGerald was an occasional glimpse in the corridors, in Jake's office, or riding down in the elevator. She had no idea what his hours were, how he spent his time. His corner office was either empty or the door was closed. He had numerous meetings. After a while she stopped dreaming about him and started concentrating on the men that were available. Unlike the fashion or entertainment worlds, Wall Street was essentially still a men's club. The women executives on the Street were attractive, but there is a difference between attractive good looks and a stunning woman. Cameron had become a stunner.

Her height; her tanned skin; her slim, tautly muscled but female body; her clean, boyish, strong-boned face; the natural grace with which she moved; the elegance with which she dressed; all made her the magnet of male eyes. And the envy of most females. Whether it was having lunch at Delmonico's, the Chateau, the Lawyers' or Bankers' clubs, or the executive dining room at the top of the Chase Manhattan Bank, or merely pacing down Wall Street with her long, easy tomboyish gait, heads turned to follow her. Wherever and with whomever she went to lunch, it was as though one hydra-headed man turned and stared in devout appreciation. Some were rich investment advisers, some not-so-rich bank officers, some thin stock analysts, some tense fund managers; some were bald, some had hair, some were young, some not so young. But one and all saluted her in silent gratitude as a woman.

For Cameron, it was a time of self-discovery. She made little effort to be selective in her choice of men. If she were not busy, or working late, she accepted the invitation. Or found another, more convenient evening. She had no favourites and no one was turned down out of hand. If she found the man attractive, interesting, and pleasant to be with, likely as not they ended up in bed. But if for some reason he did not appeal to her, she rejected him in as inoffensive a way as possible, assuring him that there would be other times. He was welcome to try again. And many did.

There was only one strict rule Cameron made with regard to men. She refused to have dinner with any man who worked at FitzGerald Associates. Lunch – a business lunch – of course. But that was it. Much to Jake Stern's disgust, there was no fishing off the company dock. None! End of subject! With a quite natural self-deception, she smugly included Timothy FitzGerald in this category. That is, should he ever notice her long enough to ask.

In truth, Cameron did not waste too much time pining over Tim FitzGerald. She was in love – desperately, overwhelmingly, uncontrollably in love – not with a man, but a place. Cameron was in love with Wall Street, and her love cast a golden glow over anyone connected with the Street. Each day when she left the office at 65 Wall Street, it seemed to her that the Street sparkled and crackled with colour and energy. She'd stand in the entrance of the building, happily watching the parade of passing people. She spotted a runner scurrying between two banking houses carrying a briefcase crammed with important papers, and noticed a trio of secretaries, giggling and chatting and hurrying somewhere to celebrate something. She watched investment bankers in their dark grey, three-button, vested suits with their white shirts and narrow, striped ties, carrying hand-tooled leather attaché cases as they strode up Wall Street towards the Lexington Avenue subway. Cameron no longer saw Wall

Street as a man-made canyon of glass, steel, and concrete but as it really was: the financial centre of the world, a place of power and majesty, a honeycomb of banking messiahs, commodity mystics, stock and bond visionaries. A place where the ordinary American citizens' financial health – even survival – rested in the hands of a few great men.

Watching the Wall Streeters pass, Cameron felt a peace and a joy she'd almost forgotten was possible. The desperate and terrifying time she'd known after her parents drowned receded into the background. She dreaded to think what her life might have been like if Geraldine hadn't taken her in. And though Geraldine treated her with real affection, Cameron knew she would never again feel secure until she could take care of herself. Now Wall Street blotted out all the past fear. She'd become a citizen of the Street. It had given her a life that was a bright, incandescent blur, far beyond anything she'd ever thought possible. In return – as payment in full – Cameron gave Wall Street her love; Wall Street and everyone who worked on the Street was made heroic by that love.

As the number and variety of men Cameron made love to increased, so did her desire to make love increase. She was like a magnificent flower that had lived too long in parched soil. She sank into her own sensuality, letting her passion grow as it would. Desires which had once been dim reveries, poetic fancies, emerged, amazing and occasionally frightening her with their strength. She became obsessed with the idea of sex. Sometimes she found it difficult to finish dinner with an attractive man before the need to feel his fingers caressing her became so strong she could hardly eat. Her nipples would grow hard, her skin hypersensitive, longing for his touch. She would wait impatiently for the dinner to end. When it finally did and they were alone, she would rapidly slip out of her clothes and, losing all reserve, respond to his desire with her own. When fulfilment came, passion undulated through her body, claiming her and leaving her spent with the intensity of

187

everything she felt. Her hunger was satisfied, but like all appetites, she knew it would soon return.

Of the varieties of men she dated, at first Cameron thought she liked security analysts best. They didn't fall asleep after sex. They had too much to say. And good professional conversation was almost – if not quite – as exhilarating as making love. Then she had an experience with Noah Greenberg, an analyst who worked for Carter and Thomas, that was thoroughly disturbing. Noah was depressed. He'd just sent out a positive report on a company that he said would end up in Chapter 10 by the end of the year.

'That's bankruptcy, isn't it? The real thing?'

'Yeah! Down the tubes,' Noah said.

'Then why did you issue a positive report? If they're in that much trouble?'

'The balance sheet is very strong.'

'If their balance sheet is strong, why will they go bankrupt?'

'The trouble is the accountants. One of our friendly Big Eight boys sent out a bunch of fools to do the fieldwork. Juniors. Kids who aren't even CPAs yet. They can't tell faked receivables from the real thing. Or that the inventories are inflated. The treasurer is too smart. He moved the same widgets around from storeroom to storeroom. So the little-boy accountants double-counted them.'

'That's awful! How do you know?'

'I know the company. And the treasurer. And the chairman.'

'Shouldn't you tell your boss?'

'I told our managing partner that the balance sheet was a farce.'

'What did he say?'

'He said, and I quote, "Farce or not, right or wrong, what the fuck difference does it make? The stock will go up."'

'It shouldn't.'

'It will. But by the time the wet, smelly stuff hits the fan, our managing partner, the company chairman, the treasurer, and all the other insiders will have bailed out.'

'What about the public?'

'They get screwed. That's why I'm depressed. If I could afford it, I'd go back to teaching.'

This experience started Cameron thinking about the way Wall Street worked. She decided that her education needed broadening, and the best way to broaden it was to be more selective in her choice of men. It was no longer enough that an attractive man ask her out. It was preferable that he have wide experience and special knowledge of the Street. She branched out from securities analysts to fund managers, to traders on the floor of the Exchange, and to what she decribed to herself as Wall Street tastemakers. Harry Byman was a stock and bond tastemaker. He was a household name to anyone interested in Wall Street.

The radio announcer was saying, 'Harry Byman, the highly regarded economist for Schwartzman Brothers, predicted today that interest rates will rise one full percentage point next month due to the budget deficit and increased demand for borrowed money. By the end of the year, this will bring a downturn in the economy, which will sharply affect the price of high-flying stocks. These stocks have been placed on Schwartzman Brothers' "sell now" list . . .'

Cameron only half listened, staring at the road. She'd been keeping track of Byman's predictions. Not one of them had been accurate in the long run. Nonetheless, when Byman said interest rates would rise, the stock market went into shock.

Byman switched off the radio. They were on their way back from City Island after a lobster dinner at Thwait's. This was their third date, and Byman had always said good night to Cameron in her lobby. It made no sense to her. She found him very bright, attractive, if not exactly a Robert Redford type. Actually, he looked like what he was: a bespectacled, slightly overweight, famous economist in his late thirties.

'Harry, the economy is not heading for a downturn,' she said. 'It's an election year.'

'You've been reading Caniglia. He works for First National.'

'Strickland disagrees with you, too.'

'Strickland works for Boston Trust.' He paused. 'How would you like to continue this at my place? We'll have a nightcap.'

Cameron was pleasantly surprised. They had one nightcap seated on a sectional couch. Then he offered to take her home. Cameron's response was simple and direct. She leaned over and kissed him. When he recovered, they really kissed.

'You find me attractive?' he asked.

'Very.' She nuzzled his ear.

'Amazing. I'm a sex-symbol type only to financial librarians, never to pretty women like you.'

'I'm a financial librarian in disguise.'

Harry was more reliable in bed than he had ever been in his forecasts. In his own way, he was a bedroom marvel – which proved that you can't judge a man by his hairline. Hours later, they smoked cigarettes and talked.

'As I was saying, you mustn't pay attention to amateurs. Caniglia works for First National. Strickland for Boston Trust.' He smiled. 'I like you, Cameron. You're smart. You use polysyllabic words. If you want to make money for yourself and your clients, listen only to me.'

'Why only you, Harry?' She kept her voice properly respectful.

'Because I'm with Schwartzman Brothers.'

Cameron remembered seeing on Jake's desk that morning the bulletin sent out by Schwartzman Brothers predicting rising interest rates, a business downturn, and the consequent

190

drop of high fliers like Xerox, Avon, and Polaroid, which are the first stocks affected when the market falls. Her mind started putting two and two together. 'So . . . ?' she asked.

'So Schwartzman is short on Avon, Xerox, Polaroid, et al. Naturally, I predict a recession so they can cover their short position and make a few million dollars.'

'That's not honest.'

'Don't be childish. You're too smart. Nobody forces anyone to believe what I say. I've been wrong often enough. You know that. The stocks will come back eventually. As you said, this is an election year.'

'But the high fliers will fall now. People will get hurt.'

'That's my point. People listen to me. Caniglia doesn't count. Strickland doesn't count. And Moore, your own economist at FitzGerald Associates, he doesn't count.' Byman stopped for effect. 'Only I count.'

'And if Schwartzman were long on Avon or Xerox, you'd make an optimistic prediction about the interest rates?'

'Sure. So they could sell into a rising market.'

'That's outrageous!'

'It's the way it is.' Byman was matter-of-fact. 'That's why I'm the highest-paid economist on Wall Street. Got it?'

'I got it.' Cameron hated it.

Byman patted her head. 'It's not what's true that matters, Cameron. It's what people believe is true.'

And the public be damned, Cameron thought.

It was Cameron's and Lucia's night to stay home. Cameron was brushing her teeth while Lucia shampooed her hair.

'Lucia, do you know that men do more talking after sex than at any other time?'

'Better after than during,' Lucia had soap in her eye.

'That's when I get my education. There are things going on on Wall Street that are not to be believed.'

'Same with the fashion business. You should see how some

191

of the staff dresses. Blue jeans. Work shirts. Sneakers. I was expecting a fashion show every day. What were you expecting on Wall Street?' Lucia stopped shampooing. She had heard the undercurrent of anger in Cameron's voice.

'Not what I'm finding.'

'What are you finding?'

'That if I stop, look, and listen, I'll know more than I want to know.'

When not concentrating on the work Jake piled on her. Cameron's mind was a chaos, a welter of contradictions. She had chosen Wall Street as her profession, and her weakness was that she loved it too well. Her love made it difficult for her to admit or accept the presence of anything that might disturb her positive vision of the Street. How could she deny the truth of everything she had learned from Noah Greenberg and Harry Byman? And having learned it how could she remain at peace with this new view of the Street? How could she explain it, excuse it? When a woman in love wishes desperately to find a way to explain the inexplicable in the one she loves, she will usually find a way. In this Cameron was no exception. She decided that there were unscrupulous and conniving men in every profession. The world was full of unprincipled charlatans. Unfortunately, the Street was not exempt. She had simply been unlucky in her choices. That was all there was to it.

Christopher Canfield called Cameron. He was exuberant, expansive. He absolutely had to see her that night to celebrate. Cameron's desk was clear. The National Toys prospectus was almost finished. Why not see Canfield? When she mentioned to Rosemary that she was having dinner that evening with Chris Canfield, Rosemary was more than a little envious.

'Christopher Canfield? That gorgeous specialist?' she

asked. 'With all that golden hair glinting with strands of silver?'

'You make him sound as if he should be stored in Fort Knox.'

'More probably Sing Sing.' Rosemary was again her usual cynical self. 'You know about specialists. They have a licence to steal.'

'What do you mean, "a licence to steal"?'

'You've never heard it before?'

'No.'

'Never mind. It's an old Wall Street joke. I keep forgetting you're new to the territory.' Rosemary sighed. 'But I forgive Canfield his sinful ways. He's so gorgeous.'

Cameron suddenly felt wary. The past months had been filled with enough disillusion. She didn't need a man who had a 'licence to steal'.

'Since you think he's so special, I'll call him and say that I'm sick, but I've got a perfect replacement. You!'

'If I were twenty-one again, you'd be on. But I'm too old, my dear.'

'Too old! He must be at least forty-five.'

'To the Christopher Canfields of Wall Street, any woman over twenty-five is too old. On Wall Street, young lady, they do it by the numbers. They total up the ages. Yours and his. For a man between forty and fifty, the total can't exceed 70.'

'You mean that if he's forty, the woman can't be more than thirty? But if he's fifty, she has to be twenty?' Cameron made no effort to hide her indignation.

'A little more, a little less,' Rosemary said with some regret. 'When a man is between fifty and sixty, the total is raised to eighty.' The idiocy of the formula got the best of her and she added, laughing, 'The men in their twenties don't know how to add, and when they pass sixty, they'd rather not add. To them I'm prime beef on the hoof.' She remembered Jake.

'There are rare exceptions, but they're the exceptions that prove the rule.'

'I never heard of anything so stupid.'

'It is silly and stupid, but Christopher Canfield lives by the rule. Just don't laugh when he gives you his apologia.'

'What apologia?'

'If he runs true to form, it goes like this. Hark! "I may not be as good as I once was, but once I'm better than I ever was."'

Cameron said nothing, but she was getting the feeling that she'd never let Christopher Canfield be in a position to 'run true to form'.

Seated in the office of Christopher Canfield, managing partner of the New York Stock Exchange firm of Canfield, Weisman, and Haig, Cameron felt somewhat reassured. Considering that the firm made the market in five major corporations plus doing the same for eight middle-sized companies, they undoubtedly traded about a million shares a day and did about fifty million dollars' worth of business each day. Yet their office at 111 Broadway looked as though they were selling pencils without erasers. The asphalt-tiled floor was uncarpeted and the tiles were chipped. The desks were old and beaten, scarred with cigarette burns and scratches. The offices of the partners were separated from the rest of the room only by a low glass partition. The water cooler was the one piece of new equipment in the office. It was clear to Cameron that these men did not throw money around extravagantly. They were all for 'go', not 'show'. If the office was any indication, they managed their stocks prudently.

Canfield was poring over a set of books with grey covers and red bindings, doing some arithmetic while evaluating the buy and sell orders of various stocks for the following day. Rosemary had claimed that he was one of the handsomest men on the Street, and Cameron agreed that he probably was. His face was lean and intense, and his blue eyes seemed never to miss a detail. He was also reputed to be one of the smarter specialists on the floor of the Exchange. That, as much as his good looks, was what attracted Cameron. Of all the people who worked on Wall Street – aside from the retail brokers – specialists worked closest to the public. They set the minute-by-minute prices of the stocks they handled. They could cause a stock to rise five points, or drop ten. This power gave them an enormous responsibility, and Cameron felt confident that here, at the heart of the Street, was living proof of the integrity of her profession.

While she waited, Cameron's eyes wandered over the various photographs of children displayed on Canfield's desk. She knew that he had one semiwife living permanently in Sweden, but his children lived with him and a housekeeper.

Canfield broke his concentration to stare wearily at Cameron. 'Sorry, baby. I guess this was the wrong night for me to see you. I can't leave here until I know how broke I am. And I won't know until that telephone rings.'

'Is there something wrong?'

'Plenty!'

'I'm sorry.' Cameron wondered which of the companies that Canfield, Weisman, and Haig handled was in trouble.

Canfield opened the bottom left-hand drawer of his desk and took out a bottle of Chivas Regal. He went to the water cooler, grabbed two paper cups, and poured a hefty shot into one of them. 'I need this,' he said, 'while we wait. How about you?'

'All right,' Cameron said. 'A small one.'

They sat barely making conversation for about half an hour. Canfield continued to work on his numbers, and Cameron slowly sipped her Scotch. Canfield poured himself two more slugs and tossed them down like water. The man could hold his liquor. Occasionally he would say something, half to himself, half to Cameron.

195

'Normally you can't give the stock away. It's a dog. It's not even a widow-and-orphans number. And here we are up to our asses in it.' Finally he looked hard at Cameron. 'You must be exhausted. I got you here straight from work thinking I'd be roaring to celebrate.' He glanced at the clock on the far wall. 'Shit! It's seven-thirty, and I might be here until – The damn tension kills my sacroiliac.'

Cameron was about to offer to make it another night when the telephone rang. Canfield almost knocked over the bottle of Scotch reaching for it.

'Hello? ... Oh, Patty. Listen, Patty ... Please, darling, I can't hear about Yum Yum now. I'm working late tonight. Honey, please! I can't tie up the telephone ... No, darling. You give Yum Yum my love. Good-bye, honey.' He hung up the telephone. 'My number-two daughter. Lovely child but no sense of timing.' He smiled weakly at Cameron. 'I know I'm acting like a lunatic, but Canfield, Weisman, and Haig is on the line. We're carrying over seven million dollars' worth of a lousy stock on our books. And if we can't get rid of it at a decent price over the next five days, we are in deep trouble. We just can't afford to hold that kind of inventory.'

Cameron was sympathetic. She tried to project support for whatever mess Canfield was in. But she couldn't understand why the firm was carrying so much stock that they considered lousy – unless they'd gone out on a limb to support the price of the stock in a bad market, to keep the price of the stock from collapsing and causing the public to lose a lot of money. 'Maybe if you talk about it you'll feel better,' she suggested.

Canfield poured himself another drink. 'Make believe this is television. There's this XYZ Company that practically doesn't trade. On a big day it moves twenty-five thousand shares.'

'What's the price?'

'Usually between thirty and thirty-one. But we've managed to get it as high as forty and a half.'

Cameron's eyes widened. 'Something is going on?'

'Of course something is going on. And the sooner it goes on, the better. At the moment we own about one hundred seventy-five thousand shares of XYZ.'

'That's a lot of shares.'

The telephone rang again. Canfield's mouth tightened. It rang a second time, and a third. 'It had better not be Patty,' he said grimly and picked up the receiver. 'Hello?' He listened for a minute and the lines in his face relaxed. 'Thank God!' he murmured in an awed voice. 'Thank God. Marty. Have a great evening.' Very slowly he hung up the telephone. His face had taken on the inspired expression of a man with a vision. He seemed exhausted, ecstatic, and dazzled into a state where he saw so much and felt so much that he did not altogether know what he felt or what he saw. Then slowly the real world seemed to come back into focus, and he noticed Cameron sitting there, seeing her as if for the first time. He took a deep breath. 'It's all right, Cameron. Everything's fine,' he said. 'I can breathe again, and we want champagne.'

At dinner at the Pen and Pencil, Chris Canfield and Cameron had champagne. Cameron had no idea what they were celebrating, but after they finished the bottle, Canfield ordered another.

'We'll make a few million dollars tomorrow, Cameron,' he said with great relish. 'Want to know what happened?'

'I would if you want to tell me.'

'I would if I could, but I can't. You'll know tomorrow.' He ordered more champagne.

Eventually they ended up in the company apartment, a luxuriously furnished one-bedroom flat on the twentieth floor of a Lincoln Towers building.

'We keep this for our clients,' Canfield explained. 'When they visit New York.'

Cameron's mind was clicking at top speed. 'Clients?

Clients don't visit you. You visit them. You're a specialist. Not an investment banker.'

'Do you want to argue with our accountants?' He laughed. 'They claim it's for visiting clients. And the IRS agrees.'

It occurred to Cameron that she damn well could argue with his accountants. Canfield, Weisman, and Haig's clients never saw this apartment. And what an apartment at that. It was a *Penthouse* fantasy. Cameron looked at her reflection in the mirrors on the bedroom ceiling and walls and decided that Canfield must have had a sex-deprived youth. The bed was a round, fur-covered circle in the centre of the room with a circular headboard that looked like the instrument panel of an aircraft. Cameron was convinced that somewhere on that console was a switch that would start a pornographic tape on the television set, and still another switch that would make the bed shiver and shake, adding its vibrations to the sexual rhythms. Her opinion of Chris Canfield, which had been slowly chilling, hit the freezing point. She did not want to spend any more time with this would-be sexual athlete.

Canfield touched a button on the headboard. The bedroom lights dimmed to a silver glow and stars came out on the ceiling. He smiled at Cameron, pleased with himself and his toy.

'A starry sky,' Cameron said, managing to smile back.

'Rain or shine.'

'Weather-proof,' she said, hurrying into the living room and sinking into a deep cut-velvet couch.

'Let me get you something to warm your heart. A cognac. The kind you have trouble getting even in the best restaurants.'

'Thank you.'

He handed her the drink. 'Here. Warm it with your hands. It's V.V.S.O.P., and I do mean Very Very Superior Old Pale. Fifty years old.'

Cameron sniffed the cognac, rolled a little around on her tongue, and agreed it was superb.

Canfield sat beside her, sipping his own drink and ostentatiously warming the glass with his hands. 'You know, Cameron, you are a remarkable young woman,' he said.

'And my age is right. The numbers work.'

'I beg your pardon?'

'Never mind. It's an old Wall Street joke. Among women.' She changed the subject. 'You're feeling better now?'

'Much. But I have a sudden impression that you're not. So, to show you that I'm a nice guy who's not just hot for your body, I'm going to tell you what the shooting's been all about. And how you can make yourself a pot of money.'

'You don't have to tell me anything.'

'I know I don't have to. I want to. You put up with me earlier, and I want to make it up to you. Consider it a present. A solid-gold, eighteen-carat present that can make you a bundle.'

'I thought it was a pot,' Cameron said resignedly. 'The pot at the end of the rainbow.'

'That's exactly what it is, and no strings attached. You don't owe me a thing.' He assumed she would be properly grateful and not take him at his word. 'Now listen . . .'

Cameron couldn't help listening. He was practically breathing in her ear.

'The stock we were stuck with is National Rec. Symbols NRC, not XYZ. Buy a chunk at the opening tomorrow. NRC is selling forty-one and a fraction. At eleven A.M. Meridian, symbols MRI, is going to make a tender offer for NRC at sixty-five glittering dollars per share.'

'And you bought it between thirty and forty.' Cameron never forgot a number.

'We did, and it still has nother twenty-five points to move up. Canfield, Weisman, and Haig will clear over three million dollars on the deal.'

'How did you know the Meridian offer was coming?'

'I used my brains. The boys at NRC were buying in their own stock like crazy. Exercising all their options. Something had to be going on, so I checked. A board member dropped the ball and told me that the takeover was in the works.'

'Naturally you acted on the tip?'

'Naturally. Wouldn't you?'

Cameron shook her head sadly. This was the way it was, but she was at a loss for what to say. She felt a terrible resentment at Canfield for being what he was: a cheat and a swindler. If she told him how she felt, would he understand? 'I always assumed that honesty was the best policy.' It was the best she could do.

'What are you talking about?' Canfield put down his drink and reached for her.

She tried again. 'I was taught that virtue is its own reward.' She shifted away, not wanting to be touched.

'Are you all right?'

'I'm fine. Never better. But I'd like you to understand that money isn't everything. Honesty is two per cent.' As she stood up, she emptied her glass of fifty-year-old cognac on Canfield's head. He understood that.

Cameron went back to her office. Work was her sedative. It had become a habit of hers to work at night. It helped keep her sexual energies at bay and lulled her doubts and fears. It was easier to sleep after she had exhausted herself at work. This night she bumped into Timothy FitzGerald. He was in his shirt sleeves coming out of the men's room.

'Ah, Miss Hightower.'

'Cameron, please.'

'Cameron. And I'm Timothy. Or Tim. You're working late.'

'I wanted to proofread the National Toys prospectus. It goes to the printer in two days.'

'Have you eaten?'

'No,' she lied. 'And I'm dying of hunger.' She could feel her excitement growing.

'We'll take a dinner break. I'll call down for sandwiches and coffee.'

'I love sandwiches,' she said.

They took a half-hour dinner break, during which they spoke only of Wall Street banalities, and then they went back to their separate offices.

Cameron stopped into Jake Stern's office the next morning. 'Jake, I have to ask you something.'

'You're a vampire. I ought to charge you for sucking my brains.'

'Suppose a specialist buys a lot of stock in a company where he makes the market?'

'Stupid! The public buys stock.' Jake was being pure Jake. 'Specialists accumulate stock.'

'Okay. But if a specialist accumulates stock in one of his own companies, is it legal?'

Jake didn't answer her directly. 'If a specialist accumulates stock because he's using his own business judgement – because he believes that the company is doing great and the stock is undervalued – that's legal. But if there's a golden goose nesting in one of the warehouses that only management and he know about? No. That's not legal. That's called inside information.' He paused and cleared his throat. 'Take that Meridian bid for National Rec that crossed the tape this morning.'

Cameron bit her tongue. 'Yes, take that.'

'If Chris Canfield found out about it this morning and tried to accumulate stock – which wouldn't be easy the way it's moving – that's legal. But if that motherfucker knew about the takeover six weeks ago and has been accumulating

National Rec stock, that's using inside information, and it's goddamn illegal.'

Cameron nodded. 'It is.'

'You bet your sweet ass it is. But I wouldn't put it past Chris Canfield, would you?'

Cameron said nothing.

Cameron fought desperately, with a pitiful fury, against what she'd discovered about the Street. She could not accept what she'd learned, yet she could neither escape it nor deny it. She was full of shame and self-contempt. All the glorious dreams that had led her to Wall Street were being corrupted by the recurring shocks of disillusion. Was it possible that on the Street, where she was prepared to spend her life, there was only this brand of sterile, scheming men, senseless in their greed, ceaseless in their thievery? Men who went their insolent ways, indifferent to the needs of the public? The gullible public who swallowed all the idiotic balderdash that the so-called professionals assured them was the truth revealed; advice about 'hot issues,' 'high fliers,' 'pure plays,' and even so-called solid investments suitable for widows and orphans. Cameron took the betrayals personally. They left her tortured, like a woman who has been wronged by her lover.

Spring was kinder to Cameron than winter had been. The buildings on the Street took on a new, magical glitter; the soft air worked its enchantment on the grey pavements. The pavements were packed again with swarms of people, pushing and pulling, clucking and chuckling, out to enjoy the rebirth of life. Cameron felt an incredible revival of spirit. She was glad to be alive – glad to be on Wall Street. There was no place like it. That spring Cameron met James Stuart Harrison, and she thought she was in love.

Jim Harrison was different. He had an innate dignity that one felt was a part of the decency and goodness of the man.

Regret that she had not met him sooner passed like a thin blade through Cameron's heart. It would have spared her so much pain, so much disillusionment. He warmed her spirit, filled her with relief and welcome.

Jim was tall and lean, with a shock of brown hair that fell in a lopsided way. His nose was thin and beaked. These two irregularities were all that kept him from being too outrageously handsome. But he had the confident charm and a certain ease that was recognized immediately by those with similar backgrounds; they knew without being told that he came from a fine, old family and had gone to all the right schools. And they were correct. He'd been a straight A student at Choate, graduated magna cum laude from Yale. After Yale it was the Harvard Business School and finally Yale Law School. This was the least he could do, given his family heritage. His father had been a second circuit federal judge; an uncle on his mother's side had been a cabinet officer when Herbert Hoover was President. His entire family tree was laden with distinguished names of men who were mentioned in the footnotes in American history texts. But it was from the women in the family that the wealth descended. And the women outlived the men in the family by many, many years. Jim Harrison received a handsome allowance from his mother – a fraction of the huge allowance his mother received from her mother – until he entered Wall Street. On the Street, the combination of his influential family, his keen intelligence, and his abundance of physical energy moved him forward rapidly. When Cameron met him he was already managing director of the Thomas Jefferson Fund.

Jim courted Cameron almost as men had courted women in an earlier time, and Cameron found this in keeping with her high opinion of him. Oddly enough, she had no difficulty keeping her highly sensual nature in check. At no time did she feel physically deprived. She wondered if she really loved Jim. Perhaps she wondered because she wanted so badly to be in love. Or perhaps she wondered because she wanted to love a man who would reassure her about her other love, the Street. But whatever the reasons, their intimacy unrolled in easy waves as they courted through the long, lazy May and June evenings.

Jim took charge of Cameron's free time, and together they went to the theatre, to the opera, to concerts. Cameron thought of Jim as a truly civilized man, that in him civilization – that much abused word – was properly expressed. Although deeply involved in the practical business of making money, he also took delight in the fine things money can buy – the refinements of art that please the mind and the senses. Often they walked to her apartment, hand in hand, deep in conversation about a play they'd seen, a concert they'd heard. Jim knew a great deal about many things, and more and more, Cameron wondered about love.

Finally there came an evening when Jim suggested that he cook a dinner for her at his penthouse apartment. They would dine on the terrace, and later – it was tacitly understood – they would enter into a deeper relationship. When the high-speed elevator deposited Cameron on the top floor of Jim's building, she hurried to his apartment and found, to her surprise, that the door was slightly ajar. Jim must have left it open for her. She stepped inside and looked around. No Jim. He must be in the kitchen preparing the béarnaise sauce for the steak. After closing the front door, she called out, 'Hello. I'm here. It's Cameron.' Receiving no answer, she started for the kitchen. Then she heard Jim's voice coming from the library.

'I'm in here, Cameron. Come on in.'

'I'll be right there,' she called out.

She hurried to the kitchen and placed a bottle of Romanée-Conti, which had cost her the better part of one day's salary, on the kitchen counter. A thick filet was ready for broiling. The potatoes were wrapped in aluminium foil for roasting. A splendid salad, glistening with olive oil, was in the huge, wooden salad bowl. Cameron smiled. It was going to be a magical evening. She fixed herself a light Scotch and water and went to find Jim. She stopped at the door to the library. Jim was on the telephone, deep in a business conversation.

'How many barrels?' he asked. 'You did say billion, with a *B*? . . . I understand. Be sure to thank your cousin . . . Wait a minute. I want to write that name down.' He picked up a gold pencil next to a pad. 'Lila Lee Smothers.' He carefully spelled the name over the phone. 'Is that correct?' Jim listened. 'All right, as agreed. A numbered Swiss bank account will be established within thirty days. Yes . . . See you in the office tomorrow. Ciao.'

Once he hung up the phone, Jim literally danced a jig in front of Cameron. Then he reached for her hand and half dragged her after him, indicating a chair for her to settle in, and sat down again at his desk. He blew her a kiss before starting a series of telephone calls. He was literally calling round the world: London, Paris, Milan, Frankfurt, Tokyo, Hong Kong. Each conversation was the same. Buy Louisiana Minerals. Buy cautiously so that the price does not start to rise. But buy!

What was so special about Louisiana Minerals? Cameron asked herself. The company had extensive interests in sulphur, but so what? It had to do with the first telephone call. As she considered the facts, she understood. When Jim completed his telephoning, he stretched his legs, faced her, and lit a cigarette.

'Curious about the phoning?' he asked.

'Mildly,' she responded.

'Fine company.'

'Must be. You're going to own a lot of its stock.'

'I hope so.' Jim blew a smoke ring towards the ceiling and Cameron waited. She had a strong premonition of what was coming, and it made her wish he'd stop talking.

'You don't know what that first call was all about, do you?'

'Jim . . .' She laughed uneasily. 'I didn't listen in on your other phone.'

'Of course not. Sorry. It's oil, Cameron. Oil! Barrels and barrels of the stuff. An immense discovery in the Gulf. And Louisiana Minerals owns the drilling rights in the choice sections. They'll make the announcement next week.'

'I see. But you got in ahead of the announcement.'

'We sure did.' Jim Harrison was thoroughly satisfied with himself. 'And the price of the stock is right. Naturally, this is strictly confidential. But we know each other well enough that I feel I can tell you. We start buying in New York tomorrow. Slowly. A few thousand shares at a time. And we keep on buying.'

'Thanks to Lila Lee Smothers?' Cameron asked in a careful voice.

'Thanks hardly covers it. Lila Lee Smothers is the maiden name of Mrs Malcolm Sorenson.'

'And Mr Malcolm Sorenson is important in Louisiana Minerals? The treasurer at least. Or you wouldn't trust his information.'

'Senior vice president.' Jim smiled. 'You have the High-tower brains, Cameron.'

'Senior vice president. Hmmm. That's high enough. He called you?'

'No. Ralph Sorenson, his brother, called. Big Ralph works for us.' Jim was all but strutting. 'I hired him.'

'Big Ralph will get a bonus.' Cameron's throat felt sore, but her tone was ingenuous. 'And how much will Little Old Lila Lee get in the Swiss bank account?'

'One hundred thousand dollars, and she's worth every penny.'

'She definitely is.' Cameron's heart stopped, then started beating so violently she felt sick. Her hands were damp and cold, and a trickle of perspiration ran down the small of her back. Something deep in her brain was crying out. 'Not again! Please, Lord, not again!' She managed to repeat, 'She is definitely worth every penny.'

'And so am I,' Jim said.

'You certainly are. You're worth every single penny. How much will your take be?' Cameron's eyes were full of reverence.

Jim considered the question as though it were a new idea. 'Let's see. The fund should make about fifty million dollars. My percentage is one and a half per cent.' Involuntarily, he grinned. 'Seven hundred fifty thousand dollars.'

'And it's a card trick.' Cameron dropped the role of awed spectator. 'It didn't take brains. Or work. Just inside information.' Her tone was dead flat. 'And we both know what the SEC thinks of inside information.'

James Stuart Harrison, B.A. Yale, M.B.A Harvard, L.L.D Yale, realized he had made a serious blunder. Cameron Hightower was not acting in keeping with her Hightower blood. She sounded like some 'do-good' reformer running for public office. Given the Hightower history – and the fortune for which they were famous – she should know better. Nobody made money, not the kind of money the Hightowers had, without cutting corners. Somewhere. Sometime. Possibly she was so rich she could afford to indulge herself in self-righteous superiority. She reminded him of some of his friends from law school who sought jobs as assistant district attorneys just because the law firms in which their fathers were senior partners represented the Mafia on occasion. Damn it! If Cameron were into high-minded reform, Wall Street wasn't the place for her.

'Are you suggesting that what I'm doing is . . . well . . . shall we say, unethical?'

'You might say "unethical". But more accurate words would be "illegal" and "crooked".' The iron band around Cameron's head was drawing tighter.

'You won't be able to prove anything.' Jim had confidence in the firm's legal staff.

'I have no intention of trying to prove anything.' Cameron moved towards the door. 'Do you think I'm proud of being associated with you? Hell, no! I've a much simpler solution.'

Jim followed her into the living room. 'What are you going to do?'

'What I stopped doing after I met you. Date a lot of men.'

'I don't get it.' Harrison's mind was careening about crazily: amazed, afraid, angry.

'You will. Believe me, Jim, you will. It'll be all over the Street in a day. Maybe sooner. There's been a huge oil find in the Gulf, and Louisiana Minerals owns the drilling rights to the richest sections.' She gave him a crooked smile. 'I think I'll see Hal Mayberry tomorrow night. He's been very patient waiting for me to get over my dumb infatuation with you. He deserves to be the first to find out about Louisiana's luck.'

'Hal Mayberry? Of Western Fund?' Jim saw Cameron's intention and went pale.

'That's the guy. And Thursday? Let's see? I know. Peter Epp of Mutual Trust.'

Jim was gasping for breath. 'Cameron! Don't! Those bastards will jump in with both feet. The price of the stock will go through the roof.'

'Won't it ever.' She put her Scotch on the coffee table.

'But Lila Lee cost us one hundred thousand dollars.' Jim was pleading.

'And worth every penny of it. Don't worry. I won't mention Lila Lee. Just Louisiana.'

'That's not fair,' Jim sputtered.

'Fair! What you're trying to pull is fair?'

'What can I give you?' He was all but on his knees. If she were anyone other than a Hightower, he'd offer her his bonus. But if there was one thing a Hightower didn't need, it

208

was more money. 'Cameron, please. Do you know what this will do to my reputation? I'm known as a man of integrity. A man whose word can be relied on. You'll destroy me.' What Jim Harrison couldn't say was that it wasn't Wall Street that would destroy him – he knew better than Cameron that the Street would blink, smile, and figure, you win some, you lose some – it was what his mother and grandmother would do that panicked him. They would see it as a scandal, a blemish on the family name. They could afford to be as self-righteously superior as Cameron. At a minimum they'd have him fired from Jefferson Fund. Then they'd pass the word around that no reputable firm should hire him. His career on the Street would come to a crashing end.

As angry as Cameron was, she sensed a fear in Jim, a fear that was greater than his concern about the loss of a big win. Despite herself, she felt sorry for him. That he wasn't the man she thought him to be was as much her fault as his. She had needed him to be other than he was – just another Wall Street chiseller.

'Cameron, you can't do this to me.'

'I can, Jim, and I will.' Her pity did not prevent her from adding, 'I'm lunching tomorrow with George Simmons. You know George. He writes the "Heard on the Street" column for *The Wall Street Journal*.' Her mood was resigned. 'So what was inside information tonight becomes public information tomorrow.'

'I'll kill myself.'

'You won't. I owe you something for a lovely springtime of dreams. Neither your name nor your fund will be mentioned.' She walked out of Jim Harrison's apartment and his life.

In the cab going home, Cameron felt horribly tired, sick with fatigue. She shook her head in bewilderment, a certainty growing in her that a demon was everywhere abroad in her universe, at work on the souls of all the men she met, the men she might love. An evening that had started out full of romance had ended with the loss of something infinitely precious; the possibility that anyone who worked on Wall Street was honest. She could no longer control her pain at the betrayal, and she dropped her face in her hands as the sobs burst from her throat.

In the 'Heard on the Street' column on Thursday, the rumour about Louisiana Minerals headed the column: 'Louisiana Minerals strikes it rich in oil . . .' The public swamped their brokers with buy orders all day.

On the following Monday, Lucia and Cameron had their regular Monday-night dinner at home alone. No men and no phone calls – the answering machine was turned on.

Dinner was a chit-chat affair, Lucia talking about her beginning boredom with the fashion business and deliberately avoiding what was on her mind until they had finished eating.

'The time has come.' Lucia finally took the plunge. 'Why have you taken to sitting home every night with a book? And being "out" when one of your guys calls?'

Cameron didn't quite know where or how to begin. 'I think I've fallen out of love with Wall Street.'

'You can't do that.' Lucia was upset. 'We can't both have chosen the wrong profession. Is it your job?'

'You know I got a raise last month.'

'Then what's wrong?'

Cameron began tentatively. 'You know that my parents died when I was a kid. And that I was a lonely teenager.'

'I don't think that has anything to do with now.' Lucia was gentle. 'What's eating you?'

What was it? Cameron considered the question and everything that had been happening to her. Where once she had seen great hopes dancing in the sunlight, she now saw only deceit and disillusionment. Would it help to tell Lucia about the encounters that had brought her to this impasse? Those events threatened the very foundations of her personal faith.

She had been prepared to build her life on a commitment to success. A success that would honour her father and grandfather, justify their right to the Hightower name and challenge the family's scorn – Geraldine excepted – for their seeming failure. But what would that cost? She could feel herself in the presence of a darker fear, infinitely more heartbreaking. Her mind wanted to reject it, but how could she?

She glanced over at Lucia. 'I'll tell you what I've been learning.' Cameron then described her experiences with four of the men she'd been seeing and what she had learned about the business ethics by which they lived. Essentially, it came down to: 'What's mine is mine, and what's yours is mine.' In the end, it was the public who paid through the nose.

Lucia listened, silent for once, as the stories unfolded. The enormities of the monies involved, the contempt for the law and for stockholders, and the ease with which the market could be manipulated shocked her. When Cameron finished, she was speechless for a while. Then, 'Christ! In the rag business, all they do is steal designs. That's penny ante compared to what you're describing. Have you talked to anybody about this?'

'Who can I talk to?'

What's the matter with Geraldine? Lucia wanted to ask. But she already knew the answer. Because I'm afraid, Cameron would have answered. She's my family, the only family I have. How can I ask her how she manages the Hightower Trust? Or if she involves herself in this kind of fraudulent manipulation? How can I insult her by questioning her ethics? And I'll despise myself for admitting my doubts. Lucia could understand that because, if their positions had been reversed, she would have felt the same way about questioning her father.

Finally she made the only suggestion she considered feasible. 'How about FitzGerald? He's supposed to be one of Wall Street's great brains. Talk to him about it.'

'You really think so?'

'I don't think you have any choice.'

Cameron's mouth tightened. If he were like the rest of them, she'd better find out now. The idea sickened her. But it was possible. If that was how the game was played, he'd expect her to play it the same way. Here was the hub of her fear, her wretchedness. She might be called upon to do her bit in some kind of a scam to bilk the public. And if everyone had their price – though she could not imagine what hers might be – why should she be the exception?

It was time to put away girlish illusions and to take responsibility for being herself. Whoever that was. And she needed to learn once and for all whether she wasn't just another shining example of that old cliché 'The only reason she hasn't sold out is because no one has made her an offer.'

'I'll speak to him tomorrow,' she said. It was as though she had been sitting at some high-stakes gambling table, taking huge risks, and betting far more than she could afford to lose.

11

Cameron spent a restless night. She had a series of bad dreams that faded as soon as she opened her eyes. As the night wore on, it became increasingly difficult to go back to sleep. When she saw the sky lightening in the east, she gave up the struggle. She slipped out of bed, deciding to shower and dress. Although it was only six-thirty, she'd go to the office. If Timothy FitzGerald were in the office, she would try to see him today. But first she must think it through, and she could think more clearly at her desk. She asked herself what she knew about the man to guide her in her approach. Very little.

Usually when FitzGerald returned after an absence, the firm added a new company to their client list, one for whom they would do a stock offering. Or an old client was ready to sell additional stock. Or the firm was involved in a major acquisition of some sort. All things considered, Cameron concluded that Tim FitzGerald took few, if any, vacations and many business trips.

Although Rosemary Atherton was vague on the details, Cameron learned that a tragedy had struck the FitzGerald family some years ago. An accident had killed two FitzGerald children. Rosemary also hinted that there was something wrong with Rhoda FitzGerald, Tim's wife. There were three remaining children, none of whom were interested in either FitzGerald Associates or Wall Street. Cameron tried to pry additional information from Rosemary and Jake Stern. But beyond what she'd already said, Rosemary would not discuss Timothy FitzGerald's family or his past. And Jake Stern had told her to mind her own fucking business. With so little to go on, Cameron had no idea how to open the subject with FitzGerald. But she had to work it out.

Cameron used the keys Rosemary had given her to let herself in and went directly to her office. Seated at her desk, she started making notes. In an effort to get her thoughts down in some sensible order, omitting the personal circumstances under which she'd obtained her information, she jotted down everything: names, dates, stocks, details of the manipulations. Going back and reading what she'd written made them seem even more shameful. Cameron lost track of time. The telephone ringing jarred her.

'Hello?'

'Oh, shit! I'm glad you're in.'

The voice sounded familiar but muffled. It was hard to understand. 'Who is this?'

'Who the hell do you think it is? It's the idiot who hired you.'

'Jake? You sound different.' She looked at her watch: nine o'clock. 'Where are you?'

'Mount Sinai Hospital. My Mustang got broadsided last night by a couple of coked-up kids.'

'Are you all right?'

'No! I'm not all right! What the fuck would I be doing in this asshole hospital if I were all right?'

'What's the matter?'

'I've got two broken legs, cracked ribs, a jammed neck, and a fractured jaw. How's that for openers?'

'It beats jacks back-to-back.'

'Cut the wisecracks. My jaw is wired. I can't laugh. Listen, Cameron, I'm going to be here for at least three weeks. And there's one awful mess on my desk. The most urgent thing is Beckett Pharmaceuticals. A new public offering. There's a draft of the prospectus in the upper left-hand drawer of my desk. Rosemary has the keys. But there's a pile of shit missing

214

from it. Fitz needs that prospectus. Goddamn it! Here comes a nurse.' He yelled to someone, 'Get away from me, you harpic.' He shouted at Cameron, 'Don't send flowers. I need pornographic pictures and dirty books. I'll be jerking off until I get out of here.'

'I'm terribly sorry.' An efficient woman's voice replaced Jake's yelling. 'Mr Stern should not excite himself.'

'How is he, nurse?'

'Very lucky. He'll recover.' Cameron had the impression she heard the nurse add, 'Unfortunately.' 'Keep your hands off me or I'll have them tied to the bed,' the nurse screamed. Then she asked Cameron, 'Is Mr Stern always this difficult? Perhaps there's been brain damage?'

'He sounds normal to me,' Cameron said.

'How do you stand him?'

'He grows on one.'

'Not on me he doesn't. He's in room 615, the Klingenstein Pavilion, just in case anyone makes the mistake of visiting him.'

Cameron replaced the receiver. It sounded as though Jake was basically all right. She'd tell Rosemary, who would get more detailed information from the doctors. In the meantime, she would be swamped with work.

She pushed the intercom and dialled Rosemary.

'Mr FitzGerald's office.'

'Rosemary, it's Cameron. Have you heard about Jake?'

'Yes. I've talked to his doctors. He'll be as good as new in three months. How did you find out?'

'He just phoned me. He said you have the keys to his desk. There's an underwriting for Beckett Pharmaceuticals. He wants me to take it over. In addition to the private placement memorandum I'm working on for Thompson Instruments.'

'He told me. I have the Beckett document on my desk.'

'Rosemary?' Cameron hesitated, then made up her mind.

'I'd like to see Mr FitzGerald as soon as possible. There are several things I'd like to talk to him about.'

'I would think so. This is quite a responsibility, Cameron. But Jake is confident you're up to it. So is Mr FitzGerald. Hang on.' Cameron was on hold for less than a minute. 'He'll see you right now. He's been expecting your call since I told him about Jake.'

He may be expecting me but he isn't expecting this, Cameron thought, picking up her yellow pad. When she passed Rosemary's desk, Rosemary shoved a thick envelope under her arm. Cameron assumed it was a draft of the Beckett documents. She knocked on FitzGerald's door and heard, 'Come in.'

'Sit down, Cameron, sit down.' Tim FitzGerald gestured to the chair next to his desk. As usual, his collar was open and his sleeves rolled up. The jacket of his Cambridge-grey suit was hanging on the back of his chair. He needed a shave. Cameron wondered what he'd been doing all night. He hadn't been in his office when she arrived.

'What can I do for you?' he asked. 'If you're concerned about the additional responsibility, don't be. The staff and I are here to help you in any way we can. This is the first public offering of Beckett stock. It's like bringing a baby into the world. Our job is to make the birth as painless as possible.'

As always, she was attracted by the dynamism of the man. Some people you meet every day and quickly forget: others you meet once and remember all your life. This was Tim FitzGerald. In his presence, facing him, she thought of a quip she had once heard, that by the age of fifty, a man gets the face he deserves. If this was true of FitzGerald, she found it difficult to imagine him implicated in underhanded dealings. But there were no guarantees. For better or for worse, she had to know.

'Mr FitzGerald, I – '

'Out with it, Cameron. Say what's on your mind.'

216

'It has nothing to do with the Beckett deal. I haven't yet studied the documents. This is another matter.' There was a severity in her tone.

'What is it?' He leaned forward encouragingly. 'What's troubling you?'

Cameron felt her lips tighten, and her throat went dry, blocking her words for an instant. Then the need to tell him everything swept aside her reluctance. She told it all: about Byman, Greenberg, Canfield, Harrison, all highly placed members of the Wall Street community, but men who misused their positions for personal profit and the public's loss. Although she made no mention of the events under which the information had been obtained, she sensed that Fitzgerald understood only too well. Under ordinary circumstances this would have embarrassed her. But these were not ordinary circumstances and Timothy FitzGerald was not the usual stranger. Far more was at stake for her than the admission that she was not a sexual innocent. She became eloquent under his acute and sympathetic gaze, responding to the humour in him, the worldliness, to the decency that she hoped was the other side of his driving, ambitious nature. And gradually, as she continued talking, she had the impression that he was listening more with his body than his ears. He was tense, as though he were defending himself against an old and familiar enemy.

When she finished, FitzGerald rose, walked to the window, and stood with his back to her. His quietness suggested that he was as disturbed as she was. 'What are you asking me?' he said after an uncharacteristic hesitation. 'Are you asking me what I think of these practices?'

Cameron's mouth felt parched. There were thorns in her stomach. She was afraid to answer, but she had to know. 'Yes,' she said.

'And you have another question?'

'Yes.'

'What is it?'

'I'd like to know if . . .'

Fitzgerald finished her question for her. 'If we play the same game?'

'Yes.'

Abruptly, he returned to his desk and drummed his fingers on the hard surface. He had walked down these roads before and could see his own footprints. He owed it to her to give as good an answer as he could give. Or maybe he owed it to himself? It was important that she believe him. He thought her progress in the company had been remarkable. This beautiful young woman had a rare gift for numbers, and, more important, he had the impression from Jake's reports that she had an instinctive gift for the Street, for predicting the general reactions of the public to their stock offerings, for making suggestions in areas where additional strength was needed. Yet she never overstated the case. He looked at her sitting in the chair so completely still that she didn't seem to be breathing. She should not be lost to FitzGerald Associates.

'I'll answer you as completely as I can.' He said it flatly, neither conceding nor confiding. Then he asked her a most perceptive question; one that Cameron had been deliberating for some time. 'I gather you've not reported this to the authorities, the Board of Governors of the New York Stock Exchange, or the SEC?'

Cameron bit her lip. Why hadn't she gone to the authorities? She had considered it often enough. But these confidences were given to her in private, some after the most intimate experience two people can have together. To betray them was to descend to their level, to violate a private trust. And on a practical level, she lacked proof. There was only her word. They were the kind of illegal practices that it took investigative reporting to prove. But how could she explain this to Tim FitzGerald?

Her silence told FitzGerald that he had accomplished his

218

purpose. No one goes through life without soiling their hands. It had been a hard lesson for her. 'At any rate, you considered it?'

'I considered it.'

'And dismissed it?'

'Yes.' Cameron felt defensive.

FitzGerald picked his words with tact, avoiding any implications about the circumstances under which she obtained her information. 'You were afraid your testimony would be regarded as idle rumours?'

'My word against theirs.'

'The "Heard on the Street" item in *The Wall Street Journal* was yours, wasn't it?'

'That was mine.'

'But you need something more?'

'Yes,' she said in a low voice.

FitzGerald took a moment, seeming to be thinking over Cameron's questions. 'Conscience,' he said, peering up at the ceiling, 'is a widespread disease without a cure. Very few of us go through life untroubled by it. It's one of the better signs of our humanness. I understand yours. I've seen what you've seen and shared the same quandaries.'

Cameron lifted her chin. The air around her seemed to be clearing. 'You know about these things?'

'Some of them. I know about Byman. Byman is a bad joke.'

'But people believe him.'

'People believe him. That's why there's the saying, "The public is always wrong." Wall Streeters believe him, too. And they're often as wrong as the public.'

'What about Moore?'

FitzGerald had been expecting this question about Dennis Moore, the economist for FitzGerald Associates. 'Dennis does not give out false economic forecasts to shore up our stock positions. Agree with him or not, what he says is what he believes. Period. No more, no less.'

219

Tim FitzGerald moved from his chair and sat on the edge of his desk facing Cameron. He went on to talk about Canfield, Harrison, and the firm Greenberg worked for with a conscientious frankness that was not unlike a medical diagnosis. There were such people on the Street, he said: people who took illegal advantage of insider information. Some, like Harrison and Canfield, he added, went out of their way to get it.

'I can hear you ask, "What happens to them?"' he said. 'Nothing in the short run. But in the long run ... that's another story. You're not tuned in to the rumour mill, Cameron.' He explained. 'These people are already being talked about. Eventually the proper authorities will do something about them. They have dealt with many others like them in the past. The wheels of the gods grind slowly, as we know, but they do grind.' Then, as if to leave all that behind, he set out in a new direction, his voice gaining vigour as he came to the heart of the matter. 'Cameron, neither I nor any employees of FitzGerald Associates have ever or would ever become a party to such schemes as you've described.'

The intercom buzzed and for an instant FitzGerald did not move. The call did not matter. Nothing mattered but the look of joy and relief on Cameron's face. It made possible a suggestion Rosemary had made earlier and that he'd dismissed. He lifted the phone. 'Rosemary, tell whoever it is that I'll call back.' He put down the receiver.

'Cameron, is there anything keeping you in New York this week?'

'I beg your pardon?' Cameron blinked and remembered the envelope. 'The Beckett prospectus. And the Thompson private placement that I'm working on.'

'The private placement can wait until next week. I'm flying to San Francisco this afternoon to meet with Leon Beckett. There are a few loose ends to tie up, plus some missing numbers, but nothing unusual. Ordinarily, I'd phone the information in to Jake and he'd know what to fill in and what to ask for. But you haven't his experience and you'll be putting the Beckett prospectus together. So a visit by you to the company seems in order.'

'If you think that's a good idea, of course,' Cameron said.

It all sounded sane and sensible, even to FitzGerald himself. Yet the truth was more complex than this, and far less neat. Something had happened to FitzGerald, something he had not counted on. Cameron had struck a chord; her face, her voice, her gestures worked on him in a strong, indefinable way that he no longer believed possible. And her trust, her belief in him, in Timothy FitzGerald the man, was like fresh air pouring into a room that had been closed and tightly locked for a long time.

12

There was a car waiting for them when they arrived at San Francisco International Airport. Crossing the Golden Gate Bridge, Cameron was overwhelmed by the view. The vast San Francisco Bay on the right, the city behind them, the gateway to the ocean to the left, and the steep, rolling headlands were awesome. After a short drive, the car left Route 101 and turned on to Route 1, the Coast Highway. They passed through Muir Beach and Mt Tamalpais State Park on the way to Leon Beckett's house. Throughout the trip Cameron had been acutely aware of Tim, a soft hum of passion playing over her senses. She found herself searching for things to say to him that might bring them closer. But it was uphill work because he seemed so remote, so preoccupied with his own thoughts.

When they arrived, Leon Beckett was standing on the flagstone steps waiting for them. He ushered them into a glass-enclosed patio that gave a breathtaking view across the lawn to the Pacific Ocean. A very young woman was sitting at the rattan bar sipping a pink liquid drink through a straw.

Beckett introduced them. 'Tim,' he said, 'meet Charlene, my fourth wife. Charlie, this is Mr FitzGerald. Remember, I told you he was coming.'

Tim acknowledged the invitation and introduced Cameron. 'Georgio will take your bags,' Leon said, nodding towards a man wearing white cotton pants and a white sports shirt. 'Come on. I'll give you a nickel tour. It's quite a place.'

As Cameron and Tim followed Leon Beckett around, she admitted to herself that it was indeed 'quite a place'. The house, the grounds, the heated swimming pool and Jacuzzi,

222

the tennis courts, the meticulously tended lawns, and extensive flower beds were impressive. But having grown up on Hightower Farm, Cameron found something out of key about the estate. It was too new, too artificial – almost a stage set. She had the impression it could be dismantled at any moment. The furniture, from the white sailcloth-covered couches to the plastic tables and rattan chairs, looked rented for the occasion. It was hard to believe anyone actually lived in the place. Leon and Charlene Beckett could have been typecast for contrast. Cameron guessed that Leon was about forty. She'd expected him to be tall, blond, handsome, athletic – her image of a typical Californian. Instead, he was short, swarthy, and built like an egg. His thick, black hair was loosely parted in the middle and a Fu Manchu moustache ran around his mouth, almost reaching his chin. Charlene was at least five inches taller than Leon and, at the most, twenty. She was a sun-bleached Californian blonde with a pretty face and lush body.

When they returned to the patio, Charlene grabbed her hand as though it were a lifeline. 'Come on,' she said. 'We can dunk in the Jacuzzi. It's super. The men can talk business.'

'Thank you, Charlene. Later possibly,' Cameron said politely. 'I work for Mr FitzGerald. I'm also here on business.'

'Oh! Well, of course. I see.' But she didn't see. Obviously, she thought Cameron was Tim FitzGerald's playmate, and playmates didn't work.

'Call her Charlie,' Leon said.

'Yes,' Charlene said. 'All my friends do.'

'A lovely name, Charlie,' FitzGerald said. 'Cameron will be responsible for your husband's prospectus.'

'Pro-spec-tus?' Charlene pronounced the word with great care. 'Is that right, Leon?'

'That's right, Charlie. Very good.' Leon smiled at Tim.

'She graduated from high school last year and has a lot to learn.' Beckett put his arm around Charlie's waist and drew her close. 'She's twenty. That's the way I like 'em. Young and trainable. By twenty-five they think they know everything.' Beckett whispered something into his wife's ear.

'Are you sure?' She giggled like the child she really was.

'I'm sure. Do it. Now!'

'Yes, Leon, darling.' Charlie rushed out of the room.

'How about a large, cool drink? Before you change into something more comfortable? We're pretty informal at Casa Beckett.'

Cameron had the impression that her suitcase had been placed in the same bedroom as Tim's luggage and that Charlie was upstairs correcting the mistake. She blushed as she realized that Tim also understood what had happened.

'I'll have a gin and tonic, Leon,' Tim said. 'What would you like, Cameron?'

'An extra-dry gin martini, please.'

Leon went behind the bar. He fished out a half gallon of some kind of gin and poured a small amount into a Manhattan glass with the initials L.B. etched into the glass. He added a lot of ice and more vermouth than gin and handed the glass to Cameron. 'That's a strong drink, young lady. A martini. Charlie gets smashed just looking at a martini.'

When Cameron tasted her drink, she almost spat it out. Leon had used sweet vermouth.

'Drink okay, Cameron?' he asked. She managed to nod. 'The trick is to use sweet vermouth. It covers the taste of the gin.'

Tim coughed violently over his drink. When he caught his breath he said, 'Can I taste that, Cameron?' He took a sip and shook his head. 'Leon, we're from Back East. You know. Traditional. Cameron would prefer dry vermouth. And not too much of it.'

'If that's what you want. But she's a – ' He was about to

224

say. 'She's a woman and women don't drink anything but sweet drinks.' He was interrupted by Charlie's return.

'I fixed things, Leon.' She put her arm around him and he patted her behind.

'I think I'll skip the drink and unpack. It's been a long day.' Cameron didn't want to risk another Leon Beckett concoction.

'Absolutely. Charlie, show Cameron to her room. How about eight-thirty for dinner? Charlie and I like an hour before dinner to relax. Don't we, baby?'

Charlie smiled coyly.

'Cameron, the ocean do anything for you?'

'Yes. I grew up in the Caribbean.'

'Well, the granddaddy of them all is out there.' He pointed towards the window. 'If you're ready ahead of us, follow that path.'

'Thank you. If I am, I will.'

Cameron stood on the edge of a cliff overlooking the ocean from a height of over one hundred feet. A waist-high stone fence protected her from falling over the cliff. To her left was a flight of stone steps that twisted its way down to a narrow strip of sand. Seventy-five feet or so offshore Beckett had erected a high, semicircular reef made out of huge boulders. It protected a small piece of shore from the ocean and still permitted the water to pass through. The result was a swimming pool carved out of the ocean. Cameron restrained an impulse to slip out of her white linen pants and blue silk shirt and go down to the pool for a swim. But it was almost eight-thirty.

Far out to sea, the red sun rested on the edge of the horizon. Cameron stared at the Pacific, mesmerized by its power. She sat on the edge of the stone wall and watched the sun sink slowly behind the horizon. A beam of colour flamed across the flat, endless surface of the water, aimed directly at her. The Pacific was everything and everywhere, dominating the land, even the sky.

Close behind her someone cleared his throat.

Startled, Cameron looked over her shoulder. Tim Fitz-Gerald was standing a short distance away, studying her. He'd changed from his business suit to a pair of well-worn blue jeans and a plaid shirt. He looked more at home in work clothes than the suits he wore to the office. She was reminded of the first impression she'd had of him on the stage at the New School. He'd struck her as a man from an earlier age when, to survive, men had to struggle with nature. That he could have so tamed his primal spirit, civilized it to accept the confinement of city life, seemed to her again to be a minor miracle. A triumph of the will of a single man over the demands of his blood. At the sight of him, Cameron's whole body began to throb, and she looked at him with a soft, longing glance, acknowledging the passion she felt flowing between them. She had known this feeling only once before, and then she had been barely more than a child. Now that she was a woman she understood. This was the man she had been searching for in all those other beds. This was what she needed, a union that was more than sexual. It was love, a melting together of two people into one. Somehow she must find the right moment or let the right moment find them. The hunger within her must find a way. She held her breath, waiting for him to speak.

'Leon sent me to fetch you,' he said. 'Before putting the steaks on the fire.'

Cameron blinked and focused on his words. She glanced back, regretfully, at the glowing ocean. She didn't want to see Leon or listen to Charlie. She didn't want to share Tim FitzGerald with anyone. But she had to. She reminded herself to be patient. Something had just happened between them. It was a beginning.

* * *

Despite the fact that she thought Leon Beckett a bit of a fool, Cameron admitted to herself that there was nothing foolish about Beckett Pharmaceuticals. The facility was located just outside of Santa Rosa, an easy, scenic drive from the house. The buildings were set well back from the road to give plenty of room for expansion, Leon explained. They were surrounded by lawns, groves of trees, and an artificial pond with a fountain shooting a single jet of water high into the air. The design of the one-storey building was both attractive and functional. The offices were located in a central triangle with buildings extending off each leg of the triangle. One building was devoted to laboratories, the second to production, and the third to warehousing of supplies, shipping, and receiving. Cameron was impressed by the horizontal lines of gleaming white concrete set off by rows of green windows. Leon explained that he'd selected green glass because tests had shown that green was the easiest colour on the eyes. Also, on overcast days the green made everything outside appear brighter and more cheerful.

What surprised Cameron was Leon Beckett's background. Since his company was in the pharmaceutical business, she'd assumed he had a background in chemistry or pharmacology. She was wrong. Beckett was a salesman. He'd been selling ever since he graduated from high school in Bakersfield. He had sold plumbing supplies, women's sportswear, and most recently, over-the-counter drugs. He'd started Beckett Pharmaceuticals ten years ago when he picked up from G. D. Searle a patented drug that lowered blood pressure, in a year when Searle had too many new products to market at the same time. There was little difference between this drug and other drugs that lowered blood pressure. What made the difference was Beckett's ability to hire the proper people, his knack for raising enough money to keep the business alive while he was marketing the product, and most important, his talent for selling. This taught Cameron to look beyond the

227

surface facts when estimating a new company. The vital factor in its success – even more important than the product – was the man who ran the company. The decisions he made when the company was first starting often accounted for its later success or failure. Leon Beckett had made all the right decisions. That was why Timothy FitzGerald had agreed to become Beckett's investment banker and to offer Beckett stock to the public.

FitzGerald, Beckett, and Cameron closeted themselves in Beckett's office. Over innumerable cups of coffee they reviewed the details of the proposed offering. Cameron listened, referred to Jake's draft, and made notes. It had been agreed that FitzGerald Associates would raise $20 million for the company by offering one million shares of stock at $20 a share to the public. Now Beckett wanted a change.

'I think we should sell less stock and raise the offering price to thirty dollars a share.'

'I won't do it,' Tim said flatly.

'You mean you won't or you can't?'

'I mean I won't. I could sell the stock at thirty dollars a share on the strength of my reputation alone.'

'Then why won't you?'

'Because it's my reputation that's on the line. Not yours. The earnings of Beckett Pharmaceuticals don't justify a thirty-dollar price.'

'They do. The earnings are great.'

Cameron glanced again at the audited financial statements for the past three years. While they would take further study, they showed that the firm was profitable and growing more so each year.

'They are good,' Tim said. 'Just not good enough for a thirty-dollar-a-share offering.'

'Not good enough!' Leon was exasperated. 'In fiscal 1973, the company grossed close to twenty million dollars, with an after-tax net of 1.2 million. That's a damn good return – six per cent on gross. And you say that's not good enough!'

'It's good enough for us to take your company public.'

Leon was dogged. 'The unaudited financials for the first six months of this year show a twenty-five-per-cent growth over the same period a year ago. That's growth.'

'Agreed. And if it keeps up, the stock will go to thirty, to forty, to fifty.' Tim was adamant. 'But today your earnings do not warrant a price of thirty dollars a share. At that price, my investors – the men and women who trust my judgement – will lose money when the stock drops to twenty, as it will. I don't like having my investors lose money.'

'I want a thirty-dollar price.'

Tim FitzGerald's face was impassive. 'If you insist, I'm on my way back to New York.' Tim said quietly. 'I advise you to say yes to twenty dollars.'

Leon said, 'Yes.'

At the conclusion, Leon agreed that the underwriter's discount – FitzGerald Associates' fee for taking the company public – would be $1 million, plus expenses not to exceed $150,000. What he objected to was a kicker to which FitzGerald held fast.

'But fifty thousand shares of Beckett stock at par value? Good God! That's ten cents a share! That's giving the stock to you.' Leon was irritated. 'That fifty thousand shares will only cost you – '

'Five thousand dollars. Exactly,' said Tim. 'And as the stock rises, and we do expect it to rise, those fifty thousand shares for which we've paid five thousand dollars could be worth a million dollars. Maybe more.'

'That's what I mean.'

'That's what I mean, too.' Tim was patient. 'Leon, this is not a best-efforts placement. FitzGerald Associates is guaranteeing you the money. If we can't sell one single share of the stock, you still get your twenty million dollars. And

FitzGerald Associates gets to paper the office walls with your stock. Do you understand me?'

'Yeah.'

The last negotiation – if that's what it could be called – was over Leon Beckett's share. How much of the $20 million being raised by the sale of the stock was to go to the company, and how much into Leon Beckett's pocket for the sale of his own Beckett stock?

'We originally agreed on two thirds for the company and one third for you, Leon. That seems fair.'

'I think it should be fifty-fifty. You're selling one million shares of Beckett Pharmaceutical stock. I think half of those shares should be company stock, and the other half, my stock. That gives the company ten million dollars and me ten million.'

'That's a lot of money for you that the company could use.'

'The company's in better shape than I am. The ten million – less your fee – will pay off all the company's short-term bank debt. What's left over will be used for general corporate purposes. We've got a fantastic new anticoagulant drug for the treatment of people who have had heart attacks. It needs more research to get the FDA off my back.' He shrugged. 'The company only needs a few million for the R and D.' He smiled ingratiatingly. 'I need the other ten million worse than the company. Remember, I'm the company, the chairman. If I'm worried about my personal life, I can't work at top form.'

'What do you need ten million dollars for?'

'Ever heard of alimony? And do you think that cottage where I live comes free? Also, I have a few personal loans out at the banks.'

Leon won this inning. FitzGerald saw the value of keeping the chairman in good spirits.

Through the day a current flowed from Cameron to Tim. Her avid eyes took in everything about him. The subtle changes in his voice and manner when he wanted to make a point. She could hardly wait to be alone with him. Somehow she must manage it. By four o'clock everything was locked up. Tim initialled the few changes necessary in the letter of intent he'd given Beckett weeks ago. The he outlined his plans.

'If you have no objections, Leon, I'll leave Cameron in your charge for the next few days. She can use some sun and rest. I've got to drive to San Francisco tonight. Trans-America has a piece of business they want to talk to me about. I'll return on Friday to pick Cameron up and take her to the airport.'

Leon's eyes flickered between Cameron and FitzGerald. He made no attempt to conceal his surprise. 'Sure,' he finally said.

Cameron was too shocked to question Tim's decision. She'd been so confident that he wanted her as badly as she wanted him. How could she have been so wrong? He wasn't in the least interested. He would be spending the night in San Francisco. He must know a woman there. Otherwise, why not drive to the city in the morning?

They left the office and started back towards the coast. Cameron was so distraught she saw nothing. The scenery meant nothing. She rested her head against the seat, her eyes closed to keep back her tears.

'What the hell!' Tim's voice jarred her out of her misery. She opened her eyes and stared out the window. There had been a bright sun and a cloudless blue sky when they started out. Now there was grey cotton making the world all but invisible. It was hard to see the road and almost impossible to see the trees bordering the road because of the thick fog.

'How bad is it, Leon?' Tim asked.

'Bad enough. By the time we get home, you won't see beyond the end of the car.'

When they pulled up in front of the house, Leon exhaled sharply. 'Whew! I'm glad we're here. A couple of times back there I almost pulled over to wait it out. You won't be driving to San Francisco tonight, Tim.'

They got out of the car into a warm, steamy bath of moisture that should have been rain but wasn't.

'Follow me,' Leon said, 'and be careful, there are three steps.'

Charlie was waiting for them just inside the house. Her blonde hair was plastered to her head: she was wearing a string bikini bathing suit. She hurled herself at Leon. 'I was so scared. I was swimming in the pool, then suddenly the sun went out.'

'It's all right, baby.' He patted her head. 'It's only fog. Go upstairs, dry off and change.' He patted her again. Charlie smiled down at him and ran off, leaving a trail of water behind. Leon glanced at Cameron and Tim. 'I've told her not to wear a wet bathing suit in the house, but she forgets.' He was indulgent. 'It takes time to housebreak a child. I need a drink.'

'I could use one, too,' Tim said.

At first, Cameron saw the fog as a reprieve, something sent by kind and loving gods to keep Tim near her. Then, as they sat in the enclosed porch drinking, her mood changed. Tim was politely keeping his distance to spare her from misunderstanding his intentions. Now, with a long fall of hope, she surrendered her dream. She was only surprised that she had not recognized his lack of interest sooner. But how could she? He had been kind to her, smiled at her, approved of her – and she wanted to hope. She wished now that he had driven to the city. Anything was better than being in the same room with him and yet not being with him.

After dinner, they returned to the patio. Every fifteen minutes or so, Tim would casually wander over to the window, estimate the fog, and return to his chair. Leon and Charlie were not shy about fondling and kissing each other. It made Cameron feel painfully awkward. She did not want to let anyone see how she felt, so, abruptly, she got to her feet.

'I'm still on New York time, and my clock says go to bed. So if you'll excuse me?' Without waiting for an answer, Cameron left the room, ran up the stairs, shut the door to her bedroom, and threw herself on the bed, sobbing. When she opened her eyes again, she realized she must have fallen asleep, still crying. Tears had dried on her face, and she could taste the salt in the corners of her mouth. The moonlight made the room glow with a silver sheen. Moonlight! Cameron ran to the window. The fog had cleared off. Tim must have left for the city. But she mustn't think of him, he didn't care for her. That thought aroused her instinct for self-preservation. She had to do something to numb her feelings. The ocean would dull the pain.

Cameron glanced at the clock. It was five in the morning. Still wearing the green velour jumpsuit she'd worn at dinner, she went quietly from her room, leaving the door open. She moved as rapidly as possible along the path through the trees that led to the lookout ledge. When she arrived, she stared at the ocean. It was flat and calm, reflecting the moonlight as perfectly as a mirror. The stone steps leading to the beach were sharply outlined against the cliff. The air was still and hot. Nothing stirred except the Pacific as it lapped gently against the narrow beach.

Soon she was standing on the soft sand. Cameron removed her sandals and let the warm water lap around her ankles. Quickly, she stripped off her clothes, tossed them into a dark place against the cliff, and waded into the water. The pool was shallow; at no point did it reach above her shoulders. It was like a huge, shallow bowl over which the towering reef cast deep purple shadows. Cameron began to swim laps. She was not aware of the moon disappearing behind the clouds and the soft fog gathering just beyond the reef, then overflowing the reef to reach the base of the cliff. With her face half buried in the water or lifted sideways just long enough to breathe, Cameron continued to swim.

Tim FitzGerald woke from a light sleep. He thought immediately of Cameron as she had been earlier, seated on the rock wall. He had memorized the long line of her neck, the curve of her buttocks clearly outlined by the tight white pants. The natural grace of her body against the sky had stopped his breath. He could no longer avoid the truth. From the first moment he'd noticed her at his lecture, he'd been aware of a shock of recognition. It was as if he had known her all his life. When she came to work for him, he became more fascinated than ever but made it a matter of principle to stay away. It was only her great concern about his personal integrity – which so disturbed him – that had caused him to lower his guard, dropping the barriers between them. During the entire trip west he had refused to see the truth. But he would not waste any more time deceiving himself. Cameron Hightower affected him deeply; he could feel the fury of his spirit demanding her. She had sounded a wellspring of feeling that had been tapped only once – by Rhoda when they were very young.

What a terrible mistake that had been. Their love had faded so quickly when romance became a reality and everyday life pulled them apart. Then came Rhoda's drinking and her affairs, soon followed by his own. Finally there was the accident. Driving while drunk, Rhoda collided head-on with a truck. His two oldest sons, Michael and Tim, Jr, were killed. Rhoda recovered physically but was now trying as hard as she could to drink herself to death. The three younger children, irrationally, blamed him for the accident. He'd been away so often on business trips that they never felt close to him. But as long as he stayed married to Rhoda, he maintained a tenuous position in their lives, a position he hoped would strengthen with time. So he could not divorce Rhoda. It would cost him his children.

What, then, should he do about Cameron Hightower? One by one he had listed the reasons why he should do nothing. One, he was a married man and could not offer her marriage. Two, he was more than twice her age. Three, she worked for him. It would be ruinous to office morale, and he would never be sure if his attentions were welcomed because she felt she had no choice. Which led to four. Suppose she turned him down? Could they continue to work together? As much as he wanted her, he would not permit passion to interfere with FitzGerald Associates. And Tim FitzGerald had a strong intuition – he never argued with these hunches – that Cameron would be a unique person at FitzGerald Associates, possibly the most important besides himself.

The result of his logic was bitter truth. Taking Cameron with him to California had been a self-indulgent, first-class blunder. It was imperative that he remedy his error – which was why he'd changed his plans and decided to drive to San Francisco to see another client. If there had been no fog, he would be in San Francisco now. He checked the time. It was 5:45, and the fog seemed to have lifted.

He dressed quickly and packed, hoping to be out of the house before Cameron was up. He stepped out of his bedroom, making as little noise as possible. The door to Cameron's room was open. He peered inside. Cameron wasn't in her bed, and it was still fully made. She'd never been to sleep. Seriously concerned, he dropped his bags, walked to her bathroom door and listened. There was no sound. When he opened the door, the bathroom was empty. Where was she? All thought of leaving was forgotten. Tim descended the stairs and rapidly searched the rooms on the first floor. They were deserted. The moon disappeared as the fog started to roll in again. Where the hell was Cameron? The lookout point – that must be where she was. But when he got there, there was no Cameron. He listened hard but heard nothing. The fog cleared momentarily. For an instant he thought he saw a pale form swimming parallel to the shore. Cameron must have lost her bearings in the fog and was searching for the shore. How long would she be able to stay afloat in the dark, dangerous water? If she became too disoriented, she might swim away from shore.

Desperate, Tim kicked off his loafers and dropped his jacket to the ground. He felt his way to the stone steps. Hanging on to the railing, he went down the steps. As he did, he repeatedly called, 'Cameron, over here! Cameron, I'm coming.' He heard his voice smothered by the fog and quickened his pace. Once he almost lost his footing. Finally he reached the bottom and found himself on dry sand. But where was she? Why hadn't she come ashore? Fully clothed, he waded into the water up to his knees, then to his waist. A white body passed in front of him. He reached for it and missed, falling into the water. Half walking, half swimming, he headed in the direction the body had been moving. He was about to call out when something collided with him.

'Cameron!' He grabbed her bare shoulders. 'It's all right!' He held her close to him, and was suddenly conscious that she was naked.

'Tim!' As if in a dream, Cameron was oblivious of the fog, her nakedness, and the fact that Tim was standing, fully clothed, in the water. All she knew was that she was in his arms. Half crying, half laughing, she kissed his lips. Her tongue flicked between their open mouths and touched his tongue. A wave of heat spread from Tim's loins throughout his body and he shuddered with exultation.

She guided him to a place near the reef where the sand sloped out of the water. There, she unbuttoned his shirt. She leaned forward, her tongue licking his nipples while her fingers helped him unfasten his belt. Tim stepped out of his clothes and in seconds was as naked as she. Still kissing, they sank to their knees. He entered her with an urgency he had forgotten was in him. They melted together in a blending of mind and heart, each straining to possess and be possessed. When Cameron's heart beat faster, a pulse in Tim's neck pounded. She arched her hips hungrily, her nails digging into his flesh, no longer able to restrain her body. Tremors rippled through her legs, along her thighs. She cried aloud in fierce ecstasy, giving her passion to him, and felt his powerful body shake as he poured himself into her, answering her with his own savage need. They climaxed together, with nothing held back, their need joining each to each, dissolving them into one person.

Afterwards, they held each other for a long time, letting the waves of desire recede. They lay in the warm sand, surrounded by the sensuous fog, and kissed tenderly, overwhelmed by the strength of their passion.

There was no longer a question in Tim's mind about the wisdom of making love to Cameron. He only marvelled that there ever could have been a question. He was in love with Cameron. All the preliminaries of falling in love had been bypassed beside the Pacific Ocean. No matter what else happened in the world, he would continue to be in love with Cameron and would continue to make love to Cameron.

Cameron knew only that what she'd waited for had finally happened. Timothy FitzGerald was the man she loved. Making love to him was an experience so magical she wondered how she had lived for so long without this extraordinary gift that God had given human beings: the power to love. Her love for Tim was final and soul-deep. All of her that was worth having was his.

13

Tim awoke first, reluctantly drifting up from the depths of an erotic dream. He was lying on his back and felt a delicious warmth beside him. Cameron's head was buried against his shoulder, her soft black hair falling across his face. She must have moved, because he felt the tension in her arm as it tightened around him, holding him fast against her. He remembered their lovemaking and the sweetness of the memory nearly overwhelmed him. He had somehow got inside the magic circle of life. The idea gave him the extraordinary freedom to love a woman to the outer limits of his nature. At the same time, it committed him to her forever. For a while Tim was lost in thought, piecing it together, reliving the magic that Cameron and he had shared. He had said, 'I love you.' She had answered, 'I love you.' But what did that mean? Those words were often spoken in passion and quickly forgotten. Suppose the night had been no more to her than an exciting interlude? She was a very young woman. These things happen. Should he try to hold her to some imaginary vow? Impossible.

Tim glanced at the sleeping girl. Had the even rhythm of her breathing changed? He couldn't see her eyes. Her long, lustrous lashes almost reached her cheeks, and the corners of her mouth were turned slightly up, as though she were having a wonderful dream. In her sleep she was gently rubbing against his thigh. Tim lay perfectly still, happy to be used for the pleasure of the woman he loved. Then her hand slid down his chest and crept between his legs. His desire for her returned. His sense of her skin, of her odour, of the suppleness of her body became abnormally acute. He had never before been so easily aroused.

Cameron raised her head. 'Good morning, darling.'

'You're awake,' he murmured.

'Do you think you could wake without my knowing it?' She lifted her mouth to be kissed. Gazing down into her dark eyes, eyes that told him how much she loved him, Tim realized how groundless were his fears. Cameron lost herself in the depths of their intense emotion. They didn't kiss again, they were profoundly quiet, caught in the spell of the passion building between them, a passion each could only give the other, which made them inseparable in the loving forgetfulness of self.

Only in the afterglow did they kiss. Cameron whispered, 'I love you.' Her mouth stopped his words. When she drew back, she said, 'And you love me.'

Tim's doubts were put to rest once and for all. Cameron loved him as he loved her; in the sun and the blue sky of the day as she had in the dark of night.

'Must you go to San Francisco?'

'No,' Tim confessed, grinning like a schoolboy.

'Then could we stay here this week? You said the private placement could hold until next week.'

'It can. Leon will be glad to put us up.' This will be a honeymoon, he thought. Then he remembered Rhoda, his children, and the decisions ahead.

Cameron saw his expression change. His reality was intruding on the miracle of their love. 'You must make me a promise, my dearest. While we're here, we're here. When we leave, we'll think about the future.' He started to object. 'Ssh.' She placed her finger over his mouth. 'I know what I know. All we'll ever need is here and now.'

Tim kissed her silencing finger. 'I promise.'

* * *

239

For the next few days, the point overlooking the Pacific and the pool below were Tim's and Cameron's private playground. Each morning they packed a wicker basket with sandwiches, a bottle of wine, and a canteen of water. Each evening they returned to the house after having spent a day eating, drinking, swimming, and making love. They made love in all the ways, as old as desire itself, that a man and a woman can give each other pleasure. Their love, at first so new, so astonishing, became as natural as breathing. Their prior existence faded away in the brilliance that their loving gave to each moment.

On Sunday they packed. Cameron had an advantage over Tim. Her plans for the future were simple, uncomplicated by other responsibilities. What was crucial to her was that they be together and share their lives with each other. She was twenty-two years old. There was time to think about the future, about marriage and children.

Tim was a mass of conflicting emotions. How could he love Cameron and not marry her? But could he surrender his children to Rhoda? He watched Cameron pack. Her transparent joy gave off a glow, making her even more beautiful to him. Momentarily, he was thrown off balance. How could she have happened to him?

Tim waited until the flight to New York to talk to her. He was one of those men who are not equipped for pretences and he wanted to state the case as he saw it.

Cameron gave him her complete attention. But as she listened to him recount his history, she was thinking, weighing, deciding, and she found that she was prepared. In fact, she was surprised at the extent of her preparation.

'Does Rhoda want a divorce?' she asked at last.

'Rhoda doesn't give a damn what I do. All she wants are the children. And money.'

'You can't divorce her. There are the children. We'll wait.'

'It could be a year. Two. Three.'

'We'll wait as long as we have to wait.'

It drew from him, so proud a man, a touchingly grateful 'Thank you.'

Cameron shrugged. 'We live our lives as best we can. I learned that long ago. Now let's plan our future.'

She would keep her apartment with Lucia and spend most of her nights at Tim's apartment at the Carlyle. Their love did not alter her plans for a career on Wall Street. Tim was a master, he would teach her and help her become more valuable to the firm. In the end, the clarity of her vision, the strength and confidence with which she sketched their future, gave him a feeling of standing on firmer ground. Divorce would be postponed, but the question would be reopened in a year or two. It was vital to Tim that Cameron understand that they *would* marry. Abruptly, he kissed her on the cheek.

'Did anyone ever tell you you were beautiful?'

'Yes. But I never cared.' She returned his kiss. 'I need you so much.'

Tim felt shaken by her passionate trust. 'Not as much as I need you,' he said. His eyes met hers and there was a complete understanding. So their lives would be joined in every way except marriage. And if that were lacking, their life together would not be a masquerade – unlike many conventional marriages.

During the years that followed, Cameron Hightower and Timothy FitzGerald came to be regarded as a team in the financial community. There was a wealthy sun glittering on the Street the day *Fortune* ran an article on 'Successful Women on Wall Street'. Cameron Hightower, partially because of her youth and striking good looks, was featured on the cover, with Timothy FitzGerald beaming with pride in the background. And when *Business Week* featured Timothy FitzGerald, managing partner of FitzGerald Associates, on its cover, Cameron Hightower, assistant to the managing partner, stood close to him on his right.

The thirty-year difference between Cameron's age and Tim's, and the fact that they were not married to each other, spiced what might have been dry business articles with romantic titillation. But the frequent appearance of Geraldine Hightower as a third member of their party put an end to rumours that the relationship between Cameron and Tim was a sordid affair and to snide questions about their financial arrangements. They were seen frequently with Geraldine in her box at the Metropolitan Opera. Geraldine was seated to the left of Tim FitzGerald at the New York City Ballet. When Tim speared a baseball with his bare hand in the box behind the first base at Yankee Stadium, Geraldine applauded. Tim FitzGerald was very wealthy and successful, but Geraldine Hightower was rich, in the inimitable way the Du Ponts and the Mellons were rich. The fame of the Hightower fortune went well beyond Wall Street, and Cameron Hightower was a genuine Hightower.

Insiders on the Street – the columnists, specialists, brokers, and traders – occasionally asked themselves whether Cameron Hightower would love Timothy FitzGerald if he were not the managing partner of FitzGerald Associates, one of the most brilliant investment bankers on Wall Street. It was a meaningless question. Would Thomas Edison, minus his electrical genius, have been Thomas Edison? Tim FitzGerald had become a Wall Street legend in his own time because he was the man he was. And this was the man Cameron loved.

Through it all, Cameron worked and learned. She became as much a creature of the sky as Tim. It was not unusual for them to leave Miami, sweltering under the heat and humidity, and arrive in Chicago in a driving snowstorm, then leave Chicago's slush and arrive in San Diego to find ideal weather and a glorious sunset. Time and distance became meaningless to them.

Cameron learned how to read a corporate balance sheet, not just for what was there but for what was omitted. It was no longer merely a set of numbers telling her what the corporation claimed as its annual profits, or how its current assest compared to its current liabilities. Tim explained that it was possible to manipulate the numbers. With too many corporations, the numbers were 'massaged' by management and cooperative accountants to show what management wanted the numbers to show, namely profits.

The first time this came up, Tim was considering whether FitzGerald Associates should participate in a syndicate making a new public offering of stock for the Delta Company, a corporation specializing in computer components.

'We'll pass on this one,' Tim said. 'They've done a lot of cosmetic accounting.'

'Like Equity Funding?' Cameron compared it to the giant insurance fraud.

'No. These numbers are not outright fake. Most firms don't have to resort to that. What they do is interpret the numbers.'

'I think I follow you.' Cameron fought an impulse to kiss him. There would be time for that later when they were home. 'They've changed their accounting system. They capitalized their research and development so this year's earnings would look good. They'll probably write the whole thing off next year, and their earnings will be lousy.'

Tim smiled. 'After the placement, of course. And when the earnings drop, the stock will go to hell. That's one reason why we are not going to participate in the syndicate. There's a second reason, just as important: Cyrus Hansen.'

Tim's attention was still focused on the prospectus. He was irritated at the thought of how much money was going to be lost by unsophisticated investors, and he didn't see the startled look pass over Cameron's face. Or her sudden pallor.

243

Or the slight trembling of her hands and the rigidity with which she held her head.

After several seconds of silence, Cameron cleared her throat and asked in what she hoped was her normal voice, 'What has Cyrus Hansen to do with the Delta Company?'

Something Tim heard made him raise his eyes. Astute as ever, he took in Cameron's agitated condition and remembered instantly that the Hightowers and the Hansens both lived in Princeton. Obviously, Cameron knew Cyrus Hansen; how well he had no wish to find out. So, deliberately ignoring what his eyes told him and the questions his brain asked, he concentrated on the facts about Cyrus Hansen, the corporate raider.

'You know what young Hansen does.' Tim spoke quickly and did not wait for Cameron's response. 'He specializes in taking over publicly held corporations that have been badly mismanaged. If the company can be salvaged, the first thing he does is chop out the dry rot in the management and put his own people in their place. The rumour is that Hansen is about to go after the Delta Company.'

'But if he gives new life to dying companies, wouldn't that make Delta a good investment?' Cameron asked.

Tim shook his head. 'You can't rely on Hansen. He's a loose cannonball. If he doesn't like what he finds after taking over the company, he could very easily gut the company and sell off the pieces, one at a time. Then everyone loses, including Hansen. But he's so rich it makes no difference, and he's had a lot more winners than losers. I don't know what he'll find in Delta.'

The pallor had left Cameron's face and was replaced by a deep, rich red glow as the rush of blood spread across her cheeks. That was Tim's only clue as to the emotions resonating through her body and broadcasting in the quiet air of the office. Cyrus Hansen! she said to herself. For me there is no Cyrus Hansen. Once there was, but no more. Not now. Now there is only Tim.

Cameron forced herself to look directly at the man sitting at the wide partner's desk and to rediscover who he was, what he was. The love in his wide green eyes drew her to him. Yes, her mind told her triumphantly, 'I love you, Tim FitzGerald.' Cameron was not aware that she'd mouthed the words and Tim had no difficulty reading her lips. The words and the smile that followed satisfied him.

'You see, it was Hansen's move,' Tim said, 'that prompted the Delta Company to issue more stock. It's a form of shark repellent used by a group of frightened men. But I don't believe it will stop Hansen. He'll react to the numbers just as we have. They'll make him mad. Hansen is supposed to have a violent temper. He'll eat that prospectus for lunch and chew up the management in the process.'

'What's your bet? Will he gut the company or revive it?' Cameron had regained her composure. Cyrus Hansen was only another corporate raider to be evaluated.

'Offhand,' Tim said thoughtfully, 'I wouldn't want to bet on there being a Delta Company inside a year.' He stopped, leaned back, and looked at Cameron. 'I just thought of a better bet. I've never considered the possibility, but maybe – just maybe – Hansen is practising. Someday he might want to go up against his grandfather for control of the Hansen Company. All that buying and reorganizing of companies could be Hansen's way of learning what makes business successful and what doesn't.'

'Do you really think Cyrus will fight Elmer Hansen?' Cameron asked, unable to keep her excitement at the prospect from showing.

'I don't know, but it's a genuine possibility.' Tim's face split into a wide grin. 'If he ever does, won't that be a real donnybrook?'

Cameron smothered a smile. She had the strong

245

impression that if Cyrus and Elmer ever tangled, there was nothing Tim would like better than to be there, right smack in the middle. She wondered which side he'd be on.

As they had originally planned, when Tim was visiting his children in Greenwich, Cameron saw Geraldine or spent her evenings in the apartment with Lucia. Often Lucia was not at home, and Cameron would have trouble falling asleep. She'd become accustomed to Tim's body next to her in bed. She missed the vibrations, the air currents caused by the presence of another person in the apartment. One evening Lucia was home, but this was a different Lucia, restrained, thoughtful, and silent. She made her speciality for dinner, spaghetti with a white clam sauce, to go with a bottle of Italian-style Manzone white Chianti. Then they adjourned to the living room. Cameron stretched out on the couch with her snifter of brandy, and Lucia slumped in her chair sipping something poured from a bottle without a label. Lucia's silence began to produce an awkward tension.

'All right,' Cameron said at last. 'Out with it. What's the problem?'

'No problem. I'm in love and I'm going to get married.' Lucia began to speak quickly. 'And I hope you won't be too mad, because I'll be sticking you with the apartment. You see, we're going back to California. To make wine and babies.'

'To hell with the apartment.' Cameron was almost as pleased as if she were the one going to be married. She sat on the edge of the couch. 'Your first love.'

'My first love. I got lucky.'

'Tell me about him. What's his name?'

'Bill Moskowitz.'

'What does he do?'

'He works in the advertising business, as an account executive. I met him while we were shooting a sports fashion setup and they were doing a cosmetic layout on the next stage. Both photographers took a break at the same time. We met at the water cooler.' She paused for dramatic effect. 'He asked me for a date, and I said yes. I kept saying yes to everything. I've been saying yes for six months. He asked me to marry him last week.'

'And you said yes!' Cameron's tone did justice to the event. Then she grew reflective. How would an advertising man from New York City, named Bill Moskowitz, fit in with an Italian winemaking family in California?

'I know what you're worrying about,' Lucia said. 'Don't. Life is one long, strange coincidence. Bill comes from upstate New York, near the Finger Lakes. What do you think his family does?'

'Moskowitz? Upstate New York? No!' Cameron exclaimed.

'Yes!' Lucia was emphatic. 'They grow grapes and make wine.'

'Moskowitz Kosher Wine.' Cameron was awed. 'It's a national institution. Maybe they want to go public?' she asked, half joking. 'No, forget it. What's Bill Moskowitz doing in New York in the advertising business? Why isn't he up at Lake Cayuga stomping grapes?'

'He's the black sheep of the family. He hates sweet wine, it makes him sick. I love it. That's what I'm drinking.' Lucia said this as though it were a declaration of faith. 'Anyway, his father, his uncles, his brothers all love their wine. So they run the winery.'

'And he's in New York in advertising.'

'Not for long. He's about to join the Manzone winery.'

Cameron proceeded with care. 'Do your parents know?'

'And how! We've had a couple of pretty rough conversations, about him being sort of Jewish and me being sort of Catholic.' Lucia paused, remembering the battles. 'But when I finally had the brains to say that Bill was the Moskowitz from the Moskowitz Kosher Wine family, we put away the boxing gloves. Dad's known Bill's father, Abe, for years. He hates Abe's wine, but he loves Abe. And he's sure he'll love Abe's son, especially since Bill can't stand sweet wine.'

'What about Bill's parents?'

'Same story. They gave in, too.' Lucia waved her glass of wine. 'They don't drink Manzone wine but they love the Manzone family. And since I'm not only a Manzone but I love Moskowitz Kosher Wine, they practically prefer me to Bill. Between the Moskowitz family and the Manzone family, we'll have the biggest, happiest civil wedding the Napa Valley's ever seen. You'll be maid of honour. The bride will wear white. And if you laugh during the ceremony, I'll pour Manzone-Moskowitz wine over your head.'

When Cameron and Tim arrived at Kennedy Airport after a week in California, first spent at Lucia's wedding and later calling on West Coast clients, Tim produced a white handkerchief and insisted on blindfolding Cameron. Cameron giggled and agreed, knowing that Tim had planned some kind of surprise. They were in the rear seat of Tim's Bentley with Andrew at the wheel, and the drive was too soft for her to recognize the bumps in the road. She decided it took too long for them to be going to her Fifty-sixth Street apartment. When the car did stop, she had a feeling they weren't in front of the Carlyle, either. Tim helped her from the car and guided her into a building. They entered an elevator and Tim whispered instructions to the operator. When the elevator stopped, Tim helped her out. She heard a door being unlocked and opened. Tim's hand took her arm and led her forward. The door closed and Tim undid the blindfold. Cameron blinked. She was standing in the foyer of a large, empty apartment.

'Do you like it?' Tim asked.

Cameron walked under a curved archway into a huge living room with a high ceiling, elegant moulding on the walls, a waxed oak parquet floor, and a brick fireplace at one end. 'It's splendid,' she answered. 'Did you buy this? Is it yours?' Questions were racing through her mind.

'What a suspicious woman.'

'Then it's a company apartment?'

'Look around,' he said.

Tim settled himself on the floor of the living room, his back resting against the fireplace, while she wandered through the apartment. There were two bedrooms, each with its own private bathroom and dressing room, and a master suite with a private bath, sitting room, and dressing room. Beyond that, the apartment consisted of a walnut-panelled library with a second fireplace, the living room, a dining room, kitchen, pantry, and breakfast corner. Off the kitchen were two rooms and a private bath, a small suite for servants. It was a penthouse apartment, surrounded on four sides by a wide terrace covered with promenade tile. There were doors that led to the terrace from the dining room, living room, and master bedroom. Gazing out of the living-room windows, she saw Central Park and the twin towers of the Majestic on Central Park West. That gave away the location; this apartment was on Fifth Avenue in the lower seventies. She turned to Tim.

'It's magnificent. You do own it, don't you?'

'I can live here, if you furnish it.'

'What about your apartment in the Carlyle?'

'I'm giving it up.'

'I see.' She'd known before the answers to her first two questions, but she approached the next one with some misgivings. 'And I'll live here with you?'

'Not quite. We'll both live here.'

Cameron knelt on the floor in front of him. 'This is our apartment?'

'Your lease will run out by the time you fix this place up.'

Cameron's hands rested lightly on Tim's shoulders. Her

emotions were so overpowering, she was unable to speak. Although she had never mentioned it, she'd always considered the apartment at the Carlyle as Tim's apartment where she occupied space as a welcome guest. Her real home was on Fifty-sixth Street. But this apartment would be theirs. It would be their home.

'I'm glad you bought it,' she said softly. 'I'm glad it's yours.'

'It's not. The apartment is yours.'

'No!' Cameron sprang to her feet. 'No! I won't take it. No!'

'Why not? What's the matter?' Tim was startled by her violent protest. He'd been so confident that she'd be pleased. In his desire to make her happy, he'd caused her pain, and her pain became his pain.

As suddenly as Cameron had flared up, she grew calm again. She stared down at Tim. So still, she was like a tightly strung wire that vibrates rapidly – invisibly – after it's been plucked. Giving off a sound too high to be heard. A wordless cry for help.

'Tim, darling, listen to me.' She knelt again in front of him, taking his face in her hands. 'I love your apartment. I want to live here with you. But I don't want to own it. No, that's not right – I would love to own it. But I don't want you to give it to me.'

'I don't understand. I enjoy giving you presents. But you don't wear jewellery, so I've bought you trifles. And you forget to wear your fur coats. I think you would live in jeans and sweaters if you could. That's why I haven't taken you to Paris to the couture collections.'

Cameron could only agree. She remembered her teenage concerns about taking gifts from Geraldine. She never wanted to be dependent again on other people's generosity, even those persons she loved. Things happened, they'd happened to her. Perhaps she was superstitious. But if she became dependent on someone and something happened she would be alone and helpless.

'I offer you a compromise,' she said, mustering a cheerful face.

'Compromises show a willingness to cooperate.'

'You take back the apartment, and as I earn more money, I'll gradually buy it from you. When the apartment is paid for in full, you can transfer the title to me.'

'That way it won't be a gift?'

'That's right. It won't be a gift.'

'All right. I agree in principle. With two minor suggestions.'

'Which are – ?'

'One, you promise to wear a few pieces of good jewellery I want to buy you.' He would not let her interrupt. 'Two, this for my convenience as well as the board of directors of this co-op. I want the ownership to remain in your name.'

'No!'

'Hear me out, please. The cost of the co-op will be a loan from me to you secured by the apartment. You pay off the loan just as you suggested. It will be like a mortgage. And when the loan is paid off, we'll have a mortgage-burning party. The way families did before it became fashionable to owe money.'

Cameron longed to agree. Until now, she had not realized how much she had wanted them to have a place of their own. So, with some uneasiness, she said, 'All right.'

'Wonderful!' Tim said. 'Besides, Geraldine has already selected her bedroom. She's tired of staying with Pierre every time she spends an evening with us.'

'Geraldine knew about the apartment?' Cameron pretended outrage and then gave up. As usual, Tim had planned ahead. Geraldine was his reserve force in case he needed help in convincing her.

'Would I choose an apartment for you – for us – without consulting Geraldine?'

'Never!' What chance did she have against the two of them?

In April 1978, Cameron, Tim, and Geraldine were sitting in front of the fire in the library of Cameron's apartment at 975 Fifth Avenue. They'd just returned from a performance of *I Puritani* at the Metropolitan Opera starring the tenor sensation Luciano Pavarotti. Tim was enthusiastic, but Geraldine unimpressed. She kept referring to Italian tenors of an earlier era: Gigli, Schipa, Lauri-Volpi. Those were tenors, she insisted. Tim listened, his mind a blotter soaking up information in a field where he felt anything but an expert.

Cameron sipped her brandy, half listening.

'Cameron,' Geraldine said sharply. 'We've been having a fascinating conversation about opera, and you haven't said a word. Come join us.'

'I was thinking about the country. The stock market. The Dow dropped below eight hundred last week.'

'An incredible opportunity to pick up bargains,' Tim said. 'Ben Graham's criteria can be used for the first time in years.'

'You think so?' Geraldine was no longer interested in dead Italian tenors.

'I do. The firm have been buying all week. For our own account as well as those accounts where we have discretionary authority.'

'Have you been buying, Cameron?' Geraldine asked.

'Yes. Every cent I can lay my hands on is invested.'

Geraldine finished her glass of sherry. 'That's good enough for me. The Hightower Trust has been sitting with almost 30 per cent of its assets in cash. We'll begin to commit that cash tomorrow.'

Tim's judgement proved to be as accurate as ever. Within a year, the Dow Industrial Average rose over two hundred points. The broad market did even better, so much better that in February 1979, Cameron, Tim, and Geraldine, having returned from a performance of *Tosca* at the Metropolitan Opera starring Plácido Domingo – a tenor Geraldine enjoyed – were having a celebration. Tim opened a bottle of Dom Pérignon, filled their narrow, tulip-shaped glasses precisely halfway to the brim, and proposed a toast. 'To Cameron Hightower. The owner of the penthouse apartment at 975 Fifth Avenue.'

They clinked glasses, drank, and Tim handed Cameron a paper. 'Your mortgage, my love, marked "Paid in Full".'

'Thanks to your judgement in the market.' Cameron's eyes glowed as she savoured the moment. Then she went to the fireplace where Andrew had prepared the fire before retiring. It was a wonderful fire, alive with the sound of the crackling dry white pine. Cameron opened the screen and tossed the note on the fire. It was gone in an instant. She found it difficult to believe her good fortune, her happiness. She was twenty-seven years old and desperately in love with a man who loved her with the same fierce passion as they'd known in the beginning. She now owned her own apartment, and after selling all her stocks, she would be a reasonably wealthy woman. On top of everything, she had a major career on Wall Street. Her opinions on matters concerning investment banking and the movement of the stock market were respected almost as much as Tim's. No wonder the columnists had started referring to her as 'The Woman Who Has Everything'.

On Tuesday, 4 September 1979, Tim and Cameron returned from a long Labor Day weekend in Southampton. Both were glad the hot, lazy summer was ending. Though the air was warmed by the September sun, Cameron found herself thinking about frosts and pumpkins, Thanksgiving Day turkeys and Christmas geese. After they'd unpacked, Cameron elected to help Alda prepare their dinner, and Tim decided to stroll around mid-Manhattan. What was left of the day was too beautiful to be spent indoors.

Tim walked down Fifth Avenue, glanced at the Bonwit Teller windows and continued walking. Today he was a looker, not a buyer. He could think of nothing Cameron needed. The great doors of St Patrick's Cathedral were worth a closer examination. At Saks Fifth Avenue, there was a houndstooth tweed jacket in a corner window he liked, but not now. When he reached Forty-second Street, he turned east, passed Grand Central Station and started up Third Avenue, heading for home. In the hour and a half he'd been walking, heavy rain clouds had moved in to cover the sun and a stiff wind was blowing off the Hudson River. Tim turned up the collar of his jacket and slipped his hands into his coat pockets for additional warmth. Should he hail a cab and ride the rest of the way home? He decided not to. At fifty-eight, he wasn't too old that a threat of rain or a chill in the air could drive him indoors. But he quickened his pace. It would be good to get home to Cameron. The feeling of great happiness that he had when he began the walk became more conscious.

He couldn't help feeling pride when he noted the number of new buildings under construction. It was astonishing. The city had been close to bankruptcy – there were many bankers who thought it still was – but one wouldn't know it from the boom in midtown construction. The pavements on almost every other corner were covered with wooden roofs so pedestrians would be protected when walking by the construction sites.

As Tim had been doing with increasing frequency over the past year, he thought again about Cameron and marriage. They'd been living together for over five years. Five years! It was hard to believe that it was already 1979. These last years had been the happiest and most productive of his life. But there was a dark side. He was still married to Rhoda, and all his efforts at maintaining a decent relationship with his children had failed miserably. Their watching Rhoda's continued heavy drinking had separated them still further from him, and the presence of Cameron in his life had completed the alienation. It had all been a waste of years, and it was time he talked to Rhoda about giving him a divorce. Past time, as a matter of fact.

Walking under a construction site, Tim heard a sharp crack. He looked up, saw a great steel I beam crash through the wooden roof and tried to hurl himself out of its path. In the instant when he knew it was too late, he remembered the things he'd put off. And now would never do. The I beam hit Tim across the chest, crushing him. He died instantly. Without the time necessary to curse himself for acting as though he were immortal.

The capon was stuffed with Tim's favourite – a combination of ground pork, chopped liver, onions, breadcrumbs, and white wine – and was roasting in the oven. Cameron fixed herself a martini and had everything ready to pour a gin and tonic for Tim when he returned. She glanced at her watch. It was 6:30. He must be taking a long walk. By 7:00 she was concerned. Tim must have taken a very long walk. By 7:30 the capon was almost roasted and Cameron was frantic. Where was he? If he was delayed, he would have telephoned. This wasn't like him. Should she call the police? The hospitals? She couldn't make up her mind, because when Tim did show up, he'd be disturbed because he'd done something that had so upset her. At 7:52 the telephone rang. Cameron leapt to answer it.

'Tim! Where the hell are you?'

'I'm sorry.' The voice on the other end of the line asked, 'Is this Mrs FitzGerald?'

'No,' Cameron snapped. 'This is Cameron Hightower.'

'May I speak to Mrs FitzGerald, please?'

'She doesn't live here. Try Greenwich. Who is this?'

Lieutenant Max Shapiro of the New York Police Department was a veteran policeman, wise in the ways of New York. When word of the accident on Third Avenue reached the precinct, he hurried over to New York Hospital where the body was lying in the morgue. The dead man's driving licence and other cards told him the man's name, address, and telephone number. The credit cards, cash, and expensive clothes told him the corpse was a wealthy man. Timothy FitzGerald? Suddenly it clicked into place. Lieutenant Shapiro was one of the many millions of Americans who invest what money they can spare in the stock market. He read *Forbes, Fortune, Business Week, The Wall Street Journal*. Timothy FitzGerald! The famous investment banker! The name of Cameron Hightower was also familiar. His wife had been correct. There was something – or had been something – going on between Timothy FitzGerald and Cameron Hightower. It never crossed his mind to pass judgement. As a policeman he'd seen too much of human nature at its worst. And that included the consequences of many unhappy marriages.

'This is Lieutenant Shapiro,' he answered. 'New York Police Department.'

'What happened? Where's Tim?'

'Miss Hightower, he's had an accident.' This was the part of the job he hated most, but it had to be done. 'I must inform you that Timothy FitzGerald was killed in a freak accident several hours ago.'

Cameron made an indescribable sound. She felt as though something had been violently ripped from her body, leaving a raw exposed void.

There was a silence. 'Miss Hightower? Are you there?' The lieutenant could hear her breathing. Shallow, rasping gasps as though she were being suffocated and was fighting to stay alive. 'Miss Hightower?'

256

A gagging sound. Then a low voice. 'Yes, Lieutenant. I'm here.'

Lieutenant Shapiro tried to help. 'Death was instantaneous. Painless.'

'I see.' Cameron was numb.

'Miss Hightower, excuse me, but do you live at 975 Fifth Avenue?'

'Yes.'

'So did Mr FitzGerald. Although we're certain it's him, would it be possible for you to make the identification?'

There was a long pause while Cameron tried to gather her wits. 'How did he die, Lieutenant?' She listened carefully to the explanation. What it came down to was that Tim was in the wrong place at the wrong time. Five seconds sooner, five seconds later – possibly even four, three, or two seconds – and they'd be sitting in the dining room eating chicken and drinking wine. 'Where is he, Lieutenant?'

'New York Hospital.'

'I'll be in the lobby of the hospital in fifteen minutes.'

Whenever Cameron remembered the funeral, she saw Tim's Mercedes, with Andrew dressed in a black uniform, waiting in front of the apartment for her. By dying as he had, Cameron felt Tim had anticipated her. He had been preparing for her future. Was it that he thought his work was complete, so he died? But it wasn't complete. And she had the old, visceral wish to talk his death over with him. Surely life held more for them than an empty doorway.

But there was no answer. Tall, slender, in a dark dress, her hair swept back in a knot, her summer tan still fresh on her skin, she entered the car.

The drive to the church was one mile. It seemed longer.

After the funeral Cameron retreated to Hightower Farm feeling bone-weary and possessed of a coldness within her that would not leave. The warmth of life seemed to have passed out of her. She spent her days in silence – a silence that Geraldine respected, keeping her distance saying very little. All Cameron's willpower was expended on getting up in the morning. When she would agree to eat anything, she would have lunch or dinner with Geraldine. The time she spent with Geraldine gave her a sense of human fellowship and took some chill from her heart. But the moment she was alone, she felt the reaction of redoubled loneliness. She had no impulse to return to Manhattan. What was there to go back to? Nothing but the emptiness of the apartment and FitzGerald Associates without Tim. Nothing but the silence of his office, which would be louder than the most discordant noises.

One afternoon, when the rain was gusting against the windows, Cameron went to the room that had been her study when Geraldine first brought her to Princeton and Hightower Farm. Seized with a fervour of activity, she pulled work from her briefcase, spilling the contents on her desk. Memoranda, an SEC prospectus, plans to remodel the company computer room lay scattered about. It was the work she loved. But every piece of paper brought Tim back. The ghost of him lurked on every page of every company report. Slowly she put the papers back in her briefcase, filing away with each some flash of his eyes, some note of his laughter, some stray gleam from the shores of past pleasures.

She sat absolutely still, staring blindly at the briefcase. Then she rose and walked to the shelves on the opposite wall. Within easy reach at the end of the shelf of Barnard textbooks were two worn photograph albums. Her only family albums. She had postponed again and again starting one for Tim and herself, out of superstitious fear that if she did, she would lose him as she had the others. Now she wished she had been less superstitious. Her postponements had not warded off disaster. She studied the backs of the two albums, her eyes misting. The one bound in brown leather held all her clippings of Cyrus Hansen. Cyrus! She'd stopped collecting items on him years ago.

Cyrus Hansen? Even his name sounded strange in her mind, and she shook her head to rid herself of the memory of the golden-haired young man from another life. Her eyes turned to the other album, the one with a worn yellow burlap cover. It dated from the first month she'd come to live with Geraldine. She took it down from the shelf and carried it over to her desk. Solemnly she looked at the documents in the album. The marriage certificate of Gary and Elizabeth Hightower. The birth certificate of Cameron Hightower.

Cameron closed the album and replaced it on the shelf. She felt the ice encasing her heart thicken. She saw herself forever shut out from the golden gifts of life. She had tried – tried hard – but it had all proved useless. She had to say good-bye to Tim, and to more. To the Cameron Hightower who had known love.

14

Days passed and then weeks before Cameron was finally able to face going to the office and sitting at her partner's desk without Tim facing her from the other side. Her recovery was due largely to Geraldine's tireless care. She lost track of time as she tried to bury herself in her work. Her daily routine remained unchanged; each morning she would shower, dress, have a light breakfast, and drive from Hightower Farm to the office. Then she would try to make the decisions necessary to keep FitzGerald Associates functioning. But her loss was inescapable.

When she forced herself to stay at the apartment, she was alone in the bed she had once shared with Tim. Sometimes she pretended Tim was not dead, that he was away on a business trip and would return soon with a new stock offering, or a new client. But her pretending was not successful. There was not a minute, an hour, a day when the weight of Tim's death did not threaten to break her heart and crush her spirit.

Geraldine insisted that she spend as much time as possible with her at Hightower Farm. When Cameron hadn't the energy to make the trip to Princeton, Geraldine drove to New York. She spent more time sleeping in her bedroom in the apartment than she did at The Farm. Jake Stern and Rosemary Atherton tried to help Cameron in every way possible. Jake went so far as to relearn the English language, making his points without his usual obscenities. Rosemary's remarkable memory was frequently called upon to fill in the blanks that Cameron, in her misery, could not recall.

In mid-October, Jake entered her office and sat in the chair facing her.

'The balloon has gone up,' he announced.

'What balloon? What are you talking about?'

'Today is 18 October 1979. Doesn't that mean anything to you?'

Cameron raised an eyebrow. 'Should it?'

'Yes, damn it! It should.' Jake was very angry. 'And damn him for being so careless.'

'What is it, Jake?' Cameron's voice was tired.

'Tim's will was read today.'

'Was it?' It occurred to Cameron that she'd been trying so hard not to think of Tim as dead that she'd put the will completely out of her mind.

'He never changed it. Understand? Rhoda and his children inherit everything.' Jake was close to tears.

'She should. She was Tim's wife and the mother of his children.'

'No, she shouldn't!' Jake shouted. 'He didn't intend it to be that way. We talked for years about his changing his will. But he was always too busy. It was always going to be done next week. Or the week after. His idea was to leave her his money. And you the company.'

'The company? FitzGerald Associates? Who owns it now?'

'The proud owner of FitzGerald Associates is now Rhoda FitzGerald.'

Cameron looked around the office, at the sculpture, the paintings, the furniture, even the desk she was sitting at. 'She own all this?'

'Every bit of it.'

Cameron rested her head in her hands. She squeezed her eyes shut and bit her lower lip in her characteristic gesture of agitation. 'Oh, Lord!' The full enormity of Jake's words struck home.

'There's more. Dear Rhoda and her brats don't want the company to survive. They're pulling their money out. We'll be out of business as of a week from Friday. We'll all be on the street, looking for jobs, because Tim didn't pay attention.'

'She doesn't want the firm?'

'She definitely does not want the firm.'

Cameron thought fast. Her blood started to flow again. FitzGerald Associates had been overcapitalized at $100 million, but that money was gone. What was left was the name, the reputation, the employees, and the offices. 'Jake' – her words were precisely measured – 'how much capital do you think we'd need to keep the doors open?'

Jake squinted and scratched his bald head. 'What are you driving at?'

'Let's go one step at a time. Does Rhoda have a use for the name FitzGerald Associates?'

'No. At least I don't think she does.'

'If she doesn't, will she sell the name to you?'

'I wouldn't pay her a nickel for it.' The idea of Rhoda FitzGerald getting more money on top of the hundreds of millions of dollars she'd already inherited outraged Jake.

'Drop it, Jake.' Cameron sat bolt upright. She had a sense of pieces falling into place. 'If we run a very tight ship, how much capital would we need to keep the doors open?'

'You and me?' Jake looked thunderstruck and excited at the same time.

'Yes, you and me.'

'The banks love you like a flower. We can borrow fifteen times our equity. But I'd rather not go over ten times. So, say we raise four million. The banks would do handsprings to lend us forty million to work with.'

'Five million. Six would be even better.'

Jake laughed. 'With six million cash invested, either as stock in the company or as a subordinated loan, we could get ten times that at the bank – sixty million! Boy! Then we could really operate. Sixty million dollars in working capital could take us a long way.'

Cameron knew she should do it. The only question was, could she? Could she overcome her fear of accepting help from Geraldine? The answer was clear. She was no longer a child. She would offer Geraldine a damn good business proposition so that Geraldine would not be doing her a favour.

'Listen, Jake. If I borrow on my apartment, I can raise a million dollars. In addition to that – but there's no guarantee – I think I can get another two million to come in as a subordinated lender. Can you match it?'

'I don't know.' Jake was holding a tight rein on his enthusiasm. 'But I can sure try.'

'Okay. First talk to Rhoda. See if she'll assign you the FitzGerald name. Cheap. And don't mention me.'

Jake rose. There was a bounce in his legs that Cameron had not noticed before. Becoming part owner of a Wall Street firm like FitzGerald Associates was something he had never expected to happen.

'We'll meet here tomorrow morning at eight-thirty.'

'At eight-thirty.' Cameron remained seated as Jake closed the door behind him. FitzGerald Associates without Tim FitzGerald? That was not the way she'd envisioned her future. But it was the only future she had left. If they were successful, Tim's name would remain a legend on the Street – a legend she would keep alive.

The next day Jake reported success. Rhoda FitzGerald didn't give a tinker's damn for the name. She intended to go back to using her maiden name anyway. Chuckling, he told Cameron that she'd wished him good luck. Because if he were successful in raising the money, it would save Rhoda the legal costs of winding up the business. That alone was worth half a million dollars. When she signed over the name, she said, 'Good riddance.'

* * *

263

Cameron spent the weekend in Princeton. She went over her proposal with Geraldine, item by item. Geraldine appeared to give it much thought, asking a number of pertinent questions. But these were questions to which she already knew the answers. After seemingly deep deliberation, she agreed to become a subordinated lender to FitzGerald Associates to the extent of $2 million. Then Geraldine excused herself, went to her office, and made a phone call. She returned to tell Cameron that Roberto Manzone and Lucia Moskowitz were expecting her, Cameron, the next day. Based on Cameron's investing her own $1 million, they would consider matching Geraldine's commitment. So, whether or not Jake Stern could raise his share, Cameron would be able to count on at least $5 million to run her company.

Cameron flew to San Francisco and was met at the airport by a very pregnant Lucia and a two-year-old baby strapped in a baby seat beside her. The baby was Francis Manzone Moskowitz. Cameron tried not to show her envy of Lucia or of her marriage to the man she loved, or of her baby and of the baby on the way. She more or less succeeded. But when she explained her offer to Roberto Manzone and his brother and to Bill Moskowitz, and showed them the projections she had worked up, she was completely successful. She left for New York with a written commitment stating that the Manzone and Moskowitz families would become subordinated lenders to FitzGerald Associates. They pledged $2 million.

Jake did not do as well as Cameron. He was in a position personally to invest $500,000, and he did obtain a subordinated lender who agreed to put up $1 million. But together, they had raised $6.5 million – more than enough to keep the doors of FitzGerald Associates open. Although Cameron's personal investment was twice the size of Jake's and her lenders had committed four times the money, she insisted

264

Jake and she co-manage the firm. When Jake hesitated, Cameron pointed out that they would never have been able to obtain the FitzGerald name without him. Much to Jake's pleasure, he had to agree.

As usual, the documents took longer to draft and be argued over by four sets of lawyers than anyone ever imagined possible. But on 29 December 1979, the papers were finally signed. The new funds were transferred to the company account and Rhoda withdrew Tim's money. The transaction closed.

When FitzGerald Associates opened its doors for business on 2 January 1980, there were two new managing partners, Cameron Hightower and Jake Stern. But of the two equal partners, it was tacitly agreed that Cameron Hightower was a little more than equal.

PART FIVE

The Managing Partner
1980–1984

15

In the months that followed, FitzGerald Associates had their good days and their bad days. Cameron Hightower and Jake Stern learned all too quickly that, together, the two of them did not equal one Timothy FitzGerald.

Cameron was seated in the reception room off the executive suite of Baxter Industries. She had been waiting twenty minutes for George Balasz to finish his meeting with Roland Daniels, the chairman. It was unlike George not to be punctual. Millie, George's secretary, had come out of her office twice to offer Cameron coffee, but each time Cameron declined. Millie's sympathy made her uncomfortable. They had known each other during the years FitzGerald Associates had done business with the huge corporation, raising hundreds of millions of dollars for them in stock and bond placements. Now there was a new stock issue of ten million shares in the offing and Balasz, the treasurer and executive vice president of Baxter Industries, had set up a meeting with Cameron to discuss it.

George was one the shrewdest, nicest men Cameron had met in the corporate world. This might be because he was European, a Hungarian who, with his wife, Vera, had barely managed to escape to America when the People's Republic of Hungary was established in 1949. George understood all too well that the world wasn't one gigantic corporation with a well-funded, completely solvent pension plan. Perhaps that was why he was both decent and a survivor.

Cameron was jarred out of her thinking by Millie. 'Mr Balasz will see you now, Cameron.'

George was seated at his desk. Behind him the window overlooking the trees of Bala-Cynwyd, Pennsylvania.

'Good morning, Cameron.' He waved her to a chair facing him.

'Good morning, George.' One would never have known from his appearance what an extraordinary mind he had. He was short and bald, appearing anonymous in his grey suit. Unlike Roland Daniels, he was not television's idea of what a senior corporate executive should look like.

Balasz came straight to the point. 'I've slipped into a quagmire, Cameron.' His face was as bland as ever. 'I've been having meetings with the board, and I've just come out of one with Roland. About our new stock issue.' For an instant a look of distaste tightened his lips. 'A question has been raised.'

'Yes?'

'Can you guarantee the placement? That's two hundred fifty million dollars.'

So that was it. 'No,' she said. 'We don't have that kind of capitalization.'

'I know. I checked it out. It's sixty million, isn't it?'

'Give or take,' she said. 'We'd do a best efforts. But I know we can do it.'

'So do I, or I wouldn't have opened discussions. But the board and Roland don't want a best efforts. A best efforts means to him just that – you'll make your best effort to sell the stock. But that's not a guranteed placement. They always had that when Tim headed the firm. If he couldn't sell all the stock – though of course he did – then the firm guaranteed to make up the difference. Roland wants that guarantee.'

'But we can do the deal. I've started putting the syndicate together.'

'I know you can do it, and you know you can do it. But the board and Roland feel we're too large for a best efforts. The idea offends them.'

'You're giving it to another underwriter?'

'Mason, Adams, and Fenwick. I'm truly sorry.'

'So am I.' Cameron got to her feet. 'Thank you, George.'

'For what?' He smiled wryly. 'For my best efforts?'

'It's better than nothing. Maybe not on the Street, but in real life.' Someday she'd be back, she swore to herself.

If FitzGerald Associates had its good days and its bad days, Cameron Hightower had more bad nights than good ones. She came out of her time of private mourning determined to give the present a chance. Surrounded as she was by eligible, attractive men, she never lacked for escorts to take her to dinner, to the theatre, to bed, if she chose. There were always men calling her and yet she always felt alone. Her sexual experiences taught her the hardest lesson of all, and sometimes she wondered if something in her had died. With a sense of irony, she learned again how easy it was to respond sexually, and how rare was the act of loving – if loving meant the power of another to absorb her mind and senses the way Tim had.

Her life was now at the office.

'Don Eggert wants to talk to you,' Rosemary said.

'I don't want to talk to him. Say I'm out.'

'I've said that five times. You can't be out forever.'

'Why not? His divorce isn't final yet.'

'He says this time it's business not pleasure.'

'It wasn't pleasure the first time. Do you believe him?'

Rosemary said, 'No.' Then buzzed back. 'It is business. Smith, Baldwin is putting together a syndicate on Alcoa. Do you want to participate?'

'Tell him to ask Jake.'

'I did. He wants to talk to you.'

'All right. Put him on.'

'Listen!' Don sounded eager. 'Just because I'm a lousy tennis player is no reason not to have dinner with me.'

'I'm on a diet. What about Alcoa?'

'What about dinner?'

'This is not barter,' Cameron said pleasantly.

'Okay.' He surrendered. 'Do you want to circle a piece of the action?'

'Send Jake the papers. That's his department.'

'What about dinner? I thought we had a great night.'

'Don, I like you very much much. You're a nice man. But I'm really interested in someone.'

'Oh? You are? The lucky bastard!'

'I hope so.' Bye.'

She was telling the truth. Work had now become Cameron Hightower's lover. All her energies were focused on Fitz-Gerald Associates. When, in the following year, they lost a number of long-standing corporate clients, for reasons similar to those that had influenced Baxter Industries, she was not surprised. She was also prepared for Jake's agitation when the Associated Dentist Insurance Fund moved their discretionary account.

'That's thirty million dollars, Cameron, taking a walk.'

'It had to happen. They've always been jumpy. Even when Tim was alive.'

'This is the week that was,' Jake said. 'First Associated Dentists. Then Aston and now De Witt. It's like a bank run.'

'When did it happen?'

'Yesterday, when you were in Corpus Christi seeing those hotshot kids you dug up.' Jake was impatient. 'If you'd been here, you could have talked Old Man Aston out of it.'

'He called himself?'

'In person. You know Aston liked to schmooze with Tim. But I'm no schmooze artist. That's your number. You yakety-yak fine. Aston would have lapped it up.'

'What about De Witt?'

'Blair, their legal-beagle rat, called to say that the family felt, and he agreed, that it was in their best interests to have their portfolio managed by more experienced hands. He'll be sending over the documents by messenger this afternoon, and will have everything else picked up tomorrow. Maybe they'll send a Brink's truck with a few submachine guns.'

'Hang loose, Jake. We can't win 'em all.'

'We couldn't win De Witt. Aston was something else. It wouldn't have happened if you'd been at your desk.'

With her inveterate watchfulness, Cameron sensed that there was more to it than Jake had said. 'What's really bothering you? Besides De Witt and Aston?'

'You're bothering me.' Their eyes met. 'I wish you'd stop this new-issue junk.'

Cameron gave an inward start. 'It's the heart of the business.'

'I want us out of it.'

Cameron had known Tim's death would shake up many of FitzGerald Associates, clients. She had seen the shifts coming, and she had her spells of despair. What she counted on were those clients that stayed – and many did – to form the backbone of the business. But it was the new-issue market that would put FitzGerald Associates back in the first rank of Wall Street houses, back where it had been when Tim was alive. What she had not counted on at all was Jake's opposition.

'Look, Cameron, I want to talk cold turkey. About those kids from Texas.' The softness of his voice did not conceal the tension.

'They're not kids, Jake. Al is in his thirties, Josh is forty-three.'

'I know. And they've got a tiger by the tail. Five ocean-front restaurants. Two in Texas, two in Florida, one in South Carolina. All profitable.'

273

'They plan to ring the Sunbelt with restaurants on the ocean. They haven't even touched California,' Cameron said.

'And it's a multimillion-dollar proposition.'

'It will be once we take Oceana public.'

'I don't want to take Oceana public. Listen to me!' Jake pleaded.

'Why not? What's wrong with Oceana?'

'The fact is, we don't know a thing about those Texans. Those location sites they gave you, how do I know if they're any good? What do I know about real estate?' His objections were voiced too loudly.

'You know as much as you'll ever need to know.'

'And one of those cowboys is the chef. Maybe he can cook, but maybe his expertise is chuck wagons and camp fires? Now he's going to be a superchef for a chain of restaurants. Can he do it?'

'I wouldn't have spent a week in Corpus Christi if I didn't think so,' Cameron said. 'What are you trying to tell me?'

'I'm telling you that this is their first time in the big league.'

'There's always a first time. It's ours, too.'

Jake fiddled with his tie. Suddenly he bellowed again. 'I don't want to take Oceana public. I don't want to do any more new issues. I hate them!'

The friendship between Jake and her was real, but since they'd become joint managing partners, every time she'd brought in a new company for a public offering, Jake had fought her tooth and nail. He had all kinds of objections; to the managers, the products, the industry. In those few cases where she'd been able to force him, kicking and screaming, to agree, FitzGerald Associates had made good money on the offering. Still, Jake was not placated. Now his unwillingness was out in the open and stronger than she'd expected. It seemed only partially rational.

'Let's talk about it, Jake.'

'There's nothing to talk about. I won't have it. Not now!' Jake tried to control his voice.

'Tell me why you hate start-up situations.'

'I'm sorry I yelled,' Jake said.

'Forget it,' Cameron said. 'Just tell me why.'

'Because they're the riskiest end of the investment banking business. You can lose more money faster backing a new company than during one hour at a rigged crap game,' he snorted. 'And when you lose your investors' money, you lose them as clients. Pretty soon you run out of clients. Ah, Cameron, what's wrong with what we're doing now? We take a piece of the offerings with established companies. We take positions in all the syndicates we want to be in. We make a good living. And our clients make a little dough too.'

'But our name is always at the bottom of the tombstone,' Cameron pointed out.

'What's wrong with being at the bottom of a tombstone for Missouri Power and Light?'

Faced with the question, Cameron accepted that half of what Jake said was true – but only half. 'Eventually, they'll forget our name,' she said. 'Nothing stands still on the Street. You know that. We either grow or we get smaller.'

'But why start-ups? New issues?'

'That's where the money is.' She kept her eyes fixed on his face. 'We didn't raise sixty million dollars to take over FitzGerald Associates just to disappear into the woodwork, did we?'

Jake didn't answer at once. He searched the room with his eyes. Refusing to look at Cameron, he started to talk in a low voice. 'Look, I did the sewer work for Tim. You know that. I'm the man who checked the facts. And believe me, our Tim, truffle hound that he was, could bring back some real lemons. Phony people. Phony numbers. Phony everything.'

'Also lots of winners.'

'Also lots of winners. But you never knew. I don't want to

play that game again. It's one thing to crapshoot with other people's money, but it's another thing when it's your bare ass hanging out in the breeze.' He seemed to cringe at the sound of his own voice. 'You wanted to talk, so let me tell you a short, sad story.' He paused for a moment to gather his resolve. 'Once upon a time there was a company called the Jacob Stern Company. Jacob Stern was my grandfather.'

'I didn't know.' Cameron's voice was hushed.

'I know you didn't. But old-timers on the Street know. That's why I didn't want my name on the door.' He tried for moderation, but could not keep his voice steady. 'If you know the name of the company, you know the story.'

'The corn-oil scandal?'

'The corn-oil scandal.' He cleared his throat and then started to talk very rapidly to make certain that he actually finished. 'My father, Stanley, was a decent man. He played by the rules – more than less – and the damn fool expected other people to do the same. Give a little, sure. Take a little, sure. But no out-and-out highway robbery.'

'I remember.' As soon as she said it, Cameron knew she'd struck the wrong note. ' I mean, of course – '

'You mean that there are books on the subject. There sure are. One of the biggest scandals in Wall Street history.'

'We don't have to talk about it.'

'I know that. But I want you to understand why I'm quits on gambling. No more trying to pick a winner from the pack. I want to go with what I know, with people I know – like you. I've seen you in action. And with the companies I know – the establishment.' Jake was sweating. 'There's garbage the papers never got their hands on. Though why they didn't figure it out, I'll never know.'

'Go on,' Cameron said. Jake was not a man who talked about himself, and if he wanted to talk, it was her place to listen.

'Everybody knows about Jess Thornton. How he did

commodity trading in millions. Every day he rode a roller coaster, in wheat, wool, sugar, corn oil. He made and lost a fortune one week, then made it back the next.' Jake faltered. 'He did all his trading through the Jacob Stern Company. He was their biggest account. All on margin. Lots of margin in commodities.'

Cameron nodded for encouragement.

'And then one week all the commodities old Thorny was betting on went sour, very sour, and they didn't recover. Eventually, my father had to call in Thorny's collateral, to cover his margin account.'

'The barrels,' Cameron said.

'The barrels of corn oil in the fields of New Jersey. You read all about it.'

'The barrels were empty,' Cameron said softly.

'They were. And the Jacob Stern Company did not have enough equity to cover the loss. Old Thorny vanished in South America, and the Jacob Stern Company folded.' His entire body was rigid with tension. 'But as I told you at the beginning of this gay, glamorous story about the Street, there was something the newspapers overlooked. Investigative reporting had not yet come into full bloom.'

In spite of herself, Cameron asked, 'What was it?'

'The Siegal family. After my mother died, my father married Harriet Siegal.'

'The racing-form people?'

'The same. Easily worth a billion dollars. Moe Siegal wasn't just into racing forms. He was also big in real estate. He didn't own a building here and a building there. Not Moe. He owned a square block on lower Broadway. A block on 125th Street and Amsterdam Avenue. Also Eighty-eighth and Eighty-ninth Streets between First and Second Avenues. And more. Much more. Many of the buildings were slums. You might say he was a slumlord. And his three daughters had Moe's spirit, if not his brains.' Jake's eyes bored into

Cameron's. 'My father met the beautiful Harriet at a board dinner of Temple Emanu-El. She was husband hunting. Anyway, it was love at first peck. My father couldn't see the scars of the cosmetic surgery. So they married and lived happily ever after. And Harriet owned a two-acre orchid house where she raised rare orchids to strew around the house. Harriet's collection of jewels was written up in *Town and Country* magazine. And when Moe died, she and each child inherited over three hundred million dollars.' Jake was having trouble speaking. 'So my father's firm went into bankruptcy. Chapter Ten. The New York Stock Exchange set up a collection among member brokerage houses to make sure the public didn't lose any money – fifteen million and change.'

Cameron heard the pain as he spoke. A long-buried, decayed and rotten secret being aired.

'Did Harriet Siegal do anything to save her husband's company? Or reputation?' Jake's face was tortured. 'No. Although it would have been a pittance for her to do a rescue act. A mere fifteen million out of over three hundred million.' He coughed. 'Or the Siegal family could have chipped in about five million apiece, which was chicken feed to them, as an act of family feeling.' There was silence. 'Harriet didn't. None of them did. And three months later my father died of a massive coronary.'

Jake stood up. 'So now you know why I don't like taking unnecessary risks. Everything is risky. With start-up situations, you triple the risk. Likewise with new issues of small companies with no track records. I don't like people or business situations I don't know. Most people – even those you do know – can't be trusted. Why ask for more trouble than your allotted share?' He looked back from the door. 'I understand that this is my albatross, not yours. You'll keep on doing these new issues, and I'll keep on fighting you.' He walked out.

* * *

The busy, crowded months became a year. Two years. If Cameron's nights were empty of emotion, her days were full. By dint of hard work, tireless diligence, and imagination, Cameron moved FitzGerald Associates steadily upward. More and more she came to value coolness, reserve, and her own judgement. With Tim gone, she had no one to bounce ideas off – ideas that often ran contrary to conventional wisdom.

Lucia drove the Jeep expertly along the hillside, over the straight road that ran between rows of green vines. In the background were more hills covered with vines. Cameron always had a sense of homecoming when she was in California, perhaps because of childhood memeories. The oaks and pines, the streams, the birds, the fruit trees and sunlit valleys all seemed to welcome her. Even though her business trip had not been successful, Cameron was warmed by the sun and her meeting with the Manzone-Moskowitz family.

'But we'd make millions by going public,' Lucia complained.

'You're hardly poor now. And your father and uncles, and your husband too, do not need any more money.' Cameron gave a rueful smile. 'They're almost a vanishing breed. The entrepreneur who has a first-class, profitable business and wants to keep it in the family.'

'It is a big family,' Lucia admitted.

'A very big family. If the winery went public, the family might eventually lose control. And wine, as your father said, is not potato chips, which are easy to mass-produce. Wine making is individual. Your father doesn't want the Manzone name to go on a wine bottle that falls below his standards.'

'But he's been screaming like a stuck pig every time he has to borrow money from the bank at eighteen per cent interest. And they said it could go to twenty-one per cent.'

'It could. You know, Paul Volcker may be the first chairman

279

in the history of the Federal Reserve to have brought on a recession in a presidential election year. He was one of the reasons Carter lost the election. And now he tops it by totally destroying any chance for Reagan's supply-side economics to work.'

'He's a dream,' Lucia said. 'I'm sorry I got you out here on a wild-goose chase.'

'It wasn't wild. I saw you, Bill, the children. Your family, California –'

'Ah! That's it.' Lucia made a sudden association. 'I just thought of something I wanted to tell you. You know Momma's in the hospital with this tumour thing. It's benign, thank the Lord. But when I was visiting her the other day, I bumped into Harry Horn. Remember him?'

'The name rings a bell.' Cameron started to laugh. 'Bell-shaped and pear-shaped breasts.'

'After four children, melons please.' Lucia jutted her large breasts forward. 'The man with the liquid crystals. And the paint. Anyway, he has made it into an invention.'

'The paint?'

'No. It's some kind of a device that provides an early warning for the presence of tumours. He called it a Thermoscan. The hospital is testing it. Harry says he's still working on it, but it's nearly complete. I gave him your name, address, and telephone number and told him to look you up when he's ready. I said you were interested in new companies.'

'It depends on the invention. What's the name of his company?'

'I don't think he has one. I didn't ask. You can probably get him by calling the hospital.'

Cameron agreed that she probably would. But by the time she reached the airport, she'd decided against calling. If the invention worked, it would be a breakthrough. It might be as important as antibiotics. Either Harry Horn had a unique discovery, or he had nothing. It was pointless to contact him before he was ready.

After her return from the Manzone winery, Cameron watched the economic scenario unfolding. When the Dow hit 1,000, she started pulling all the monies of FitzGerald Associates – and those discretionary accounts that they still managed – out of the market. Paul Volcker seemed to her obsessional about raising interest rates to fight inflation. High interest rates would bring on a recession and the stock market would go to hell. The year 1982 might be a rerun of 1974.

'Cameron, what the hell are you doing?' Jake was fuming. 'Coz told me you've been liquidating our entire position. Are you nuts? We're up to our ass in cash. Over twelve million. How can we make money on cash? You want to trade dollars? For what? Lira?'

'I do not want to trade dollars. Not today!' Cameron snapped back and there was a startled moment while Jake waited for her to recover herself. 'We're in money-market funds.'

'What the hell are we doing in money-market funds? The Dow is over one thousand.'

'We're collecting interest. The Dow will be under one thousand by the time you buy Christmas presents.'

'Who told you?'

'I know.'

As irritated as he was, Jake was set back by Cameron's confidence. 'Why do you think that?'

'Because I read and I listen. The market is about to break. It could start a free-fall any day now.'

Jake glared at Cameron. He was divided by a need to trust her and a reluctance to buck the general market trend. 'I don't understand you. Maybe I'm stupid.'

'You don't have to understand me. The trading desk is my responsibility.'

281

'All right. Do as you please. Only heaven help us if you're wrong.'

'If heaven can.' Cameron appreciated Jake's concern. 'But I'm not wrong.'

Forbes, Business Week, Barron's, and all other business publications were filled with articles in a variety of tones – gloomy, appalled, righteous – on the collapse of the stock market. The Dow Jones average fell into the low 800s just in time for the holiday season.

Jake stuck his head in through the door of Cameron's office Wednesday morning before the long Thanksgiving weekend. He was not a man to admit that he was wrong, but he did have the grace to give her a twisted smile. 'You're one smart broad,' he said. 'You know what I mean?' Cameron knew what he meant. 'Yeah, a very smart broad.'

Lucia's monthly letter was full of family news. Mike had cut his first tooth, and after Bob and she had returned from celebrating in San Francisco, the result of the celebration was that she was pregnant again. If the new baby was a girl, she'd give her Cameron as a second name, since all her children's first names had to be saints' names to ease her parents' concern at her lapse from Catholicism. She hoped Cameron was happy and had found a man to occupy her at least one quarter as much as Wall Street, and –

'Faint!' Rosemary said as she entered the office wearing a stylish Calvin Klein wool dress and flashing a three-carat square-cut diamond on the third finger of her left hand.

Cameron put down Lucia's letter. 'I'm on the floor.' She laughed with an odd absence of surprise. Rosemary was long overdue. 'It's wonderful! Who's the lucky man?'

'Ronnie Haig. Remember him? He's retired.'

How could Cameron forget Ronnie Haig, who was one of the partners of Canfield, Weisman, and Haig? 'Retired' was a polite way to describe what happened when the board of governors of the New York Stock Exchange finally called a halt to their operations by suspending the firm indefinitely.

Cameron didn't know what to say. The hardest lesson she had had to learn on Wall Street was not to expect even her friends to have the same values as she did.

'No. He was never part of the operation.' Rosemary was vehement. 'Don't you remember?'

Cameron remembered that Ronnie Haig had the sanctimoniousness of a rich, ageing sinner. He had put up the original capital to fund the firm, but had never done a day's work in his life. He owned one per cent of GM stock, worth approximately $250 million. The specialist firm had just been one of his many toys. But if he hadn't known that something was happening, he was either very stupid or very canny. Yet, why push the matter with Rosemary? She would receive no thanks for hovering like a protective deity weighing the scales of justice. Anyway, she questioned her own motives. She had dreamed her own dreams of marriage and disliked intensely the throb of self-pity in her throat.

'Then congratulations are in order.' Cameron made a valiant effort to sound as cheerful as her words. She smothered the thought that of the three people in the office who she really cared about – each in a different way – two would now be gone. Tim was dead and Rosemary would be leaving. Only Jake remained, and if anything should happen to him, she'd be alone.

'The hell congratulations are in order,' Jake said from the doorway. 'You come to my office, Mrs Atherton.'

'Mr Stern, I do not take orders from anyone but Miss Hightower as long as I am in the employ of FitzGerald Associates.'

'You come with me.' Jake grabbed Rosemary's arm, yanking her squirming body out of Cameron's office and into his. Once there, he slammed the door.

283

'What the hell do you think you're doing?'

'I'm getting married, Mr Stern.'

'To that limp reed. If he can get it up once a month, you'll be in luck.'

'He can get it up.' Rosemary gave Jake a smug grin.

'And he's a horse's ass. Old enough to be my father. He's been married three times.'

'There's safety in numbers. He can afford the alimony.'

'You'd marry him for money?' Jake shouted.

'Dear heart, no one asked me to marry him for love.' A smile flickered over Rosemary's face. 'Not even you, you charmer.'

Jake glowered for a moment and then paced the floor. 'Damn it! Why do you have to get married?'

'It looks better for the children,' Rosemary teased him. 'You should be pleased. You're free of my proposals.'

Jake gave her a sharp look. 'You're immoral.'

'And you're a fool.' Rosemary was aware that Jake was bargaining with her. 'What are you offering that's better?'

'Nothing!'

'That's what I thought.' Rosemary started towards the door.

'You stay here!' Jake shouted.

'Why?'

Jake didn't answer. He was a confirmed bachelor, and now his long-entrenched view of himself was tugging at its moorings. Could a woman be trusted?

'Well, what are you offering?' Rosemary repeated.

'A little adultery?'

'No, dear, I am not a complete idiot.'

'Damn it!' Abruptly Jake saw himself in a new way. Something had changed in him. Something had been discovered. He couldn't let her go. They were a semi-established corporation. 'Damn it! Will you be faithful?'

'How do I know?'

'I'll kill you,' he roared.

'I'll be faithful.' Rosemary primly lowered her eyes.

'Or I'll kill you.'

'Or you'll kill me,' she agreed.

'Damn! Damn! Damn! Will you marry me?'

Rosemary raised a pair of glowing eyes. 'No. I will not.'

'You won't?'

'Not when you ask me like that.' Rosemary was enjoying her innings.

It was too much for Jake. 'What the hell do you want?' He tried to sound reasonable. 'Do you want a formal proposal, for Christ's sake?'

'Yes.'

So Jake got down on his knees and proposed.

When they told Cameron of their engagement, she gave them her truly enthusiastic congratulations. Privately, she thought with amusement, she wasn't losing a secretary, she was gaining a silent partner.

Cameron made all the wedding arrangements. The early June sky was in a bridal mood; the terrace of her apartment smelled rich and green from the variety of plants lining the walls and the breeze that drifted across from Central Park. The living and dining rooms had been cleared for sixty guests. There were ten tables, each seating six people. The china was nineteenth-century Staffordshire and the glasses, Baccarat. Seasonal flowers were arranged in tulip-shaped glass holders on each table. The name of each guest was engraved on place cards.

Cameron thought that Jake's Aunt Annette, in her Lagerfeld suit and her Harry Winston jewels, looked like an intelligent serpent poised to strike. Since Harriet had recently died in London, Annette represented the Siegal family at the wedding.

'I don't believe that woman's name is Atherton,' Annette

285

said. 'One of my friends is Lord Atherton. She's hardly related to him.' Her tone became mocking. 'It is true that responsible housekeepers are at a premium. Perhaps she cleans silver well, polishes crystal, dusts and scrubs efficiently. Although I would not use her to serve dinner.' She considered this. 'I can understand his needing a housekeeper. But to marry one?'

Geraldine intervened. 'Lord Atherton – Bunny – is an old friend of mine.'

'Is he?' Annette asked archly. 'And who are you?' She appraised Geraldine's Saint Laurent suit curiously.

'Geraldine Hightower.'

'Oh! Geraldine Hightower. Of course. I'm Annette Siegal.' She quickly climbed down off her high horse. 'What a pleasure to meet you. So you know Bunny.'

'Yes, and Bunny adores Rosemary.' Geraldine was smooth, feeling that insincerities were in order. 'She's a distant cousin. I believe she's an honourable.'

'Is she?' Annette Siegal had a dim feeling that Geraldine was making a fool out of her. Then she submitted. 'Well, I'm glad she's not a charwoman. One never knows with Jake. He has his father's blood.'

'Stanley Stern? I met him years ago. A bright, pleasant man.'

The two women stared at each other, Annette assessing Geraldine's far greater wealth and social position, and Geraldine thinking that Annette was a cartoon.

'You're more forgiving than I am.' Annette drew herself up in scorn. 'The man left a great deal to be desired.'

Geraldine's attention rested momentarily on the unmentioned scandal of the Jacob Stern Company. 'And so did your sister Harriet.' Her tone was only mildly sardonic.

Later, Cameron and Geraldine stood side by side on the terrace staring out into the long, late afternoon of Central

Park. The servants were still tidying up. Cameron was more weary than the occasion had demanded, and the paleness of her skin accented the gleam in her hair as though what was left of her vitality had all centred there. Her eyes had a faraway look, and her face was suffused with the pain of an animal that is hurt but cannot tell what is wrong.

'Try breathing deeply,' Geraldine said protectively.

'I am. Zen breathing.'

There was a long pause, neither wanting to speak about Tim. Now that the festivity was behind them, tears came to Cameron's eyes.

'I did catch the bouquet,' Cameron said.

'A good omen.'

'Or it would have fallen to the floor. It hit Annette first. She wouldn't touch it.'

'The wedding was superb. If they live happily ever after, it's to your credit.'

'No it's not. If they live happily ever after, it's up to them.'

Geraldine looked at her with kindness. 'You're as realistic as ever.'

'I've had no choice.'

'Some of us are so burdened. Or blessed. I've had no options either.'

Cameron picked up a note in Geraldine's voice that warned her. She faced the older woman. 'Are you all right?' Geraldine's face was imperturbable, and Cameron filled in the silence as though she had answered. 'You're not all right. What's wrong? Tell me.'

'I'm getting on. I'm old.'

'You are not.' Cameron's eyes surveyed her cousin with love, admiring her strong-boned face, her erect posture. People usually thought Geraldine much younger than she really was, but at that moment she looked close to her eighty-odd years. 'What is it?'

'Nothing.' But there was the merest dissent in her voice.

'It's not nothing, or you'd tell me.' Geraldine's determined composure did not reassure Cameron. Then it struck her. 'Your heart?'

'Maybe. I don't know.' Geraldine seemed relieved to have had it said and not to be the one to say it.

'What do you mean, you don't know?'

'I'm going into hospital for a checkup.'

'When?'

'Next Monday.'

Cameron felt awkward, uncertain of how much or how little to say. 'I'll drive down Monday evening.'

'Thank you. For worrying about me.'

'Of course I worry about you. Why shouldn't I?'

In the face of Cameron's concern, any effort at pretence seemed frivolous. 'Again, thank you.'

The women had a mute exchange and abruptly all glibness and fear and grief fell away, cleaned by the ordeal upon them. There was no time for anything but recognition. Cameron reached out for Geraldine's hands, and they clung together for seconds, sharing their future.

Cameron had hired a new secretary. She wasn't Rosemary, nobody ever could be, but she was intelligent, willing, and energetic. Her name was Della Halpern. Although she did not have Rosemary's memory, she had a mind that was at home with a filing system. She could find any information she was asked for in a matter of minutes. Late Monday afternoon she buzzed Cameron.

'There's a Dr Jordan on the telephone. He insists on speaking to you. I don't have his name on file, but he says he's calling from Princeton.'

Cameron's stomach turned over and her mouth went dry. 'Put him on.'

'Miss Hightower, I'm Dr Jordan, Miss Geraldine Hightower's personal physician. I'm at Princeton General Hospital.'

Only Cameron's ears heard his words. Her mind heard another voice. 'Yes?'

'Miss Hightower has asked for you. She's here in the hospital.'

Cameron caught her breath. 'What is it? What happened?' But she knew and what she knew was no small matter.

The doctor kept his medical detachment. 'She's had a mild heart attack, and she's in intensive care. I think we can pull her through.'

'I'll be there as soon as possible.' Cameron put the receiver down, and then she heard clearly the second voice in her brain, a voice out of the past – Lieutenant Shapiro. It was Tim, all over again.

Dr Jordan met her in the hospital lobby within minutes of being paged. One look at him told Cameron all she needed to know.

'She's dead?'

'Yes. She died about ten minutes ago.'

'Where is her room?' Cameron held herself steady.

'She's going to be moved – '

'I know. Please. Before she's moved.'

'But it's not – '

'I want to say good-bye.' Her words had such a childlike simplicity that Dr Jordan agreed. Cameron followed him down the long corridor to Geraldine's room.

Geraldine Hightower's will was read some weeks later. Cameron Hightower was named executor and Geraldine's three brothers were designated trustees. Hightower Farm and all its furnishings, all the mahogany, pine, and oak chairs, tables, sideboards, armoires – everything that had been accumulated by generations of Hightowers – was left to

Cameron Hightower. The remainder of Geraldine's estate, including the $2 million subordinated loan that Geraldine had made to FitzGerald Associates, reverted to the Hightower Trust. Geraldine recommended that the stock and bond portfolio of the trust be managed by Cameron Hightower and FitzGerald Associates. She also left Cameron an envelope containing a note from herself and a postcard.

There was a subsequent meeting in the library of Hightower Farm to discuss the matter. Cameron had been in the library hundreds of times since that first day – it now seemed eons ago – when the Hightower family had had its meeting to decide what to do with her. The colour, the feel, the texture of that time was more vivid to her than the present. The only difference between her relatives now and her relatives then was that they were older and, if possible, more cavalier than they had been before. Cameron sat in what had been Geraldine's chair and watched as they arranged themselves about the room.

Leo Hightower, looking plump in a dark suit, sank into a leather chair that sagged alarmingly under his weight. 'I'm glad that's over with,' he said with a sigh. 'Funerals are depressing.'

'Yes,' George Hightower said in a vaguely effeminate voice. 'It was most unfortunate that Geraldine died when she did. Monaco is in season. We had to send our regrets to the palace. I don't think the prince will ever forgive us.'

Raymond Hightower stood with his back against the unlit fireplace. 'I liked Gerry,' he remarked coolly. Raymond was taller and more burly than his brothers, but he would never have dared to call his sister 'Gerry' when she was alive.

It was painfully apparent to Cameron that no one in the library, except herself, mourned for Geraldine. If anything, they were sadly indifferent.

'I think we ought to tell you what we've decided, Cameron,' Raymond said.

'We do hope you'll understand and not make any difficulties.' Leo smiled at Cameron and George nodded.

'As the spokesman for the three of us,' Raymond continued, 'I would like you to know that we've come to a decision. A unanimous decision, I might add.' He smiled briefly. 'One that cannot be appealed. We question the wisdom of Geraldine's suggestion regarding the Hightower Trust. We find it not to our liking, so we have made other arrangements. We will not hand over the trust's stock and bond portfolio for you to manage.'

'Why not?' This was exactly what Cameron had expected, but she was prepared to go through the motions. 'FitzGerald Associates has the staff and the expertise to manage the trust.'

'It is possible that Timothy FitzGerald had the expertise.' Raymond was patient, if obviously bored. 'But the fact is, you do not. And as for your staff, we know nothing about them.'

'If Geraldine didn't believe I could manage it, she would not have recommended me. She had your best interests at heart.'

'That's true, but Geraldine was, shall we say, getting on in years. Time does take its toll on all of us. And she was devoted to you.' Leo stated this with mild surprise. 'I must say it shows a generosity of spirit – if a bit quixotic – that she left you The Farm. But if you'll forgive me for saying so, we do not believe you are capable of managing the few hundred million dollars we have in the market. Naturally there is no question as to our oil and real estate holdings. They run into the billions.' He paused to collect himself. 'But, my dear girl, even a few hundred million is not for anyone lacking in experience.'

'Who will manage the portfolio?' Cameron asked as a courtesy.

'Willums Smyth. You have heard of Willums?' Raymond said cheerfully. 'He's chairman of Dickenson, Smyth, and

Company. We've all known Willums since childhood. You may have known his granddaughter, Cassy Smyth, at Paddington. Willums will give us the personal attention we require.'

'Willums Smyth,' Leo echoed. 'Please don't press us, Cameron. We realize that this is a bitter disappointment to you, and we regret the necessity. But don't argue. Arguments cause unpleasantness. We wish you well with your enterprise. Since there is no need for further discussion, I believe this concludes the meeting.'

'It does not,' Raymond said with some irritation. 'There's the matter of the loan.'

'Oh, yes. The loan.' Leo was flustered. 'Is it necessary, Raymond?'

'It's necessary. We all agreed. You know that.' Raymond turned to Cameron and stared at her with cold detachment. 'Geraldine's loan to your company comes due in about eight months. The Hightower Trust expects payment in full.' His eyes narrowed. 'I assume you will be able to meet that obligation.'

'The money will be repaid on time,' Cameron replied with equal coldness.

After her relatives had left, Cameron considered the meeting and the pretentious naïveté of her Hightower cousins. They did not even know what was public information; that Harrison, Smyth, and Company was about to be acquired by the Prudential Insurance Company. And their dear chum, Willums, who would give them special attention, was due to retire to Palm Beach. They would end up dealing with strangers far less astute and conscientious than she. But Geraldine was gone, and her brothers free to do as they wished. It was fortunate that only a portion of the Hightower Trust's holdings was in the stock market.

Cameron thought carefully about Raymond's statement

that they would pull the trust's money out of the firm. FitzGerald Associates could not afford to lose that much capital. There was only one thing for her to do. Like it or not – and the fact was she hated the idea – she would have to mortgage Hightower Farm and use that money to replace the trust's funds. It was not in Cameron's nature to wonder why Geraldine had not taken care of the loan in her will. She hadn't, and leaving her Hightower Farm – the land she loved more than any place in the world – was more than enough for her.

She looked at Geraldine's note. There were a few lines of poetry enclosed.

> When I am dead my dearest,
> Sing no sad songs for me;
> Plant thou no roses at my head,
> Nor shady cypress tree.
> Be the green grass above me
> With showers and dewdrops wet;
> And if thou wilt, remember
> And if thou wilt, forget.

As if she could ever forget Geraldine. Then she recalled the note attached to the postcard. 'When this card arrived, you were still a student at Paddington. Nothing followed. So I saw no reason to add to your grief, since there was no return address and no hope offered.'

The postcard was scribbled in a bold scrawl in green ink. 'Greetings from Paris! Nineveh next stop!' It was signed by Cyrus.

Cameron stared at the card and sat with her chin in her hand, brooding over the past and Geraldine's decision. She felt a twinge of the old pain and brushed it aside. She went to her desk in her room on the second floor and found the old, cracked leather album. Slowly she opened the album and looked at the clippings about Cyrus. She added the postcard to the collection.

16

Once having heard the story of the Jacob Stern Company, Cameron understood the source of the differences between Jake and herself. They were almost negative and positive poles. Jake's mind was neither agile nor brave, and he shied away from risk. It wasn't his caution that Cameron objected to most; that was a necessary and useful quality. It was the fact that caution was almost the only response in his repertoire. His mind wore blinkers to protect him from new ideas, and as a result, he had no judgement. In a world where every idea seemed equally perilous, he could not select among the perils.

She stared at the papers he had given her to read, then glanced at him across the desk from her, searching for the right words. But she could have spared herself the effort. He had become prepared to do battle.

'Cameron, don't argue. You know old Jake. Usually I hate start-up situations.' His enthusiasm was extravagant. 'But not this time. All my old buddies are making fortunes in small computer companies. It's the wave of the future. And one of them just tipped me off on Weldyne. They're looking for money. We could take them public.'

'No,' Cameron stated, brisk but resigned.

'Why not? What's the matter with our Warrior Woman? You running scared?' He said this more with surprise than sarcasm. 'It's perfect! All my pals – Gilbert, Russell, Kane, Golden – are making fortunes in the new-issue market.'

'We've made money on new issues, too.' Cameron reminded him.

'Yeah. You did it over my dead body.'

'Bleeding from every pore,' Cameron said gently.

The reproach brought the righteousness wide awake in Jake. 'Sure, I've been wrong. But I've also been right. You need me to stop you from building castles in the air.'

'Or along the ocean?' Cameron remarked casually.

'I said I've been wrong. Yes, Oceana, if you want to make a for instance. I know it's now listed on the Amex.'

'And soon on the Big Board.'

'True.' He became deferential. 'Maybe I've seen the light at last. Weldyne, a small computer company – '

'No! You know that IBM recently settled their case with the antitrust division of the government.' This time Jake had the sense to wait for her to continue. 'All those small companies are like the pilot fish that are parasites around a whale. The whale is IBM – or Big Blue, as the in folks call it. Now that Big Blue is clear of legal barnacles, it's going to turn like a whale, and the waves it makes will swamp most of those small computer companies.'

'But Gilbert? Russell? Kane? They've made fortunes.'

'And so have Harper and Dowles and all the brokers and brokerage houses that tout those stocks. Even some investors have made money.'

Jake screwed up his face, perplexed. 'That's what I mean. You see it, too.'

'*Some* of the investors have made money. A very small percentage. But not the majority. The majority won't get out in time. They don't know the time is now, *before* Big Blue makes a wave. So we will not fund your computer boys, Jake. It would be a bad speculation, and we do our best not to speculate with other people's money. OPM – you've heard the term?'

Suddenly Jake was in a hurry to leave, saying he had some phone calls to make and giving Cameron a queer embarrassed glance.

Impatient with Jake and with the way she'd handled him,

Cameron slipped on her jacket. Her dental appointment was at eleven. As she opened the door, she heard Della on the phone, her tone distracted, staving off boredom. 'I'm sorry. She's not available at the moment. You can give me a message . . . Yes, she will be in this afternoon, Mr Miller, but – '

Something went '*Ping!*' 'Mr Miller? What Mr Miller?' Cameron asked. 'Who are you speaking to?'

Della put her hand over the phone. 'He says he's an old friend, but he's never called before.' When she saw the expression on Cameron's face, she stopped.

'Is his name Byron Miller?' Della nodded. Cameron grabbed the receiver. 'Byron!'

She was surprised by her feeling of relief at hearing Byron's voice. It was deeper than she remembered but just as buoyant. She'd be delighted to see him that afternoon.

'So, look, Cameron, I'm not asking you for something for nothing.' Byron was still the same animated Byron.

Cameron thought how little we all change. When is the die cast? When are we moulded? Today, Byron seemed to be a highly respected, very bright man. Gone were the sneakers and the sweat shirt, the jeans, the windbreaker. His hair was combed, his business suit pressed, his loafers shined. He looked like another Byron. But he was still the same Byron, an authority on Wall Street.

'. . . and so the minute I spotted you in *Fortune*, I said to myself, "Hooray for Cameron Hightower, lady tycoon!" There's a woman who doesn't have to learn the hard way, from experience. She can learn from other people's mistakes. She doesn't have to do the corporate number to find out it's not for her.'

'Thanks to you,' Cameron insisted in her most sincere tone.

'You betcha,' Byron said. 'And I'm not in the least shy about taking credit. Look at what Byron Miller hath wrought.'

296

Cameron was more than generous with her praise. In fact, she was so generous that Byron wondered if she might be overdoing it. Besides, he had the feeling that her kind of ability would have found a way without him, and he said so. When that was made clear, he told her about Reliance Pharmaceuticals.

'As a senior chemist, meticulous in my reports on the new antioxidant additive for pickles, I make a quick forty thou a year. I'm not in line to be a division manager – too young. Reliance promotes on seniority. Merit is okay, but how often you've eaten in the company cafeteria is what makes it for you. That's fine for those who love cafeteria cooking, but it does a number on my enthusiasm. I'm not married, with a wife and kids to support. And I have this juicy morsel to trade – '

'You don't have to trade with me.'

'I don't want a freebie, out of the goodness of your heart.' Byron gave a forced laugh. 'You know what I mean.'

'How did you know we were looking for someone?'

'On Saturdays I take a joy ride to Wall and Broad and put my ear to the pavement.' Cameron's expression told him to stop the clowning. 'Okay, I have a friend, a young woman friend who writes PR for Goldman Sachs, and she knows my heart belongs to Wall Street. She gossips in the best circles and is a mine of information. She's offered sex but I'm holding out for marriage.' Byron locked his fingers together and caught his breath. 'Well, anyway, she keeps me posted. But until recently I wasn't ready to make the move.'

'But you're ready now?' Cameron asked encouragingly, adding to herself, in fact you want to make the move so badly you can taste it.

'Yes. Everything's fallen into place. You have an opening, and I'm qualified. I've a master's in organic chemistry. An MBA from Rutgers. Night school kept me off the streets.

297

Furthermore, I come bearing gifts: Reliance Pharmaceuticals – not the biggest, but big enough.'

'Eight hundred million. A solid operation,' Cameron said, wondering what Byron knew that she didn't.

'Eight hundred million. And the chairman has the jitters. His digestion is shot.'

'B. J. Vance is nervous?' Cameron cocked an eyebrow.

'B. J. is as nervous as a cat. And guess who he's mad at?' Byron lowered his voice to a conspiratorial whisper.

'Morgan Stanley.' It was an easy connection for Cameron.

'Bull's-eye!'

'Why?'

'Why not? Why the hell break your balls to become chairman if you can't flex your muscles once in a while.' Byron dropped into sotto voce again. 'His glorious chairmanship doesn't like what Morgan Stanley didn't do with the last Reliance bond offering.'

'What didn't they do?'

'They didn't meet his standards. The interest Reliance pays on the bonds is too high. And the chairman's brother-in-law who handles the account is retiring.' Then Byron added, as though he were saying the unsayable, 'B. J.'s ego is on the line.'

'His ego?'

'B. J. thinks now he'll get short shrift because he's not Bristol-Myers, or Warner-Lambert.' He stopped to bow to Cameron's superior wisdom. 'Do you think he will?'

'What I think doesn't matter,' Cameron said. 'It's what B. J. Vance thinks.'

This reminded Byron that although Cameron was an old friend, she was also a professional. 'Right,' he said earnestly. 'And naturally you want to know how I know all this?'

Cameron did.

'I have a friend who works in the treasurer's office. The secretary's assistant.' Byron coloured slightly. 'Well, you know. A bachelor gets around almost as much as a bachelor girl. She told me Vance has been having meetings with the treasurer about Morgan Stanley and whether Morgan Stanley has the proper respect.'

Cameron was listening, but with the portion of her mind that never rested, she was thinking about Byron working for FitzGerald Associates. She handpicked her security analysts. They had to know more than just the industry in which they specialized. Nor was it enough that they could read a balance sheet upside down and spot the inconsistencies. They had to be people watchers, too. Looking for shoulder tensions, backaches. They had to be doubtful, suspicious – yet not too cynical.

'You know the industry?'

'Ask me anything.'

Some instinct advised Cameron to ask instead, 'How is your father?'

'He's dead.'

'I'm sorry. And your mother?'

'Like all mothers, she complains.' Byron was growing restless. He gave Cameron an anxious glance. 'Look, I don't want any charitable donations to guarantee your place in heaven.'

A softening came over Cameron's face. She was confident Byron's credentials were as he'd claimed. She knew nothing of his history except that his father was dead, and she had the distinct impression that he was relieved about that. She was tempted to ask, 'When did he die?' because she had a hunch that his death had something to do with Byron's finally contacting her. But she decided not to ask.

'No charity. You're hired,' she said at last. 'I want you to meet my partner, Jake Stern.'

Jake agreed to hire Byron partially because Cameron had known him years ago and partially because Byron had given

299

the firm a solid lead. Reliance Pharmaceuticals was a client worth having. Considering both facts, he decided that $40,000 a year wasn't too much for a senior analyst of the chemical and pharmaceutical industries.

Leon Beckett strode into Cameron's office with his usual swagger, looking much as she remembered: heavy with a little grey in his moustache. In Manhattan he seemed like the tourist he was; his suit was too beige for March, and his raincoat too light.

'You run this whole shop!' He made a sweeping gesture with his arms, his face full of too blatant admiration. 'Two floors in this building! That's not granola.'

Cameron wondered if he'd ask how much rent they paid per square foot.

'And you're young enough to be my daughter. That is, if Gilda and I – she was my first – had had a child. Instead of a Merce.' His appreciative eyes ran over her body. 'I am impressed.'

'I'm only one of two managing partners. Jake Stern is the other.'

'The hell you say! My information tells me you're the man they salute. Or woman.' He chuckled ingratiatingly.

Cameron glanced at the latest annual report of Beckett Pharmaceuticals. 'Your company has made progress.' Her tone became excessively polite to hide the irritation she felt for those who flattered her for their own purposes. Anyone less dense than Beckett would have sensed her impatience. 'Revenues have more than doubled in the last nine years. You're netting eight per cent on gross.'

'Up from six per cent, young lady.'

'Due to a change in accounting practices.' She could almost hear Tim's caustic comment, 'A little cosmetic accounting.' Beckett was crude, he was uneducated, he was greedy; but a native shrewdness had put him far ahead of

300

men whose business successes were limited by their lack of total commitment to making money.

'Why not cosmetic accounting?' Beckett was offended. 'Women do it every day. A little eye shadow here, mascara there, lip gloss. So why not a little cosmetic bookkeeping? It makes the best of the company's good points. And it's strictly legal. Like eye shadow.'

'It is legal, and it does make your profits look good,' Cameron had to agree.

'Of course! Or else the price of the stock would be nowhere. It's thirty and a quarter now. But thirty and a quarter is not good enough. Not for me. The company has to grow. New factory space. More personnel. You understand that?'

Cameron understood. Guts and determination had always fascinated her, still did, even though seeing the qualities carried to an extreme in Beckett went against her nature. But the fact was that she could make Beckett's case even better than he had – without the change in accounting principles.

'How many shares do you want to see?' she asked.

'Same as the last time, one million. But they're worth more now.' He was smug. 'At the market price – thirty, thirty-one – they should bring . . .'

Cameron waited while he pretended to do the grade-school arithmetic that he must have done a hundred times before.

'To pick a round number, I would like FitzGerald Associates to raise thirty million dollars,' Leon said nonchalantly.

Cameron did not say, thirty times one equals thirty, and when you add zeros, it comes to thirty million. Instead she asked, 'For the company? For expansion?'

Having been impressed with Cameron, Beckett was now impressed with himself. 'Fifteen million for the company. To fund our new product.'

'I see. And fifteen million for you.'

301

'You got it. Fifteen million for little old Leon. Why not? Five hundred thousand of the million shares you'll be offering will be mine.' He was thoroughly satisfied with himself. 'A man has to live. Mr Thin – that's the working name of the new product because it thins blood – prevents clotting. Mr Thin, if you'll pardon the pun' – he laughed – 'will do the hearts of the stockholders good. Aside from the reduction of deaths after a heart attack, it will keep the stock moving up, and that's very good for a stockholder's heart.'

Thinking of the product, Cameron hoped Beckett was accurate. She knew he was prone to self-serving exaggeration. 'It works?'

'Perfected to perfectamente! We are now a two-product company. And this second one's a real biggie.'

'How long will it take to get FDA approval?'

'That's just a formality. I've lain an inside track there. Say about six months.'

'But you want the stock sold before you get the approvals?'

'You better believe it. I have to plan for expansion. And I've exes aplenty. I just dumped my sixth. She wasn't up to me.'

'I'm sorry,' Cameron said for lack of anything else to say. She smiled inwardly. Clearly, the affair between Leon Beckett and Leon Beckett was the only one that mattered.

'I'm not. Okay. When do we get started on the placement?' Beckett's moustache beamed at her.

'I have to have the clinicals analysed.'

'Naturally.' Leon was thrown slightly off stride. 'How long will that take?'

'Three weeks. Maybe a month.' While Leon thought this over, Della buzzed her. 'Good,' Cameron said. 'Send him in.' As she hung up, Byron Miller opened the door.

'Hello, Byron. I want you to meet Leon Beckett.' She nodded towards Leon. 'Leon, this is Byron Miller. He'll be reviewing the material you sent us. Byron is our analyst in the pharmaceutical industry.'

'How do you do, Mr Beckett.'

Beckett heaved himself from his chair, and the men shook hands. 'Hi,' Beckett said after a long silent moment. He had a way of not looking at men he did not consider his equal that could, if the men were sensitive, be intimidating. Disturbing as this was to Byron's self-esteem, it gave him the advantage of observing, unobserved, as Beckett resumed his speech to Cameron about the clinicals.

But Cameron was having none of it, and she referred all Beckett's comments to Byron, forcing Beckett to give the younger man serious attention. A curious appraisal flashed between them as each recognized something of himself in the other. They were both born salesmen. Although Leon was irritated at finding himself dealing with a young man he did not employ, he accepted that business was business. This was all part of the show. Once the presentation was concluded and Byron left, Leon came up with a new theme.

'How about dinner with a client while the client's still in town, Cameron? Show me a good restaurant. New York claims them all.'

It was a moment for tact, and then Cameron remembered that it was the first Beckett stock offering that had brought Tim and her together. For that reason, if nothing else, she owed him the courtesy of a social evening.

'Of course,' she said. 'Tomorrow? At seven?'

They spent the evening at the Oak Room at the Plaza. It had been one of Tim's favourite restaurants. 'The neighbourhood joint,' he had called it. He liked the big armchairs and comfortable atmosphere of an older New York and the international flavour of the men and women who floated through the room.

Cameron and Leon discussed Leon's business, Leon's

prowess as a golfer, Leon's expertise on skis, and Leon's political ambitions when he had enough millions. Cameron listened patiently to the blasts of self-approval, saying, 'I see,' and 'Oh, yes,' and once, feeling him urging her to applaud, she said, 'Really? How clever of you.' Then, as though preordained, Leon came to Leon's high level of sexuality.

'I may be shorter than you, Cameron, but I'm bigger than big in bed.' His expression became intimate. 'Want to try me? I'll give Tim's ghost a run for his money.'

Cameron sat quietly, giving off no scent of her distaste. Finally she said, 'Leon, I appreciate the compliment, but I never mix business with pleasure.'

'Horseshit!'

Cameron bent her head. If necessary, she'd give up Leon Beckett as a client. She sipped her coffee. 'I mean it,' she said.

In the cab to her apartment, Leon insisted on being invited up for a nightcap. He was not a man to leave well enough alone, and Cameron resigned herself; she might as well get it over with.

Seated in her living room, over brandy, Leon Beckett put his offer on the table. 'Look, Cameron, we're business associates. You're young enough. Beautiful enough. You're not eighteen, but your flesh is still firm. I need a change of pace. Six young wives is too many. I ought to marry and stay married. So how about it?'

The ridiculousness of the speech reached Cameron through a thickening haze of irritation. There were times – and this was one of them – when she wished she were a man. A female client was unlikely to suggest to her investment banker that he marry her. Or go to bed with her. Controlling her anger, she said, 'Again you compliment me too much.'

'Cut it out. We're a matched pair. Tim's dead. You're alone. Sure, you have lovers, but they're not me. I'll be your husband.'

304

'You're proposing marriage?' she asked, hoping that the words "proposing" and "marriage" might bring him to his senses. Then she realized she'd made a tactical error. No man with six ex-wives would flinch at the words.

'That's what I'm doing. I'm proposing marriage. What an old-fashioned phrase. Anyway, as I said, you're alone. I'm great in the sack, and I'll bet you are, too. You move FitzGerald Associates to San Francisco, and I go on inventing new products.' Raising his hand, he silenced Cameron's objections. 'You raise the money for the new products. Beckett Pharmaceuticals becomes another Baxter Travenol. We'll make millions. Hundreds of millions.'

'Thank you, Leon, but no.'

'You don't mean that.' Leon's porpoiselike eyes surveyed every curve of her body. 'You need me. You should have kids. And we'll have them. I have two now – they're brats – but our kid would be a genius.' He put his glass on the side table and walked over to her, quite unruffled. 'We'd found a dynasty, Cameron. A dynasty! Put your glass down, I want to kiss you.'

'Please, Leon,' Cameron said, holding her glass between them.

'You don't have to be shy with me. I know you're no plaster saint.'

Cameron made an inspired confession in a halting voice. 'Leon . . . I . . . well . . . You see, I can't have children. We can't found a dynasty.'

Leon stood very straight, the greed and excitement gone from his face. 'You can't? Why not?'

'An accident some years ago.'

'Oh,' Leon said. He stared at her, half with disbelief, half with contempt. What healthy woman would say such a thing unless it was true? If she had said she didn't want children, he could have convinced her. But this! He stepped back. 'I apologize, Cameron.' A considerable prize had been

305

arbitrarily snatched from him and he wanted to let fly. But she was still his investment banker so he had to maintain his composure.

Cameron did her best to look contrite, even dismayed.

'Forget everything I said.' Leon tried to make amends. 'I drank too much wine. And then the brandy. You know how it is.' He headed for the door.

Three weeks later Byron went over the Beckett Pharmaceutical clinicals with Cameron.

'The FDA won't license Mr Thin,' Byron said. 'There are side effects. It does thin the blood but continuous use in animals shows neurological damage. There's severe sensory dysfunction, like the inability to coordinate voluntary muscular movements.'

'You mean?'

'Yeah. It needs a lot more work and new clinicals. You know some biology, don't you?' Cameron nodded. 'Then let me explain what happens and show you the lab reports.'

Leon Beckett was indignant. What did she mean, FitzGerald Associates would not do the stock offering? He couldn't believe it. He flew to New York to argue with Cameron, disguising his real fury behind his salesman's talent for persuasion.

'Cameron, I can't believe that a professional of your stature would make such a mistake. The FDA will approve the drug.'

'If they do, then we're wrong,' Cameron said.

'Who is this idiot, Byron Miller? What does he know about a complex molecule like crystalline warfarin sodium?' He added, sarcastically, 'I'm referring to Mr Thin.'

'You met him. Our security analyst in pharmaceuticals. He has a background in chemistry.'

Leon remembered Byron the salesman. 'You let that clown make a decision like that for FitzGerald Associates?'

'That's one of the things he was hired to do.'

Abruptly, Beckett made an oblique connection. 'You're sleeping with that idiot.'

Cameron did not think the remark warranted an answer. It was no longer possible to pay him the compliment of anger.

'There's no other explanation,' he ranted. The idea infuriated him, but when he recovered his composure, he took it as a narrow escape: proof positive of female incompetence. 'I'm sorry for you, Cameron. You're allowing your sex life to get in the way of your business judgement. Like any ordinary woman, like one of my exes.' That was his parting shot.

Jake had a similar reaction. 'Why the hell did you do it? Beckett was Tim's client. We've made a bundle on the Beckett stock. And it's rising. It closed at thirty-three yesterday. Beckett's been leaking Mr Thin all over the Street. Mr Thin reduces the chance of having a heart attack.'

'The FDA won't approve it.'

'He says they will.'

'Byron and I went over the lab reports. They won't.'

'Byron!' Jake was irate. 'What the fuck does he know?'

'If he doesn't know, why did we hire him?' Cameron asked. 'Besides, I know. We'll start getting rid of our Beckett stock at the end of next month. The FDA report should be issued in six months. Then watch what happens. Stop worrying, Jake. When the report comes out, Beckett Pharmaceutical stock will drop like a lead balloon. And you'll have a grandstand seat to enjoy the show.'

Byron had dinner at one of his favourite restaurants, a small Hungarian hole-in-the-wall in the west eighties. The owner was the chef, his daughters were the two waitresses and his wife sat behind the cash register. There were ten small tables. The room, for it really was not much more than a room, was always full at dinnertime. The price was right, and the goulash tender and tasty. This night, Byron couldn't taste the food, so it didn't matter where he ate.

When the discipline of eating was over, he ambled home, took off his shoes, stretched out on his bed, and thought about Leon Beckett . . . which was the same as thinking about himself. In a surge of memory, he began again the long trek down the corridors of the past, to stare at the various images of his father on those Sunday afternoons in Central Park. He recalled again the determined voice, the calculated silences, and then heard the litany. 'It's the biggest con game in the world, son. The biggest!' The mouth was opening and closing against his ear. So much of him was in turmoil, it was no longer possible for him to lie to himself. His father had been his model, his teacher, his advocate for a certain kind of success. Promoting a company, or a product, making it big on the stock, owning it at 10 cents a share and selling it to the public at $5 or $15 a share. Those things did happen.

Forbes had done an article on Leon Beckett, who had found a product, bought it, and built a company. When Beckett was forty, Tim FitzGerald took the company public. Beckett made $10 million then, and now he had his hand out again, asking for $30 million – $15 million for himself. Fifteen million dollars! Whew! Byron knew he could think circles around Leon Beckett. The damn fool didn't even know that his new product wouldn't be licensed. But bigger fools on Wall Street would give him the money. Fifteen million dollars for Leon Beckett.

Byron went to his desk. He stood still and stared at the grey ledger containing a record of his market trades. He had started with $5,000 six months ago, and as of today, he had made over 30 per cent on the money. Much better than the mutual funds did, but still chicken feed. Unless he made a lucky buy in the new-issue market, it would take decades before he made enough money to support his mother and to live the kind of life he dreamed of, maybe buy a partnership in FitzGerald Associates. But he would not think of Cameron.

Byron shut his eyes as all the frights and terrors that whirled about him constantly grew louder. He heard his father say, 'It's the only way to make a big buck, son.' And Leon Beckett was the living proof it could be done. That's what his father had been reaching for, the big win. Byron laughed, semihysterically, trying to drown out the fear. 'No!' he shouted to the empty room. 'That's not for me.' Then he added to himself, thank the Lord it wasn't being offered.

In June, three months later, a tombstone appeared in *The Wall Street Journal*. Wallace and Royce had sold one million shares in Beckett Pharmaceutical stock at $33 a share. Through the week the stock had a nice zigzag upward curve to reach 36¼. Jake read the tombstone and wished he'd never seen Byron Miller. Byron read the tombstone and had some bad nights. Wallace and Royce had made a hell of a commission from the sale of Beckett Pharmaceutical stock, a commission FitzGerald could have made – over $1 million. Was he wrong? he asked himself. Beckett had called the product Mr Thin. Suppose Mr Thin turned out to be Mr Clean? Suppose the FDA gave it a clean bill of health? Byron could feel the sweat on his sheets.

The plump little man slumped on the bed in his hotel room on the West Side of Manhattan. The telephone receiver was so fixed to his ear it might have created a vacuum. His eyes were red rimmed, and his plump cheeks drawn with fatigue lines. His shirt collar was frayed and open, his tie askew, and his thinning grey hair uncombed.

'Miss Halpern?' His voice revealed more than his words. He was a man who had regularly been kicked, and pleading was second nature. 'When will Miss Hightower return?'

'She's expected next Wednesday.' Della Halpern was brisk. 'I'm sorry I can't help you.'

It was a question of setting up an appointment to see Cameron Hightower, Harry Horn explained. In his meekest voice he added that he'd been told by Lucia Moskowitz that Miss Hightower would be interested in his invention.

Della relented somewhat at the mention of the Moskowitz name.

'I didn't plan to stay later than Tuesday morning.' There was no use in saying that he couldn't afford to stay another day. 'If she comes back before then . . .?'

'I doubt that she will, but I'll give her your message. Do you want to leave your number?'

'No. I'll call back. Thank you,' he said. 'Thank you very much.'

Harry Horn hung up the phone, stumbled to his feet, and went to the window. There was nothing to see but the windows of another room. It made no difference. All he could see was his mistake. Like a fool he'd counted on seeing her. Why hadn't it occurred to him to write her first? Why? Because he was so concentrated on his work that he could think of nothing else. That was why he was no good as a businessman. Business had to do with things like money, and money didn't interest him. Science had to do with life. He sighed, as if there were someone in the room to listen to him. He would have to call every Wall Street firm in the telephone book. But who could he ask for? He was just wise enough to know that he ought to go downstairs and have a cup of coffee first. He was in no state to deal with any more disappointments, and he had to prepare for his lecture on Monday.

Just before the stock market closed on Friday, news came across the tape that was of passing interest to Herbert Coz. The good or bad fortunes of every stock of every company did not interest him, but this company was one that Tim

310

FitzGerald had originally taken public, and Cameron High-tower had refused to handle its new stock offering. In fact, at her instructions, he'd liquidated their entire holdings of Beckett Pharmaceutical stock. Good for her, Coz thought. 'The FDA reject Beckett Pharmaceutical's application to market commercially its antiblood-clotting drug. Further testing is needed for possible side effects.' Beckett Pharmaceuticals would hit the silk.

Byron Miller slept like a baby that night.

17

Cameron returned from Seattle late Monday afternoon. One look at the unfinished construction of the Washington State nuclear power plants was enough. She wouldn't touch the bonds. On a hunch, she called Byron at the office.

'You're not supposed to be back until Wednesday,' he said.

'Think of this as Wednesday. Have you any plans for the evening?'

'No,' he lied.

'This is the night for the Hall of Science and Industry lecture. Who knows what undiscovered Edisons are waiting for us? Want to break bread with me at the Hungry Plate?'

'Sure. I was going to the hall anyway.' He had planned to go with Wanda, a new girlfriend.

'See you at seven.'

At the hall on East Twentieth Street, a small, plump man stood on the stage. The audience was a motley assortment of Village characters who were interested in poetry, art, science; of itinerant chemists and physicists; of science teachers, science addicts, science faddists. But where were the industry people? Cameron wondered. Business was missing, as was Wall Street. The hall was optimistically misnamed.

A small, plump man held up what looked like three strips of black plastic. 'These strips are impregnated with liquid crystals,' he said. 'Liquid crystals exist in nature and have remarkable qualities. They change colour in response to heat.' Harry Horn stepped down from the platform and distributed the strips to the audience. Byron reached for one.

After he returned to the platform, Horn said, 'Wrap the strips around your wrist like a watchband. What do you see?'

'I see red and blue lines running up and down,' a man said.

'Jesus! I must be freezing to death,' a girl said. 'The thing is turning blue.' Another voice agreed.

'What does it mean?' Byron asked.

'That's normal,' Horn replied.

'It's very colourful,' a woman said. 'But what is it? A toy?'

Everyone tittered, but on the subject of liquid crystals, Harry Horn was unflappable. 'Liquid crystal is a wonderful discovery that should be used in the service of mankind.' His eyes sparkled. 'They are, as I said, responsive to heat. People think of red as hot and blue as cold, but liquid crystals reverse the sequence. Red is cold, blue is hot. The colours go from red to orange to green to aqua to blue, showing heat variations. And they do this with great accuracy. The reason the strip turned blue is because the veins carrying blood are close to the surface of your wrist, and blood makes the skin warm.'

'Jazzy, but what do you do with it? Use it for art? Or fashion?' one person asked.

'I've already done what I want to do with it,' Horn said. 'But first . . .' He glanced around the room. 'I see there's a small boy in the audience.' He smiled at the girl in jeans sitting next to the child. He had already given her a strip of liquid crystal plastic. 'Young woman, are you the child's mother?'

'I'm not his daughter.' She laughed.

'Would you mind placing the strip of liquid crystals on the child's forehead?' She did as Horn asked and the strip turned a faint rose. 'Oh! He has a fever! Red is hot!' She looked confused. 'No. You said red is cold.'

'Red is cool. Blue is hot. His temperature is normal.'

313

The woman grinned. 'Can I keep this? I'll use it as a thermometer.'

Horn nodded. 'Sure. That's only one of the uses of liquid crystals. Disposable thermometers. More accurate than touching your child's head with your hand.' He gave the audience a look of utmost seriousness. 'Now I'll show you something that's more than a convenience device. I've devoted twenty years of my life working on it, and I've finally achieved something worth all my time and effort.'

Horn walked to the rear of the platform and pulled down a screen. He signalled to a boy in the rear of the hall who had set up a table and a slide projector. The boy dimmed the lights and placed a slide in the projector. A pair of women's breasts encased in a brassiere-like contrivance with swirling colours ranging from bright blues to soft green and rose appeared on the screen.

Horn used a long pointer.

'What you are seeing are the breasts of a healthy woman wearing what I call a Thermoscan, made of liquid crystals. You'll notice that the colour on each breast is symmetrical. And there are no hot spots.'

A man called out, his voice full of scorn, 'It's a bra. Women burn bras.'

Harry Horn shook his head. 'It is not a brassière. It's a Thermoscan. When women find out what it does, they won't burn them. Just watch.'

The next slide showed a pair of breasts covered by a series of small coloured circles. Each circle had a dark blue centre.

'You can easily see the circles. Blue is a hot spot. This woman had a number of cysts. They were detected by my liquid-crystal Thermoscan a year before palpation found anything. Perhaps a mammogram would have picked them up, but the woman had no reason to take a mammogram.'

A wave of excitement swept over the audience.

'The cysts were discovered when they were no larger than

a pinhead. At such an early stage, a malignant tumour could be removed with no danger to life, and with little damage to the breasts.' He took a deep breath, as though to hold himself in check.

A woman in the audience started to clap. 'Where is it? Where can I buy a bra . . . a Thermoscan?'

'I'm sorry. You can't buy one, madam. Not yet, anyway. That's why I've come to New York – '

A man interrupted. 'I'm a chemist. I know about liquid crystals. But would you explain how it works?'

'It's simple. A tumour or a cyst forces more blood to circulate closer to the skin, generating more heat than normal. If the liquid crystals in the Thermoscan form a distinct circle with a blue centre, that tells you that something – it could be anything from a cyst to a cancerous growth – is there, and it's time to go to the doctor to find out what's happening.'

'Please! Where can I buy a Thermoscan?' the woman shouted. 'Is the medical profession keeping it off the market because surgeons make so much money on us?'

Harry Horn shook his head. 'No. I believe the medical profession would be glad to have every woman own her own Thermoscan. Think of the grief it would save. I'm trying to raise the money to manufacture the product for the mass market. What I need . . .'

Cameron remained seated while Byron waited for the crowd milling around Harry Horn to disperse. Eventually, they wandered off, with everyone murmuring that they wished Harry Horn's dream were a reality. Left alone, Horn seemed deflated and depressed.

'Mr Horn,' Byron said, 'I would like to talk to you about your invention.'

'I don't have much more to say.'

'I'm with FitzGerald Associates, and we're interested in your product.'

Horn stared at Byron. 'FitzGerald Associates?'

'We're a Wall Street firm. We're interested in new products.'

Harry Horn's face first went blank, then became incredulous. 'I came to New York to see Cameron Hightower,' he said.

'She's sitting over there. She asked me to speak to you.'

Harry Horn saw Cameron seated in a chair in the rear of the empty room. Slowly his face took on a visionary's radiance. When he recovered, he said, 'Would you introduce me, please?'

'If it's what Horn claimed,' Cameron said to Byron when they were alone later, 'it's a major invention. Think of it! An early warning tumour test for home use. It's as important as the pill!' For a few minutes Cameron mused over the miracle of liquid crystals while Byron silently begged her to give him a crack at doing the evaluation. To be on the inside of something like this would make his career and satisfy something else in him that wanted more than success.

'Liquid crystals do respond the way he says,' Byron said. 'They're called cholesteric liquid crystals. They do react to heat. There's a lot of experimental work being done, but this is as advanced a use as I've read about.'

'Is it possible?'

Byron nodded.

'Should we contact liquid crystal experts or is that jumping the gun?'

It was the use of the word 'we' that resolved it for Byron. 'I know enough to give you a preliminary evaluation of the technology. And then – '

'And then we go to the experts and ask the right questions,' Cameron directed.

* * *

Byron absorbed every page of Harry Horn's report, committing them to memory. He responded to the diagram of molecules as a man might respond to a woman. His hands started to sweat, and soon he was bathed in perspiration as he studied the way the molecules behaved under heat. Mentally, he tore Horn's work to shreds, scattered it about, and put it back together again. He got up, walked around his living room twice, then hurried to the kitchen. He opened the refrigerator, took out a triangle of cheese, and absentmindedly unwrapped the silver foil. Unaware of what he was doing, he put the cheese on the counter and returned to his desk – forgetting to close the refrigerator door. He devoured the pages looking for flaws. But the report was absolutely unique. It was no scam or promotion. It wasn't a phony tax shelter. 'It is a major breakthrough,' he said aloud as though testing a theory. So Byron Miller fell in love.

It was three in the morning by the time Byron dialled a private number.

'Yes?' Cameron was wide awake.

'Do you know what he has?' Byron said quietly.

'Tell me,' she said.

'If I know what I think I know, it's a miracle. I'll start calling the experts tomorrow, and I'll be out of the office all next week seeing them.'

Cameron said, 'Take all the time you need.'

The next morning Cameron called the Hotel Amsterdam at nine A.M. and discovered that Henry Horn had checked out. The information brought her up short. What a lunatic thing to do! Where was he? The desk clerk said he might be at the bus terminal. Della called the bus terminal to determine the bus Horn would take to return to San Francisco, where he had said he lived. At ten o'clock, Cameron, Della, and another secretary prepared to leave the office for the bus terminal on Fortieth Street and Eighth Avenue. They were

317

standing at the elevator door on the thirtieth floor when the doors opened and Harry Horn stepped out, carrying his luggage. As usual, he looked distracted.

'Miss Hightower,' he exclaimed. 'Are you leaving? I was just coming to say good-bye. And thank you for everything.' He was oblivious of the other women staring at him.

'Good-bye? Now? But we have a lot to talk about.'

Horn was bewildered. 'You have the Thermoscans. All we need is a company to manufacture them.'

'Exactly. And to form a company we need you here.'

'But-but,' he stuttered. 'I ... Not m-me. I can't run a company. I'm a scientist.' He flushed. 'I mean I'm an inventor.' His voice took on authority. 'I am that. As soon as the company is formed, I'll move east, and I'll be around every day to consult.'

As he spoke, Cameron started moving imperceptibly towards the glass doors of FitzGerald Associates. Muddled and disorganized, Harry Horn followed, and the two other women fell in line behind them.

'Harry, your invention has patent protection, hasn't it?' Cameron asked.

'Yes. It's covered by seven issued patents and four still pending.'

'That's why we need you here to help form the company.'

'But I can't stay.'

Cameron started to ask why, and then she knew what was troubling him. 'Come into my office. It's private, and we can work things out there.'

And they did. Cameron opened an account for Harry Horn at the Citibank branch at Broad and Wall by depositing $5,000. Then she told Harry to call the lab where he worked and arrange for a leave of absence. When the company was formed – as she believed it would be – he could resign. Harry Horn acquiesced with the passive fascination of one watching a magician.

* * *

Some weeks after Byron's meetings with three experts, the feasibility studies on Harry Horn's invention dribbled in. All three chemists agreed that Mr Horn had produced a stable liquid-crystal system. Without judging the value of the product, they believed his patents would hold up. Dr Felix Hobson of the Liquid Crystal Institute at Kent State added a personal note: if he could be of any use, he was offering his services. Someone for Mr Horn to interact with as the product was developed. Not exactly a consultant, more of an associate, was Hobson's idea. His fee would be quite reasonable.

Cameron began putting together a company around Harry Horn and his invention. She decided to call it Life Sciences, an appropriate name for a company built on a lifesaving invention.

A pity, she thought, that Harry Horn couldn't run the business. The company needed a chief executive officer, but the kind that Cameron had in mind was not for hire. What was needed was a genuine entrepreneur, a man like Edmond Land, or even a Leon Beckett. Someone agile and ambitious. Cameron had an idea who might fill the slot, but when she mentioned the name of her choice to Jake, he objected violently. He insisted she do her executive search in the traditional way. She tried; she put ads in *The Wall Street Journal* and called three major headhunters. To give Jake his due, she admitted to herself, it was the right way to go; and strange things do happen. Someone unique might turn up. Weeks passed and she found herself swamped with résumés. None of them struck the right chord, but she saw the most promising candidates just in case.

'You interviewed only eleven?' Jake asked.

'How much time do you want me to waste? I saw six sent by headhunters and four from résumés. Nobody was right.'

'What was wrong with them?'

'Nothing. They were right for themselves but wrong for

the job. What any company needs to prosper is a product, a marketing instinct, and good administration. We have the product. The market will be banging on the door to get it. As for administration, Life Sciences does not own a building on Park Avenue. There's no organization chart. The company will employ five people to start and fifty later.' Her lips tightened. 'What the head of Life Sciences needs is something rare called business creativity – which Byron has.'

'Balls!' Jake exclaimed. 'What does Byron Miller know about business?'

'He was at Reliance. He works here. He went to a B school.'

'Not Harvard. Not Stanford. Not Wharton.'

'Rutgers is a fine school.' Cameron grew firm. 'The president of Life Sciences also must get along with Harry Horn, the foggy, semi-genius of this act, and Byron does. He must understand the technology. Byron understands it. He must grasp the financial realities. Byron grasps them. He's worked on enough of our placements and he lives and breathes Wall Street. He has everything except experience. If he had that, he wouldn't be available.'

'Have you offered Byron the job yet?' Jake asked.

'No. Byron works for FitzGerald Associates. It means offering him a new position.'

'For which he is highly unqualified.'

'For which he is highly qualified,' Cameron insisted. 'I've followed your instructions to the letter.'

'And found no one but Byron who pleases you.'

'Do you want to read the résumés? Do the interviews?' Cameron disliked nailing Jake, but there was no option.

Jake didn't answer, and that ended the matter.

Byron listened to Cameron's proposal without moving a muscle. Ever since he had read the patents, he'd avoided the

320

thought of any such opportunity. He had studiously side-stepped all conversations about the applicants.

'It's a big change,' he finally said.

'I think you can handle it. But do *you* think you can?' she asked. Byron agreed to think it over.

Byron's apartment was not furnished according to the American fantasy of the pad of a reasonably successful bachelor. The fact was, it was almost unfurnished. There was a bureau in the bedroom where he kept his underwear, socks, shirts, and other such things that most men keep in bureaus. There was a double bed that was usually unmade, with two parallel, concave indentations on either side, announcing their history. In the living room there was a mahogany table eight feet in diameter that once had seated ten for dinner. There were five chairs around it. It served as a desk and was piled high with papers and books: books on chemistry, on finance, on business, some history and some art.

Alone that night in his apartment, Byron perched on one of the chairs and stared, unseeing, at the jumble on the table. The strength of his need to accept Cameron's offer took him by surprise. He had laboriously buried it as though it were some obscene crime, shovelling dirt over the corpse's coffin, even planting shrubbery to distract the passerby, hiding it beneath the pressures of his usual day. He had given himself fully to wilful amnesia; and at the very moment when he felt himself free – his desire sufficiently anaesthetized so that he believed he didn't care – Cameron blithely informed him that it was all his. He was not only in the race, he'd won.

If he wanted to hear arguments against his accepting the offer, all he had to do was ask his mother. Her reasons could fill a book. The ones she would give and the unspoken reasons they both knew by heart and tacitly agreed be shunned. She would start with: 'Your job as a security analyst is secure.' That would be her launchpad. 'You're not

321

prepared to run a company . . . You're bound to fail . . . And then where will we be? After all my years of work . . .'

It all swept over him – the ancient terror of his childhood, of his mother and him adrift in the world with no anchor; of being unwanted, no one giving a damn if they lived or died.

But why must he fail? An intensity of hope was at work within him. As long as he didn't discuss it with her, if he made his own decision, he needn't confess to fear. He could be steadier in his struggle with himself, against himself.

Facts, like people, have their limitations. They are subject to human interpretation. He need not see the world the way his mother did.

'I want it!' Byron shouted suddenly.

'Then take it!' he answered himself silently.

He'd tell Cameron tomorrow.

PART SIX

The Corporate Raider
1984–1985

18

Cameron and Byron were seated on one of the wooden benches backed by a stone wall that enclosed Central Park. They faced the building across Fifth Avenue where Cameron lived. They had had dinner at Vasata, a small Czechoslovakian restaurant on East Seventy-fifth Street that specialized in roast duck. It was a minor celebration and Byron loved roast duck, but he barely touched his food. Nor was he as talkative as usual about Wall Street, and he did not try to make high entertainment out of business.

'Everything is going on schedule,' Cameron said matter-of-factly.

'It is.'

'Then what am I missing? Why are you wringing your hands and howling at the moon?'

'Who's howling?'

'You are.'

There was a visible tightness around Byron's jaw muscles. He glared up and down Fifth Avenue, at the towering apartment buildings, the windows of which were almost all darkened.

'Tomorrow and tomorrow and tomorrow. All those fucking whorehouses.'

'Byron.' Cameron tried to make a joke of it. 'You are speaking of Wall Street venture capitalists. One of them once offered to buy the Bronx Zoo. That shows some imagination.'

'No understanding of real estate. How did he miss Central Park?' Byron shut his eyes, repeating in his mind, venture capitalists. Sometimes he couldn't stop his memories from affecting his thinking. This evening they had taken over his

325

mind; and though he tried like hell to incinerate them, hell wasn't hot enough to burn them to ashes. He searched for the words and could only find the anger that he tried to moderate. 'They're damn fools.'

'They are a fact of life.' Cameron gave Byron a steady look. 'Household words on Wall Street, like Dow Jones and Standard and Poor's. Chartists.'

Byron's voice was muffled. 'I don't like them.'

'They're no better and no worse than the other flora and fauna on the Street.'

Byron gave a wry laugh. 'There are no rules in affairs of the heart.'

'Try to love someone not your intellectual equal,' Cameron said.

'I'll do my best. Shoulder to shoulder.'

'Please. And remember, I'll have no chance for shin kicks.'

'Or rabbit punches.' Byron's eyes gleamed.

'And your reward will come long before heaven,' Cameron said.

'Good. I lack spiritual vision.' He stood up.

Cameron followed him, and hearing his strangled humour, did not probe further. They crossed Fifth Avenue, neither of them smiling. When they arrived at her apartment building, Cameron reached with sympathy across the silence that had grown between them.

'I don't know why you're as concerned as you are, but it's your business. If Tim were alive, FitzGerald Associates would put up venture capital. Tim did do a few start-up situations. But, as you know, Jake and I have not. It's hard enough getting his cooperation when I take any small, private company public. But to put down the first nickel for a start-up deal would be jingle bells in July to Jake.'

'I figured.' The irritation in Byron's voice was reflected in Cameron's face.

'You know the drill as well as I do,' she said. 'Either we

raise the start-up money from friends, friends of friends, or relatives – anyone who can be collared to make a campaign contribution – or we go to the professionals, the venture capitalists.'

'I hear you.'

'If I could do it, I would.' She made her confidence, her goodwill, almost tangible. 'You'll be fine.'

'Fine? Sure. Everything will be fine. Okay, tomorrow at nine-thirty A.M. in the lobby of the Seagram Building. Wellington, Wall, and Pinkus, here we come.'

The offices of Wellington, Wall, and Pinkus on the fortieth floor of the Seagram Building had a westward view of the United States that implied invisible cornfields, the Rockies, the Pacific Ocean. It spoke of the power of the country and, by association, of Wellington, Wall, and Pinkus. The venture-capital arm of the firm was headed by Tony Wall. Cameron had known Tony Wall for years and had attended several of his candlelit dinners at his home on Lily Pond Lane in East Hampton. Cameron had put Tony first on her list of venture capitalists because he could be trusted to be the most conventional, and she wanted to test the waters on what would probably be the least receptive of minds.

Byron spent an uninterrupted fifteen minutes describing Harry Horn's invention and the market for the product in detail. He began by sketching the scientific basis. He reported on the clinical tests performed at three major hospitals that validated the invention. He glowed as he spoke of its benefits to the human race. Tony didn't understand; even worse, he didn't want to understand. When he realized he was speaking Esperanto to Tony, Byron switched tack. He gave the projected size of the market. Tony's face was oatmeal until the market size was mentioned, then he licked his lips. Byron wound up his presentation by saying that they were looking for $300,000.

'What will you use the money for?'

'A small factory space. We need office supplies, a receptionist-type secretary, lab equipment. You can't use a hot plate and a Bunsen burner to purify liquid crystals. We want to make more prototypes – samples of the Thermoscan.'

'How long will the three hundred thousand last?'

'Long enough for us to make the Thermoscans.'

It was a meaningless question. Tony's interest was in Cameron. 'You plan to take the company public when they have the samples?'

'Yes,' she told him.

'It's an interesting product, all right, if it can be developed. Send me the proposal.' He was speaking to Cameron. Byron might as well have been in the men's room. 'I'll see if it meets our criteria.'

'Which are?' Byron asked.

Tony's expression said, you don't count. His mouth said, 'That's private information.'

'Do you think I'll tailor the proposal to meet your criteria?' Byron asked.

'Of course not.'

'Then why not give it? So we won't waste each other's time.' Tony stared at Byron and Byron stared back until Tony blinked.

'We never give out that information,' Tony insisted.

'I'll bet you don't.' Byron was full of good fellowship. 'Because you make it up as you go along. Don't you, Tony?'

Waiting for the elevator, Cameron said nothing about Byron's attitude. She felt like his mother, his sister, his girlfriend, all rolled into one. She wished she could help him. But how?

'I'm sorry,' he said. 'But I'm really not.'

Cameron waited for more but nothing came. Byron took a handkerchief and wiped his lips. 'What I'm sorry about is not what I said. It's my lack of pragmatism. Sheer practicality. What I said was true. He has no criteria.'

'I know. But why hit him with a dead fish?'

'Isn't his name on the door because his parents bought him a partnership? Didn't his grandfather form American Latex? There's no calcium left in his bones. Deep down where it counts, he's pure jelly. The original typewriter would not have met that rag doll's criteria and Remington would have gone begging. But once Mark Twain bought a Remington and made the typewriter a religious symbol by typing *Huckleberry Finn* on it, Tony baby would be calling, hat in hand, on old Remington. To paper his walls with money Remington no longer needed.'

Cameron knew he was right, but she said nothing. All she could hope for was that whatever private vampire was after Byron would stumble on a stake.

The next day they tried Venlong. Cameron had made a strategic change of plan. Since Byron was looking for blood, he might as well have it where it didn't count. Venlong, owned by the Longstreet family and located in Rockefeller Center, was venerated for its wealth and occasional flamboyant ventures, clear examples of the hereditary acumen and guts of the Longstreet family. Even when the companies they backed got into trouble, raising new money for Venlong was easy because of the respectability of the Longstreet name. Adrian Haveworth, who managed Venlong, and Avery Longstreet were childhood friends who both had gone to Groton and Yale, as had their fathers before them. The Haveworths were quite comfortable, and their comfort was derived from living off the very rich. They were a sycophantic family by inclination and they taught each other the velvet techniques of sponging off those who could afford them. They raised parasitism to an art form.

Adrian, the youngest member of the Haveworth family, did

not study law or medicine or even literature. Instead, without premeditation, but with a remarkable exhibition of the inheritance of acquired characteristics, he attended the Harvard Business School. No one in the family had any idea what he had in mind. Neither did Adrian, but everyone trusted his genes. And they were proven right. There was scuttlebutt on the Street that Venlong was created expressly for Adrian to manage, but that was hearsay, and both families laughed at the gossip. The fact was simply that the Longstreets were doing what Longstreets always did. They took care of their own.

Adrian Haveworth was a chubby man with curly blond hair and a blond moustache. He was credited with a taste for adventurous projects. His selections were by and large poor, and those that worked out did so by pure chance. Avery Longstreet didn't give a hoot or a holler whether Adrian's batting average was high or low as long as he stayed within the budget.

Byron and Adrian disliked each other on sight because Byron was exactly what Adrian wasn't. Worse, he was not wealthy or Adrian would have known him. Still, good manners prevailed, and Byron gave his presentation in a sensible, seasoned voice with just the right amount of fact and optimistic fiction called projections.

When he concluded, Adrian asked, 'What was your experience before Horn?'

'I worked for a year and a half as a security analyst in the pharmaceutical industry. For FitzGerald Associates.'

For an instant Adrian almost looked impressed. He glanced at Cameron. 'He worked for you?'

Cameron said, 'Yes.'

Adrian thought about this. Although it was his understanding that Cameron was not one of the real Hightowers – the rich Hightowers – nevertheless, the fine name was hers by right of birth. 'What did you do before that?'

330

'I worked for Reliance Pharmaceuticals. I was a senior chemist.'

'Have you a PhD?'

'No.'

'What do you know about liquid crystals?'

'A great deal. And I've discussed the invention with the experts in the field.'

Adrian chewed on his exasperation. Eventually he managed a response. 'That hardly makes you an expert. Does this Horn have a PhD?'

'No. But he's done outstanding work in liquid crystals. The invention is feasible. We have reports documenting the fact. All from liquid crystal experts. One is the head of the Liquid Crystal Institute at Kent State.' Having said this in too loud a voice, Byron wished he hadn't.

It was his first tactical mistake, and Cameron flinched inwardly when she heard it. Adrian Haveworth could be intimidated, but less by scientific credentials than by multi-zeroed fortunes. But science, like art, had its place in his firmament. Now, Byron's temper had given Adrian the advantage. Temperament was not suitable for business. He shifted his attack.

'It's possible that the invention has a sound scientific basis, but it clearly needs development within a business environment. What experience have you had, Mr Miller, along those lines? Running a business to begin with, and one that requires technical know-how at that?'

Byron lowered his gaze briefly. 'I have a degree from the B School at Rutgers.'

'That hardly prepares you to run a new business venture. You've had no on-the-job experience.'

Byron lost his balance in his distaste for the hypocrisy of the man. 'And I suppose you've had years of experience backing fledgling companies?'

'I've backed quite a few.'

331

'And made a fortune doing it?'

Adrian said something unintelligible.

'You mean you haven't made a fortune?' Byron pushed on. 'Perhaps you've lost a fortune?'

'In venture capital there are always losses.'

'There are, indeed. Adrian, first name. Haveworth, family name. Adrian Haveworth. Why isn't it Networth? Then I could make a funny. Adrian Networth hasn't much net worth.'

A frozen stillness descended over Adrian Haveworth.

'No, you didn't make a fortune. But then again, you didn't lose a fortune, either. In fact, you didn't lose a cent. What you lost were the Longstreet pennies.' He paused long enough to enjoy the expression on Haveworth's face. 'You're bought and owned, body and soul, by the Longstreets. You're their windup doll. If, now and then, you lose a few pennies by investing in some harebrained scheme, they scold you. Or if you make them a few dollars on something, they pat your head.'

'Get out of here!' Adrian's voice choked. He had never been so outraged in his life.

'See you, buster.' Byron walked quickly out the door.

'I'm sorry, Adrian.' Cameron's expression was frozen, barely disguising her shock. 'There are some chemistries that simply don't mix.'

Byron was waiting for Cameron downstairs, at the end of the elevator bank. They left 30 Rockefeller Plaza, neither of them saying a word. They both remained closeted with their own thoughts during the cab ride to Acorn Ventures. Acorn was housed in an elegant limestone mansion on Beekman Place. From the rear of the house, one had a view of the East River. The ground on which the house stood was valued in the many millions of dollars.

Norman Mann, the manager of Acorn Ventures, was the kind of man Byron understood. He was stocky, with thinning brown hair, and he wore steel-rimmed glasses. Prior to joining Acorn, he had been a partner in Reginald and Billingsley, the largest international tax law firm in the world. His tour of duty had included the entire world. In more than a dozen Eastern and Western nations he had interpreted the vagaries of the American legal system to multinational corporations with arms extending to the United States. His naturally good mind had been honed and stretched by experiencing a variety of cultures with a multiplicity of values and lifestyles. He could look at what might seem to others to be an outlandish business venture with a lack of cynicism and estimate its possiblities. Conversely, he could evaluate standard ideas – such as a software company – and see them for what they were and calculate if there was room for one more in the field. Acorn Ventures had made some very discerning investments.

Byron gave Mann a lucid description of the Life Sciences project. He was neither too expansive nor too modest; he was sane, even conservative. He noted the downside risk and explained exactly what it was; that it lay in the developmental stage of bringing the product from a handmade item to one that could be mass-produced. He concluded by alluding to the potential profit once the Thermoscan was developed.

Norman Mann asked all the right questions, and Byron gave all the right answers. He behaved exactly as Cameron would have wished. When Mann asked to see a written proposal, Byron handed it to him.

Cameron and Byron walked slowly to First Avenue and hailed a cab.

'Two outs and one positive maybe,' Byron said. 'By the way, I am sorry.'

'Apologies accepted,' said Cameron.

'I'm improving with practice.'

333

'You are. Mann could say yes or he could say no. I want to review my list of venture-capital firms.'

'Have you changed your mind about me?'

'No. You can do the job. Now that we've scouted the territory, I don't want to buckshot. It's time to switch to the rifle.'

'You mean the types I can deal with – the positive maybes.'

'Something like that.'

Byron cast about for a way to make reparations. 'Look, I'm open to change. I swear to heaven I'll never pull the kind of stunt I pulled with Haveworth.'

'I believe you, but I still want to go over my list.' Cameron said. 'I don't want to shop the prospectus around. Venture capitalists lunch together.'

'It sounds like a club.'

'It is,' Cameron said.

334

19

Usually Cameron spent the time while Andrew drove her from her Fifth Avenue apartment to her office thinking about the coming day, reviewing the work that routinely passed over her desk, planning what action – or lack of action – Coz would take on the floor of the exchange. Lately, a lot of her time had been taken up with Byron and Harry Horn in trying to raise the seed money for Life Sciences. But today was an exception. Byron, Harry Horn, and his Thermoscan never crossed her mind. Cameron's total attention was riveted on an article she'd read that morning in *The Wall Street Journal* while finishing her coffee: 'Cyrus Hansen Acquires 11% of United Bronze Corporation.'

It stated that in Hansen's 13 D filing with the SEC he would continue to purchase stock in United Bronze with the intention of ousting the current board of directors as well as the senior management. Evan Perry, chairman of the board of United Bronze, said the corporation would resist Hansen's raid with all the resources available to it, including the courts.

Over the years Cameron had come upon numerous similar articles concerning the activities of Cyrus Hansen. *Forbes* magazine had likened him to the fictional Rhett Butler, a gunrunner during the Civil War who had sailed his badly needed cargo of arms past the Union blockade. Hansen acted partially for profit but mostly for the sheer thrill of thumbing his nose at the less courageous, less able captains of industry he left far astern. *Forbes* added that once Hansen decided a corporation was ripe for the plucking, there were very few executives fast enough on their feet to escape. He could not be paid off with 'greenmail,' a variation on blackmail that the

Mafia had somehow missed. Strong companies were never raided. Only weak ones with assets that an inept management had clumsily mismanaged. In such cases the corporation paid the raider through the nose, multimillions in 'greenmail' to avoid the takeover bid. Thus the executives protected their jobs and their incompetence by using corporate assets to fend off the 'housecleaning' that followed a successful raid. And the stockholders footed the bill for the battle because their stock was worth less.

Cameron had never thought of United Bronze as a target, but clearly Cyrus Hansen had. Earnings were down, but that happened with the best of companies. What made this announcement even more unique to Cameron was that this was the first time Cyrus's erratic path had crossed hers. FitzGerald Associates were the investment bankers for United Bronze. As such they would be called upon to advise the chairman what to do. How best to fight this attack? What was the most effective 'shark repellent' to use against the raider? Even as Cameron turned these thoughts over in her mind, far below the surface only one thought held her. She would see Cyrus again. What was more, she would be opposing him. The very idea momentarily winded her.

Then she asked herself, why not? What was Cyrus Hansen to her but the blurred, bittersweet memory of a teenage girl who had fallen in love by mistake? He'd known where and how to reach her for years, and had chosen not to. The fact that she could just as easily have located Cyrus was irrelevant. He was the one who'd left without saying good-bye. It was up to him to return. Deep inside her Cameron could feel a familiar tension. She was gearing up for the fight that was bound to come. She was going to enjoy taking on the corporate buccaneer.

By the time Andrew pulled up in front of 65 Wall Street, Cameron was so charged up she was out of the car and into the building before Andrew had a chance to open the door for her. She brushed by Della and entered her office, where Jake was sitting, waiting for her. Despite her genuine affection for Jake, her words were curt, almost rude.

'What is it?' she snapped. 'I'm very busy.'

'What the fuck has your ovaries in an uproar? Could it be the huge fee we're going to earn from United Bronze?' He chortled, mentally rubbing his hands together. 'Look at your messages. Perry's called three times from his limousine. I believe he's marooned somewhere on the Long Island Expressway.'

Cameron grabbed the pile of pink slips Della had stacked in the centre of her desk. 'Seven forty-five. Evan Perry. Call me please. Important.' Cameron recognized the number of his car phone. 'Eight o'clock. Evan Perry.' The same message. 'Eight-fifteen. Evan Perry.' Again. Her intercom buzzed. 'Yes, Della?'

'Guess who's on the phone?'

For reasons Cameron never cared to probe, Evan Perry was not one of Della's favourites on their client list. But it was a dislike Cameron did not share, and she was in no mood to coddle Della this morning. 'I have no time to play games. Is it Evan Perry?' Both Della and Cameron were surprised by the intensity of Cameron's reaction.

'Oh, my! We are in a fine mood today,' Della remarked. 'Yes, it's your Mr Perry.'

'Not my Mr Perry, Della. It's Fitzgerald Associates' Mr Perry. One of the men who helps pay your salary. Put him on.' Waiting, Cameron shook herself with irritation. She'd never talked that way to Della. What the devil was the matter with her? She answered her own question. Cyrus Hansen was the matter with her. After sixteen years, just the possibility of seeing him again made her moods swing back and forth violently. One moment she felt irritable, combative, even rude, the next moment she was eager, excited. Here she was, thirty-two years old, acting like a sixteen-year-old teenager.

'Cameron?'

'Good morning, Evan. What can I do for you?'

'Nothing until this damn traffic opens up. I've been sitting for an hour and a half between Great Neck and Little Neck. It's ludicrous! I'm the chairman of the board of a nine-hundred-million-dollar corporation, and I have to wait until every little assistant product manager in a broken-down Datsun gets out of the way. I should have bought a helicopter years ago.'

'You mean the company should have bought you a helicopter years ago.'

'Same thing,' Perry growled. 'Anyway, I have a ten o'clock appointment with Cyrus Hansen. I want you in my office at nine forty-five.'

Perry's lack of concern that she might have a previous appointment momentarily jarred Cameron. Then she relaxed because she appreciated the tension a corporate executive might feel when threatened by the notorious Cyrus Hansen.

'Have you dug your trenches, Evan? Got your barbed wire strung and the machine guns in place?'

'This is not funny, Cameron. Oh, hell! Can you hold on? My other phone is ringing.'

Two phones in his company limousine. I wonder what he'd do if the company was making money? Cameron thought. 'Never mind, Evan. I'll be at your office at nine forty-five. But I still think at a minimum you should dig a few trenches. Ciao.' Cameron hung up on her sputtering client.

Cameron stood on the sidewalk at Third Avenue and Thirty-ninth Street, staring up at the sleek tower with bronze-tinted glass and elegant bronze-anodized aluminium finishing details. Even the sidewalk was a mixture of concrete, stone, and some kind of brown plastic. The four-foot bronze squares were separated by rubberized expansion joints that were supposed to prevent the sidewalk from cracking due to the extremes of heat and cold in New York. They prevented nothing. The sidewalk was cracked.

A cold April wind was blowing off the East River, and Cameron pulled the collar of her mink-lined Burberry higher around her neck. The name United Bronze Corporation was spelled out in huge bronze capital letters that ran above the length of the four revolving doors. It was supposed to impress the passersby, making them think that United owned the building. This was a bit of corporate aggrandizement, since United Bronze only rented the top four floors. But at the signing of the lease, the company paid a king's ransom to have its name on the building, just to satisfy Evan's vanity and desire for publicity.

At precisely 9:45, Cameron entered Evan's office. He was standing at a bank of windows staring out at the river. His profile was etched against the tinted glass, and the sunlight seeping through the window gave his skin a bronzed look. Evan was a movie casting director's dream of a chief executive officer: tall, erect, broad shouldered, lean. His nose was thin and straight, and he held his head at an angle that made his jaw appear strong. His iron-grey hair was cut short in almost military fashion and brushed back from his broad forehead. His voice was well modulated, and his eyes looked directly at whoever he was talking to. Cameron glanced around the office. The walls were crowded with photographs of a younger Evan Perry leaping high to catch a football. Evan Perry three feet off the gound shooting a two-handed jumper on a basketball court. Evan Perry at net smashing a tennis ball. Evan Perry teeing up a golf ball.

His desk was a large rectangle of slate set on bronzed steel legs. There were no drawers and nothing on the top except two bronze baskets marked 'In' and 'Out'. Both baskets were empty. Behind the desk was a slate-topped credenza which held nothing but a multibuttoned phone.

As though taken by surprise at her sudden appearance,

Evan roused himself from his contemplation of the world and strode towards Cameron.

'Really glad you could make it, Cameron.' Though Cameron knew from his official biography that he'd been born in Kansas City, Evan had spent most of his adult life in the Northeast and had mastered the mashed-potatoes-in-the-mouth accent of the New England socialite. She was aware that much of what Evan did was a performance, but it was such a good performance that Cameron had to restrain herself from applauding.

'I read the papers, Evan,' she replied quietly. 'And I know an emergency when I see one. But I am curious. Why are you meeting with Hansen? Isn't he the enemy?'

'Well, Hansen is a large shareholder. I thought a meeting would smoke out his intentions.'

Cameron snorted with impatience. 'It seems to me he's made his intentions quite clear. He's out after your hide.'

Evan appeared pained at her words. 'We really don't know that,' he said. 'Talk is cheap, and the papers have to print something.'

'What do you want me to do?'

'Listen and take notes.'

'You pay secretaries to take notes.'

'Come on, Cameron. Where's the old team spirit? I remember one time when Dartmouth was playing Harvard – '

Cameron interrupted. 'This is not a football game. What are you doing to defend yourself?'

'I called a special board meeting last night and gave the team our game plan.'

If Evan didn't stop treating this like a college sports event, Cameron thought she might be sick all over his Dartmouth green carpet. 'Would you kindly clue me in on what you decided?'

'We went into a huddle, and we're going to come out – '

The phone on the credenza rang and Evan interrupted himself to answer it. 'Yes? . . . Send him up.'

'Evan' – Cameron became insistent – 'before Hansen gets here I want to know what you've decided to do.'

'Not now. I'll tell you later. Hansen is on his way up.'

Cameron exhaled through clenched teeth. She glanced at a reflection of herself in the window and was not too pleased with what she saw. While her loose-fitting beige jacket and navy skirt with starched white shirt and string tie were efficient, they were not exactly the most feminine clothes in her wardrobe. She became irritated with herself for wishing she looked more female and seductive just because she was about to see Cyrus Hansen again. But the fact was, nothing would have pleased her more than if a good fairy had appeared, waved her magic wand, sprinkled a little fairy dust, and transformed her suit into a soft and sinuous dress.

A knock on the door announced Cyrus's arrival. The door opened and Cyrus Hansen stood for a moment, framed by the doorway. Cameron repressed a gasp. Except for his blond hair he was no longer the golden boy she remembered as a teenager. His skin was a mottled combination of red and tan. His strong face was marred by a deep white scar running down his left cheek. There was another scar across the bridge of his nose, which must have been broken and badly set. Cameron had the distinct impression he had been in a number of nasty brawls with men who had used more than their fists. He'd put on weight. But it was muscle not fat. His shoulders were massive, filling the open doorway, and his body was powerful. Unlike Evan, his chest did not taper down to a narrow waist and hips; instead, his torso resembled the trunk of a tree. There was an elemental maleness about him that reduced other men, Evan included, to the status of 'boy'. Cameron was struck by the similarity between this Cyrus and the Tim FitzGerald she remembered.

Despite his bulk, he glided across the floor gracefully to

stand toe-to-toe with Evan Perry, his hand outstretched. The two men were about the same height, but there the similarity ended. Instead of wearing a conventional business suit, Cyrus had on a pair of white corduroy pants, a black turtleneck sweater, and an old blue blazer with leather patches at the elbows. What appeared to be rubber-soled boots disappeared under his pants.

After hesitating, Evan accepted the outstretched hand. There was a moment of unexpected tension as Evan tested the strength of Cyrus's grip. Cyrus's wide mouth curved into a slight smile as he waited for Evan to stop playing his schoolboy game. When he didn't Cyrus grimaced in disgust and, without any seeming effort, tightened his own grip. Evan Perry was a strong man with large hands, but in the knuckle-squeezing bout, he was badly outmatched. His face turned white with pain, and he dropped Cyrus's hand, acting as if nothing had happened.

'Cyrus Hansen,' he said. 'I've been wanting to meet you for some time. Really good of you to make it.'

Cyrus's grin grew bigger. His lips curled over large, strong white teeth. 'It would have been cavalier of me to ignore the opportunity to meet you.' His voice was deeper than Cameron remembered, a genuine bass baritone rumbling effortlessly from his chest.

'I can understand that.' It appeared to Cameron that Evan's smile was pasted on. 'By the by,' Evan continued. 'I thought it a good idea to have United's investment banker present at this meeting.' He turned in the direction of Cameron. 'Cameron Hightower, Cyrus Hansen.'

A swift and unexpected grin passed like a breeze over the surface of Cyrus's face. 'Cameron?' he repeated her name as though relearning a language with which he was once familiar. 'Cameron Hightower. You grew up.'

'I grew up.'

Their eyes brushed. He glanced quickly at her left hand. 'Not married?' he asked.

'No,' Cameron replied, sensing that he already knew the answer to that question. 'And you?'

'No. How is Geraldine?'

'She died. Three years ago.'

'I'm sorry.' And his voice held true regret. 'I must be getting old. I'd forgotten FitzGerald Associates are the investment bankers for United Bronze.'

Before Cameron could remark on that, Evan Perry broke in.

'I didn't realize you two knew each other.' There was the merest hint of suspicion in his voice. If Cameron and Cyrus were old acquaintances, where did that leave him?

Noting Evan's anxiety, Cameron immediately tried to smooth his ruffled feathers. 'We grew up together, Evan. But we haven't seen each other in . . .' She paused, unwilling to admit that she knew how many years had passed. 'Let's say a long, long time.'

'Relax, Perry,' Cyrus added, clearly not giving a damn how Evan Perry felt. 'FitzGerald Associates are your investment bankers, not mine. And from everything I've read about Cameron Hightower, I'm certain she's professional enough not to allow whatever there was between us' – Cyrus smiled intimately at Cameron, deliberately encouraging Perry to assume a type of relationship that had not existed – 'to cloud her judgement.'

Cameron could feel the heat rising to her face. It exasperated her that she would blush at the veiled suggestion that she'd been to bed with Cyrus Hansen.

Evan cleared his throat. 'Of course. I'm as aware as you what a really splendid investment banker Cameron is. A credit to her sex.' Cameron winced at Perry's patronizing tone. Oblivious of her reaction, he said, 'I'm being rude.

Won't you sit down?' He gestured towards a round, slate-covered conference table in the corner of the huge office.

Cyrus waited for them to settle themselves before saying, 'I'm a little tight on time, so I'll come to the point. After I take control of the company, I intend to select a chief executive officer. How about convincing me it should be you?'

'I read your announcement, Cyrus,' Cameron said. 'Unless you were misquoted, it seems to me you've made up your mind about Evan.'

'I wasn't misquoted. Do you blame me, judging from what's happened to United's earnings since Perry took over? Still, one can always change one's mind. Given enough good reasons. I'm familiar with your official biography, Perry. What might interest me is the inside story of how you got to be the CEO of the corporation.'

'Sure. Why not?' Cameron was amused to note Evan trying to deepen his voice to match Cyrus's. 'You know I went to Dartmouth. I was a three-letter man for three years – football, baseball, and basketball. But basketball was really my game – all-American in my senior year.'

Cyrus appeared to be impressed.

'Of course, it didn't mean then what it does now. Sports have become a big business. A real money game. When I was at Dartmouth, sports were for fun,' he said cheerfully. 'And it did teach me to keep in shape. Where did you go to college, Hansen?'

'Princeton, Oxford. The London School of Economics. And the Sorbonne.'

Cameron's eyebrows shot up. That was an impressive collection of schools. But then again, Cyrus wasn't a three-letter man.

'What did you do after graduation?' Cyrus's question was too casual. At least it was too casual to Cameron, who had begun to pick up a pattern in Cyrus's questions.

'I did graduate work and accepted a teaching post at Dartmouth. Teaching English literature.'

'A challenging field. Excellent preparation for a business career. Makes a well-rounded personality. What period of English literature?'

Not even Evan Perry could miss Cyrus's sarcasm. For a moment the pasted-on smile became unstuck, then he recovered and said, 'Eighteenth and nineteenth century. Jane Austen is my favourite novelist.'

'Marvellous writer,' Cyrus said, 'I think of myself as Janeite. Whenever I reread one of her novels, I find it difficult not to laugh out loud at the satire.'

'Laugh at Jane Austen?' Evan was appalled.

Cyrus corrected him. 'Laugh with Jane Austen. Not at her. Anyway, what happened then?'

'Well, you remember Chester Bancroft?'

'A good man,' Cyrus said. 'The chairman before you. As I recall, he built United Bronze from a fifty-million-dollar corporation to a company grossing close to a billion dollars.'

'Right. You see, Chet was my best friend at Dartmouth. He was the batboy for the baseball team, the waterboy for the football team, and the student manager of the basketball team.'

'Not much of an athlete.'

'Chet? God, no! Chet was only about five feet six inches tall and weighed well over two hundred pounds.'

'He must have really looked up to you.'

'He did. He really did.' Without saying so, Evan gave the impression that everyone looked up to him. 'Anyway, Chet was a born manager. The minute United hired him, I could see it was in the cards that he'd be chairman someday.'

'But you didn't go to United with your friend?' Cameron asked.

'Oh, no! English lit was my field. I stayed at Dartmouth and eventually became an associate professor.'

'Then how . . .?' Cameron had become intrigued with the saga of Evan Perry.

'How did I get to United?' Evan gave Cameron his most irresistible smile. 'When Chet became president, he offered me a job as vice president for public relations at a salary' – he chuckled contentedly – 'I really couldn't afford to refuse. You see, Chet was never comfortable speaking in public to large groups. Security analysts and the like. He didn't think he made a good impression. So he'd tell me what to say, and I gave the speeches. I made a good impression on everybody.'

'So did Trilby,' Cyrus muttered.

Evan Perry began to assume a new personality in Cameron's eyes. Until now she'd considered him a surprisingly literate, very attractive – if a bit pompous – man who, trapped by changing economic conditions, was reduced to fighting for his business life against Cyrus Hansen, a brilliant, ruthless corporate raider. Suddenly, she saw the exploitiveness of a possibly incompetent man.

'Anyway, I went to work for Chet, and he sent me to Harvard Business School. When Chet became chairman, I became president of the company.'

'I see. A natural step.' Cyrus was suitably encouraging.

'Chet was a real take-charge guy. And I carried out Chet's orders.' Perry hesitated before resuming on a properly mournful note. 'Then Chet had his coronary and I became chairman.'

Feeling Cyrus was not a receptive audience, Evan explained how different he was from Chester Bancroft. He said that Chet ran a one-man show and made almost every decision – except for the colour of the toilet paper in the ladies' room which he assumed was white. Evan Perry preened and ran a hand through his hair. He explained that he took seriously what he'd been taught at the B School. And he did his best to run United Bronze in the B School case book system with 'decision trees' and all the other techniques.

346

He set up committees to make decisions on policy and chaired all of them. 'But the damn-fool division heads had been handpicked by Chet. They were used to carrying out Chet's orders. And they expected me to make all the decisions,' Evan explained irritatedly. He tried to tell them this was a new regime and whatever they had to say would be listened to. 'It went right over their heads.'

'You didn't want to replace them with men of your own choosing?' There was nothing but courtesy in Cyrus's question, no hint of doubt or faultfinding. Merely a wish to understand. 'You don't like firing people?'

'I'd have fired the lot of them and not lost a minute's sleep. But replacing them would have been just as hard – if not harder – than keeping them. It's tough to find good men. The best thing I could do was nothing. Struggle along and try to teach that group of third-string substitutes how to play winning ball.'

Three years of wasteful committee meetings passed and, frankly, Evan stated, he was tearing out his hair. The company was coming apart for the lack of a decent first-string team. 'Not a starter in the bunch. We're losing money hand over fist.' He looked at Cameron. It wasn't the look of a man who was about to lose something he valued highly. It was the triumphant look of a man who had just put something over on everyone. 'As I mentioned to you, Cameron, I called an emergency meeting of the board last night.'

Cameron felt her anger begin to rise. After hearing Evan Perry's real history and how he came to be chairman of United Bronze, she had to accept that it was a position for which he was totally unqualified. She realized he had no intention of putting up a fight for control of the company, but had gone in the opposite direction. She glanced sideways at Cyrus, who was slumped in his chair, his face impassive except for the corners of his mouth, which had developed a suspicious curve, something akin to a suppressed smile. It came to her with absolute conviction that Cyrus had known Evan's history all along and had encouraged Evan's detailing of it for her benefit. She thought she knew why.

'I get the picture, Evan.' She sounded approving. 'You very intelligently persuaded the board that it was in their best interest to provide you with a safety net.'

'Exactly.' Evan smiled. 'And they were cooperative.'

'In other words, they gave you a golden parachute, as the media jokingly call it. After all, if the company is taken over by a raider, you certainly should be compensated for your heartache and anguish at the loss of your chairmanship. And be handsomely repaid for the years of good work you've already put in. How large a settlement did they agree you should have if Hansen takes over?'

'Not that much, Cameron, I'm really an English lit instructor at heart. Not one of your typical, greedy corporate types. We agreed on three million if Hansen takes over the company. You do remember, Henry Ross asked for seven million and got it.'

Cameron suddenly flared up. 'Then I don't understand, Evan. What the hell am I doing here? If you've arranged for a settlement of three million should Hansen take over, you have no plans to fight him. And you don't need my help!'

'But he does, Cameron. Very much.' It was becoming more and more difficult for Cyrus to continue to smother his amusement. 'The board's cooperation wasn't as cut-and-dried as Perry would like you to believe.'

Evan Perry jumped to his feet, knocking his chair over backwards. He slammed his hand on the table, 'What's that supposed to mean, Hansen?'

Cyrus shook his head slowly. When he spoke there was a dangerous edge to his voice. 'Sit down, you big-man-on-the-campus, and we'll try to keep this meeting civilized.'

It was perfectly obvious – even to Evan – that Cyrus Hansen was prepared to run an uncivilized meeting if necessary. Remembering what had happened to his hand when he'd tried to intimidate Cyrus physically, Evan abruptly picked up his chair and sat down.

'What it means, Cameron,' Cyrus continued, 'is that the board wasn't quite so incompetent as to vote Perry a three-million-dollar settlement in the case of a takeover without double-checking him.'

Evan's face was growing red. 'Their suggestions were quite sensible.'

'Extraordinarily sensible,' Cyrus said with a smile. 'They attached a few strings to the settlement. And you, Cameron, are the strings. As United Bronze's investment banker, the board wants you to decide if my offer for the company is fair. If you don't think it is, you're to set what you consider a reasonable price, with which I'll either agree, or I won't. Also, Perry only gets his three million if you decide his performance as chief executive officer entitles him to it. If you don't think it does, then he doesn't get it.'

'How the hell do you know that?' Evan shouted.

'Friends in high places, Perry.'

Cameron considered what had occurred during the past half hour. She decided Cyrus had known all along that FitzGerald Associates was United Bronze's investment banker. Once he'd discovered she was at the meeting, he'd led Evan down the garden path and made a bit of an ass out of him, only because the board had passed on to her the decision on Evan's safety net. Although she didn't like it, she had to admit it was a masterful performance, fully up to Cyrus Hansen's reputation.

'I want to see a signed copy of the minutes of last night's meeting,' she said. 'Signed by you, Evan, and by corporate counsel. If the minutes read as Cyrus claims, my company will meet with your auditors, your outside counsel, and other senior executives. I'll have an evaluation of the company ready in two weeks. Is that all right with you?'

Evan answered sullenly, 'I suppose it will have to be. And what about my severance agreement?'

'That depends in part on the evaluation we come up with.' Cameron's look challenged Evan to voice any objections. He didn't. She turned to Cyrus. 'Are two weeks agreeable to you?'

Cyrus shrugged his shoulders.

'One more thing. No one in this room is to do any trading in United Bronze stock until we agree or do not agree on a price.'

'I'm surprised at you, Cameron,' Cyrus drawled. 'That goes without saying.'

'Nothing goes without saying. So I've said it. Is it agreed?'

'Agreed,' Cyrus said mildly.

Cameron studied Evan Perry. Her refusal to go along automatically with his golden parachute appeared to have been a serious blow to him. For the first time in Cameron's memory Evan wasn't either standing ramrod straight, or sitting, head held high with what she now saw was a slightly weak jaw jutting out. She felt a surge of pity for the man and an urge to offer some comfort. But Cyrus had done his job too well, and the knowledge of the means by which Evan had become chief executive officer and how he'd allowed his company to disintegrate helped her check the impulse.

'If you have no further need of me, I have a business to run,' she said. Evan waved her off with a dispirited flick of his hand. 'Cyrus, it's been, ah . . .' She laughed, suddenly self-conscious. 'Shall we say, interesting, seeing you again.' She held out her hand.

Cyrus took hold of it with both his hands. A shock Cameron hoped was imperceptible passed through her entire body. Hurriedly she broke the connection and left the office.

That afternoon Cameron had scheduled a meeting with Byron for three o'clock. He arrived at five minutes to three.

Before they could begin to talk, Della buzzed the intercom, thoroughly rattled. 'Miss Hightower, there's a Mr Cyrus Hansen here. He's a wild man. He says he wants to see you. Shall I call the police?'

Cameron stopped seeing and hearing. Cyrus Hansen! A white-hot anger swept over her and a part of her wanted to scream, What the hell do you want? Are you trying to influence my evaluation of United Bronze? Because if you are, God help you, Cyrus Hansen! But deep within her was the Cameron who was raised to follow compass points in a storm. Cyrus Hansen was not going to break her pace.

'No. I'll see him.'

Cameron glanced at Byron. 'I'll see you after I dispose of this old friend. Sorry, Byron.'

On his way to his office, Byron passed a man whose face was familiar. Cyrus Hansen. That's who it was. He stared at him with straight, unclouded vision, and among other things he noticed was that Cyrus Hansen didn't notice him. Byron was wrong. He also decided that Hansen was not only a big man, he was smart. And he could be a son of a bitch. In that Byron was right.

Cyrus entered the office looking much as he had earlier in the day. The sight of him threw Cameron into an untypical state of agitation. Here, as in Evan's office, Cyrus seemed to fill the entire room. Her office was no longer hers. He had laid claim to it. Or was it herself he had laid claim to? She clasped her hands in her lap because they were trembling.

'Good afternoon, Cameron.' They might have been speaking to each other regularly – not as lovers but as friends – on a daily basis for years.

'What brings you here?'

'I was in the neighbourhood so I thought I'd drop in.'

The arrogant bastard! For a moment Cameron felt she had lost the capacity to breathe. Then she quickly pulled herself together. 'I see.'

'I realize I'm interrupting your day.' There was not the merest hint of an apology in his tone.

'You are.'

'But among old friends – '

'Old friends!' Cameron's throat was sore from the strain of holding back the furious words she couldn't say. 'Is this a social call?'

'In a sense. In any case it has nothing to do with your evaluation of United Bronze.'

'That's nice.' Icicles dripped from her voice.

'I'm flying to Cannes tomorrow with a friend. Thanks to you, I have two weeks in which to play.' He gave her an unhurried, intimate smile that told her everything she was thinking was true. 'So tonight would be a good night for us to have dinner.'

'I can't believe you have nothing better to do.'

'I haven't.'

Cameron's resentment flared up and she started to say no, but then she found herself laughing. He was so arrogant, it was funny. And what was one evening? The work she had planned could be tabled for tomorrow. 'All right. We'll have dinner.'

'And mix business with pleasure,' he said. 'We'll discuss Horn's invention.'

'Horn's invention? Harry Horn?'

'Harry Horn and Life Sciences. And Byron Miller.'

'What do you know about Life Sciences?' She was glad she hadn't fumbled the sentence.

Cyrus took his time. 'Everything that you put into the proposal you dropped off at Acorn Ventures.'

'I see.' She was starting to, at least.

'I'm the money behind Acorn Ventures. It occupies the first floor of my New York home. When I'm in town, I live there.'

352

'I thought you raided sick corporations. Sort of a corporate undertaker,' Cameron said weakly.

The expression on Cyrus's face didn't change. All she could see was that he was continuing to measure her.

'I do. I also make venture-capital deals. For every sick company I bury, I try to father a new baby. It sort of balances things out.' His voice had a smile that never reached his mouth. He rose and started for the door. Over his shoulder, he said, 'We'll talk at dinner. I'll pick you up at seven. Wear jeans.'

Cameron wore a trench coat over white jeans and a pale blue-green silk shirt, the colour of the sea at dawn. A small emerald set in an enamelled pendant was suspended from a thin gold chain. Tim had given it to her, and this was the first time she'd worn it since his death.

Cyrus was standing in front of her apartment building beside a waiting cab. 'I'm working on the boat.' He seated himself beside her in the back seat.

Cameron tried not to smile. 'I guessed that.'

'Sorry. I had no time to shower. You can probably smell me.' His smile was merely polite.

'Yes.'

The musky male odour of the man seemed to caress Cameron's body.

'I'll shower when we get to the boat.'

'For me? Please don't.'

'For me.'

The schooner, *Acorn II*, was the biggest boat moored at the West Seventy-ninth Street marina on the Hudson River. The far ends of the U-shaped pier were reserved for boats of such size. The schooner was rigged with fore and aft sails that were neatly furled.

'It's beautiful,' Cameron said.

'She'll do. A boat is a woman. She needs almost as much attention. She's a hole in the water that has to be constantly filled with money,' he said carelessly. 'Still, she's livable. Of course, we've never won the Palm Beach to Bermuda race.'

'Oh, dear. And have you come in second?' Cameron parodied Queen Victoria's famous question.

Cyrus followed her lead. 'Your Majesty, in that race there is no second.'

Dinner for two was set on a small, rectangular table in the main cabin. There was a white Irish linen tablecloth covering the dark walnut table, white-wine glasses, and a bottle of Montrachet 1979 cooling in the ice bucket.

'I had Franz, my houseman, bring everything over from the house,' Cyrus explained as he went to the shower. 'He's a fine chef. I hope you like salmon. What do you drink?'

'Martinis – if it's easy.'

'The fixings are in the refrigerator,' Cyrus said. 'Make yourself one. The liquor cabinet is under the shelves. Pour me a Pinch straight, water and rocks on the side.' He left for the shower.

By the time Cameron had made the drinks, Cyrus came out wrapped in a towel. He took the Scotch and disappeared into the stern of the boat. His body was bronzed and muscular, and Cameron could hardly stop staring at him. She made herself sip her martini with elaborate disinterest. In minutes he returned dressed in white ducks, a white cotton shirt, a rope belt, and bare feet. He drank the glass of water and poured himself a second Scotch. He raised the glass, giving Cameron a glance of amused and tolerant speculation, lacking in any sexual interest.

'To Life Sciences,' he toasted.

'To Life Sciences,' Cameron echoed.

Over dinner he outlined his position. He thought the Harry Horn invention remarkable. He had no opinion of Byron

Miller and Cameron was aware of his suspended judgement. 'Do you vote for him?' Cyrus asked.

'Yes. I would not have selected him to be chief executive if I didn't believe he could handle the company.'

'That'll do. I'm prepared to invest three hundred thousand dollars seed money on two conditions. First Acorn gets thirty per cent of the company's stock.'

Cameron was unprepared for his reasonableness. If Cyrus took 30 per cent of the stock – or 300,000 shares – that left 700,000 shares to be split between Byron and Harry Horn. This was less than many other venture capitalists would demand. She saw no gain in further bargaining.

'Good enough. In fact, generous. What's the second condition?'

'The company, Life Sciences, is never to do business with the Hansen Company.'

His voice was devoid of emotion, but Cameron could tell he had said the words before. Repeatedly. Suddenly their shared past came back to her, and she heard Geraldine's careful voice: 'Elmer Hansen is a very complicated man.' She glanced around the cabin and then at Cyrus's face, searching for the smallest clue, a confession of feeling, a willingness to share. His face was a closed door. She had nowhere to go but forward, so she quickly ran through in her mind the companies that might market the product if the Hansen Company couldn't. There were enough. Life Sciences did not need the Hansen Company.

'Second condition accepted,' she said.

'Good. I'll have Acorn call you in the morning.'

When dinner was over, they each sipped a Courvoisier and talked. They spoke of Geraldine, of Princeton, of Cameron's managing FitzGerald Associates. Cyrus told how he had journeyed around the world, to the Forbidden City in Peking, to Kyoto, the ancient capital of Japan, to the Temple of the Tooth, to the Alhambra, to Knossos. They touched on his penchant for gobbling up corporations and laughed together at Cameron's not knowing he was behind Acorn. They were glib, gossipy, and newsy. They talked the way old friends who are catching up do. It was a triumph of tact.

However, they omitted more than they said. They said nothing about Tim FitzGerald or about Elmer Hansen. Nothing about the death of Cyrus's parents. Nothing about Cameron's hurt when Cyrus vanished into thin air all those year ago. They danced a graceful minuet on a minefield.

Cyrus finished his second cognac and stood up.

'Come. I'll escort you to Riverside Drive and Seventy-ninth Street. I keep a cab waiting when I'm in town. We have a flat price. The driver's name is Max Freud.'

On the way to the cab, Cyrus made no mention of seeing Cameron again, and Cameron was glad. The evening had been very hard work; being alone was less painful than all the artificial warmth.

20

As Cyrus promised, his corporate counsel, Norman Mann, called the next day. In short order a draft of a contract was drawn, and the legal negotiations between Acorn's lawyers and Life Sciences' lawyers began. Lawyers being human and legal fees always being an unstated consideration, it took a tiresome two months before the closing took place.

In the meantime, Cameron met only once with Cyrus Hansen and Evan Perry. She handed each of them a bulky looseleaf notebook containing her evaluation of United Bronze Corporation, and explained how she'd arrived at the numbers. The total price was more than Cyrus had offered but not more than he was willing to pay. Perry did not receive his golden parachute. Instead, she suggested he receive a bonus of one year's salary and a pension of $40,000 a year. That was about equal to the pay of a full professor of English Literature. At first Evan objected strongly to her decision, but when Cyrus made it clear it was this or nothing, he quietly walked off the field. After all, he reasoned, there'd be another ball game next week or next month – and another Chet Bancroft somewhere ready to look up to an ex-all-American basketball player.

Once the $300,000 from Acorn was deposited at Citibank's private banking division, Byron Miller rented factory space in Somerville, New Jersey. Harry Horn and he ordered laboratory equipment and a minimum of office furniture. The telephone, the gas, and the electric companies were notified; they hired Ann McDougal as a receptionist-secretary, and interviewed chemists and lab technicians. Life Sciences was off and running.

* * *

A heavy July rainstorm had flooded the Jersey Turnpike, forcing Cameron to forgo her usual weekend escape to Hightower Farm, her refuge from the pressure cooker of Wall Street. Relaxing in her New York apartment on a leisurely Sunday afternoon, she lay on a couch in front of the unlit fireplace, drowsy, sections of Sunday's *New York Times* scattered on the floor. Somewhere in the distance the house phone rang. It didn't register. The sound of the front doorbell was more penetrating and she opened her eyes for a moment, then closed them again. But when Alda stood directly over her and spoke in an excited voice, she made an effort to keep her eyes open. 'Miss Cameron! Miss Cameron! There's a man at the door with a large package for you.'

'What is it?' she asked sleepily.

'He says he has strict instructions to give it only to you.'

Unwillingly, Cameron roused herself. Automatically she ran her fingers through her hair and shook the loose blue linen caftan she was wearing so it hung properly from her shoulders. Barefooted, she padded across the living room to the entrance hall. And stopped dead in her tracks, her sleepiness gone. Instead of a bonded delivery boy, a tall, sleek – that was the first word that came to mind – handsome man with thick, wavy black hair and a pencil-thin moustache was standing just inside the open door. He'd unbuttoned his raincoat, and she could see he was wearing some kind of a dark uniform with a lot of gold braid.

'Miss Hightower?' Her name was spoken with a liquid accent that brought back memories of her youth. His dark eyes ran knowingly up and down her body, taking in her slightly mussed hair and her bare feet. Suddenly she felt embarrassed. She was naked under her caftan and sensed that the man was aware of that fact. Damn it! Why hadn't Alda warned her? The least she could have done was put on a pair of slippers.

'Yes?' she said.

The man managed a graceful salute while still holding the large package under his left arm. 'I am Captain Mendez. Iberia Air Lines of Spain. My good friend Cyrus Hansen asked me to deliver this personally to you. It comes straight from Madrid.' He handed Cameron the carton.

Startled, Cameron accepted the package. It was so large she had to cradle it awkwardly against her body. She remembered her manners and said, 'Thank you for delivering this on such a wet day. Would you care to step in and have a cup of coffee? Perhaps something stronger? A cognac?'

Captain Mendez coughed discreetly into the back of his hand. 'Unfortunately I cannot. My friend is waiting downstairs in a very damp taxi.' He gave Cameron a courtly smile that left no doubt as to the sex of the waiting friend. 'I have been careless. Knowing Cyrus, I should have anticipated delivering his gift to a beautiful and charming woman. But ...' He raised his hands in a fatalistic gesture. 'A fool deserves his fate. Perhaps another time?'

'Mmmm ...' Cameron mumbled, a prickle of irritation running through her at the captain's high opinion of Cyrus's taste in women.

After shutting the door, Cameron walked slowly back to the living room, placed the carton on the floor in front of the fireplace, and stared at the box. It was a plain, corrugated brown carton about three feet long, over a foot wide, and about a foot deep. Heavy, reinforced tape had been used to seal the carton. She hurried into the kitchen and returned with a sharp carving knife. The tape slit cleanly and the carton opened. Cameron caught her breath in surprise. Inside the carton was a black guitar case. She placed the case on the couch and, kneeling, opened it. When she saw what was inside, she swallowed, forcing down the sudden lump in her throat. Though the case was new, the guitar was not. It was a beautiful instrument, inlaid with a variety of woods and black

359

and white ivory. Everything glowed with the patina of age and loving care. A note had been taped on the inside of the case.

Impatiently, Cameron ripped open the envelope and then cursed herself. In her hurry, she'd torn part of the note. As she smoothed the paper, her fingers seemed thick and unsure. Finally she read what Cyrus had written.

Remember Sam's guitar? This one was made by the same master, Antonio Torres. Play it. Enjoy it, as you once did.

Cyrus

Lovingly, Cameron lifted the guitar from its case and strummed the strings. The instrument had a warm, mellow tone, but it needed tuning. Although it had been years since she'd last touched a guitar, there was nothing wrong with her sense of pitch. The six ivory pegs creaked as she tuned the strings. Her fingers were badly out of practice. And her voice no longer floated effortlessly. She was close to weeping at what she'd lost. Singing and playing the guitar were part of her heritage, a gift from her parents. No matter how different her life was now, she had no right to forget her past. Cameron made herself a promise to practise on this wonderful instrument. And if she ever saw Cyrus again, she would thank him for his reminder and play and sing for him as she had that long-ago sunny day that had once seemed the happiest day of her life.

Cyrus telephoned Cameron on a warm afternoon in September. Her heart leapt and so did her anger over the fact that he had taken so long to call. It was a social call for that evening.

'I'm busy,' she said. She was dining with a recently divorced investment banker who had been waiting in line for a month to see her. She was about to thank him for the guitar, but he cut it briskly.

'We'll have a quick bite at the Four Seasons. I have business in the Seagram Building.'

'I can't.' She should have said her polite good-byes then and there.

'Then we'll take in a show. It should be interesting.'

'I've seen everything worth seeing on Broadway. Besides, I'm busy.' It was her last chance to say good-bye and make it stick.

'We're going to a backer's audition for a new Broadway musical called *Cats*. It should be lively. I'll meet you at seven at the Four Seasons.' He laughed. 'They keep a table for me. I'm the last of the big spenders.'

The backer's audition told Cameron that the show would be a smash hit. If it were a stock, she'd have invested in it. Cyrus did. To the tune of $200,000, almost as much as he'd invested in Life Sciences. After the audition, Cameron thanked him warmly for the gift of the guitar and was about to offer to play for him, then stopped herself. The time wasn't yet right. When he took her home, he stayed in the cab and watched her walk up to the glass door of the apartment building. Once the doorman appeared, the cab drove away.

Two nights later, they went to an auction of fine English and early American furniture held at Christie's. It included silver table services, table porcelains, crystal, and linens. Cyrus bought a George III Sheffield hot water urn for $12,000. After the auction and dinner, Cyrus took her home and said good night in the lobby of her building.

A week later, they had dinner after attending a gallery opening of Cowboy Art. Walking slowly up the now deserted Madison Avenue, they talked about the paintings, especially those devoted to cattle. They spoke of the roundup, the trail, the chuck wagon. Cyrus remembered Russell and Remington, who painted at the turn of the century, depicting the lifestyles of both Indians and homesteaders. He said that the

361

two painters were responsible for the partly mythical, partly true fantasy of the American West that the American people subscribed to in their calendar art and motion pictures.

'One of their biggest collectors is the Twenty-One Club,' Cyrus said.

At this point, four teenagers jumped them. Cameron had been watching the approach of the quartet out of the corner of her eye. The boys were tall, gangling, with Afro haircuts, wearing leather jackets, jeans, and green sneakers – all looking for someone to rip off. She was aware that to look at them directly was to invite trouble. Maybe they would pass them by; she held her breath.

What happened next happened so quickly that only afterwards could Cameron sort it out. All four boys jumped them at the same time. Cyrus pushed Cameron behind him. Obscenities were shouted. Arms and legs flew as Cyrus's right arm swung in a powerful backhand that slammed one boy against the building wall. A second boy knifed out to slash at Cyrus, but before he could do anything, Cyrus caught his wrist and bent it back until Cameron heard the wrist snap. The boy slumped to the pavement. At what seemed the same time, Cyrus grabbed the third boy and flung him bodily at the fourth, who had started to run away. The two of them landed in a heap. Then they staggered to their feet and ran, leaving behind their screaming friends.

'Shall we call the police?' Cameron asked.

'No. I have no intention of spending the night explaining to lawyers how I assaulted those innocent children. We'll go home.'

This time, to Cameron's surprise, he took her upstairs to her apartment.

'Would you like a nightcap?' Cameron's smile bore no trace of intimacy.

'Maybe. We've had a busy evening.'

Cameron searched in her purse for the keys, her fingers

trembling, pressing down the excitement of her body. Whenever she was near him this happened, but she was constantly aware of the need for caution.

Abruptly, she stopped her feverish searching and raised her face to his.

'Kiss me,' she said.

'I think not. Not tonight.'

'Why not tonight?'

'I don't like starting things I can't finish. Tomorrow I sail for Martha's Vineyard.'

'Tomorrow is hours away.'

'Tomorrow is soon enough. I'll skip the nightcap. Thanks anyway.' Cyrus pressed the button for the elevator.

Cameron was very near to hating him, but his voice, the way he held his head, the set of his shoulders, his walk – all the trivial details of the man were involved with her deepest self. Her desire for him overcame her resentment. 'Another day, another $1.98. Another nightcap.'

'Good night Cameron,' Cyrus said as the elevator arrived.

In the starry silence, Cyrus stretched out on the deck of the schooner, smoking a cigar and scanning the sky for an answer. The stars were brighter than the darkness within him. He thought of his planned trip to Martha's Vineyard and of Tracey, the beautiful woman who eagerly waited to crew for him. But the boat was rigged for one and he could handle it without her if he wished. Then his mind veered to Cameron. She had grown into the woman he had foreseen when she was still a shy, lonely teenager. Now, in his imagination, he saw her afresh, her beauty, her sensuality, her intelligence. When we first met, he thought, she was older than her years. She is still older, still wiser.

Since the day of his father's funeral, he had been viscerally opposed to the idea of seeing anyone from Princeton and anyone who was in any way contaminated by his grandfather.

Including Cameron. He was sure of his feelings for her, but he was not sure of her. At this critical moment, she posed a special danger. He was unable to dismiss his sharp intuition that in some way Cameron would weaken him in his fight with Elmer. A leaden feeling settled over his mind and body. He had to maintain a cool detachment with Cameron. But the detachment was becoming increasingly difficult. He did not know how to harden his defences against his feelings for her. It was a mistake to have made the Acorn investment. Yet he had made it, knowingly. It was no use trying to deny he was falling in love with her. He had probably loved her from the beginning, a lifetime ago in Princeton. Her nearness cast a spell over his mind.

But could he risk it? Could he trust her? Who was she? What was she? What were her passions? Some women, some men, breathed only for money. Some for sex, some for power, and some for love. What did Cameron Hightower want?

He put his cigar into a two-thousand-year-old Greek copper bowl that served as an ashtray, stood up, stretched, took a step, and stopped. He watched her walk down the dock towards him. She was wearing a loose shift, thongs, and carried a Pan Am flight bag and a guitar case. Within seconds she was standing on the gangplank, her eyes brilliant in the ship's light.

'I've come to crew,' she said, putting her bag and the guitar case down on the deck.

He reached for her hands as she stepped on board.

It was like a sudden tropical rainstorm. Once they were in the cabin, they started making love, without preliminaries. Their pent-up desires took command of their mouths, of their hands, of the movements of their bodies. Holding her hard with one arm, he slipped his hand gently under her shift, and lovingly caressed all the contours of her body, until she swayed against him, moaning with pleasure, meeting his desire head-on without restraint. Her eyes were closed, and a pulse beat in her neck as she slipped the shift over her head.

'I want you.' Her voice was ragged. 'I want you.'

He stopped her words, licking her with tiny strokes of his tongue, teasing her and then moving away. His touch sent a flush to her brain, heightening the sensations radiating from his fingers. When he lifted his head, the passion in his face matched the passion in hers. All the erotic fantasies she had had about him in the last months now erupted. Her legs weakened, and her eyes were wide and almost wild as her trembling fingers stroked the nape of his neck, unbuttoned his shirt, her hands feeling the muscled texture of his skin, the curling hair on his chest. The hands slipped downward, searching to know all of him, his strength and his need. To learn of him as he was learning of her. When her hands found and stroked his hardness, his body went taut with desire. In seconds he was out of his clothes. He moved quickly, almost roughly, pinning her to him.

'We waited too long,' he murmured, kissing her eyes, her cheeks, her throat.

He lifted her up and carried her into the cabin, laying her gently on a bunk. There, stretched out beside each other, they abandoned themselves to an orgy of kisses and caresses. Cameron was barely able to breathe for her desire. The hunger consuming her became a core of fire. She leaned backwards in his arms, her fingers running like a delicate spider over his face, touching his mouth as though to discover its shape, trailing over his chest, lightly teasing his nipples, and dancing onto his stomach. The sensual patterns caused a shiver of desire to run through him. And when her hand slid downward, lingering over his hard sex, he bit her nipple gently to keep from crying out with pleasure.

' Cyrus . . .' Her voice was husky. 'I always wanted you. Even when I didn't know it.'

'My darling. I always knew.' Cameron found herself

imprisoned in his grip while his tongue, his lips, roamed over her body, boldly, provocatively, enjoying every secret place. Making a choked sound in her throat, she opened herself to his most intimate kiss, crying out at the pleasure he gave her. Her eyes, drugged by the violence of feeling, begged him to take her. Then the earth seemed to tilt, and she had no more words, only her body running liquid fire, twisting and dissolving around him. With a deep male sound, he entered her, his hips moving against her, telling her how much he needed her. Each thrust sent a wild current speeding through her body, demanding more, giving more in return. The world fell away as a cry of ecstasy broke from her and from him in the same instant. And nothing existed but the rapture they shared with each other.

In the morning, a high wind caught the sails of the schooner as it sliced through the water. Cameron and Cyrus were mutually content, at peace with themselves and each other. Finally Cameron strummed her guitar and sang for him as she had when they were very young. And once again, the day became the happiest day in her life. Each had a double identity for the other; the self of the past and the self of the present. Their history gave a special authenticity to their passion. A dream forgone had come true. The alchemy of time made its own rules. Under the compulsion of the present, they did not speak of the years they had been separated. Those years were consigned to another existence. They formed a private boundary not to be crossed. Neither had to be told to avoid what lay in wait beyond the barrier.

The first months were a charmed time for Cameron. She and Cyrus spent every night they could together in her apartment or his house. His bedroom was not a rich man's room. It was a seaman's quarters, almost ascetic, clean and male, darkened to the glare of all city noise and lights, slumbrous as a boat drifting on the waves. It was the simplest of places for the simplest of pleasures. Sometimes they had a brandy before making love. Often, they could not wait. Anything besides their melting together was wasting time.

Occasionally when they lay side by side, drained after their nighttime wanderings over each other's bodies, furtive memories surfaced in Cameron's mind. She had glimpses of a state such as she had only known before with Tim, of such a merging of herself with another that she was bereft of her own identity, yet exalted by a heightened sense of individuality.

During the day, it seemed to Cameron that her eyes, ears, and other senses had become more acute. There were colours in the world she'd not noticed before, wide expanses of odours, ranges of sounds; all the sparkle and variety of life around her now crowded in on her as never before. Everything amused her: the long hours of meetings with Jake on a new issue, the bargaining with managing partners over points in a syndicate, the trading strategies she relayed to Coz, the Ping-Pong with Byron over Life Sciences' progress. All were interlaced with her anticipation of the night with Cyrus.

Cameron never asked herself if this miracle could last. She had learned the hard lesson when young that the heart asks more than life can give. When that is known, all is known. She was content with the warming sun on the here and now. Cyrus had vanished before; he might do so again. He was a man who had never dropped anchor. Something she didn't understand was driving him before the wind. She had thought he was like Tim – a younger version. What a joke on her. Tim had been a rock of a man. Remembering him in the light of Cyrus she recognized for the first time that Tim had fought his big fights before she knew him. He was a man at peace with the world and himself. There were no more wars, no more terrible confrontations for him, except the one with

Rhoda and his children. And for that, she had been a touchstone, his ally. Her life with Tim had been almost easy.

Cyrus was another matter. He was caught in some inner maelstrom. Nothing was settled for Cyrus, least of all his feelings about her. Who hurt you so? she sometimes wondered. Who, long ago, did something so ugly, so indecent that the memory breaks your heart? Cameron loved Cyrus deeply but she didn't understand him. The only time she was sure he was with her was when his passion for her dulled his caution. Then she could feel his love, hard and strong and absolute.

Yes, he might hurt her; and if he did, she would outlive the anguish. Women do. As for now, she would not trade the sweet violence of their nights for money, fame, wealth, or peace of mind; if such a trade were offered.

Imperceptibly, like the first workings of autumn after a long, hot summer, deep changes began to affect the lives of Cameron and Cyrus. On the surface, things seemed much the same. They would go to the theatre, to parties, to galleries, to movies. They would sail on the *Acorn II*, drive to Hightower Farm for the weekend. They would go to out-of-the-way restaurants in the Village, Little Italy, and Chinatown. And Cameron came to know Cyrus. When, in an expansive mood, he talked and played with ideas, Cameron would feel the strength of his mind and be hypnotized by his thinking, sometimes against her will. She would sense too the implacable rage that ran like an undertow beneath his sardonic wit. What did it mean?

There was another, even stranger note. Wherever they went, and whatever they did, she was becoming aware of a hovering phantom. Her very presence seemed to call it forth. They were never alone. There was always someone with them.

Once she alarmed herself when he was overly silent by spontaneously bursting out, 'Cyrus, what is it?'

And Cyrus, like a good priest, calmed her. 'I'm thinking, that's all. You remind me of many things I'd forgotten for years. It's not you, it's me.'

Thanks for easing my conscience, Cameron thought. To know all is to forgive all. I am forgiven. But for what am I being forgiven?

Cyrus Hansen and Norman Mann met in Cyrus's office to review the state of Acorn's investment portfolio. The holdings in new companies backed by Acorn Ventures had gone from the first $2 million when Acorn opened its doors some ten years ago to $60 million. Not all the new companies Acorn backed had been winners, but some were well on their way. A discount brokerage firm started by two brothers on the West Coast was flourishing. They offered no advice but simply executed customer orders cheap and fast. So was a fast-food training centre for promising personnel from fast-food chains. It was a specialized MBA school for those dedicated to fast eating and to making a living by supplying the demand for speedy hamburgers, fried fish, fried chicken, hot biscuits, tacos, and the like. A computer-game company had doubled its sales. About Life Sciences, one of the more recent ventures, Mann had not much to report.

'Naturally, they need money. Two million dollars, more or less. The question is how to raise it. Miller wants a public stock offering.'

'Less stock dilution for him,' Cyrus said.

'For him and for us,' Mann said. 'I have mixed feelings. If the prototype machine can be built before the two million is spent, it makes sense.'

'We own almost as much of the company as Miller and Horn,' Cyrus noted.

'Also, if we go public it could make a lot of small investors rich. That's good publicity. The American dream come true.'

Mann pursed his lips. 'The problem is, suppose the machine takes longer to complete and more than two million is needed?'

'Then a 146 private placement is in order. And we all take a big stock dilution.'

'Yeah. It's a judgement call,' Mann said.

After the meeting ended, Cyrus sat alone doodling on his notepad, glancing intermittently at the blank screen of the computer on his desk. Abruptly, he switched the machine on and started punching buttons. In a matter of seconds a full report on the Hansen Company lit the screen.

Everything was flat. The gross was flat, profits were flat. The reason was no new products. The price of the stock was dropping, down to 62 this morning. Cyrus made a note. It had been as high as 110. The Hansen Company was like an apple ripening. Cyrus switched off the computer and considered his holdings. He owned 10 per cent of the company, worth about $620 million. When the right moment came, he would make his move. He stood up and walked around the office restlessly. When would the right moment come?

Elmer Hansen was no Evan Perry, nor did he bear the vaguest resemblance to the other incompetents Cyrus had fired after acquiring their companies. Those men, like Perry, were primarily interested in their inflated salaries, their too lavish perks, their lucrative stock options. And, of course, by surviving until they reached sixty-five, they could retire to Palm Beach or Palm Springs or Palm Desert or Palm Wherever. They could then practise hitting 5 irons, in the hope of playing golf with professionals in celebrity tournaments and being seen on television, while the corporation they left behind continued to struggle with still another indifferent, unqualified chief executive, selected by the same inept board. As for the shareholders, fuck 'em. Who the hell cares about the shareholders' money? Cyrus grimaced in disgust. Business was his love. He despised men who reached for positions of responsibility and then behaved irresponsibly. Such men were like termites. Often there was little worth saving in the companies they ran. But if there was, once he took over, he placed men in charge who could do the job expected of them. He saw to it that they benefited substantially; the company then revived and prospered, and the shareholders profited from a higher stock price. Everyone gained, he most of all.

His gain was more than financial. Nothing that he'd done since he'd stopped trying to break up every bar from Rio to Hong Kong was simply to make more money. Cyrus suppressed a short, harsh laugh at the frequent implication in newspaper reports that greed was what motivated his corporate raids. He was worth over half a billion dollars. What in God's name could he do with still more money?

But he could do a great deal with the experience he gained. Every move he made was designed to teach him yet another aspect of what it took to run a multibillion-dollar corporation. He must learn everything, from corporate finance to new-product development, including production, internal operations, and marketing. He had to test and season his judgement of people and business situations. Learn what a business school could never teach him. Learn in the real world where a wrong decision could bankrupt a company. He was preparing himself, with what amounted to religious zeal, for the major task of his life: to take over the Hansen Company. He was as ready as he would ever be. The only question was, when would the Hansen Company be ready for him? When would it be most vulnerable? When was the right time to take on his grandfather? To prove that he was the Hansen of the Hansen Company?

Cyrus hated his grandfather with a cold, unrelenting hatred that had increased as he grew older. He hated him for what he had done to his parents. All these years later, Cyrus understood that Elmer had destroyed his son out of frustration, because Ellie was incapable of managing the Hansen Company. It meant nothing to Elmer that his son's ability to use his hands to make things work was a rare and wonderful gift. All it meant to him was that Ellie couldn't think. He wanted his son to be a brilliant executive, not a toolmaker. A toolmaker wasn't good enough. So he flushed his son down the drain. Then there was Cyrus's mother. Cyrus hated Elmer for murdering his mother. Not actually killing her, but somehow, in some way, he knew Elmer was to blame for his mother's fatal fall from her horse. Cyrus wanted revenge, not the physical vengeance he had thirsted for as a young man. That was meaningless. He wanted a true vengeance. He would take from Elmer the only child Elmer ever loved – the Hansen Company itself.

It would be a bloody fight. Cyrus had no illusions about his grandfather's strength. He'd never allowed his hatred of Elmer to blind him to what an extraordinary man he was. The Hansen Company was a monument to Elmer Hansen's ambition, brilliance, and endurance. But time was with Cyrus. Cyrus remembered reading an interview with the great heavyweight boxing champion Joe Louis. In his prime, Louis said, he never saw an opening. He just hit his opponent. Later, he saw all the openings, but by the time he threw a punch, the opening was gone. Judging from the latest reports of the Hansen Company, the same thing was happening to Elmer. Ten years ago the company had been growing at an annual compounded rate of 15 per cent, both in sales and profits. Elmer never had to look for new products, they came to him. Now, Cyrus thought, by the time he finds them, it's too late. Another company has taken over the market and the opportunity is lost, Elmer, like Joe Louis, was an old champion who should retire.

Cyrus shook his head. Who was he kidding? Elmer would never retire. He'd fight like a cornered wild boar. And Elmer was just as violent, just as dangerous. But Cyrus was Elmer Hansen's grandson. It would be Hansen against Hansen. The timing of his attack must be perfectly calculated because timing was everything.

This made him think of Cameron. His palms were wet. Memories as thick as wasps buzzing about their nest invaded his brain, stinging him so deeply he froze with the beauty and pain of what had happened. Cameron reminded him constantly of things he must forget until after he'd finished with his grandfather. Though her face was beautiful and her body now the body of a woman, she remained the Cameron of his youth. The boy who was a girl. Who he'd almost killed himself to save. He'd charted a course years ago where Cameron was concerned, and he looked back only to wince at the degree to which he had lost his bearings. How had he managed to go so far off course? What was he doing with her? What was he going to do about her? Her presence in his life stirred him profoundly. Yet, at the same time, something as vivid but totally different continued to move him still more. It was the warning he'd felt at the beginning. Now that he was gathering his strength for the battle with Elmer, he felt a dark apprehension. Something within him argued against making any decisions about Cameron. It left him with a dry, bitter taste in his mouth, be it right or wrong. All he did know was that he could do nothing. He could only take half-measures – and wait.

21

All signals were go for Life Sciences.

An assistant chemist was hired by Harry Horn. A top-drawer machine designer, Peter 'Pee Wee' Spokane, came on board as a consultant; his assignment was to draw up sketches for the prototype machine that would make the Thermoscan. The machine would manufacture Horn's unique creation in quantity. If the prototype machine – Junior Wheel as it was called – could make 500 Thermoscans a day, it would be the model for the King Wheel that would make 50,000 a day.

Cameron, Cyrus, Jake, and Byron met in Cameron's office to discuss infusing more capital into Life Sciences. Byron had come prepared with cash-flow projections and Spokane's preliminary designs for the new prototype machine. They needed money in pretty short order, Byron explained. The seed money of $300,000 had slipped through the cracks into the dirt beneath the factory. What was needed now was $2 million to get the company past the start-up stage.

'I think a public offering is in order,' Byron said. 'Two hundred thousand shares of Life Sciences stock at ten dollars a share. That should carry us until the prototype machine is built.'

Cyrus disagreed. 'I don't think the company is ready for a public stock offering.'

'When will it be ready?' Cameron asked.

'When the prototype machine is completed,' Cyrus said.

'That could be a year from now. It would be 1986!' Byron exclaimed.

Cameron was crisp. 'Cyrus is not arguing the need for the

374

money. He believes it should be raised privately, not publicly. Isn't that correct?'

'Thanks for the translation,' Cyrus said. 'I was thinking about a 146 private placement.'

That was the logical way for Cyrus to go, Cameron realized. She should have seen it coming.

'Why?' Jake asked. 'A 146 is for sophisticated investors only.'

Suddenly Byron erupted. 'What a crock that word is – "sophisticated"! Pardon me if I throw up. They're big-buck investors, period. That's what a 146 is. In Pennsylvania, I believe, a so-called sophisticated investor refers to someone who earns two hundred thousand dollars a year and has a net worth of one million dollars. Excluding real estate – meaning their home. In some states it may be more than a million in net worth.'

'I gather you don't like the idea,' Cameron said.

'That's an understatement. The only thing I like less is a news announcement saying, "We're on red alert." '

'It does protect the small investor,' Jake said mildly.

'That's the party line. The 146 private placement protects the public from chancy investments. If the "sophisticated" investor wants to play it fast and loose and drop a few hundred thou, he doesn't go without filet mignon. But if the local grocer drops a five-thousand-dollar bill, he might run short of money for his mortgage payments. So goes the press release.' Byron snorted. 'However, the bread is buttered on both sides for the snappy swingers who qualify as "sophisticated". For them we issue more stock.'

'Probably another million shares,' Cyrus said.

'Naturally. Another million. So those gourmet scavengers can buy in at two dollars a share. Unlike the working stiff, whose ticket of admission could be ten dollars a share.'

'The theory of a 146 private placement is that the risk is greater, so the rewards are greater,' said Jake.

'I know the theory. It's like the theory that the sun revolves around the earth. It's ass backwards,' Byron protested. 'The laws are busy protecting the poor middle class against itself. Also against the horror of making any real money. The public can't buy stock in a 146 placement because the public's money would be at risk. But for taking that risk, which they can afford, the rich buy in for less, and get more. Whoopee! So the rich get richer and we all know what the poor can do.'

'Go fight the system,' remarked Jake.

'I intend to.' Byron looked straight at Cyrus. 'Do you know that if we did a 146, I couldn't buy stock in my own company?'

'Not even if you wrote a certified cheque,' Jake agreed.

'That stinks!' Byron was shaking his head. 'Friends, I want to spread the goodies around. Everyone's welcome. Come one, come all. At ten dollars a share. Buy one share for your kid's birthday. Five shares for an anniversary present. Five hundred shares for a nest egg. That's how the public gets in on the ground floor of a big new oil gusher.'

'We should be so lucky,' Jake commented.

'If I didn't believe it was going to happen, what the hell am I doing here?' Byron asked heatedly. 'Two dollars a share? It's un-American. It makes some men less equal than others.'

There was a moment of quiet in the office as everyone digested Byron's vehemence.

Cyrus spoke first, 'Your concern for the ordinary investing public is touching. Is it possible this burst of patriotism has something personal about it?'

'You bet your sweet bippy! I too am one of the great unwashed. If we go the "sophisticated" investor route, we'll have to issue those extra million shares. And that dilutes my ownership. Harry's, too.'

'It would do that. From thirty-five per cent to seventeen and a half per cent,' Cyrus said flatly. 'And mine from thirty to fifteen per cent. But I'm willing.'

'That's mighty generous of you, Cyrus,' Byron said. 'But

you don't have to give that much of a damn about your ownership in Life Sciences. You're up to your everlasting in Hansen Company stock.' The flush that appeared under Cyrus's skin should have warned Byron off, but he was too far gone to pay attention.

'Add that to your sizable investment portfolio. And add to that the payout from the corporations you've taken over. Plus the other companies like Life Sciences that you've backed with your nickels and dimes. I've read some of them are doing very well. Life Sciences has not exactly cost you your heart's blood.'

'Cyrus is in the venture-capital business. Naturally he owns shares in companies, Byron.' Cameron had not missed the danger signals and she was trying to head Byron off.

'And a very good business it is. If you can afford to be in it. And Cyrus can afford it very well.' Though Byron spoke to Cameron, he never took his eyes off Cyrus. 'With all due respect, Cyrus, you don't take a full pound of flesh. I speak from experience. But you don't give your money away, either. That's not the capitalist way. And we both believe in capitalism.'

'Cut it out, Byron.' By now, Jake had had enough.

'I won't,' Byron insisted, his eyes still fixed on Cyrus. 'What does Life Sciences matter to Cyrus Hansen? If it falls out of bed, he won't lose a night's sleep. A company is like a bus to Cyrus. Never run to catch a bus. There'll always be another one in five minutes.' Byron swallowed. 'But what is it to me? It's my life. And Harry Horn? It's also his life – and his soul! And that's why I want as small a dilution as possible, I want a public offering.'

People shifted position again as they do in the theatre after a highly emotional scene. Cyrus was the least impressed. He'd been through similar arguments too many times before.

'You've forgotten one important point, Byron,' Cyrus said. 'Things can and do go wrong. This is a complicated machine.

377

You could run out of money before it's completed. Two million dollars stretches only so far. Then what? You could go back to your sophisticated investors. They have the resources to back up their original investment with more money. It'll be a lot harder to get a refill from the Street if you go into the public market.'

'Nothing will go wrong! Spokane is the best form, fill, and seal man in the business. He designed the machine used to package sleeping pills.'

'Sleeping pills are a reasonable size,' Cyrus pointed out. 'This machine must form, fill, and seal dots that are almost microscopic. It's never been done before.'

'Spokane can do it. He could design a machine to print on the head of a pin,' Byron insisted. 'With space for angels to dance.'

'I realize FitzGerald Associates makes less on a private placement than they do on a public offering,' Cyrus said to Jake.

Jake reared up at the implication that profit was influencing his position.

'If we do decide on a public offering, it will be too small for FitzGerald Associates to handle.' Cameron gave Jake a hard look. 'We'll probably take it to Claxton, Mazlow.'

'I didn't say anything,' Jake muttered into his chest.

Cameron read the printout in her mind with sharp distaste. Byron was pulling one way and Cyrus another. The decision was up to her.

'Your point is well taken, Cyrus. We're all concerned about the risks involved in building the prototype machine,' Cameron said carefully. 'But with two million dollars in the bank, I think Life Sciences buys enough time for Spokane to do the job.' After seconds of silence she added, 'And I have to admit that I lean towards a public offering. It does give the average investor a chance to get in on what could be a major American corporation.'

Cyrus abruptly rose to his feet. There was a note of both irritation and concern in his voice. 'None of you' – he pointed at Byron, Jake, and Cameron – 'have the foggiest idea of what you're doing. You don't see the risks. All you see are the rewards.' He shook his head disgustedly. 'I'll see you tonight, Cameron. Until then, you might consider if Wall Street is the place to make a philosophical statement about the right of the public to lose money.'

That night Alda had prepared baked pompano espagnole. It was one of Cyrus's favourite dishes, and since Cyrus was Alda's favourite guest, she delighted in crushing the peppercorns and kneading the butter and flour together for him. While waiting for dinner to be served, Cameron and Cyrus had been having desultory conversation. 'Junk gossip,' Cameron called it in her own mind; a way of talking, yet saying nothing that mattered. Cameron was waiting for the real topic to be raised.

Now she stretched out on the couch in the library, nursing her martini and watching Cyrus pour himself a third double Scotch from the bottle of Haig and Haig Pinch. Being alone with Cyrus, knowing that in a short time they would be making love, was like a drug that blurred all her senses. She could not remember a time, not even when she was starting out on Wall Street and first discovered the magical gift of high sexuality that nature had lavishly bestowed on her – not even in the years she'd lived with Tim – when her body had so needed the fulfilment of having a man. Specifically, of having Cyrus.

The sound of his voice broke through her reverie. Very casually the subject emerged. 'Cameron, did Tim FitzGerald ever put together any pure venture-capital deals?'

That was a novel opening. Time, indeed, Cameron thought. What was this sudden resurrection of Tim, whom they had barely mentioned since they met? With a certain reluctance she sat up.

'You mean start-up situations? Not new issues of already existing private companies?'

'Yes, start-up situations.'

'In the time we knew each other, no. But he had in the past.'

'Then you've had no real experience with them?'

'Not first hand,' Cameron admitted. 'But I did listen to Tim describe his experiences, and I'm a good listener.'

'Yes, you are. When you want to listen. By the way, how did you get Jake to agree to your getting into Life Sciences at this stage?'

'I didn't. Rosemary did.'

'I should have guessed,' Cyrus said. 'Look, FitzGerald was brilliant and experienced. By the time you met him, he'd learned that certain risks are not worth taking.'

'You believe he would have done the 146 private placement.'

'Yes. He would want to protect the public. As Byron put it so neatly, "from itself".'

'I can't say I like the implication.' Cameron's back went up. 'And as for what Tim would or wouldn't have done, we'll never know.'

'That's true. So let me remind you of Arthur Stone and Charlie Fargo. Two of the biggest venture capitalists around.'

'They were on my original list for start-up money.'

'They should have been. They do start-up situations all the time. But out of ten investments they expect five to go belly-up within two years. Either the product doesn't work or the entrepreneur can't hack it. Four others will limp along with no one making much money on them. So the tenth one has to be a big winner. Arthur Stone looks to make twenty to thirty dollars for every one dollar invested in his winner. To pay for the nine that don't make it.'

Cameron said, 'I know the numbers.'

'You know Stone's numbers but you don't know mine.' His tone was cutting. 'I don't work the same way. I don't like to lose. Ever! I don't back ten ventures in order to lose with nine and make it big with the tenth. I expect all my deals to be winners. And I fight to make them winners. I let Miller spout that bus routine at the meeting because it was your meeting. But the fact is, I've caught the bus, paid my fare – three hundred thousand dollars to be precise – and I expect it to take me where I'm going. To become a major company.'

'Isn't that where we're going?'

'It is not. And you're going to get yourself hurt. Your optimism and your belief that Byron can walk on water has stopped you from looking at the downside risks. If that machine takes longer to develop than you've estimated, you're heading into a very nasty collision with Wall Street psychology.' He sat down beside her and placed his drink next to hers. 'Cameron, you've made a mistake. It could be a serious one.'

'Because I believe that the public should have first crack at Life Sciences' stock?'

'Yes. They should have a crack, but not first crack. Not at this stage,' he said, clearly disappointed in her. 'Wall Street has its favourites. And its out-of-favourites. If Life Sciences doesn't live up to its promises and fails to satisfy their fantasy lusts, Wall Street can turn on a dime. Then, should you need another injection of money, there may be a shortage of donors.'

'You're thinking about the machine. It will be ready on time,' Cameron said stubbornly.

'I hope so. I told you. I don't like losing. I don't like being wrong. Even more, I don't like being wrong about you.'

Suddenly Cameron felt herself struggling with an unwanted shyness.

'Cyrus, do you mind telling me what we're talking about?

Do you mean if I make a mistake, you'd be wrong about me?'

'Yes. You'd be wrong, and when you're wrong you get hurt.'

'I've been hurt before on the Street. I can handle it . . .' Her words trailed off as she watched his face.

'If you're wrong, you will get hurt,' he repeated. 'If you get hurt, I get hurt. And I don't mean financially.'

'I don't understand . . .'

'I'm falling in love with you. That's what's wrong.'

'Oh.'

'And I can't seem to stop it.'

'Well,' she said.

'And what about you?' he asked, as if wanting to know the day of the week.

'I have been for years.'

'The exact words, please,' he said, not giving any concession.

Cameron closed her eyes for an instant, then plunged. 'I love you. I've loved you since the first day, when you crashed the car.' She went to him, putting her arms around his body, burying her head against his chest.

'Must we have dinner?' His voice was hoarse.

To everything there is a season, and to Claxton, Mazlow this was their season. The small Wall Street house never had a private dining room where the silver was initialled with the housemark, as Lehman Brothers did before the company was taken over. The wall panelling had not been purchased from some great old mansion on an estate in the throes of becoming a housing development. Instead, there was one large office, almost a bull pen, and men of all sizes, shapes, and ages – a few women too – were hunched over their chairs at their overcrowded desks. Here and there, one would wolf down a sandwich and grab a swallow from a container of coffee. Their motto was to sell! Sell! Sell! Whatever the house was selling that day. And they did it in New York nasal tones, Southern accents and Western drawls.

To any casual observer happening to stop in at Claxton, Mazlow, the brokers pushing their wares, coaxing and cajoling their clients, might have sounded like circus barkers. To Byron, who did occasionally drop in, they were his barkers. And the mention of Life Sciences was music to his ears, an angel choir.

'Yes, Mr Jorgenson, it's gonna be a big winner. The biggest! You can retire to Stockholm on the money you'll make. One hundred shares? Don't be foolish. It's the chance of a lifetime. At least three hundred. At ten dollars a share it's a steal. A lousy three thousand dollars to get you set for life, Mr Jorgenson. For life, I said. With Life Sciences.'

One former used-car salesman said, 'Rufus, I wouldn't steer you wrong. Cyrus Hansen put his own money into this thing. Now that's strictly QT. But it's the truth. May God strike me dead! I got it from Claxton himself. It's a new technology. Technologies are in! No, Rufus, forget about utilities. Utilities are lights-out. Banks got bad loans. Can I write you down for six hundred? Come on, man, this is no time to be a piker. You wanna run a drugstore all your life?'

The following tombstone was published in *The Wall Street Journal* four months later:

This announcement appears as a matter of record only

> May 3, 1985
> LIFE SCIENCES, INC.
> 200,000 shares
> common stock
> price $10.00 per share
>
> ---
>
> The public placement of these shares was
> arranged by Claxton, Mazlow, Inc.

Once the money was deposited in the Life Sciences account at Citibank, Harry Horn hired two more chemists and Pee Wee Spokane finished the drawings for the prototype machine that would eventually be the model for the mass-production machine that would make the Thermoscans by the tens of thousands.

Margo Bayless, a small young woman with a slightly too round figure, had a pleasant, if uninspiring face. To look at her one would never suspect that the sexual act in all its variations was her second greatest pleasure. She had started out in the advertising business and then opened a marketing consulting firm in her apartment on East Fifty-seventh Street: Margo Bayless Associates. She had an instinct for marketing, and a man could talk business to her, ideas and products, both in and out of bed. One of her off and on again steadies was Herbie Claxton.

It was Herbie who explained to Margo that for a marketing pro she didn't know her own market. What she should look for was a dedicated entrepreneur who had a product with potential, or at least a product with pizzazz and, hopefully, some substance. Such were the men she should cultivate, not the corporate executive types she was cosying up to, with their marketing directors, staffs, and services, all ready to argue against any proposal Margo submitted. She was up against the NIH factor – Not Invented Here – that scotched any chance she might have with a corporation. But the new boy in town, the entrepreneur, who had no marketing director or staff, was the bandwagon to jump on. That was the bandwagon Herbie had jumped on. There was also, of course, the tender, loving care she could offer along with her professional services.

So quite naturally, when Margo saw the Life Sciences tombstone with Claxton, Mazlow as the underwriter, she questioned Herbic about the new venture.

He nodded. 'You catch on fast. Byron Miller is a live one.'

'What about an introduction?'

'I was wondering when you'd ask.'

If Byron's recent life could have been graphed by a chartist, it would have been a jagged line with many highs and lows. While Harry Horn searched for chemists, Byron interviewed marketing men and women. He wanted to get a handle on what it would take to get national distribution for the Thermoscan.

'Okay. What's your pitch? A marketing study? A marketing director? Registered reps? What?'

'Don't be naïve, Mr Miller,' Margo Bayless smiled. 'What you need is not a marketing staff, a marketing director, or registered reps. Not for a company as small as yours. What you need is a marketing contract from a big company whose speciality is selling. That's all they know how to do – market, sell – sell mouthwash, toothpaste, adhesive bandages, baby powder. Why not Thermoscans? And I have the connections to just the right people. Together, we should come up with a very profitable marketing contract.'

Byron eyed her with a certain detachment. 'Beautiful. So they market the product for us,' he said, 'and pay us a snappy ten per cent royalty over factory costs, and maybe fifteen per cent if we're lucky. Why don't I just give it to them for free?'

'Mr Miller! The way they market – which is their lifeblood – that lousy fifteen per cent would add up to millions.'

'You haven't thought it through,' Byron insisted amiably. 'But why don't you try convincing me over dinner tonight? And you can tell me about all your connections.'

Byron and Pee Wee Spokane had a series of nuts and bolts meetings with the tool and die maker at Pentacol Tool and Die. Pee Wee's detailed drawings for Junior Wheel were theoretically beautiful.

'It's a pisser!' Ivan Leonderoff, the owner of Pentacol, enthused.

'Then what's taking so long to finish it?'

'It's also a killer, that's what,' Ivan said, chewing on his cigar. He went on to say that in the tradition of form, fill, and seal machines, a star had been born, but with one tiny flaw. The star had an eye in the middle of her forehead. She needed cosmetic surgery.

'Damn it! What's the problem?' fumed Pee Wee.

Byron, having heard all this good news on the telephone from Ivan, got busy pacifying Pee Wee. 'Don't take it to heart. There are bugs to be ironed out.'

'What bugs?' Pee Wee asked belligerently.

'Bugs!' Leon said, getting mad. 'What do you think? I like bugs? I hate 'em. They keep me awake nights. My wife, she knows about beetles, ants, roaches, mosquitoes. She should know about bugs in machines.'

'What bugs?' Byron asked, patience personified.

'The fills in this machine have to be absolutely exact. Am I right?' He didn't wait for an answer. 'There are two thousand fill holes in this machine, one-twentieth of an inch in size. Teeny-tiny tots, those fill holes. And every damn one of them has to be perfectly sized.' Leon spat out cigar chewings into a spittoon. 'This reminds me of my wife and her embroidered pillows. We have to embroider two thousand fill holes. It's a bitch!'

Things went from bad to worse, as they sometimes do. Byron, Pee Wee, and Leon had seven more meetings in five months and then slowly but surely, by reason of perseverance, imagination, sweat, and obscenities, things went from worse to somewhat less worse. Eventually Byron could say, 'Look what us kids hath wrought.' Although he wasn't Alexander Graham Bell, and the invention wasn't a telephone, it was a totally original form, fill, and seal machine that he had somehow pushed to completion.

The Junior Wheel was finally shipped to the factory at Life Sciences.

'This is not a dirty phone call,' Byron said when he telephoned Cameron.

When he relayed the news Cameron said, 'Great!'

'Don't swill any champagne. Not yet. Our fun is just beginning. They filled the holes with oil. We have to fill those little buggers with liquid crystals.'

'I'm on your side.'

'We ought to have a meeting.'

'You're thinking about money.'

'Cameron Hightower, I am obsessed with money. I just wrote out a cheque for one million two hundred thousand to Pentacol Tool and Die. For the creation of the Junior Wheel. That does not mean we're flat-ass broke, but a young executive has to think of his future.'

Byron went to Cameron's office. Jake was sitting in, lusting for a brawl.

'I suspect you recognize something familiar about my anxiety,' Byron said.

Before Cameron could answer, Jake jumped in. 'Having a nice time?' he squawked. 'Eating well? I notice you bought a new jacket, also a new Ford. Two million can buy some trinkets.'

'I leased the car to get to the factory,' Byron shouted. 'The IRT subway does not run to Somerville, New Jersey.'

Byron and Jake went at each other. Jake screamed, Byron yelled, and both beat the table like a married couple having a long-repressed fight. What had happened to Byron's promise of progress? Jake demanded. Where was the finished prototype machine? he asked. Nowhere, he answered himself. 'Sure, I lost faith. You got two million American dollars. That's money. Over a billion pesos in Mexico. We've got no results to show for it.'

Cameron allowed the battle to take its natural course. If

Byron believed enough, he would prevail over Jake. Jake's spine needed constant testing; it was too prone to caving in under pressure.

With this in mind, she was silent, forcing Byron to explain why the machine had taken so long and how much more money was needed to complete it. He had to lobby his heart away to get the concession from Jake that perhaps another public offering was in the cards.

'We should have gone the 146 route as Cyrus wanted,' Jake pouted.

'No, we shouldn't have. What's wrong with another public offering?' Byron asked.

'Nothing,' Cameron said. She was remembering all too well what Cyrus said originally, 'Nothing at all. But you have no news. And on Wall Street no news is bad news. What can we say? The prototype machine isn't quite ready? It will take another six months, maybe a year? "See you around the ball park," they'll say.'

'There are unforeseen complications,' Byron gave Jake the placating smile of the underdog. 'I am sorry.'

Jake was sorrier and forgave him nothing.

Cameron decided a cooling-off period was necessary. 'We'll take the weekend to think. If we bring out a second stock offering, it will have to be at seven and a half dollars a share. That's the current market price. We could raise six million.'

'For how many shares?' Byron asked in pain.

'Eight hundred thousand. That should give Life Sciences six million dollars. Enough to carry it until the prototype machine is completed.'

Cameron saw Byron's sick expression. He hated the idea of selling company shares at what he considered a deep discount price. So she searched for an option. 'Byron, what you need is someone of stature – someone who Wall Street respects – to say the Thermoscan works. That it's a break-through invention, like the pill. And once the machine is ready, it will move at full speed. Someone like David Sarnoff, for instance.'

'But in pharmaceuticals,' Byron's mind started to stretch.

'Yes, someone like Sarnoff, but in pharmaceuticals. Sarnoff had scientists working on twenty different inventions at the same time. He'd walk through the labs and say, "We'll go with this. Junk that." He was right often enough. That was how he built RCA.'

'He also had his off days. Didn't he dump the dry photocopier, known today to their admirers as Xerox? And videotape, which those horse traders at Three M picked up for a song.'

'He missed some. But Wall Street forgets that. What they remember is the legend of the man. That Sarnoff looked at the group who was tossing dots around and said, "Let there be colour television." And one year later there was. You need someone like him to say, "Aaah, yes, the Thermoscan." Now that would be news. Then we could ask fifteen dollars a share for the next stock offering.'

'Thirty dollars,' Byron whispered as he left Cameron's office thinking about David Sarnoff. Where was he now that a new technology needed him? Suddenly Margo Bayless appeared on Byron's inner TV screen. He grinned. He had always believed in serendipity. He used a street phone to call, and a woman's voice answered.

'Margo Bayless Associates.'

'This is Byron Miller. Don't I know you from somewhere?'

'From dinner some months ago. And that delicious dessert afterwards. What took you so long to call?'

'To everything there is a time. I was thinking about your pithy comments between cigarettes. Do you happen to know a David Sarnoff?'

'You mean a David Sarnoff of pharmaceuticals?'

'You follow my thinking exactly.'

'Why don't you drop by my place? We'll comb my Rolodex. And maybe sample another dessert.'

22

Cyrus Hansen sat in his office, his features set in a rigid grimness which the computer screen on his desk seemed to intensify. The readout was a repeat performance. As he had anticipated, earnings were flat, profits down, and company stock off another six points at 55, or more than 50 points below its high. The Hansen Company needed new products badly. The research and development division had not had a new idea in years. Word came back to Byron regularly that Elmer was beating the bushes looking for a winner, but nothing had materialized. Another few months, and it would be time for him to move. Thinking about the Hansen Company brought Cameron to mind, and as always the association disturbed him. He was still undecided what to do about her. He loved her and she said she loved him. Did he really then have a choice? Unlike his usual behaviour, he had procrastinated, searching for some compromise. He thought he'd found one, but he was worried about Cameron's reaction when he told her what he had in mind.

Margo Bayless and James Taylor, vice president in charge of marketing for the Hansen Company, had been friends for years, until James's wife had sensed trouble. Then James had reluctantly bowed out, knowing that Elmer fired employees for even rumoured infidelity. Elmer had no patience with sexual peccadilloes, which he regarded as a detriment to dedication. What the old monk himself did when his gonads were on the march, James couldn't guess; maybe he fucked the balance sheet. Still, James always took Margo's calls, and this time the talk extended to a brief afternoon tête-à-tête at

Margo's apartment. Afterwards, James Taylor was entranced with the Life Sciences project.

Margo had three Thermoscans sent to Taylor, and he promptly brought them to the attention of Sidney Shotz, head of research and development. Shotz knew his name was near the top of the list of those destined for the Elmer Hansen firing squad. During the past year, he had developed no new products, he had found no new products. The price of Hansen stock was running neck and neck with the price of his stock options, so they were currently worth zilch. He was mortgaged to the hilt and he had two daughters in college. If he was fired, his wife would leave him for her dentist. In short, he needed a new product badly.

James Taylor's call was proof of divine grace. Yes, Shotz wanted to see the devices immediately. In point of fact, he marched into Taylor's office to pick them up himself. He read the Life Sciences proposal, and the reports on clinical tests and made notes. Then he called Hobson of the Liquid Crystal Institute and a few others who had done feasibility studies. He made vague promises of perhaps putting them on as consultants. Everyone was enthusiastically cooperative, because PhD's need money like everyone else. Sidney went back to James Taylor and said, 'Let's have a meeting.'

'With Elmer?' James asked cautiously. He knew as well as Sidney that they were entering the lion's den.

'Yes, with Elmer,' Desperation made Sidney brave. 'The material checks out. I'm preparing a report. Would you mind telling Elmer, when you do your memo, that I put you on to the Thermoscan?'

'Of course,' James said, taking in Sidney's pleading smile. But it aroused little sympathy in Taylor. Sidney's troubles with Elmer, of which Taylor was well aware, were Sidney's troubles. James would give credit where credit was due – to himself.

In the privacy of his office, Elmer Hansen read Taylor's

memo. His expression showed nothing, registering none of the scorn he felt for Taylor. The man was a liar, as all good salesmen are. His very sales ability made it impossible for Taylor to distinguish one product from another. As for his mention that Sidney Shotz had reviewed the device and found it plausible, there was the slim chance that Sidney had found the new product. But Elmer didn't believe in slim chances. Sidney was a hack; Sidney lacked imagination. However, he was a good work horse, which was why Elmer employed him. Given something to work on, he would know how to test it, and if need be, develop it. If the Thermoscan was as sound as Shotz's report stated, it would give Shotz something to do and relieve Elmer of the need to fire him. Elmer did not want a new head of R and D with imagination. A man with imagination couldn't be trusted. If he stumbled across something, he might go into business himself, leaving behind only a coded file. Sidney would do, if this was real.

How it had really come to the Hansen Company was something Elmer would delve into later. For now, he wanted to meet the Life Sciences people responsible for it. He buzzed his secretary and told her to call James Taylor and have him contact Life Sciences to set up a meeting for eight-thirty tomorrow morning. He told her to invite Sidney Shotz, and be prepared to sit in and take notes.

Meeting in Elmer Hansen's office, besides Elmer himself and his secretary, were James Taylor, Sidney Shotz, Byron Miller, and Margo Bayless. Shotz and Byron Miller talked, Taylor and Shotz talked, then all three talked together. Elmer listened and Margo observed his close attention. She noticed that he watched Byron most attentively, seeming to sift Byron through his mind. Margo was correct. Byron Miller was not a man Elmer knew, but he recognized the breed. Elmer's expression of mysterious contentment made Margo shudder.

For as long as it takes to cause a chill in the room, Elmer

Hansen remained silent at his desk. The conversation between the other men became stumbling, hesitant, and finally ground to a halt. Then Elmer spoke into the waiting silence. 'Do you have patent protection?' he asked Byron.

'Yes, Mr Hansen. Originally the patents were in Harry Horn's name. He's assigned them to Life Sciences.'

'Who is Harry Horn?'

'Executive vice president. Our research chemist. I'm the business brains.'

Elmer's eyes almost twinkled at the use of the word 'brains'. 'And these are samples of the Thermoscans?' he asked, picking one up from his desk. 'It works on the principle of thermography. As I understand it, it can detect cysts and tumours, benign or otherwise. An advance warning system.'

'That's right. It detects anything. Even down to half a centimetre in size.' Byron spoke with authority. 'A hot spot would indicate a blockage in the circulation. Something to be looked at while the looking is still safe.'

'The product would make a great demonstration for your salesmen,' Margo said, slipping off her jacket and unbuttoning her blouse.

'What are you doing?' Byron was flustered.

'I'm demonstrating,' Margo explained, slipping off her blouse and showing one of the devices that Harry Horn had designed just for her. The Thermoscan was a swirl of blues, greens, and rose. 'See. I'm healthy,' she said, smiling her sweetest smile at Elmer. 'Swirly blues and greens and red. No round blue hot spots.'

'Thank you for the demonstration, young lady. You've made your point,' Elmer stated coldly.

Feeling vaguely deflated, Margo slipped on her blouse, buttoning it with her eyes fixed on her fingers as if they were performing a delicate surgical operation.

'What price were you thinking of asking?' Elmer said to Byron.

'What were you thinking?' Byron parried.

'Fifty cents.'

'Fifty cents!' Byron swallowed glass. It was hopeless. 'It costs us fifty cents to make.'

'You'll show me those figures?'

'They're in the proposal.'

'All right. I agree to the normal one hundred per cent factory markup. We'll pay one dollar apiece and market it.'

'A deal!' said Byron, who had been expecting 60 cents or 70 cents at the most. So it was done! Fantastic!

'We'll have some meetings to iron out time frames,' Elmer said. 'Delivery dates. When we can start marketing the product. And so forth.'

'Absolutely,' said Byron.

'I'll have my lawyers contact you tomorrow. Holden, Hennesy, and O'Neil. You'll be talking to Hennesy. Who'll represent you?'

Byron surprised himself. 'Caldwell and Smith.'

Later, Margo asked him who the hell were Caldwell and Smith. Life Sciences' lawyers were Sweeney, Sullivan, and Weiss, the same as FitzGerald Associates'. What was Byron doing changing lawyers in midstream?

'I met Caldwell playing chess at the Seventy-second Street Chess Club. He's very good. And he's cheaper. Sweeney is four hundred dollars an hour. Caldwell is two hundred dollars.'

Margo had done more than a bit of finessing in her day, and she could spot it under any flag. Byron didn't want Sweeney because Sweeney would discuss the contract with Cameron Hightower. And Byron wanted to make a grandstand play, walk into Cameron's office and flourish the contract like a peace treaty with Russia. Margo wasn't even jealous. If anything, she felt a modicum of pity. Byron was good enough for her. But Cameron Hightower, she thought in a rare spurt of modesty, was in another league. Also,

Margo's network had informed her that Cyrus Hansen had staked out a claim on the property.

Elmer Hansen sat alone in his office reviewing the Life Sciences proposal for the second time. Nothing in him stirred except his mind, which was like a magnet picking up details. When he finished reading, he reached for the private telephone on his desk and dialled a number. 'I want you to find out everything there is to know about Byron Miller,' he said to the man at the other end. 'He's chief executive officer of Life Sciences, a small company located in Somerville, New Jersey.'

'Sure. How soon?'

'Three weeks.'

'I'll be in touch.'

The library in Cyrus's limestone town house was a large room with a scrolled ceiling and dark walnut panelling. There were leather chairs and a great open fireplace that was now warm with the heat of a blazing fire. The long, uncurtained windows looked out over the East River and the low lights of Queens.

Cyrus was squatting, Persian fashion, a short distance from the fire, staring pensively into the flames. A bottle of Taittinger Blanc de Blancs was cooling in the ice bucket; two rock-crystal champagne glasses stood beside it. The new blueprints for the *Acorn* were spread on the floor, blurred by the dancing shadows cast by the fire.

Cameron slipped to her knees beside Cyrus, leaned over and kissed him on the ear. Cyrus smiled, running his hand through her hair.

'I like it more when it's mussed,' he murmured.

'I like it any way you like it.'

'The champagne is chilled. And waiting for our toast.'

'The champagne, the toast,' Cameron said almost

reluctantly. She would have been content to rest a while longer. It was pleasant not to talk, just to be there and listen to the fire singing its own song. She wished to hold on to this precious moment of peace. Looking at the *Acorn* plans meant change. The future stretched away into the mist, never predictable, unknown, unseen – perhaps not what she wanted, not what she hoped for. But this moment was safe and could not be touched. It was odd, she thought, how much she wanted to hold on to this fragment of time. Probably Cyrus would forget this moment as soon as it was over, occupied as he always was with his plans for the future. He wasn't afraid of the future. Why was she?

She accepted the glass. 'To the *Acorn*.'

'To the *Acorn* reborn.'

'To the *Acorn* reborn,' Cameron repeated.

The clinked glasses and Cameron took a deep swallow of the fine champagne. The future was upon them.

'Let's see what you plan to do with that already perfect boat.'

Cyrus gave her a half-smile. 'Not *Acorn* the boat – *Acorn* the house. The plans are for remodelling the interior of this house. I'm going to have it pulled apart and put back together again.'

'Why? The house is perfect. A jewel. Why tear it apart?'

'For us, my darling. I think we should make a change in our lifestyle. I'm tired of sleeping in your bed. You must be just as tired of mine. It's time we started sharing our bed and our bedroom. My bedroom is completely a man's room, yours a woman's. I want the bedroom enlarged into a master bedroom for a master and a mistress. My offices are already set up on the ground floor. But you need your own work space at home. Possibly the top floor?'

'I'm not following you,' she said.

'You have no work space here. You need a place to work in our house.'

Cameron heard his words and it seemed to her then that her vision had cleared. The world had become hallowed and harmonious. How lovely the night was. How it overflowed with softness.

'Cyrus, are you asking me to marry you?'

There was a heartbeat of silence and it seemed to Cameron that his lips formed the word 'yes'. But he said, 'No. Not exactly. Not at this moment. I'm suggesting we live together. Like normal, healthy people in love.'

'Live together? But not marry?'

She heard the strain in his voice as he repeated. 'Not at this moment.'

Cameron felt a pale foreboding. Meagre mementoes of the early morning of her life went streaming through her mind like a series of stop-action snapshots. Memories of Tim, days of wine and wishes.

'I love you. And you love me. Yes?'

'You know that.'

She called on all her strength. 'Then we can wait.'

'You don't want to live with me?' There was an odd note in his voice. It sounded almost as though he were relieved. For an instant her back went up. Why ask her if he didn't want her to accept? She glanced for reassurance at the blueprints. They were real enough. They must stand for something. But he was taking her rejection all too well.

She handed him her empty glass. 'More champagne, please.'

He poured her another glass and refilled his own. She sipped the wine while mulling over the idea. Reality had met her often enough in ugly shapes, and she knew all too well the pranks that fate could play.

'We're happy as we are,' she said at last.

'And you don't want to live with me.'

'Under the circumstances, I don't think it's a good idea.'

The air was heavy in the room, seeming to hold a moment

397

of crisis. It hung before them, dark, menacing, a drop in which all the potential for explosion had collected. Then it gently subsided into the ebb and flow of ordinary conversation.

Cyrus spoke first. 'You're probably right. We'll junk the idea. Forget it.'

'No. I think it's a wonderful idea. Let's not forget it. Let's keep it as something . . . something to look forward to . . .'

'We have enough to look forward to as it is,' Cyrus said as he rose to his feet and gathered the plans. He rolled them up and reinserted them in the cylinder in which they had been delivered. 'I'll send them back.'

'Oh, Cyrus! Don't!'

'Why not? We don't need them.'

But we might someday, was what she wanted to say. Instead, she took his hand and placed it against her cheek. 'I'm sorry, darling,' she whispered. 'Forgive me, please.'

'There's nothing to forgive.'

A flash of pain crossed Cameron's face, so brief it was merely a suggestion. It occurred to her then that it was completely out of character for Cyrus to suggest they live together without getting married. Why did he do it? Because he wanted her, but for some reason did not want to marry her. And this was a kind of compromise that he expected her to turn down. This new idea unnerved her and, to blot out her sudden anxiety, she kissed the back of his hand and then his fingers, one by one.

Cyrus dropped the cylinder on the rug and took her face between his hands. He looked at her long and hard. For the first time he saw how close she was to tears.

'How much do you love me?' he asked.

A thousand expressions struggled beneath the surface of Cameron's features but were erased too quickly for Cyrus to decipher. Finally, she said very softly, 'With all my heart. More than you need. More than anyone needs.'

The only sound in the library was the crackling of the fire. A frightening premonition filled her. Time was running out for them. She put her hands behind his head and pressed her body against his. He began to kiss her in a way he never had before – violently, desperately, murmuring her name. Disappointment, concern – but above all, relief that Cameron had turned down his poorly conceived compromise – mingled with and were lost in the urgency of his desire.

Few men who have longed for success know the exact moment it arrives, but Byron knew it Tuesday morning as he waited for Cameron in her office.

'What is it?' Cameron asked when she arrived. 'What happened? You look like the cat who ate – '

'The cage full of canaries. I did. I have news. News for Wall Street, news for all fund managers and trades, and news for the public. News that means our new stock issue can come out at thirty dollars a share instead of that crummy seven and a half.'

'What is it?'

'You said to find a David Sarnoff. I found one.'

'Tell me,' Cameron said.

'I have a marketing contract for the Thermoscan with one of the greatest living authorities . . .' Byron's voice was full of glee.

'Who? What are you talking about?'

'One of the great pharmaceutical houses has agreed to market the product of Life Sciences. The chairman of the board signed a contract agreeing to pay one dollar per item. Each Thermoscan costs fifty cents to make, so that's fifty cents profit. They'll sell in the supermarkets and drugstores. Discounted, of course, to the medical profession, hospitals, doctors. They'll market it in France, in England, in Kenya – worldwide.'

'That's wonderful!' Cameron's spirits were almost as high as Byron's.

'It is wonderful. The contract validates the Thermoscan. Elmer Hansen would not have signed it if he didn't believe he could make millions on it.'

'Elmer Hansen?'

'Elmer Hansen himself. The Hansen Company – big, bright, and one of the Dow Thirty.'

Byron saw Cameron's head turn away; when she looked at him again, she had an expression he had never seen before.

'You can't sign the contract.'

'You've lost your marbles.'

'You can't do it.' Cameron took a cigarette from a jade case on her desk. The cigarette was stale but she hardly noticed.

'What the hell's the matter with you?' Byron asked.

Cameron purposely glanced towards the window. But she saw nothing; for an instant she thought she might have gone blind. Then her vision cleared and she saw the towers of Wall Street and the Hudson River. 'I promised Cyrus we would never do business with the Hansen Company.'

'Unpromise him.' Byron tried on a big, comforting smile. 'There's nothing in our contract that says the Hansen Company is off-limits.'

'It's illegal to make exclusions like that. We had a verbal agreement,' Cameron felt haunted and was sure she looked it.

'I didn't know,' Byron fumbled for excuses. 'You never mentioned it. I thought that was what you meant by find a David Sarnoff.'

Cameron's voice was unsteady. 'I didn't realize you were looking for a marketing contract.'

Byron felt a sharp sense of outrage followed by confusion. 'I didn't know,' he repeated lamely.

'You could refuse to sign the contract. There are plenty of other companies.'

'It's too late.'

Cameron's eyes grew dark, stricken with knowledge. 'You signed the contract?'

'We closed Friday.'

'Byron!' Cameron's voice broke.

'You never told me.' Byron's feelings clashed and blurred amid a mixture of protests, guilts, resentment of Cyrus, jealousy, and with it all a deep compassion for Cameron's obvious anguish. Finally he said, 'Look, I didn't know. Or I wouldn't have . . .' His voice trailed off.

'Why the hell were you so secretive?' Cameron was beside herself.

'I wasn't secretive.' Byron's voice was rising. 'I only wanted to surprise you.'

'Surprise me! What are we, children playing hide-and-seek? We're supposed to be in business together.' A spasm of anger and chagrin twisted her mouth. 'You must cancel the contract.'

'I told you the contract is signed. Signed by Elmer Hansen. Signed by me. It's done. I can't wish it away. Throw it away. Wash it away. Magic it away. I can't unsign it. Much as I might want to.'

Cameron was fighting to hold herself together. After a moment she said, 'How did this disaster happen?'

Byron didn't like being wrong any more than most people. And this was more painful because he'd been certain that she'd be pleased.

'I have this friend, Margo Bayless. She's a finder of sorts. She found J and J, Bristol-Myers, and others. But no one would play by my rules. They wanted to test-market forever. Or redo the clinicals almost forever. Or they would pay fifty cents. Anyway, Margo came up with the Hansen Company.

401

And it was love at first sight between Elmer Hansen and our Thermoscan.'

'Why didn't Ned Sweeney tell me? He's your corporate counsel.'

'I didn't use Sweeney,' Byron chose his words cautiously, not wanting to make any more mistakes. 'I knew he would keep you informed, and as I told you, I wanted to surprise you. To show you that you were right in picking me to head up Life Sciences.'

'I was right,' Cameron said softly. Too right, she thought. But Cameron was not one who took pleasure in quarrels with anyone, let alone Byron. 'If only it wasn't Elmer,' she said in a whisper.

'I did it for you.'

Cameron groaned. 'Stop it! You did it for yourself and for Life Sciences.' But even as she rejected Byron's excuse, she had a flash of recognition. In a way he was telling the truth. She had always known how much Byron longed for the success of the company and for his own success. Now she felt the shock of familiarity mingled with utter surprise. As much as he wanted success, he wanted her approval. He hated that she wasn't applauding his coup.

'What's done is done,' Cameron finally admitted.

'I'm sorry about Elmer Hansen.' Byron said the words bleakly. 'And about Cyrus, too.'

There was a sense of violation in the air; if much more were said, it would become unforgivable.

'Just go away and let me think,' Cameron begged.

Byron stood up. 'But I'm not sorry otherwise.' He had the look of a child who has dropped his candy in the sand. He couldn't bring himself to ask her what she meant to do about Cyrus or how she would explain what he'd done. As he hurried from the office, he thought that he should have been walking on air, but all he felt was a sense of failure and loss.

His high hopes had died. Jesus Christ! What the hell could he do to make it up to her?

Left to herself, Cameron felt bone-cold, alone in some grim, alien world. A sound like a sob came from her throat. There is such a thing as pure accident, and yet the consequences of such an accident could attach itself to one as surely as if it had been wilfully premeditated. Why hadn't she told Byron about the Hansen Company restriction? How could she have been so careless? How could she explain the oversight to Cyrus? How could she ever convince him that it was purely accidental? Her eyes closed wearily for an instant. Instinctively, she felt that there were heavy odds against Cyrus's accepting Byron's actions as the result of a slipup in communication on her part. Cameron Hightower was not known for such blunders. She could almost hear the crackle of mistrust and anger in Cyrus when she started to explain. Then she ran her hands through her hair in a strange half-gesture of bewilderment. Why was she so afraid of Cyrus? He loved her. He would understand. She must make the call now. The situation must be resolved immediately. Cameron picked up the phone and dialled Cyrus's number. It took her three attempts to touch all seven buttons correctly.

'Acorn Ventures. Good morning.'

'Good morning. This is Cameron Hightower. I would like to speak to Mr Hansen, please.'

'I'm sorry, Miss Hightower. Mr Hansen has already left for Dallas. You just missed him. Is there any message?'

Cameron could barely hear herself. 'No.' Very slowly she replaced the receiver.

That afternoon Elmer Hansen made a telephone call. For years he had contemplated the pleasure of making this call, and had waited with oxlike patience for the right time. Finally the right time had arrived. Nothing could dull his satisfaction.

The fact that he did not reach the party in question was a minor annoyance. It was enough that he leave a message. The party in question would understand perfectly. Particularly since he left his name: Elmer Hansen, Sr.

23

Cameron was meeting Cyrus at five o'clock on the observation deck at La Guardia airport. He'd been in Dallas for three days and was scheduled to land at 4:45. From La Guardia they planned to take a Pan Am flight to Bermuda and the Coral Beach Club. But she was held up in traffic and reached the airport fifteen minutes late and out of breath. A quick glance at the terminal monitor showed that his flight had arrived on time. She hurried to the observation deck, more disturbed at having kept Cyrus waiting than the situation warranted. But when she arrived at the deck there was no Cyrus to be seen. She walked the full length back and forth looking for him. Finally she picked a spot where she had a clear view of the doors opening onto the deck. While waiting she pretended to watch the planes taxiing down the runway for a takeoff or gliding in for a landing. Actually, she saw nothing. She was trying to decide when would be the right time to tell Cyrus about Byron and the Hansen Company. She realized there was no right time. The real question was, when would be the least wrong time?

The past three days had been full of careening ups and downs. She had promised herself that she would call Cyrus in Dallas and tell him everything that had happened. It would come as a shock to him, but she was convinced that she could make him understand. It had been her mistake, not Byron's. She had never meant to cause Cyrus the slightest pain. But even as she thought those things, it was difficult for her not to feel guilty, deceitful in a way she had never felt before. She found herself in need of constant self-reassurance. Cyrus loves me, she told herself over and over again. He'll forgive me. He'll accept that I am human and human beings make mistakes. All the things she told herself were not enough to calm her. She had no excuse for her negligence. Her instincts about Elmer Hansen had warned her from the start that Cyrus had reasons for the restriction. Still – she reminded herself again – Cyrus loved her, and that love would help him to forgive her.

Yet the first day passed, and she could not make the call. Then the second day, the third. All the while she was aware that the longer she postponed making the call, the worse it would be. But what surprised her most was her own need to delay. Then she was saved by a happy notion. She allowed herself to believe it would be wrong to call Cyrus. It would be making too much of Byron's innocent error. She would tell him when they met, face-to-face.

Cameron checked her watch, 5:30. Where was he? She felt vaguely apprehensive and shrugged it off, certain the feeling came from the unpleasant news she had in store for him. Once they saw each other, it would straighten itself out. She was reluctant to leave the deck and go look for him. They could easily miss one another in the crowded airport and waste more time trying to find – Then her heart leapt. There was Cyrus's tall figure striding towards her. She blinked. He was not carrying his suitcase. Of course, that was it; he had checked it through. That was what had taken him so long. She would have done the same thing if she had not been concerned about being late.

'Cyrus!' Cameron called out and waved as though he could miss her.

'Good evening, Cameron,' he said, coming to a stop in front of her.

For the length of a pulse beat, he stared down at her while she waited for his glad-to-be-home kiss. When it didn't come, she stepped back and studied him.

'Are you all right?' she asked.

'No. But I'll recover.'

Cameron's heart turned over. 'What is it?'

He stood with a stiff grace, appraising her as though she were some kind of object whose price he was estimating.

'Did you check your bag through? Is that what took so long?' She said the words mechanically.

'No. I'm not going.' He took his time. He could do that. 'I dropped off my bag in Max's taxi, but it seemed important to say good-bye in person.'

'Good-bye?' For an instant Cameron thought she was going crazy. 'Cyrus! Stop it! Please!'

'I'm being as polite as I can be under the circumstances.'

'What circumstances? What are you talking about?' Cameron refused to admit that she knew only too well what he was talking about.

'You know damn well!' He flared up in spite of himself. 'I'm talking about Byron Miller and Life Sciences. They have a marketing contract with the Hansen Company.'

Cameron became aware of the constraints masking his fury. 'I was going to tell you,' she said, but her words were not delivered with her usual authority.

'Were you? When?'

Cameron was too distraught to notice the few people on the cold observation deck who glanced curiously at the handsome couple near the door. The man and the woman were having a heated dialogue in low, civilized tones, but their bodies seemed to be shouting at each other.

'I was waiting to tell you. Now. Or on the plane. Or . . .' Cameron felt hot and her clothes were rough against her skin. 'When did you find out?'

This morning. I telephoned in and Norman Mann told me. My grandfather called Tuesday to announce the good news. He thought I'd appreciate hearing directly from him.' Cyrus's expression mirrored his disgust. 'You had to do it, didn't you?'

'Do it? Do what?'

'Set up the marketing contract with the Hansen Company. After you promised me you wouldn't. The lure of all that money was too great, wasn't it?'

'I had nothing to do with it,' Cameron all but screamed. 'Byron did it himself. He found the Hansen Company himself.'

'You can't expect me to believe such a remarkable coincidence. Particularly since you know my grandfather.'

'It's true. Byron knew nothing about our private understanding. It's not in the contract –'

Cyrus laughed. 'And of course, you never told him.'

'I didn't know he was looking for a marketing contract. He never mentioned it.'

'Naturally. And it's pure accident that he didn't use Ned Sweeney to represent him. I called Ned, he knew nothing about the contract.'

'Byron used a different law firm. He wanted to surprise me.'

'Stop it, Cameron! I'm not a fool. Ned Sweeney is an old friend, you know that, Sweeney would have told me.'

Cameron remained silent, and Cyrus slowly tilted his head to one side. Something in her face fired his anger even higher. The restraints he'd attempted to place on himself snapped. 'Cameron Hightower, you're a whore! Your own special kind of whore! Your price is higher than most, considerably higher. You don't rent your body for a couple of hundred dollars. Not you! With the Hansen contract to toss around the Street you'll make millions on the public offering. But the price you charge doesn't change a thing. You're still a whore!'

Cameron finally found her voice. 'Have you anything else to tell me, Mr Hansen? Do you wish to make any more moral points to justify this scene?' Her temper now matched his. 'Damn you, Cyrus Hansen! I didn't and I still don't understand why you wanted that private understanding, but I didn't break it. I had nothing to do with the contract.'

'I don't believe you.'

Cameron made one last effort. 'If you look at the agreement, you'll see Margo . . . Margo . . . Margo Something was the finder.'

'Margo Something?' Cyrus towered over her. 'Do you think my grandfather would do business with a Margo something? It took a Cameron Hightower to put that son of a bitch Byron Miller in touch with him.'

Cameron's head rattled like a loose marionette, and her breath came in choked sobs. 'I love you. I wouldn't do that to you.'

Cyrus stared at her across the ruin of their lives. 'I loved you, too. Once.'

For a moment they stared at each other, seeming to see all they had lost. Then Cyrus wheeled and ran for the exit. He was gone within minutes.

In deep shock, Cameron boarded the flight to Bermuda and checked into an impersonal tourist hotel. She was shaking with fever and thought, dear God, how can I sleep tonight? There should be a lock on my brain. Instead of dinner, she ordered a bottle of Scotch and a bucket of ice and fell into bed after all but finishing the bottle. When she woke, she felt hung over, stifled, and numb. Somewhere inside her a door had slammed shut, and it would neither let her in nor let her out. She tried to sleep in the sun. She tried to read. She tried to eat breakfast. She did very little better with lunch. She skipped dinner. On Sunday she caught the noon flight back to New York. Sitting in the first-class cabin, she had a deep perception that something vital in her had been murdered by Cyrus Hansen.

A leaden feeling settled over her as she realized how completely she had lost Cyrus. The lonely, grey years she saw stretching before her were all that she would have. The life she had longed for with him, the love and happiness she'd reached for – Cyrus as her husband, their children, rich years of growth – had all seemed possible. Now she knew, once and for all, that happiness was beyond her, try as she might to have it otherwise.

Cameron paused in her barren vision of the future. There were other things to which she did not want to give a name. She observed herself in the act of mentally ducking and dodging, but the more she avoided, the more vividly she knew what she feared. She found herself compelled to come to terms with an alarming reality. The rock to which she had always clung for support, which had never failed her in time of need, was crumbling. FitzGerald Associates was her rock, and she no longer cared what happened to the company, whether it flourished or failed. She knew Byron Miller was waiting for her, expecting her to perform miracles in a world that had stripped her of a belief in the miraculous. She would do for Byron what had to be done. No more and no less. She could not allow herself to do less, but she was incapable of doing more.

On Monday afternoon, Byron appeared in her office for a meeting. Not much was accomplished. Underneath Cameron's surface commitment to the future of Life Sciences – now that they had the Hansen contract to flaunt on the Street – Byron felt only a mechanical response to his enthusiasm. Her heart and mind were elsewhere.

Byron's reaction to this apathy was redoubled fervour. 'But Cameron, you don't get it. We have the contract! And we have the prototype machine. The machine finally works. Junior Wheel ran all weekend without a single glitch. It can turn out five hundred Thermoscans a day!'

'That's very good,' she said listlessly.

'Good? It's fantastic! And it's news for the Street. You said just a few months ago that the Street needed news. Well?' A feeling of desperation began to work its way through Byron's nervous system.

'All right. I guess we can push the offering through at ten.'

'Ten! That's almost as big a freebie as seven and a half!'

'Five hundred Thermoscans is not fifty thousand. You still can't mass produce them.' Cameron wished he'd stop pounding at her.

'Of course not. Junior Wheel is a prototype machine. You know that as well as I do. Everyone knows it. But we're on our way.' Byron was having a terrible time with Cameron's lack of support. 'We should price the stock at fifteen. Maybe twenty dollars a share.'

'I'll have to think about it,' Cameron said wearily.

'Think about it?' Byron struggled with a way to bring Cameron to her senses. Finally, he decided on a direct approach. 'Cyrus Hansen resigned from the board of directors. His resignation arrived by registered mail this morning.' Byron watched Cameron closely, convinced that what was wrong with her was linked to the resignation. Perhaps something had gone wrong in Bermuda.

The deadly apathy, the dullness in Cameron's expression did not change. 'I know. He sent a photocopy here.'

Byron realized he must not press her too hard. Yet he had his own needs with which to contend, and he could not restrain himself, 'I hope that whatever happened between Cyrus and you hasn't influenced your thinking.' He tried to sound casual. 'The board of directors is not a basketball team. We don't need five players. Any number can play as long as there are three. And in fact, we have four.'

'No, it isn't a basketball team,' Cameron agreed vaguely.

'So we don't need his vote on how much we ask for the stock.'

'That's true.'

'Listen to me, Cameron,' he said in a firm voice. 'I'm flat

against asking ten dollars a share for the stock, but we're not getting anywhere. Suppose we call a special board meeting and talk about it here?'

'We could do that,' Cameron said with too much relief.

'All right, I'll set it up.' Byron did his best to be gentle, while wondering how Cyrus Hansen, that all-American prick, could cause such raw, devastating grief.

After Byron left, Cameron glanced at her calendar. Nothing urgent pending, no meetings, no major decisions. The market would go up. Or down. But there was no big question looming over it that might cause a violent swing. In any case, since she had a tie-line from The Farm to the office, she could follow the floor trading from her desk in her study. She just wanted to go home.

Cameron had not been to The Farm in three weeks, and only when she arrived there did she realize how much she missed it. Hightower Farm was her real home. The house was full of memories of generations of Hightowers. She, who had had her family for such a short time, had generations of family at Hightower Farm. It was her safe place.

She turned up the driveway and smiled, it seemed, for the first time in ages. The lights on either side of the front door cast a golden glow across the lawn. She barely had a chance to put her key in the lock when the door was opened by a smiling Grace, the housekeeper, who had stayed up to greet her.

The next morning the sun streamed through the window, and Cameron stood in a shaft of golden light, examining her naked body in the full-length mirror. Her period was six weeks late. In the past she had occasionally skipped a month, and it had always turned out to be nothing. She'd been careful about taking precautions and had her IUD regularly checked. So how could she be pregnant? Cameron picked up the phone and called her longtime gynaecologist.

* * *

Dr Allan Jarvis completed his examination and told her the news. Her IUD had slipped, and she was six weeks pregnant.

'At your current stage, we could do the abortion here in the office. It's like a D and C.'

'When?' Cameron asked dully.

Dr Jarvis consulted his appointment book. 'How about tomorrow at ten? No fuss or fanfare. You'll go home, go to bed, rest, read a book. Be as good as new by Thursday.'

'Not tomorrow.'

'Oh.' Dr Jarvis waited for her to add something. He'd seen this before, too. When she remained silent, he asked, 'Do you want to think about it? Talk to the father?'

'No.'

Dr Jarvis understood. Either the father didn't know, mustn't know, or didn't care. He waited. As the quiet minutes ticked away, his compassion for the woman he'd known as a teenager overcame his professional reticence. 'Cameron, I know this is a hard decision, but don't think about it too long. Make up your mind. The longer it takes, the more difficult the decision will become.'

Cameron listened. 'How about Thursday?'

Dr Jarvis consulted his appointment book again. 'Thursday at two. How's that?'

'Fine,' Cameron said without thinking. She left the office quickly, her body perspiring and shivering at the same time.

Back at The Farm, Cameron fell across her bed. She closed her eyes. For a moment she was alone with the baby that lived inside her. It was Cyrus's child, but everything that Cyrus and she had together was over. For the good of everyone, including the baby, she should have an abortion. Yet for some reason, she wanted to postpone the inevitable, and that was impossible. There was one thing she could do. If she couldn't postpone the baby, she could postpone Byron. She couldn't face the argument with him over the price of the stock. She'd be stronger next week. Then she could hand the deal over to Jake and be done with it. She reached for the telephone and pressed the button that connected her directly to the office. When Della picked up, she spoke quickly.

'I'll be staying here at The Farm for the rest of the week. Cancel the appointment with Byron and set it for Friday of next week . . . Yes, I'm fine . . . Thank you.' She hung up.

Cameron fell back on the bed, unable to think of anything other than the baby. There was no one to protect her from the lonely decision she had made. For better or worse, the baby would be gone by next week; and for an instant, Cameron had a sense of her own nonexistence. She raised her hands to her face as the tears streamed down her cheeks, and she wept for her baby and herself with a fresh, first grief.

Della postponed the meeting with Byron, explaining that Cameron was out of town.

'Damn!' Byron swore as he hung up, feeling a mixture of compassion and anger at Cameron. He was doubly infuriated by the lingering presence of Cyrus Hansen, who he was sure was responsible for Cameron's being unavailable. Added to the unexpressed love he felt for Cameron was the guilt that his signing the Hansen contract was the cause of her anguish. He understood clearly that Cyrus had done a vanishing act. His stomach began to churn as if from a long, self-imposed fast. He hungered to put his arms around her, to soothe her, but a cluster of ingrained inhibitions held him back. Still, in his rapidly calculating mind there was the hope that maybe, not now but someday – God granting him luck and success – he would rescue Cameron from that dungeon where that bastard Hansen had tossed her. He agonized over Cameron for a few minutes longer. Then resentment, jealousy, and the bitter conclusion that there was nothing he could do made his decision for him. If she was going to waste her time lighting candles on the altar of Cyrus Hansen, he'd damn well do things his way. It was time to make Wall Street sit up and take notice of Life Sciences. He told himself that it wasn't simply his high level of anxiety that was gnawing at him, or a craving for personal recognition. It made good business sense. Furthermore, a little astute public relations might be just the medicine to bring Cameron back to life.

Public relations was unknown territory to him. But, with his true gift for the carnival, it was only a matter of trusting his instincts. He recalled hearing Jake talk about Leon Beckett's leaking information about Mr Thin. What was good enough for Beckett was good enough for him.

Byron did not hire a pulic relations firm, or a press agent. He did it his own way. He called *The Wall Street Journal* library and asked the lady librarian in what issue could he find an article on Life Sciences. It was a new company that manufactured a special kind of high-technology brassière called a Thermoscan. When he finished telling the librarian what the Thermoscan could do, the librarian was very interested. She hadn't seen such an article. If she had she would have remembered it. Byron and she chatted. He explained that he wanted to buy stock in the company and Thermoscans for his mother and sister. The librarian understood and was sympathetic; she'd also like to buy one, so he should be sure to tell her when he found out where they were being sold. She gave him the name of a reporter, Bob Anderson, to whom to speak. Anderson was heavily into high-technology companies.

Margo called Anderson and explained that her brother had talked to the librarian, who had given him the reporter's name. Anderson was interested, even though he hadn't heard of the Thermoscan or of Life Sciences or of the Hansen contract. But he'd look into it; he had his sources. By the time he had thought to ask Margo her name and thank her for the tip, she had hung up.

In no time Anderson arranged to meet with Byron Miller.

Two days later there was a piece in the 'Heard on the Street' column of *The Wall Street Journal* about Life Sciences, the Thermoscan, and the Hansen contract.

Cameron Hightower did not see the *Wall Street Journal* article. For the first time in years, FitzGerald Associates was not in the forefront of her mind. Seated at her desk at The Farm, eating her meals which somehow she managed to get down, driving many miles along solitary roads, going for long walks on the estate, awake or asleep, her mind went ceaselessly around the question: to have or not have the baby? The logic and the illogic. On Thursday morning she postponed her appointment with Dr Allan Jarvis. It struck her how hidden away from her own sight was her longing to have the child. What she hadn't seen, what she couldn't have foreseen, was what she'd renounce by having the abortion. It could be precious indeed – quite like gold coins sewn into the coat lining of a fleeing refugee to be spent someday for survival. But if she had the baby, she'd be an unwed mother. Was that what made her consider an abortion? Or was it that her baby would not have a father?

On Monday morning while she was reviewing the estate bills, the telephone rang. It was Dr Jarvis.

'Cameron,' he said gently. 'If I hadn't known you since you were a teenager, I wouldn't now presume. But I've done some thinking about you . . .' He hesitated.

'Go on, Allan.'

'Well. I think you want to have the baby, and since you do, I think you should. If you have the baby and the circumstances leave you no alternative . . .' He stopped again, floundering.

'You mean if the father won't marry me?'

'Yes.' He hurried on. 'In that event, I can put you in touch with a top-grade adoption agency. All strictly confidential.

They have a waiting list of the finest families. The best names.'

'The best names? You mean the Hightower name isn't good enough for my child?'

'No. I don't mean that at all. Hightower is a fine name.'

'But it can't be passed down by a woman? There's a law against that?' Her sarcasm silenced him. 'I'll be in touch with you when I make up my mind.'

Cameron hung up. Dr Allan Jarvis had made her look at a possibility she had not even remotely considered. Give the baby out for adoption? To Cameron that amounted to the same thing as abortion. She glanced at the bills on the desk in front of her. There was the mortgage on The Farm to be paid. The half-year taxes were due. The servants' salaries. Running Hightower Farm was a lot like running FitzGerald Associates. The baby came back into her imagination in a scene that would never take place if she had the abortion. Or permitted an adoption. A young man – she was certain it was a boy – looking exactly like Cyrus did all those years ago, in his room in The Farm. A room filled with afternoon sunlight, enjoying his life, never knowing that his mother had almost decided not to have him. Her mind veered back to the bills she was paying. If there was no one of her lineage to inherit it, Hightower Farm would suffer an ugly tear. The other Hightowers didn't love the place. They would sell the land off to developers. And now that she was looking at the future, who would take her place at FitzGerald Associates when she was ready to step aside? A stranger she'd groomed? Or someone of her own flesh and blood?

'Why not?' she asked herself. Damn it! Why not? The baby was hers. Cyrus's and hers. She had loved Cyrus. Despite what had happened, she loved him even now. But what had happened to her sense of self? Long before Cyrus, she had a life of her own, a business of her own. His behaviour with her had been outrageous. If he could believe what he believed

417

about her, what kind of man had she been in love with? How little we know of each other, she thought. Still, she had seen the Gorgon's head before. And it hadn't blinded her. It had simply dried her tears. Cyrus had given her future back to her own care. Now she must do her best to hold it fast. Which brought her back to the baby. Why let the baby go when there was nothing to stop her from having it? What if she were unwed? She was Cameron Hightower, and she was her own person. Prudently she faced the implications of her thinking. How to explain the baby to Jake? To the world? Did she owe Jake an explanation? No! Did she owe anyone an explanation? Again no! Her caution snapped, and the matter was settled. She would have her baby and raise it herself.

She picked up the telephone and called Dr Jarvis. She impressed on him that she expected complete confidentiality. The delivery would not be at Princeton Hospital. She would choose her own time when she would introduce her child to the world.

By Wednesday she was ready to return to the office. As she drove to Manhattan, she was calm, supported by a strong sense of being alive, of her baby being alive. She knew precisely what was to come and what she had to do. She would raise the baby at Hightower Farm with a sleep-in nurse and spend her weekends and as many midweek nights as possible at The Farm. She looked at her brush with abortion – adoption had never been a reality – and she was appalled by the narrowness of her escape.

When she arrived at the office, Della beamed a welcome, and the relief on her face was obvious. It flew over the office grapevine that Cameron Hightower was back. Minutes later, Jake Stern was standing in her office, holding a copy of *The Wall Street Journal*.

'I'm glad to see you looking rested and fit,' he said. 'You will please thank me for running the office single-handed.'

He said this proudly, 'But the next time you plan to take an extended vacation, please give me fair warning.'

'I'll tell you now,' Cameron said, thinking of her baby. 'I'm planning a trip around the world over the summer. It should last about three months.'

'A trip around the world? For Christ's sake, why?'

'I want to study other markets. There are things we should know firsthand.'

Jake whistled between tightly closed teeth, accepting that Cameron's mind had a further reach than his. 'All right. But as to the here and now, did you see Monday's *Journal*?'

'No,' Cameron said, making an excuse. 'The mail in Princeton is occasionally slow.'

Jake opened the paper to a page with a column outlined in red. 'Read that. A piece on Life Sciences.'

Cameron scanned the article. 'Is that why I have a message from the OTC Fund at the Pru? They want to buy ten thousand shares.'

'That's undoubtedly why.'

'How did they find out so fast?' she asked.

'The *Journal* or OTC?'

'The *Journal*! Who told them?'

Jake gave Cameron a probing look, 'I'll tell you who. Our boy. The stock has had a three and a half point rise this week.'

'More buyers than sellers,' Cameron said, 'Come on, Jake. You have to admire Byron's media sense. Give the devil his due.'

'That's what I'm afraid of. The devil isn't in the market for stocks. He buys and sells souls. Byron's? Or maybe ours?'

Byron showed up for the Friday meeting full of purpose. Cameron stared at him in bewilderment. Byron had undergone a remarkable transformation. He was wearing jeans and a sports shirt. All that remained of the past few years were the Gucci loafers and the Burberry trench coat with the brass rings on the belt. He looked remarkably like the Byron she'd known when she was in college.

'You look fetching,' she said.

'I am fetching. I'm me. Through with the business-suit blues. Have you ever seen a real trailblazer, a frontier man, a successful entrepreneur in a buttondown shirt?'

'Yes. Quite a few. It's called accommodating the system.'

'The system can accommodate me for a change. It's time I started being myself. Wall Street can take me as I am. In fact, they'll love me. Inside every tight-assed prisoner in a business suit is a radical fighting to get free.'

'You're about to radicalize Wall Street?'

'Yes. At least in their thinking about the pharmaceutical industry. To hell with Bristol-Myers and the rest. Life Sciences is about to become the new boy on the Street. You're going to price the issue at twenty dollars a share.'

'Twenty dollars. It's selling at eleven and one half this morning,' Cameron pointed out. 'And by the way, I thought the board of directors was going to make the decision about the price. Where's Harry Horn? Where's Rosemary?'

'Harry votes the way I vote. Call him and ask. And Rosemary votes with you. Jake'd break her arm if she didn't. Now that our great and good friend, Cyrus Hansen, has resigned from the board, we have a tie vote.' Byron glanced at Cameron and tried not to be to affected by how beautiful she looked. The vacation actually seemed to have done her some good. She was not tired and dispirited and drawn the way she looked the last time he saw her. He had meant to rescue her, but she might have rescued herself.

'Twenty dollars is too high,' Cameron commented, although she lacked conviction.

'Twenty dollars isn't high enough,' Byron had conviction enough for both of them. 'Cameron, you are about to commit a mortal sin. Against Life Sciences, against FitzGerald

Associates, and against yourself.' He watched Cameron closely for a reaction.

'FitzGerald Associates makes the market in the stock. We'd have to start accumulating shares to drive the price of the stock up. A new offering at twenty dollars seems possible, but we'd have to start today.'

'You're thinking about it?' Byron was nonplussed. He'd come to do battle and there was no battle.

'I've been thinking about it.'

From the moment she decided to keep her baby, scar tissues had been forming over the wound left by Cyrus. He'd called her a whore, and she'd been cringing like a whore. It was enough – more than enough. Once she accepted the fact that she could have a life without Cyrus, she was herself again, committed to doing the very best for Life Sciences and FitzGerald Associates.

'Byron,' she asked, 'which investment banking house do you think is big enough, strong enough, and fast enough on its feet to do the best job of placing the new issue of Life Sciences stock?'

'Mason, Adams, and Fenwick. Ask me something hard.'

'Exactly,' Cameron buzzed Della. 'Get me John Mason please.'

John Mason was at his desk when his secretary rang. Cameron Hightower? He repeated the name to himself. She wasn't a real force on the Street, not yet anyway. But there was something about the young woman that flagged his attention. She was smart enough for Tim FitzGerald and smart enough to manage FitzGerald Associates, which made her smart enough for him to take the call. He told his secretary to put her through.

Cameron and John Mason had a pleasant exchange of greetings, and then, dispensing with small talk, Cameron got down to cases. She would like to see John Mason and the sooner the better. She had something of importance to discuss with him, a new piece of business. She would bring Byron Miller with her. Miller was chairman of Life Sciences, a small company she'd been instrumental in putting together. It had a big product.

John Mason did not show either by a blink or a muscle flick that Byron's jeans and tennis shoes were other than what he had expected. In fact, Byron in jeans was far more effective than Byron in a business suit. Ruefully, Cameron admitted that Byron had caught the Wall Street fantasy life. The jeans were right – particularly with the Guccis – and a beard would have been even more effective. She wondered when he'd grow one.

The official introductions being taken care of, Cameron gave the floor to Byron, and he proceeded to perform as though a spillway at Hoover dam had been opened. He was engaging, congenial, informative, and entertaining.

'It's the new frontier of medicine. The great forward leap. More than a wonder cure. The wonder prevention. Preventive medicine. The Thermoscan is the wave of the future.' Nor was Byron merely a brassy promoter and cheap charmer. He had the facts and figures, and he had clinical studies. And above all, he had a marketing contract for the Thermoscans with the Hansen Company. Byron was like a guru who had generously reached out to bestow a gift on mankind.

To John Mason, Byron Miller appeared as a brilliant innovative businessman. 'Cameron,' he finally said, 'Tim would be proud of you. How much were you planning to raise for the company?'

Watching Byron hypnotize Mason, Cameron's thinking underwent a 180-degree turn. The excitement and euphoria Byron had created suggested a much higher figure than she had originally considered.

'Fifty million,' she said, her voice brimming with confidence.

'At how much per share?'

'At the market price. Which will be at least twenty-five dollars a share,' She cast a swift, sideways glance at Byron.

'Exactly,' Mason agreed. 'Fifty million at the very least. And we'll get your twenty-five dollars a share. I know the Street. They'll fall all over themselves to climb on board, so two million shares will be easy to place. And that's only the beginning.'

Byron's eyes were shining as Mason and Cameron made arrangements for another meeting the next day, when the three of them would decide details such as how many millions in commissions Mason, Adams, and Fenwick and FitzGerald Associates would receive for doing the placement. As well as how much stock the two firms would split as additional compensation. This should be done before the lawyers got into the act. Cameron and John – call me John, he said to Byron – would put the syndicate together. Still overwhelmed by the opportunity that had walked through the door, Mason generously agreed the tombstone would read, 'FitzGerald Associates – Mason, Adams, and Fenwick.' The FitzGerald name would be first.

The glut of success made Byron appear to swell in size. Cameron was more circumspect. But her feelings of exultation quite equalled Byron's. The order of the names on the tombstone stirred Cameron. It was a huge step forward. On Wall Street, as in Hollywood, the billing of your name mattered. And FitzGerald Associates would head the list – lead banker – even ahead of Mason, Adams, and Fenwick. That was progress.

PART SEVEN

The Street
1987–1989

24

Once Byron Miller had signed the letter of intent and the red
herring had been deposited at the SEC, the word flew around
Wall Street like wildfire. FitzGerald Associates was back.
John Mason, the 'Silver Fox' of the Street, was the champion;
and if he was in there pitching, this was hot merchandise.
Della and Mason's secretary, Ivy Levine, were swamped with
calls from other secretaries. Managing partners of funds,
trusts, and even a few banking houses wanted to speak to
John Mason and Cameron Hightower. Everyone wanted to
participate in the placement.

Adrian Haveworth of Venlong asked for 10,000 shares.
Cameron debated with herself and almost said, 'No, our own
syndicate members are still buying.' But the Longstreets were
big money, and who knew what the future might hold? So
she allowed Venlong to have 5,000 shares. They were already
oversubscribed.

There was a happy blue sky and a hot June sun looking
down on Wall Street the morning Byron Miller arrived at the
office of FitzGerald Associates for the formal closing of the
offering. His hand was steady as a rock as he accepted a
cashier's check for $50 million made out to Life Sciences
and drawn on the Morgan Guaranty Trust Company. He
managed an easy smile as he slid a cheque for $2 million
across the table to John Mason, the cash part of Mason,
Adams, and Fenwick's commission for the sale of Life
Sciences stock. His grin was broader as he gave Cameron
Hightower another cheque for $2 million, FitzGerald Asso-
ciates' share of the cash commission. Not even two additional

cheques totalling $230,000 to cover the out-of-pocket expenses of both investment banking houses made the slightest dent in the magic of the moment. But when Byron handed John Mason a stock certificate for 100,000 shares of Life Sciences and recieved a cheque for $10,000 – equalling the 10 cents par value of the stock – anyone knowing Byron well would have recognized that like a hospital patient, he was smiling through pain. The additional compensation of all those shares at such a price gave him a stomach ache. The cramp cleared when he handed Cameron a certificate for 100,000 shares of his company, also at 10 cents a share. It was made out to FitzGerald Associates and was their part of the additional compensation. Cameron Hightower was a different matter to Byron. He would have gladly given her 200,000 shares for no money at all. A drink was had all around, and the closing ceremonies were over. It was back to business as usual for all concerned.

John Mason returned to Mason, Adams, and Fenwick to prepare for a meeting with George Balasz of Baxter Industries. He had an uncomfortable feeling that something wasn't quite right, and they might not get to do Baxter Industries' new $40 million tax-free bond placement to clean up pollution. But if they weren't going to get it, who would?

Cameron Hightower studied a draft of an agreement between Baxter Industries and FitzGerald Associates covering the terms of Baxter Industries' new $40 million tax-free pollution bond placement. Now that FitzGerald Associates was in a position to offer Baxter a guaranteed placement, George Balasz had been pleased to give Cameron a nice piece of new business. Her attention wandered briefly from the document. She would give a lot to see Cyrus Hansen's face when he read the Life Sciences tombstone that would appear in tomorrow's *New York Times* and *Wall Street Journal*.

Byron Miller slipped into the Rolls-Royce limousine that

had been parked on Wall Street waiting for him. Margo Bayless was in the rear seat. He brushed away her eager hands, reminding himself of the necessity for business before pleasure. His first stop was the twentieth floor of the Citicorp Building on Fifty-third Street and Lexington Avenue, the Private Banking Division of Citibank. Mary Jane Simons, Life Sciences' loan officer, was waiting for him. Even in the largest bank in the United States, a deposit of $50 million commanded a certain amount of respect, and Byron graciously allowed everyone to congratulate him before he left the bank. Then he was off on a shopping spree for Margo: a Calvin Klein suit, an Oscar de la Renta dress, Charles Jourdan shoes, Kenneth Lane jewellery, and a brief stop at Harry Winston. After that, Byron bought three pairs of jeans at Bloomingdale's, a half dozen Lacoste tennis shirts, and two new pairs of Gucci loafers. They had lunch at the Palm Court at the Plaza Hotel before ending the day in bed in Byron's apartment.

Four months later, having returned from her world trip, Cameron gave birth to a seven-pound boy. She named her son Gary for her father and Gerald for Geraldine Hightower. Two weeks after giving birth to Gary Gerald Hightower, Cameron was back at her desk at FitzGerald Associates. She'd managed to keep her pregnancy and the birth of her son a secret from everyone in the firm. Though Rosemary Stern guessed what had happened, she kept her own council.

The invitation was printed by Tiffany. Cameron recognized the heavy stock and the choice of embossed lettering. It was a duplicate of Geraldine's invitations. Cameron stared at it, feeling more irritated than surprised. 'Mr and Mrs Raymond Hightower request you to join them at a gala ...' Something to do with one of the many 'causes' the Hightowers supported. Not necessarily because they believed in the cause but as a way to pass the time. Cameron smiled, thinking how Geraldine would have smiled. She 'respectfully regretted . . .' and returned the invitation.

In the middle of a hectic trading session, Coz was paged. It broke his concentration on the movement of the stocks, the numbers, and the floor traders. Inwardly he cursed, giving vent to a remarkable list of obscenities that would have done justice to a dockworker. Still, Cameron never interrupted his trading unless it was an emergency. He walked to the post at a rapid pace and picked up the phone.

'Coz here,' he said softly.

'Herbert, this is Doris.'

'Doris? Doris who?'

'Doris, your sister, Herbert. You might remember your only sister's name.'

'Doris, I'm in the middle of a very heavy trading day. I'll call you at home this evening.'

'Herbert, I'm in your neighbourhood, and I thought we might have lunch.'

'Lunch?' Coz accepted that Doris was even more bubble-headed than he'd suspected. 'I never lunch, Doris. Until the floor closes. At four.'

'I'm your sister, you can make an exception. It's important.'

'No!'

'I need your advice.'

Coz reconsidered. 'Okay. Meet me at four-fifteen at the door to the New York Stock Exchange. The one on Wall Street. We'll have a drink.'

'I don't drink. You know that.'

'You'll have a Coke. I'll drink.'

'Herbert, I have nothing to do until four-fifteen.'

Coz almost said, go fuck yourself. He didn't. 'The door to

430

the New York Stock Exchange at four-fifteen.' He hung up the phone and quickly regained his concentration on the activity swirling around the floor.

At 4:20, at the Chateau, the restaurant he selected, Coz ordered a double Scotch and Doris had tea. Doris looked to Coz as Doris always looked these days, expensively unstylish. Once she'd been very pretty. Now she was overweight, overdressed, overcurled, overmadeup. Coz had learned a few things about women in his years on the Street. He recognized that Doris had no class.

'What's the problem?' he asked, eager to get this over with.

Doris hemmed and hawed, and fumbled for her usual sense of superiority. After all, she'd been married to a professional man. She'd taken classes in English literature at NYU at night. Coz had never been to college. It didn't matter. Here, on Coz's territory, she somehow felt inadequate. She needed his advice.

'Herbert, I belong to this stock-investment club.'

'So?'

'So we had a speaker last Friday. A financial planner who recommended we all buy stock in a company called Life Sciences.'

'So?'

'It's over-the-counter.'

'So?' Coz repeated again.

'I mean it doesn't sell on the New York Stock Exchange,' Doris persisted. 'It's like a new issue.'

'I know,' Coz said.

'I understood from the speaker, the financial planner, that the company has a very fine product. Something that detects tumours. And that the stock in the company is now selling for fifty-five dollars.'

'It closed at sixty-one dollars today.'

'Oh! Then you know about that stock?'

431

'I know that stock.'

'Well, this is my dilemma.' It took a few minutes for Doris to explain that she was torn between buying 100 shares of Life Sciences, as many of her investment-club friends were doing, or buying 200 shares of Sears. Mr Hefflin was very much for Sears. He had no faith in over-the-counter stocks. But Doris wasn't quite convinced of Mr Hefflin's omniscience in this case. She liked the product. What did Coz think she should do?

Coz waved to the waitress to bring the check. 'You do what Hefflin says. You always have. You always will. He has a college degree.'

'Would you buy the stock?' Doris's voice was hoarse. She hated having to ask Coz anything. 'It will cost more than six thousand dollars. That's a lot of money. But all the girls in my club are buying it.'

'Hmmm . . .' said Coz, studying the check. 'I own Life Sciences stock.' He gave the waitress a twenty-dollar bill.

'You own it!' Doris was stunned.

'Five thousand shares.' Coz relished his triumph.

'Five thousand shares?' Doris slumped. She was stricken. That was an awful lot of money.

Coz didn't add that he'd bought the stock when it was selling for 7½. 'Yes, Doris, five thousand shares. Tell that to Mr Hefflin.' He stood up. 'You keep the change. But leave a decent tip.'

The second time the Hightower family made contact with Cameron they were more direct in approach. George Hightower telephoned to ask her to have drinks with him at the King Cole bar in the St Regis Hotel. He was in town for the day. Cameron had an immediate previous engagement.

* * *

432

In September, the Life Sciences plant was in the midst of moving to much larger quarters in Fairlawn, New Jersey. The machine, the lab equipment, the coffeepot, everything was being packed. Only the phone was still connected.

Ann McDougal called Byron, who was working with the packers. 'Your mother is on the phone, Mr Miller.'

Byron, sweating like a pig, went to the phone. 'Splendid!' he said under his breath. 'Yes, Momma? What is it?'

'Byron.' Sara's voice floated plaintively through the telephone. 'Is the name of the company you work for Scientific Life?'

'No, Momma, Life Sciences,' Byron said, controlling his exasperation.

'Life Sciences,' Sara said as though memorizing the words. 'Life Sciences. That's what Aunt Rose said. She read about the company in *The Wall Street Journal*. She reads that paper, though I must say I don't know why.'

'Aunt Rose is right. The name is Life Sciences.'

'Byron, Aunt Rose asked me to ask you for a favour.'

'What is it, Momma?'

'The Scientific Life stock is selling for seventy-five dollars.'

'Life Sciences, Momma. It's seventy-seven this morning.'

'Seventy-five or seventy-seven, it's all the same. Byron, your aunt Rose wants to buy ten shares. I tried to talk her out of it, but she was always stubborn, even as a child. She says it's an investment.' Sara's voice was full of disbelief.

'It is an investment. Have her call her broker and buy the stock.'

There was a silence at the other end of the telephone. Then Sara made her statement. 'Byron, Aunt Rose can't afford ten shares of Scientific Life at seventy-seven dollars a share.'

'I can't help that, Momma,' Byron said. 'We're moving the plant. I have work to do.'

'You listen to me, Byron Miller. I'm your mother.' Sara's voice became authoritative. 'I want you to get your aunt Rose that stock at a wholesale price, fifty per cent off. What's the sense of your being employed by that company if you can't get the stock wholesale?'

Byron shook his head in resignation. He'd give Aunt Rose ten shares of his own stock free.

The third contact the Hightower family made with Cameron could not be refused. Leo telephoned and set an appointment a month in advance. All her Hightower relatives – Leo, George, Raymond, and their wives, Roselind, Amy, and Ellen – would be present. It was to be a family reunion at Lutèce, to discuss family business.

'You know we own ten thousand shares of your Life Sciences stock,' George Hightower said expansively. 'We bought it at twenty-five dollars a share and got in on the ground floor.'

'Yes, you did,' Cameron agreed.

'It's hitting the eighties now,' said Leo.

'How do you keep your figure?' Amy asked. 'You eat so much. You even had bread and butter.'

'I exercise and I worry,' Cameron said.

'Speaking of worry,' Leo said, 'Willums moved to Palm Beach.'

'It wasn't sporting of him,' George said huffily. 'He said his doctor advised him he needed sun and air and golf.'

'A man does need rest. Willums worked very hard.' Cameron said reasonably.

'There's a pip-squeak named Craig Comstock handling the account. I don't like him,' said George.

'I don't either,' agreed Ellen. 'He can't tell a salad fork from a dessert fork.'

'Oh, my!' said Cameron.

434

'He wears hand-painted ties with scenes on them,' said Raymond.

'Well!' Cameron was properly aghast.

'His wife has long, frizzy blonde hair,' said Roselind. 'She wears gold jewellery with everything.' Roselind understood that everyone present knew she could buy a gold mine if she wanted one.

'He's lost us thirty million dollars in five years,' Leo said.

'That's a bit of money.' Cameron continued to eat.

'It is a bit,' said George. 'Now we're thirty million short in our original account. The last statement said we were down to one hundred ninety million.'

'Thirty million is quite a loss. But still ...' Cameron reiterated while she ate.

'So we've been thinking.' Leo came to the point. 'Since Geraldine originally recommended that you manage the stock and bond portfolio of the Hightower Trust, we might consider moving the account to FitzGerald Associates. But you must agree to supervise the account personally.'

Cameron ruminated on fate while the white wine gently marinated her senses. Some remote, inherited, atavistic streak of survival was revealing itself in the Hightower brood. Though they were foolish and vain, with an intolerable attitude of superiority, they were not so incompetent that they couldn't smell trouble in the wind.

'Are you offering me the management of the Hightower Trust portfolio?' Cameron said.

'On one condition,' Amy interjected.

'Which is?' Cameron's back went up.

'It isn't much.' Leo noted her stiffening. 'The girls here want you to have this Life Sciences company make each of them a custom-made Thermoscan. They don't want their Thermoscans to be mass-produced. Everything else they own is custom-made. Dresses, coats, shoes. So the same goes for Thermoscans.'

Cameron almost burst out laughing. If the mass-production machine took forever to complete, Byron and Harry could go into the custom-made Thermoscan business. For rich women who wanted everything custom-made. Maybe it should be a separate division? Life Sciences Couturier Thermoscans. They could charge . . . Oh, could they charge! Repressing her smile, she said in a sober voice to Amy, Roselind, and Ellen, 'It will cost you a pretty penny to have them custom-made.'

'We expect to pay,' Amy said. 'Thousands of dollars if necessary.'

'I don't care what it costs,' Ellen chimed in.

'Money is no object,' Roselind agreed.

'All right. I'll speak to Mr Miller, the chairman of Life Sciences, and see what can be done.'

'We're available for fittings any time next week,' Amy said. The women smiled with satisfaction at each other.

'I'll be in touch,' Cameron said.

Leo heaved a big sigh. 'Okay, girls. You've had your innings. Now let's get down to business, Cameron. We'll have the Hightower Trust account transferred to FitzGerald Associates tomorrow.'

'Tomorrow is a fine day,' said Cameron.

25

Cameron glanced at a note John Mason had sent over by messenger. 'That young man of yours certainly is a showman. See page 40.' She opened the copy of *People* magazine that had accompanied the note. There was a four-page article on Byron and Life Sciences with full-colour pictures of three well-endowed young ladies wearing Thermoscans. Byron had timed the publicity perfectly, since the shareholder meeting was two weeks away. Cameron was still trying to sort out her reactions when Della buzzed her.

'Yes?' Cameron asked.

'Mr Stern is on his way in,' Della said.

He was already in when Cameron clicked off.

'Cameron!' Jake exploded. 'Have you seen this week's issue of *People*?'

'Did John Mason send you a copy, too?'

'He sure did. Look at it!'

'I already have,' Cameron said quietly.

'Byron's gone crazy.' Jake was sputtering. 'His notice to shareholders of the meeting is bad enough. Pure promotion! But to have the notice printed in a magazine!' Jake collapsed in the chair opposite Cameron, flourishing the magazine wildly in the air. 'Look at that picture. Jeans and a tennis shirt. Hair over his ears. The barefoot boy with cheek. "I'm not in hiding," says Byron Miller, chairman of the board of Life Sciences.'

'I know. I read it.'

Jake was not to be stopped. 'The caption under the picture. "Will Byron Miller set a new trend in the style of corporate

437

management?" I could kill him! Promotion and more promotion. He's begging for some damn-fool shareholder to bring a malpractice suit.'

'You're right, Jake. The shareholders could bring a class-action suit for one hundred million dollars for malpractice on the grounds that Byron has made them too much money.' Cameron didn't like what Byron was doing any more than Jake did, but she was not about to admit it.

'It's not funny. Listen to this. "The annual shareholder meetings of corporations are theoretically held to elect a board of directors and discuss any business that might properly be brought to the board's attention by the shareholders. Sadly, however, many corporate chairmen are allergic to questions. So they hold their meetings in the Jersey swamps at three A.M. after the garbage is dumped. Or in a log cabin in the Rockies during a blizzard. I am not in hiding. I will hold the annual shareholder meeting of Life Sciences at seven o'clock on Friday, May 30, in the grand ballroom of the Waldorf-Astoria. Come one, come all. Freeload and ask all the questions you can. Your ticket of admission is a share – one single share – of Life Sciences stock." He goes on like that.' Jake was having trouble breathing.

'I read the article.' Cameron was resigned. 'They also printed everything else he included in the notice of the annual meeting to shareholders. The chart showing the rise in price of Life Sciences stock from the original offering of ten dollars a share to the second offering at twenty-five dollars a share to its current price of eighty-nine dollars a share. His projections show the stock hitting one hundred ten.' She stopped and stared at Jake.

'They also printed that Cracker Jack prize he sent out with the notice. The sticker with the four broads wearing the thing. We are now in the tit business. I threw up when I saw it.'

'He does have his own way of doing things,' Cameron said, mustering a brave front.

Suddenly Jake became very quiet. 'Cameron, I know you run the trading desk, so let's dump our Life Sciences stock. I want to run for my life.'

'We can't. I used the stock as collateral at the bank.'

'Oh, shit! Did you have to?'

'We're growing fast, Jake. We needed a bigger financial base to cover our operations.'

'Isn't there any way we can get out? Byron is beginning to smell a little like corn oil to me.'

Cameron tried to reassure her partner. 'I ride herd on Byron all the time. I'll keep him out of trouble.'

'I hope so. One Jacob Stern Company in a lifetime is enough.' He heaved himself to his feet. 'Okay. Keep me informed. While I give my all for Philadelphia Electric. Now there's a company with style. Their bond offering is my type of deal. Solid. Respectable. My firm, guiding hand will make their prospectus irresistible.'

Cameron watched Jake leave. It was obvious he hadn't faced the reality of their situation. Philadelphia Electric was a guaranteed offering, their second. They were the lead bankers and the whole thing was like a nest of Chinese boxes. They would never have been given the offering without the guarantee. And they would never have been able to guarantee it without their new line of credit – seventy million dollars. The Morgan Bank had not given them the credit out of the goodness of their heart. They had given it because she'd pledged their very hot Life Sciences stock as collateral. Cameron glanced at the magazine on her desk, then opened the file that lay beside it. It contained the notice of the shareholder meeting. Stock price projections! Half-naked women! Soon to appear in live colour at the Waldorf! She brought her hands together sharply. It was clear what Byron was doing. He was selling tickets like a circus barker! Sending up the price of the Life Sciences stock on publicity and promotion. There were moments when Byron's jazz worried her as much as Jakes's jitters.

John Mason could tell that Tom Ucciarde was puzzled. Life Sciences' stock was still rising and there was nothing in the rumour mill to stop the rise. So why did he want to sell the stock?

'You're sure you want me to tell the boys to unload our entire position?' Ucciarde asked.

'Our entire position – one hundred thousand shares. Listen, Tom. We picked up that stock at ten cents a share as a commission when we put together the syndicate. It's now selling for almost ninety dollars. We've made money.'

'Over nine million,' Ucciarde agreed enthusiastically.

'So why so greedy?'

'Yeah. Why? You know what they say. The bulls and the bears go to the bank, the pigs go to the slaughterhouse.' Ucciarde agreed too quickly.

The minute Mason heard his floor trader, he realized he'd made a mistake. Ucciarde knew how greedy he was, and he didn't believe the reason he'd given him for selling the stock. He should have remembered his own maxim: never explain, never complain. Mason shifted gears. 'What's the trading like?'

'Twenty-five to fifty thousand shares a day.'

'That's good. It's big enough to bury our selling. Tell them to dribble the stock out slowly, five thousand shares one day, forty-five hundred the next. Take a month to get rid of the stock. And try to make sure no one knows we're selling. If they do find out, it's important they don't know we're selling for the house account. It's for a widow. An orphan. A lunatic.'

'I understand,' Ucciarde said, though he really didn't. 'I'll

440

have them feed it out slowly. There won't be a ripple. Nothing to scare the fishes.'

'Good. I'm counting on you.'

After Ucciarde left, John Mason considered his decision. His years on the Street had given him a second sense. The genius, Byron Miller, was giving him a very uncomfortable feeling. Byron's performance was becoming a shade too flamboyant for his taste. Byron was running up a big tab, and John Mason wasn't sure the genius would be able to pay the cheque.

On Friday, May 30, the day Byron had selected for the Life Sciences shareholder meeting, Cameron and Coz were going over the results of the week's trading. Nothing spectacular, but they both knew a little here and there added up. On his way to the door, Coz casually said, 'Someone is accumulating Hansen Company stock. A tender offer or a proxy fight may be shaping up. If there's a takeover bid, the stock will have a nice move. Think about it.' He left without noticing Cameron's sudden loss of composure.

A profound sense of desolation seized hold of Cameron's heart. In a surge of memory she reconstructed all the buried images of Cyrus Hansen. Her grief was as corrosive as acid. Like some pockmarking childhood disease, she was afraid she would carry the scars of their last ordeal together for her entire life. The wounds had only partially healed, but at least she had her baby. Their baby. A part of Cyrus. She accepted all over again how hopeless it was to hope, and how impossible it was not to hope.

Later, at the Waldorf, Cameron pushed through the revolving door and stopped dead in her tracks, gaping at the sight that greeted her. At the top of the stairs leading to the main lobby stood four attractive models directing people towards the grand ballroom on the left. They were dressed in skintight jeans and 'poor boy' shirts with Life Sciences printed in liquid crystals across their breasts and on the seat of their pants. The colours of the printed words changed with every movement. Alternately, they called out in beguiling tones, 'Anyone for the big Life Sciences show?' and 'The shareholder meeting in the grand ballroom – step right this way.' Whenever anyone responded, one of the girls took the shareholder by the arm and escorted him or her, or both, to the stairs leading to the ballroom.

Cameron brushed aside her eager escort and made her way up the ornate staircase to the ballroom. To the left of the long corridor leading to the ballroom was a table and a banner proclaiming Life Sciences Friendship Circle. Six men and women were seated around the table. When Cameron headed directly for the ballroom, she was stopped by a uniformed guard.

'Sorry, ma'am. Get your admission pass at that table. Or you can't get in.'

'Where is Mr Miller?' Cameron's temper was starting to fray.

'He's inside, getting ready for the entertainment.'

'Damn!' Cameron muttered under her breath and strode back to the table. She approached a young woman. 'My name is Cameron Hightower. I'd like an admission pass.'

'Hightower?' The woman tilted her head towards the man seated next to her. 'Bobby does H, I, J, K. I do D, E, F, G.'

Cameron moved sideways towards Bobby, who smiled in welcome. 'Hightower?' he said. His bored eyes opened wide. 'Hightower! Of course. Your pass, Miss Hightower.' He handed her a small piece of black plastic. 'Peel off the back. It's pressure sensitive. Put it on your forehead.'

Cameron followed instructions and Bobby produced a mirror. Cameron watched the plastic go through a change of colour; the background remained black, but C. HIGH-TOWER appeared in brilliant green.

'It's liquid crystals,' Bobby explained.

'I know,' Cameron said through tight lips.

At the entrance to the ballroom, she was stopped again by a small man, also dressed in blue jeans and T-shirt, who peered nearsightedly at her forehead. 'Hello, Miss High-tower. I'm Allan Kotes. With Sweeney, Sullivan, and Weiss. I'm checking off the numbers of shares represented by every shareholder who shows. We need a quorum.'

'I'm surprised Mr Miller accepts the tradition,' Cameron remarked caustically.

'Yes, I've never seen anything like this shareholder meeting.'

'Neither have I, Mr Kotes. Where is Mr Miller?'

'Floating around in there somewhere. What a blast!'

It was a blast. The atmosphere of the ballroom was permeated with an air of expectation, an electricity that Cameron associated with the opening of a Broadway play just before the curtain rose. Her eyes searched the crowd for Byron. Instead of the rows of seats facing a raised dais, there were round tables with eight chairs per table. In front of each chair was an envelope. The room was set up for a banquet, not a shareholder meeting. Two bars, one at each side of the room, were doing a land office business. The balcony that ran around three sides of the room was festooned with huge blowups of girls wearing Thermoscans, the same girls Byron had included in his notice of the meeting. Balloons and streamers hung from the ceiling fixtures. A crowd of share-holders milled about, talking excitedly in loud voices.

The crowd spanned about sixty years, from the mid-teens to the mid-seventies. People gorged themselves at the canapé table on red caviar, blinchini, pâté, sweet and sour spare ribs, shrimp, and all manner of cheeses. There was a drifting hum

443

of conversation, an undercurrent of anticipation. These people weren't here to participate in a shareholder meeting. They were here to have a good time. They expected and wanted to be entertained. The announcement had set them up for that.

'Cameron!' A feverish Harry Horn approached her. He was also wearing blue jeans and a T-shirt, and looked even more ridiculous than the lawyer. 'Isn't this something?' he enthused. 'Let's find Byron.' He urged Cameron towards the centre of the room.

Cameron allowed Harry to propel her along.

'There he is.' Harry pointed to Byron standing with one foot on the stairs leading to the dais and dressed in his usual jeans, sports shirt, and loafers. He was regaling a ring of admiring shareholders and paused for a moment, his eyes canvassing the milling throng. Even at this distance, Cameron could tell he was counting the house.

Cameron moved closer and caught a few words over the hubbub. 'Sure! It's going to one hundred twenty. I suggest you buy now,' Byron was saying. 'That's right. We'll be shipping product in six months.'

Cameron's disquiet deepened. He shouldn't keep promoting the stock so blatantly.

Byron spotted her, excused himself, and hurried to greet her. 'Pretty terrific shareholder meeting, isn't it?'

'Frankly, I don't like it.'

The look of a small boy who had just had his backside slapped appeared on Byron's face. But Cameron sensed a difference. In the past, the look was real. Now it was just another pose that Byron put on, just as he put on his pants and his shirt or any other costume that he thought would work to his advantage.

'Come on, Cameron,' he said. 'Don't be a wet blanket. Shareholder meetings are notorious for being so deadly dull,

444

the few diehards who attend become comatose. And we both know that's deliberate. This time, all the little people who've been salting away our stock will be alive and kicking. Ready to speak their piece.'

Cameron glanced at the bar. 'Providing they're sober enought to speak.'

Byron grinned, and the sly, small boy peeked out. 'Nobody makes them drink.'

A well-rounded young woman joined them. Like everyone else connected with Life Sciences, she wore jeans and a skintight T-shirt. However, her shirt was so stretched you could see her nipples pressing through the material. She linked her arm possessively through Byron's.

'Byron,' she said. 'Mr Haveworth is one of our big investors. He wants to say hello.'

'Yes, I do. I certainly do. I must say I'm very impressed with what you've accomplished with Life Sciences. It's a pity we could not see eye to eye at our first meeting,' Adrian Haveworth said graciously.

'That's the way the jelly shimmers,' Byron answered, starting towards the dais. 'See you around Mr Haveworth. Or was it Net . . .?' Seeing Cameron's expression, he shut his mouth.

'No,' Adrian rambled on. 'Not Mr Haveworth. Why don't you call me Adrian?'

Byron stopped, turned, and stared at Adrian Haveworth. He smiled a generous smile. 'Thank you, Adrian. I will. And you can call me Mr Miller.' He turned and strode towards the platform.

Cameron remained a few minutes with Adrian Haveworth, making an effort to smooth his ruffled feathers. When she caught up with Byron, she said, 'That wasn't nice.'

'It wasn't meant to be nice.'

'Your forehead says your name is C. Hightower. I guess

the C stands for Cameron,' the big-breasted young woman said.

'And you're Margo Bayless. Was this circus your idea?'

'I'm not that inspirational. Byron gets the credit.'

The women measured each other. Cameron tried to forget that Margo Bayless was the woman who'd introduced Byron to the Hansen Company and in so doing had lost her Cyrus. That wasn't fair, she admitted to herself. She never had Cyrus to lose in the first place. Margo's reaction to Cameron hadn't changed: she was out of her league, as was Byron. There was nothing to worry about. Byron was hers.

Byron looked at his watch. 'Time to get the show on the road.' He pointed to the dais. 'You sit here, Cameron. Mason couldn't make it, and Rosemary may or may not come. So Harry, you and I are the only board members here.' He jumped the two feet to the platform and walked to the microphone. 'Testing. One. Two. Three. Four.' His voice resounded throughout the room. 'Everyone,' Byron called out. 'Grab a seat. It's showtime.' It took fifteen minutes before Byron could get the shareholders seated.

'Before we start the formal meeting, I want you to know how much Life Sciences appreciates your taking time to come to our meeting. And to show you our appreciation, there's an envelope in front of you. Each envelope contains a card. When you get home, fill in your Thermoscan size, or your wife's or daughter's, or your girlfriend's size. Remember, even if a woman doesn't wear a bra, she should own a Thermoscan.' There was an outbreak of applause. 'The card is stamped and addressed. Drop it in the mail, and Life Sciences will send you your own Life Sciences Tumour Detection Thermoscan. Absolutely free!' Byron paused dramatically, allowing for a second and louder round of applause. When it died down, he continued. 'Now for a preview of what you'll receive in the mail. We've set up a dressing room

446

in the wings. I'd like to call on five volunteers to model our Home Tumour Test Thermoscan for you. Ladies only, please.'

The men chortled and the women giggled. There was scattered applause, much louder than the joke warranted.

A substantial group of women raised their hands. The shareholders of Life Sciences were definitely into the spirit of things.

'Margo,' Byron called out. Margo was seated at a table just to the left of the stage. 'Pick five ladies at random.'

Margo flitted around the tables. She selected a woman here, another there, and soon all five were herded into the curtained-off area.

By now, Cameron's antennae were alerted. What appeared to be a random choice wasn't. The women were all young and pretty, and had excellent figures, if oversize breasts. A hand tapped Cameron's shoulder.

'Sorry I'm late.' Rosemary Atherton Stern's clipped British accent had become more clipped since marrying Jake. 'Jake and I had a small tiff, as to whether I meet my responsibilities or keep him company at a musical. He lost.'

'Glad to have you,' Cameron said. 'I need a shoulder to lean on.'

'Relax, ducky,' Rosemary said cheerfully. 'Give the boy his due. He was born to have his name in lights. Now, look at that!'

The five volunteers, wearing their skirts and Thermoscans, trooped out of the dressing room to join Byron at the microphone.

'Examine our volunteers closely,' Byron exhorted the audience. 'Look at those colours.' From under the lectern he produced a long pointer and illustrated that each woman had healthy breasts by tracing the colours on the Thermoscans. Then he watched as the women snaked their way through

447

the tables to permit the shareholders to get a better look. The women eyed them, the men ogled them; everyone fully appreciated the women's natural endowments. It was hard to say if there was more appreciation of the female shape or of the medical achievement.

'What if one of the girls happened to have a problem?' Rosemary whispered.

'Don't worry about it. I'll explain later,' Harry Horn, sitting next to Cameron, whispered.

'All right, ladies,' Byron called out. 'Thank you very much. If you'll be kind enough to change to your usual attire, we'll begin the formal meeting.'

Once the women disappeared behind the curtain, Byron rapped on the microphone. 'I would like to call the annual meeting of the shareholders of Life Sciences to order. Mr Kotes, as assistant secretary of our corporation, do you have a record of the number of shares present?'

'Yes, Mr Chairman. Of a total of 3,200,000 shares issued and outstanding, the shareholders present represent 2,258,300 shares. In addition we have proxies for another 570,000 shares. That comes to 2,828,300 shares. More than enough for a quorum.'

Cameron guessed that a majority of the missing shares were held by Cyrus Hansen. She had not expected him to attend the meeting, and she would not permit herself the merest hint of regret.

The next business at hand was the election of the board of directors of Life Sciences. Byron conducted the election in the traditional manner. The nominees were Cameron High-tower, Rosemary Stern, John Mason – in absentia – Harry Horn, and Byron Miller. There was no opposition, no abstentions, no nominations from the floor. The five members were reelected unanimously.

448

Byron clasped his hands over his head like a prizefighter proclaiming victory.

'It is customary at this time for the chief executive officer – that's me' – he gave the shareholders a broad smile – 'to give you a summary of the year's progress. I would say the chart included with your notice of the meeting showing the price rise of Life Sciences' stock speaks for itself, and does it far more convincingly than any words of mine could do. So rather than discuss the progress of your company, I would like to discuss the philosophy motivating Life Sciences.'

Forty-five minutes later, Byron finished. His closing words resounded through the grand ballroom. 'We must appreciate how our evolving intelligence has flowered into the glory that we call man. As it is with the human race, so it is with Life Sciences. Your company's growing intelligence will add to the glory of mankind, and your profits will be rich in both financial and personal rewards. Rewards from the products we are evolving that will benefit the world.' Without pausing, Byron called out, 'Is there anything more you need to know about Life Sciences?' He waited five seconds. 'No? Then I move the annual shareholder meeting of Life Sciences be adjourned. Do I hear a second?'

Margo Bayless shouted, 'I second the motion.'

'All in favour?'

There was a rousing chorus of 'ayes'.

'Opposed?'

Silence.

'The meeting is adjourned.'

'I do not believe it,' Cameron said to Rosemary.

'Believe it,' Rosemary shrugged. 'Jake should have come. He loves show business.'

'Jake would have had an attack of hives,' Cameron snorted. She spotted Harry Horn standing alone, mumbling disconcertedly to himself. On a hunch she rose and joined him.

'What is it, Harry?'

He held up the Thermoscans. 'One. Two. Three. Two of those women kept theirs.'

'So what? You're going to send out five hundred as samples.'

'You don't understand,' Harry moaned. 'These are special. Remember Mrs Stern asked how we could be sure all the women would be healthy?' Cameron nodded. 'Well ...' Harry fumbled around. 'Byron insisted I rig them.'

'Rig the Thermoscans?'

'I fixed them so that no matter if something was wrong, it wouldn't show up.'

Cameron felt sick. She had to hold on to a table to steady herself. 'Why did he do that?' she asked.

'You know Byron. His motto is "No bad news for the Street". He said that if one of the women had a tumour or cyst, it would have wrecked the mood of the meeting.'

'And if one of those women does have something wrong, that'll do a lot more than wreck the mood of the meeting. It will mean a multimillion-dollar lawsuit and rotten publicity from here to Outer Mongolia.' Cameron was furious. 'Can you find out the names of the women who modelled them?'

'I think Margo Bayless has the names.'

'She would. Tell her to get those things back, Harry. Make any excuse. Say they were experimental and got into the batch by mistake. I don't care what you say, but you have to get them back. Then you can send the women finished Thermoscans that work properly. And tell Byron I want to see him on Monday, first thing. Of all the damn-fool stunts, this takes the cake.'

Cameron left the ballroom with Rosemary. As she walked down the stairs, she thought of Harry's words: 'No bad news for the Street.' She wondered how far Byron would go to prevent bad news from reaching Wall Street.

26

Cameron rubbed her temples. The headache came in low, slow waves as she read *The Wall Street Journal*. She had never had headaches before, but during the past year, whenever she went over the press clippings she'd collected on Life Sciences, she experienced a short bout with a throbbing forehead. Byron had been in orbit for almost two years, and the stock was at a record high. But delivery of Thermoscans for national marketing by the Hansen Company had been postponed repeatedly – with Byron using any number of excuses. Now again in September 1989, Byron had announced in the newspapers that delivery was starting almost immediately. What gave Cameron a headache was Byron's idea of what 'immediately' meant. She had Della get him on the phone.

'Hi!' Byron said in his feeling-fine, everything-is-first-rate voice.

'Byron, I saw the piece in today's *Wall Street Journal*.'

'They didn't give Harry proper billing.' Byron was still resting easy.

'And I didn't know you had a PhD. Night school again?'

'I don't have a PhD. Who said that?'

'The article, Byron. It quoted Dr Miller.'

'Oh, sure, I remember.' Byron's broad grin was almost visible through the telephone. 'You know the press. They like to give away titles. It hypes the article.'

'Not *The Wall Street Journal*.' A thin feeling of tension crept into Cameron's body. 'You didn't happen to mention that you had a PhD did you, Dr Miller?'

451

'Cameron!' Byron sounded indignant. 'Why would I do such a stupid thing? The reporter must have just assumed it. Liquid crystals is a complicated technology. And everybody has a PhD these days.'

'And it does add to the stature of the chairman.'

'As a matter of fact, I wish I did have a PhD. But it was either an MBA or a PhD. I couldn't afford both,' Byron said sadly. 'That bloop was a reporter's mistake. He wrote a "D" instead of an "M".'

'This is the second time it's happened. That's once too often.'

'Well, have you noticed that the price of the stock is holding around one hundred twenty-five dollars? I must be doing something right.'

Cameron glanced out the window at the clear, brisk sunshine. It smiled at her, but she didn't smile back. 'When will you be shipping product?'

'Any day now.' Byron spoke lightly, as if it were a matter of no consequence.

'There've been three announcements and three postponements.'

'I know. There are still a few bugs in the machine. But we're working them out. They should be cleaned up before Christmas.'

'Sure. Well, keep me posted.' Cameron put down the receiver, feeling frustrated. And if she felt this way, she could well imagine what Elmer Hansen was feeling. She shook her head. Elmer Hansen could take care of himself. Her job was taking care of FitzGerald Associates.

She switched on her desktop computer. The Hansen Company stock was still quoted at 45½, the same as yesterday. The trading volume, given the size of the company's capitalization, was on the high side; 150,000 shares one day, 185,000 the next. Yesterday, it had gone over 200,000 shares.

As Coz had said, someone was accumulating Hansen stock. Possibly Cyrus? If he was, it could lead to a proxy fight. There was money to be made in that stock. It was time to start buying. Cyrus Hansen! She permitted herself exactly five seconds of torment over the name, then she wiped it from her mind. She called Coz and told him to start accumulating Hansen Company stock for the firm account.

Cyrus Hansen worked with his computer. The Hansen stock had risen three quarters of a point, on higher volume than usual. Was someone else buying? Probably it was just a blip. At least, he hoped so. He'd been planning his move for a long time, waiting for the proper moment. But the Life Sciences contract with the Hansen Company had forced his hand. He studied the numbers on the screen. That was no blip. Someone else was accumulating Hansen stock. The fight with Elmer could no longer be delayed.

His sleep, which was never good, had deteriorated badly. His world seemed lonelier than it had been. Sometimes, in the dark, he thought about the nights with Cameron, the mingling of their bodies that obliterated time and thought. But they were not memories he often permitted himself.

'No, Byron! Absolutely no!'

'Come on, Cameron. What's the matter with you? Do you have any idea how many strings Margo and I had to pull to get *Inside America* interested in Wall Street? And get us on the programme?'

Cameron struggled to control her temper. These days it was becoming more and more difficult to talk to Byron. She chose her words precisely and spoke slowly. 'I don't care what you did. It's a lousy idea.' Her irritation got the best of her. 'Maybe if you worked as hard to get the production machinery running as you do to get all that damn publicity, you'd be delivering product by now.'

'Cameron! That's not fair. I'm doing my best.' The sincere, easily hurt Byron took centre stage.

As always, Cameron retreated. Her instincts told her that Byron was fragile, his bravado all show. 'It may not be fair, but it is accurate.' She tried another approach. 'Have you ever seen MacDonald Wilson, the host of *Inside America*, in action?'

'Sure,' Byron lied with conviction. 'I watch the programme as often as I can.'

'Then you know he's a butcher. He'll cut you to pieces.'

'Not if you're with me. You can be my shield.'

'They'll end up carrying us home on it,' Cameron said sarcastically.

'All right.' Byron stopped fencing and played his trump card. 'If you won't appear on the programme, I'll do it without you. Wilson can find another investment banker who is into new issues to take your place. Maybe Herbie Claxton.'

Cameron's silence told him he'd struck the proper chord. Reluctantly, she surrendered. 'Game, set, and match. We'll both appear on the programme.' Under no circumstances would she allow the Byron Miller who had emerged in the last two years – since the $50 million stock sale – to appear on national television without her hand on his shoulder to control him. 'Listen carefully, Byron. Tell them we'll do it under the following conditions – '

Cameron did not want to give the producer of *Inside America* an opportunity to edit the videotape of the programme. It would be too easy to slant the tape to make any points Wilson wished. So her most important condition was that the programme be live. Privately, she hoped that her demand would kill the entire project, but to her dismay, MacDonald Wilson agreed to the live format.

* * *

454

Cameron spent half an hour with the makeup man before someone came to get her.

The cameras were already in place, circling a set that was supposed to be an office, presumably hers. The director had suggested she sit at the desk and Byron be seated in a chair next to her. She spotted Byron off to one side. Byron's makeup man had done too good a job for her taste. His hair was even more rakish than usual, and its studied, tousled look was held in place by spray; his hollow cheeks were accentuated by shadow that made him look hungry, even underfed; and his dark eyes seemed to glint with mischief. Byron looked too theatrical – the schoolboy charm was exaggerated. This was Byron Miller, young man on the make, the Huckleberry Finn of Wall Street. With a vengeance.

'Nervous, Byron?' she asked, knowing the answer.

'Why did we agree to do this?'

'We didn't. You did, and you blackmailed me into coming along.'

A man approached. He was tall, well groomed, with big shoulders and blue-black hair. 'Good evening. I'm MacDonald Wilson.'

'Cameron Hightower.' They shook hands.

'And you're Byron Miller. Hi.' He extended his hand. 'I still think it was a mistake not to tape this show. We could have edited it together.'

'But you would have had final say as to programme content,' Cameron said amiably. Wilson's smile acknowledged the fact.

The charm radiating from Wilson was more effective on camera. His eyes were long, narrow slits topped by heavy, black eyebrows. They were canny, cynical; qualities TV viewers interpreted as wise. Up close they were chilling.

A voice called out, 'Everybody, sixty seconds to air time.'

Wilson whispered, 'The first minutes are taped, followed by two commercials. Take your places during the commercials. I'll make my comments from that stool next to your desk. That's your cue. Then I'll ask you a question.'

'I don't suppose you'd give us a hint as to the question?'

'No, Cameron. You insisted on a live format. You got it.'

The programme began. An outline of the map of the United States with the *Inside America* logo appeared. The centre of the map showed a youngish woman and two small children. The woman said, 'I heard about Life Sciences and their wonderful new device for the detection of breast tumours. But I couldn't buy one, and I didn't find out I had breast cancer until it was too late. I had to have a radical mastectomy.' Several quick shots of women wearing a Thermoscan followed. Three were healthy. One had cystolic breasts.

'Where did they get those?' Cameron asked in a low voice.

'I gave them to the director,' Byron whispered. 'He said he needed examples of how the thing works.'

A second picture followed. A close-up of a middle-aged man. 'I should never have bought stock in the Alpha-Beta Computer Company. The company went broke and I lost all my savings.'

'What's Alpha-Beta got to do with us?' Byron asked.

'I've an idea, and I only hope I'm wrong.'

The map of the United States reappeared. Inside the map was a series of pictures of stock certificates. Each one was a different company, and a big, black 'BANKRUPT' had been stamped across the face of each. The final certificate was unstamped. It was for 100 shares of Life Sciences. Wilson spoke.

'Tonight, *Inside America* will be looking at the phenomena of the new-issue market. A few Americans have made fortunes on the new-issue market, but many have gone broke.

Recently the new-issue market has collapsed, due in large part to the bankruptcy of many high-technology companies. But one high-technology company has been weathering the storm. That company is Life Sciences.'

There was a close-up of Wilson's face. 'I'm Mac Wilson. In a departure from our usual format, because of the importance of tonight's subject, *Inside America* will devote the entire hour to an in-depth look at the new-issue market and, in particular, Life Sciences. We will also review the activities of our guests, Cameron Hightower, managing partner of FitzGerald Associates, the Wall Street investment banking-house for Life Sciences. And Byron Miller, the chairman of the board of Life Sciences.'

The two commercials were aired, and then the programme began. Wilson delivered a monologue using charts and statistics detailing the frightening number of women who died of breast cancer each year. He dwelled on the import-ance of early detection in successful treatment of the disease, which took him to Life Sciences. He said nothing to which either Cameron or Byron could take exception. But Cameron waited. She couldn't believe that they had been invited to appear on *Inside America* so that MacDonald Wilson could extol the wonders of the product Life Sciences had devel-oped. She was right.

'Of course,' Wilson continued, 'there are a few important questions about Life Sciences that should be brought to the public's attention. While clinical studies appear to show that the Thermoscan does what the company claims, the fact is that Life Sciences has yet to manufacture for sale to the public one single device. They have a small prototype machine that can make about five hundred Thermoscans a day at substantial cost. Yet, without one penny of income, the company has raised over fifty million dollars from the

American public by issuing three million two hundred thousand shares of stock. Although the original price was $10.00 a share, the stock is currently selling for $125.50 a share. Which means that Wall Street, as of this moment, placed a value on Life Sciences of over four hundred million dollars. To put this into perspective, Pan American World Airways – the flagship line of the United States – has a current market value of only four hundred fifty million dollars. About the same as Life Sciences.'

Across the country, in living rooms, family rooms, TV rooms, and dens, men and women visualized Pan Am. Its huge fleet of modern jet planes, its thousands of employees, its worldwide facilities, the Pan Am Building in New York City. And wondered how this was possible. How could Life Sciences, a small company which had not sold a single Thermoscan, be worth as much as Pan Am, a giant international airline? What was wrong with Wall Street?

When Wilson turned to Cameron, she was prepared.

'Miss Hightower, Mr Miller, would either of you care to comment on this?'

'I can understand your puzzlement when comparing huge Pan Am to tiny Life Sciences,' Cameron began. 'At first glance, it does seem strange. But one tends to forget that Pan Am no longer owns the Pan Am building and they had to sell their Pacific routes to raise cash. The airline has lost hundreds of millions of dollars. And continues to lose money. Maybe that's why Wall Street values the company at only four hundred fifty million dollars. They question the ability of the airline to survive. Maybe – just maybe – Wall Street and the investing public are fairly astute. They see Pan Am as a loser and Life Sciences as a winner. So they sell Pan Am and buy Life Sciences.' She paused and then said with great

458

confidence, 'I myself will stand on the valuation of Life Sciences at four hundred million dollars.'

Around the country people had second thoughts about Pan Am World Airways. Maybe Wall Street wasn't so foolish?

There was another break for commercials. When Wilson resumed, he explained how Cameron Hightower had found Harry Horn – the inventor of the Thermoscan – and selected Byron Miller to head the company. He described how she'd raised the seed money from Acorn Venture Capital, taken the company public, and put together the second, huge sale of stock. Then he said, 'At the moment things appear to be coming up roses for Life Sciences. But let's examine what has happened to other small companies that once appeared to be equally as promising.'

A series of short, taped interviews with men and women who had invested their savings in new, small companies followed. One elderly accountant had retired to Miami Beach on a $3,000 investment he'd made in Digital Equipment Corporation. A former hairdresser lived in Palm Desert, California, on the proceeds of a flier she'd once taken in Polaroid. But most of the vignettes told of monies lost that the people interviewed could not afford to lose. There were stories of mortgages foreclosed, children unable to complete college, reluctant wives who had never worked being forced into the job market to help support their families: a litany of broken dreams. The final tape – of a short, round man on a chaise by a swimming pool and a pretty, young blonde in a tiny bikini next to him – made Cameron gasp: Leon Beckett!

After a few desultory comments from Wilson, Beckett explained why he was lounging poolside at his California home instead of being in an office.

'Beckett Pharmaceuticals ran into some bad luck a few

years ago. The FDA turned down our new drug that thinned out the blood of a person who had had a heart attack. We called the drug Mr Thin.'

MacDonald Wilson remained congenial. 'By "bad luck," do you mean that Beckett Pharmaceuticals was forced to declare bankruptcy?'

'Chapter Ten,' Beckett announced without regret.

The camera panned around the vast estate and back to Leon and his seventh wife.

'You don't appear to be suffering any financial hardship from the bankruptcy of your company,' Wilson remarked.

'Me? Hardship? Hey, Mac! You think I'm some kind of dummy? I unloaded enough of my stock before the company fell apart to set me up for life.'

'Let's make sure I understand. Even though your company went bankrupt, you were able to sell enough personal stock to the American public to make you a rich man.'

'You're damn right.' Beckett was not the least abashed.

'But the American public, the people who bought your stock, they lost their money?'

Beckett shrugged. 'There are winners and losers. I'm a winner.'

'Were there any other winners at Beckett Pharmaceuticals?'

'A couple. FitzGerald Associates, the Wall Street firm that took the company public. They got a fee of a cool million dollars. And stock in the company that they sold for a lot more money.' Beckett grinned knowingly at the camera.

'That gives us the picture, Leon. And thank you for allowing *Inside America* to visit you in your pleasant retirement.'

There was another break for commercials. When they ended, Wilson spoke to Byron and Cameron.

'It would appear, Cameron, that Leon Beckett and your company, FitzGerald Associates, were about the only winners at Beckett Pharmaceuticals. Would you care to comment on this?'

'I'd be glad to.' Cameron went into an explanation of the history of Beckett Pharmaceuticals and its relationship with FitzGerald Associates. She dwelled at some length on Byron Miller. On how, when he was working for her company, he had done an excellent analysis regarding Mr Thin and why it wouldn't be licensed by the FDA. Because of that analysis, she had declined to do the second placement of stock. Another Wall Street firm had done it, and it was from that placement that Beckett derived most of his money. Cameron talked and kept on talking. Her idea was the more time she took, the less time Wilson would have to attack Byron and herself. By the time she finished, the director called another commercial break, and there were only fifteen minutes left to the programme.

'So far this programme has focused on the men and women who have made and lost money investing in the stock of new companies. But for them, investing in stocks is not a full-time job. It's something they do to try to make extra money. We will now interview a man who is a professional investor. A man who makes it his business to put money into new ventures. And he, probably better than anyone else, knows the real story behind Life Sciences and what are its chances for success.

'For the conclusion of this investigation of Life Sciences, its investment banker, and Wall Street, we take you to the home of Cyrus Hansen.'

Cameron's pained cry – 'Damn it!' – was heard across the country. Byron and she stared at the image of Cyrus on the monitor. He was dressed in his usual blue blazer, tan slacks, and open-necked shirt. His golden hair gleamed under the bright TV lighting. His size, his obvious great physical strength and startling masculine good looks made even the

461

imposing MacDonald Wilson look pallid. Cameron's heart pounded wildly as she stared at the picture of Cyrus in his study. Memories of the times they had made love sent shivers up and down her thighs, making her face burn under the TV makeup.

'Mr Hansen,' Macdonald Wilson said, his voice coated with something resembling awe. 'May I call you Cyrus?'

'Certainly, Mac.'

'Cyrus, would you be kind enough to describe the part you played in Life Sciences?'

'By profession, I buy and reorganize companies. I'm also a bit of a gambler. But I don't gamble at the crap table, or play roulette, or bet on the horses. I gamble on concepts and people. I'm what is called a venture capitalist.' Cyrus went on to detail his involvement with Life Sciences up to the signing of the Hansen Company contract, including his resignation from its board of directors. Cameron noted grimly that he made no mention either of his restriction against doing business with the Hansen Company or his reason for resigning.

This last fact was not lost on Wilson. 'Why did you resign, Cyrus? Is there something wrong with the Hansen Company contract?'

'Plenty!' Cyrus said with great intensity. 'For openers, look at the result of the contract. The stock of Life Sciences, a company with a product that has yet to be mass-produced, is now selling for about one hundred twenty-five dollars a share. What if they're never able to mass-produce the Thermoscan?'

'The stock would drop,' Wilson speculated. 'But why should they be unable to mass-produce the product?'

'Because designing the machinery to do it is very compli- cated. I gather you've seen the prototype machine?'

'Yes. It seems to work very well.'

'It does, but it also works very slowly. As you already said,

462

it can turn out about five hundred Thermoscans a day. Hardly mass production.'

'Then why did the Hansen Company, one of the giants in the industry, sign a contract to market a product that has not yet been commercially manufactured? And, according to you, might never be mass-produced?'

Cyrus reached for a folder lying on the table next to him. The folder contained the recent history of the Hansen Company. He pointed out how the Hansen stock had fallen, how its sales and profits were flat.

'The Hansen Company wants that product badly,' he said. 'Elmer Hansen, my grandfather, was perfectly willing to allow the company name to be used in what amounts to a stock promotion. Remember, the only investment the Hansen Company has in this product is in the paper on which the contract was drawn, the time several house lawyers spent on drawing up the contract, and the ink from the pen Elmer Hansen used to sign the contract. The point is, Elmer Hansen and the Hansen Company have very little at risk in this venture.'

'Would you care to comment, Cyrus, on the commissions FitzGerald Associates received from the sale of Life Sciences stock to the public?' MacDonald Wilson asked.

'They were on the high side, but within reasonable Wall Street guidelines. Considering the risks involved.'

'What risks, Cyrus? Judging from what we've heard and what you've said, doesn't the public take all the risks? The investment banker gets his fee no matter what happens to the company later.'

Cyrus shook his head. 'That's too simple. Assume for the moment that FitzGerald Associates were producers who sold their shows to your network. And all they produced were flops. What would happen to them?'

Wilson considered the question. He knew exactly where

463

Cyrus was heading, but he saw no way to avoid answering the question. 'The shows would be dropped and the producer would find it difficult to make another sale.'

'Precisely. If FitzGerald Associates continuously loses money for their clients, they'll lose their clients. And go out of business.'

Cameron swallowed hard as memories filled her mind. She saw Tim, she saw herself. She'd been so young, so naïve, when she'd asked Tim FitzGerald the same question. And he had given her almost the same answer Cyrus had given Wilson.

'Let me make a final point, Mac,' Cyrus said. 'I do not like the way Life Sciences was put together. The product itself, the Thermoscan, is an important invention. But the company management leaves much to be desired. First it gives Byron Miller the same opportunity that Leon Beckett had to sell his stock in Life Sciences to the public before the company is a successful business, not merely a stock promotion. He could walk away from its failure a rich man. Also, Miller is not a proven businessman. He's a successful promoter, as one can see from the ridiculously high price of Life Sciences stock. And Cameron Hightower, while she is highly professional in many aspects of Wall Street, has little knowledge of the pitfalls connected with offering small, high-tech companies in the public market. Miller put together a contract with the Hansen Company, and Hightower used it. As it now stands, the public's money is at great risk. If for any reason the Thermoscan cannot be mass-produced, many investors who cannot afford it will lose their money. What the public must understand clearly is that the Hansen Company contract is meaningless.'

Cyrus leaned forward and the camera zoomed in. The earnestness and concern on his face was magnified one hundredfold. 'I say this to the American public. You have

464

bought stock in a promotion. Not a successful company. Sell your Life Sciences stock. Sell it now. Get out while you still can at a decent price. Tomorrow may be too late.'

Cameron checked her watch; only five minutes to go. She'd think about Cyrus later. Right now, she had to do something to stop what was likely to be a selling panic when the market opened tomorrow morning.

'Cameron, Byron, you've heard Cyrus Hansen's views. Anything to say?'

'You'd better believe it.' Byron had been quiet for most of the programme, having told himself repeatedly that this was no time to shoot off his mouth. But the direct assault Cyrus had made on Cameron, on him, and on the Hansen Company contract was more than he could stomach. Cyrus's personal vendetta with his grandfather was drawing blood, their blood. He went on the attack. 'You are aware, Mac, that Cyrus Hansen is a very rich man?'

'I would imagine so.'

'He owns over half a billion dollars of Hansen Company stock. Plus other investments worth many hundreds of millions of dollars. He's loaded, and it's his idea that only the rich should get richer. By that, I mean that only the rich should be allowed to invest in small companies like Life Sciences. Let me tell you, dear friends in the middle-income brackets, there's a particular SEC regulation called a 146 private placement that Cyrus Hansen loves. Do you know why? I'll tell you. The rule varies slightly from state to state, but generally speaking, to invest in a company under Rule 146, you have to be worth at least one million dollars. Yeah! A cool million. Plus have an income of over two hundred thousand dollars a year. Cyrus Hansen is angry because he didn't want Cameron Hightower to take Life Sciences public so all you folks could have a crack at getting rich. Not our boy Cyrus. He believes in protecting the public from itself. If

465

we'd done a 146, every single buddy of Cyrus Hansen's would have gotten in on the ground floor, cheap! But not you. Oh, no! Not you! Not me, either. *We* wouldn't have qualified.'

Cameron picked up on Byron's sentiments. 'Byron is right. It's up to each and every one of you to decide how to invest your money. You may lose your money. It happens. But if you hit a winner, then you' – she pointed at the camera – 'you and you may become as rich as Macdonald Wilson. And maybe – who knows – even as rich as Cyrus Hansen. The question to ask yourself is, "Do I really want to be rich?"'

Cameron had timed it perfectly. As she said 'rich' the director cut away for a commercial. The programme was over. Wilson approached them. He bore no personal animosity, because *Inside America* was a combination of news and entertainment and the more entertaining the show, the higher the ratings. He hadn't been able to decimate Cameron Hightower and Byron Miller as he had hoped, but the show had enough fireworks. That was all that mattered.

Byron shook hands with him and nudged Cameron. Now that the show was over, she seemed dazed. 'Shake hands,' he murmured. 'And let's get the hell out of here.'

After having their makeup removed, Cameron and Byron left the studios together. Andrew was waiting to drive them home, but Cameron gave the car to Byron. She felt a strong need for fresh air, light pockets, and solitude. Something, a shrinking from Byron's fierce attack on Cyrus, had built up inside her, and she could not have sat quietly beside him in the car. She was glad to be alone, alone with the human race at large. While walking, she could dream and wonder what Cyrus was thinking, wonder if he was as starved for her as she was for him. Strangers didn't feel sorry for her. They

466

didn't care that she had failed with Cyrus. That all she had left of the man she loved was a baby who would never know his father. She felt a sharp sting of loneliness and a sense of injustice.

Then there passed just below the surface of her consciousness a recognition that something quite extraordinary had happened. Slowly her face took on an expression of guarded hope. Perhaps she was attaching too much importance to her idea. But perhaps – only perhaps – Cyrus's rage at her had something to do with his upcoming battle with his grandfather. Maybe when that was over, he might begin to see her more clearly. After all, he didn't have to appear on the programme. To fight Elmer, he could have continued doing what he'd been doing: accumulating Hansen stock. But his appearance had been a signal. It sounded an alarm, telling Elmer more than Elmer needed to know. Surprise was always a major element in a successful attack. Cyrus knew that. Why had he thrown it away? Why had he appeared on *Inside America*? To attack Byron and her? Possibly. But also possibly to warn her. Beware of Byron. Beware of Elmer Hansen. If he had tried to warn her, at risk to himself, was it because his caring for her overcame his caution? The question led down a blind alley. There was nothing for her to do but to wait and hope.

PART EIGHT

The Takeover
1989

27

'Harriet, call Miss Goody. I want the daily closing price of the Hansen Company stock over the last six months. I also want Sam Penn's report covering the last six months.' Elmer Hansen clicked off, with the air of a man about to confirm something he already knew.

In the early afternoon, his secretary placed a list of the daily closing prices of the Hansen Company stock on his desk, starting with May 10, 1989. The Hansen Company librarian was meticulous. She'd included the daily trading volume along with each price. Harriet added the report from Sam Penn, who was listed in the company's organization table as assistant to Miss Goody. However, his salary was many times Miss Goody's; and in the matter of research, he was a bloodhound. He not only read the important newspapers, he listened to and recorded the news broadcasts of several radio stations and watched videotapes of television news programmes. He studied the employees of the Hansen Company, compiled private dossiers on all the senior executives, and did the filing of the clippings provided by the company's clipping service. He was in charge of the collection and cataloguing of everything that related directly or indirectly to the Hansen Company.

Elmer Hansen studied Miss Goody's report with obsessive attention, all the while smiling faintly. The price of the Hansen Company stock had reached a plateau. About three months ago its slow but inexorable downhill slide had come to a halt, and the daily trading was up. Why? The company had not yet announced the marketing of the Thermoscan.

There was nothing to keep the stock from falling further. Except Cyrus. Elmer was pleased. If it had no other value, the slipping of the stock had smoked out Cyrus, who was finally making his move. He was accumulating stock, preparing for a proxy fight. Elmer momentarily relished the prospect of dealing with an adequate adversary.

He looked next at Sam Penn's report on Cyrus, his eyes half closed. Penn stated, as if this fact had not been filed with Elmer long ago, that Cyrus Hansen had put up the original seed money for Life Sciences. Since then, Cyrus Hansen and Cameron Hightower had evidently had a serious falling out. Penn described the reasons for their dispute as it was stated on *Inside America*. He underscored Cyrus's emphasis that the Hansen Company contract was completely misunderstood by both Wall Street and the public. Because it had been used to pump up the price of Life Sciences' stock, it smacked of being a con. Elmer felt a surge of pride, recognizing in Cyrus the same bladelike acuity that he himself exercised. Penn added – in an editorial aside – that he believed the Hansen Company contract was the reason for the rupture in the relationship between Cyrus Hansen and Cameron Hightower.

Elmer Hansen looked up, gazing past the papers, his face very still, as if he'd long ago lost the capacity to feel. Then, for an instant, his eyes glinted as if he were mocking an invisible presence. The fall of the stock was meaningless, and he had no interest in the failure of the relationship between Cyrus and Cameron. But the possibility of a proxy fight for power? That was another matter. Cyrus thought he had a mission to accomplish: to take over the Hansen Company. But the Hansen Company was more than a business to Elmer. It was his creation, the living proof of what he had achieved and of his strength, his genius, his early struggles and triumph. It was the source of his pride, his power. The

Hansen Company was blood of his blood, more his child than a flesh-and-blood child could ever be. It meant more to him than his life. He would never have surrendered it to an incompetent fool such as his son had been. And he would not hand it over to Cyrus. Not now. Not until Cyrus proved himself able to run the company, to make it grow, to build on what he'd created.

Elmer was aware that in any struggle with his grandson the one point where he was vulnerable was his *need* for Cyrus. It was this need with which he must contend. He must fight against the knowledge that Cyrus had a hold on him because he carried the Hansen name. So Elmer knew that he had to move with caution. He must not break Cyrus as he had broken Ellie. At the same time he must trap him, bind Cyrus to him. He was Elmer Hansen, the Hansen of the Hansen Company: Cyrus was not. Cyrus must accept that truth. Only when he was dead would Cyrus succeed him as the Hansen of the Hansen Company.

An odd sparkle came into Elmer Hansen's eyes, and when he buzzed his secretary, his voice seemed threaded with an unnatural gaiety.

'Harriet, get me Byron Miller.'

Totally mystified, Cameron read the announcement. It was a routine release sent to all brokerage houses and security analysts by the Hansen Company and was signed by James Taylor, vice president of marketing. The Hansen Company would do a limited test-market of the Thermoscan in several weeks. This was all very exciting, yet it gave Cameron an uncomfortable sensation. Why hadn't Byron told her the great news? She picked up the phone to call him.

'LSI,' Ann McDougal, the company's long-time telephone operator, said.

'Ann, this is Cameron Hightower. Would you give me Mr Miller, please?'

A short pause, then, 'I'm sorry, Miss Hightower. Dr Miller . . . Ahem . . . I mean, sorry, Mr Miller has given instructions he's not to be disturbed.'

'I don't care what instructions Mr' – and Cameron further emphasized the Mr – 'Mr Miller has given you. Get him!'

'I can't, Miss Hightower. He's out of the building.'

'Why didn't you say so in the first place?' Cameron snapped. 'Where is he?'

'Outside. Supervising the construction.'

'What construction? Never mind. Send someone to find him and tell him I want to speak to him immediately.' Cameron was never rude to defenceless telephone operators, but at the moment she was so upset that she hung up on Ann in the middle of the girl's aplogies. Dr Miller! Ann's slip confirmed what she'd suspected for the past year. Byron had given instructions that he was to be referred to as Dr Miller, except to those few callers who knew better. What on earth was Byron doing? What kind of construction was he supervising? When her phone rang she grabbed for it, certain it was Byron. It wasn't.

'Cameron, have you read the Hansen announcement?' For once Jake sounded pleased. 'Thank God it was Hansen itself. Not Life Sciences. Hansen doesn't kid around. That clown must be finally making product delivery. Praise be!'

'Yes.' Cameron tried to keep her voice noncommittal, but its very quietness alerted Jake.

'Okay. Spill it. What the fuck's bugging you? My office faces west. Why haven't I seen rockets or fireworks or skywriting over New Jersey? Or at least a star rising?'

'The star rose in the east, nitwit. And delivery of the Thermoscan does not rank with the second coming.'

'It's enough to cause my second coming. I told Rosemary

474

to meet me at the door tonight, martini in hand and stripped for action.' Jake gathered himself. 'Let's take it from the top. What the fuck is wrong? Why aren't you in orbit?'

'I am in orbit, Jake. Can't you hear me celebrating? Singing and dancing on the top of my desk? Talk to you later.'

She broke the connection, leaving herself free to ask the same questions. What was wrong with her? It was pure vanity, yet the fact was she was hurt. This wasn't their way, Byron's and hers. Wasn't there a bond between them? He should have told her the great news first.

Her private line rang a second time. Once again she reached for the phone but now with a studied casualness. This time it had to be Byron. Again, it wasn't.

'I don't know what he's doing!' The voice panted in a whisper. 'He's acting so crazy I don't know what to do.'

Cameron let the panic-stricken voice stumble on. The more the person talked, the more disjointed his words became and the less Cameron understood.

'He's going to get us into trouble. I can feel it. You have to help!' The voice sounded close to tears.

'Who is this?' Cameron asked quietly.

'Harry!' he almost screamed. 'Harry Horn!'

'Harry?' Cameron felt giddy. Harry was either hysterical or drunk. 'What is it? What's the matter?'

'I can't talk on the telephone. And anyway I could be wrong.'

'About what?'

'Byron.'

Harry kept rambling wildly, but gradually Cameron pieced together a series of alarming facts. Byron was building a high cyclone fence around the factory area. He had closed the plant yesterday, but actually it wasn't closed. The factory was working around the clock. Guards now patrolled the grounds, and the parking-lot area was going to be floodlit at night, to

475

keep out spies. The place was more like a fortress than a factory.

'Spies? What spies, Harry? Why is he doing this?'

'Listen to me. I've mailed you a key, with a sketch of the grounds and the building. There's a small gate behind the plant. You'll be able to tell from the sketch how to reach the skylight on the roof. You have to see for – ' Suddenly Harry's voice changed. 'Hello, Byron. I was calling the garage to see if my car would be ready by noon. The line is busy.' Cameron heard the sound of the phone being slammed down.

Cameron slowly replaced the receiver. Before she could remove her hand, the phone rang for a third time. Cautiously, she brought the receiver to her ear.

'Cameron! Hi!' It was Byron. He radiated jaunty confidence. 'Have you heard the great news?'

'Yes, I read the announcement.' Cameron tried to sound enthusiastic. 'By the way, Ann said you were supervising construction. What construction?'

'Now that we're finally in production, I don't want any security leaks. So I'm having a fence built.'

'Security leaks? You sound like a character in a spy novel. When do I get to see King Wheel in operation? How about my coming out this afternoon?' Cameron asked, conscientiously casual.

'I'd love to show you the King Wheel, but we're closing for a few days. Getting ready for the production run. I need a break, so I'm taking a long weekend with Margo in Puerto Rico.'

'How about next week?'

'Next week is great!' Byron's relief was apparent. 'Next week you'll get the full treatment. The King Wheel in action. It turns out Thermoscans like cookies.'

'Does it?' Cameron tried to keep the scepticism out of her voice.

'It sure does,' Byron said, full of conviction. 'Wait'll you see it. Gotta run now, Cameron. Talk to you next week. 'Bye.'

Cameron's original feeling of unease when she read the Hansen Company announcement came back stronger than ever. Either Harry had gone haywire or Byron was lying to her.

Cameron cancelled her Friday night date with the president of a pension fund. The keys from Harry had arrived and she intended to find out exactly what was happening at the plant. She put on jeans, a dark sweater, and a long black stocking cap, the end of which she wound around her neck like a scarf. A glance in the mirror told her that what she was doing was too theatrical for her taste. She hated the whole idea. She didn't want to think about what she might see at the plant, but she had to find out what was going on.

She searched among her ski clothes, found a powerful flashlight, and strapped it to her belt. Finally, she clipped on a small leather purse with a zipper that had been designed to fit onto the belt. As she left her apartment, it seemed impossible to believe what she was going to do – impossible, but she would do it.

Cameron pulled her Mercedes to the side of the road about a quarter of a mile from the factory. She had no intention of being spotted by one of the guards, if there were guards as Harry had claimed. Feeling somewhat foolish and frightened, she made her way along the deserted tree-lined street towards the rear gate of the plant. She tried to walk in the shadows and blend into the dark background, while her heart thudded fiercely and every nerve jangled. She was grateful for the heavy jacket she had put on and the warm cap. It was the middle of November, and the night air was cold with a brisk wind out of the northeast. But it was more than a physical cold that was making her shiver.

Life Sciences occupied an entire 50,000-square-foot building in a medium-sized industrial complex. Cameron silently gave thanks that the building was on the perimeter of the complex, backing up on a grove of tall evergreens. If it had stood in the middle of the complex, there would have been no way to approach it unseen, because as she drew near she could see the glow from the floodlit parking area.

Just before reaching the corner of the property, Cameron slipped noiselessly into the grove of trees. She made her way warily between pines and blue spruces to the rear of the Life Sciences property. She used her flashlight sparingly, only often enough to keep from bumping into a tree. The grove ended about ten feet short of the property. Cameron crouched in the shade of the last line of trees and stared, amazed, at the sight below. She was on a low bluff overlooking the Life Sciences factory. What she saw made her think the world had gone mad. She checked her watch: it was 11:30 P.M. and the Life Sciences parking lot was brilliantly lit and jammed with cars. Harry Horn had told the truth: they were working 24 hours a day. Why?

Here and there she spotted big, burly men wandering about, looking into car windows, kneeling to check under the cars, inspecting the newly erected fence. Cameron's heart missed a beat as a guard passed directly below her. She heard him rattling the chain and padlock on the gate. She held her breath, trying to get a sense of the way the guards moved. There seemed to be about fifteen minutes between each inspection of the rear fence. She visualized the crudely drawn map Harry Horn had sent her. The gate was about thirty feet to her right and opened outward.

Cameron crept quietly through the trees. The thick bed of pine needles absorbed any sound her shoes might have made. When she estimated she was opposite the gate, she lay flat on the ground and wormed her way forward to the edge of the bank. She raised her head to look for the gate just as a man started whistling below. She flattened instantly and froze. The chain rattled as the man tested it. Drops of sweat ran down Cameron's forehead. After a few moments, she heard the shuffle of feet moving away, and looked up just in time to see a black raincoat disappear around the corner of the building as the guard moved off.

The slope had been graded at about a 45-degree angle. Here and there were a few bushes, but for the most part, the bank consisted of raw dirt. Cameron rolled over on her back and twisted her body around so that her legs were stretched out in front of her. Then she carefully inched forward along the ground. But as her buttocks passed over the edge of the slope, she lost her balance and slid down the bank. The noise of loosened dirt and small stones falling sounded to her like a landslide. Surely the guards heard her! She resisted a frantic impulse to scramble back up the embankment. The seconds ticked away but no one came running towards her. She struggled to her knees and crawled the few remaining feet to the small shadowed spot next to the gate. About two yards inside the fence was a shed where some chemicals were stored. There was a barrel next to the shed that Harry had placed for her to stand on and climb to the roof of the shed. From there, Harry had written, it would be an easy stretch to the roof of the one-storey main building. There were four skylights on the roof. She was to go to the far skylight on the right and watch.

Cameron unzipped the small purse she'd attached to her belt, fished out the key Harry had sent and inserted it in the padlock. Before opening the lock, she gave one last frightened look around. There was no one who could see her. She opened the lock and the well-oiled tumblers moved smoothly. Within seconds she passed through the gate, put the padlock

479

and chain back in place, and scrambled from the barrel to the tin roof of the storage shed.

The top of the parapet was considerably higher than Harry Horn had indicated. Standing on her toes, she was barely able to reach it. Cameron felt grateful for all her tennis playing at the West Side Tennis Club and squash playing at the Columbia University Club gym, because she needed every ounce of strength she could muster. It took a well-coordinated spring, aided by her arm and shoulder muscles, to vault over the parapet. She landed lightly on the stone-covered tar roof. Moving quickly, she scuttled across the roof to the far skylight. She knelt and wiped the glass clean to get a better look. Her eyes went wide and then filled with horror. She choked back a cry. She could not believe what she saw.

The giant King Wheel stood silent and dark in a corner of the room, but everywhere else there was frantic activity. Three or four hundred men and women were jammed into the room. Each wore a long white coat and a white surgical cap. A small group around the Junior Wheel were taking Thermoscans as they slowly came off the machine, one at a time, and hand-packing them into boxes. A box was then passed to a second person who inserted printed material. Cameron guessed that these were the instructions on how to use the device. From there, the box went to a third set of hands that sealed it and put it in a shipping carton.

Cameron's head throbbed violently. Momentarily, her vision jumped about and blurred. The lunacy got worse. When she scanned the factory, she saw many workers seated at long tables holding syringes. As a thermoscan was passed down the line, each worker filled a number of cavities with liquid crystals. It dawned upon her then that they were also making the product by hand! Hand-making it! When the unit reached the end of the line, it was placed in a mould and a lining was heat-sealed into it. The completed Thermoscan was then folded and placed in a box. The rest of the process was identical to what went on at the Junior Wheel. Cameron opened her mouth to scream 'Stop it!' and found she had no voice. She could only kneel on the roof and stare through the skylight.

Byron, dressed in a white coat and cap, was dashing about the room helping one worker pack, instructing another in the hand-filling operation, checking the heat-seal station and the finished product. He was also counting the filled cartons that were stacked and waiting to be carted off to the shipping area. Harry followed Byron everywhere. Periodically, he'd put his hand on Byron's shoulder as if to stop him. Byron would impatiently shrug him off and continue his frantic instructions.

As Cameron watched, the muscles in her thighs began to cramp. Her concentration was total. It took several minutes for her to feel the gusts of wind and the downpour of rain and sleet that soaked her clothes. Water was running down her cheeks, dripping off the end of her nose, trickling under her scarf. She remained paralysed, as though turned to stone. She was witnessing a colossal, criminal fraud! It was a fraud against the Hansen Company, against Life Sciences and its shareholders, against FitzGerald Associates – and against her! Her heart turned over. Most terrible and shameful of all, Byron was committing a crime against himself.

Why was he doing this? He couldn't actually believe he could fool everyone and turn out millions of Thermoscans by hand? Not millions. Why was he committing a criminal act that would destroy everything he'd worked so hard for and believed in so strongly? Something in Byron must be forcing him to cheat, to lie, to commit a crime – something he couldn't control.

Silently as she'd come, Cameron ran across the roof, surveyed the ground quickly for the guards, and then let herself down to the roof of the storage shed. Soon she was through the gate and scrambling up the rain-slick dirt slope. She was too shocked to pay attention to the noise of the sliding dirt and stones and the danger of attracting the guards. Twice she lost her footing and went crashing back against the fence. With a burst of energy, she gathered herself for a third attempt. Digging in with her fingers and toes, she managed to reach the top of the bank where she sprawled exhausted on the wet grass. The rain and sleet poured down her face, covering it with a thin film of ice-cold water.

Eventually, Cameron managed to rise to her feet. She snapped on her flashlight, ignoring the risk of discovery, and staggered more than ran through the trees. When she reached her car, she scrambled behind the wheel, locked the door, and collapsed, trembling with cold and shock. She was too weak, too weary, too fragmented to do anything other than sit. It was only when the sky began to lighten in the east that Cameron roused herself sufficiently to start the car. She drove carefully over the icy streets to the George Washington Bridge and then back to her apartment.

Cameron lay exhausted in her tub, allowing the hot water to soak into her bones and drive away the chill. But the heat could not melt the icy fear within her. Byron Miller, her oldest friend, the man she trusted, the man she chose to head up Life Sciences, the man she loved like a younger brother – Byron had betrayed her trust. Why? Why was he doing this? So what if the King Wheel didn't work? A new and different wheel could be designed. Life Sciences didn't need money. She had gone over the corporate books only last week and found that the company had almost $20 million in cash and securities; Life Sciences was solvent. Then the full horror of the situation struck her.

Cameron sat bolt upright in the tub, her eyes fixed,

unseeing, on the opposite wall. It wasn't Life Sciences that needed money. It was her company. FitzGerald Associates. The firm needed money desperately. Not next week or next month, but now! Right this minute. The moment she exposed Byron, the value of FitzGerald Associates' Life Sciences stock would drop from over $12 million to zero. The Morgan Bank syndicate had lent her company $100 million based on the collateral of their Life Sciences stock and its rising market value. What market value?

Cameron gave a short, dry laugh that sounded more like a choked sob. If she made the fraud public, the value of the stock would be reduced to zilch, and the syndicate would call their loan. Even if by some miracle the banks held off, FitzGerald Associates' debt to equity ratio would exceed the 15 to 1 allowed by the New York Stock Exchange. The Exchange would force the firm into bankruptcy. Everything she'd worked for for so long would be lost. Panic laced with despair ran through her as she visualized the future.

A city marshal's notice taped to the front door of the office. Bankruptcy proceedings. Everything would be sold at auction to pay off debts. The furniture, the rugs, the paintings – things that were her own – would all be ticketed and knocked down to the highest bidder. And what would happen to the people who worked for her? All the people who depended on their salaries to pay the rent, buy food, clothes? They counted on her, and she'd failed them.

Cameron tried to bring her racing mind to a dead stop. She didn't dare to think. And she didn't dare not to think. Every nerve in her body had suddenly awakened. It was as though a great blaze of light had been turned on. In the centre of that was Gary's face. Her son.

Hightower Farm was their home. Gary's home. The place where she wanted him to grow up. He was to have the long, magic years of boyhood there. A safe time such as she had never known. She sat absolutely still, stupefied by the future she saw before her. Gary's and hers. With bankruptcy she would be unable to meet the large mortgage payments on the farm. She would lose Hightower Farm as well as her company.

Not only had she failed the people at FitzGerald Associates, she had failed her own ancestors. And even more devastating, she had failed Geraldine, who had left Hightower Farm to her.

And beyond all these ugly realities, there was one more dreadful question: From where would the money come to take care of Gary? Bankruptcy proceedings and the loss of things precious to her would not be the final disaster. No! Not by a long shot. The case could – and probably would – be made that she had looked the other way every time Byron had promised to deliver Thermoscans and then had called off the delivery. The high price of Life Sciences stock made it possible for her firm to borrow the money it needed to expand. Cameron closed her eyes in pain. She'd be barred forever from working in the securities field. Her career on Wall Street would be finished.

Cameron sank back into the huge marble tub, barely able to breathe. She would insist on meeting with Byron tomorrow and put an end to the charade, then and there. She'd tell Byron . . . What would she tell Byron? You're a fraud? I'll expose you? How could she sit in judgement on her old friend, knowing how severely she judged herself? She'd run out of self-righteousness. All long-held theories and ethical precepts broke down entirely in the face of the human situation, Byron's and her own. Wittingly or not, wasn't she an accomplice in his crime?

There must be a way to stop Byron's madness and not ruin herself.

A name came to mind; Elmer Hansen. Yes, he might be

the answer. She would meet with Elmer Hansen and tell him the truth. Once he knew the facts, Elmer Hansen would not accept delivery. They'd find an acceptable reason why. Would he then cancel the Hansen Company contract? That must not happen. She would reason with him. Byron would have to resign as chief executive officer of Life Sciences, and a man acceptable to Hansen would replace him. Possibly Byron could stay on and concentrate on new-product development. That was really what he did best. Life Sciences would announce that the King Wheel needed redesigning. The stock would drop, but it wouldn't drop that much, not as long as the Hansen contract was still in place. FitzGerald Associates could cover itself at the banks. It would be a tight fit, but with any luck, they'd squeeze through the knothole. She needed luck. More than luck, she needed the cooperation of Elmer Hansen.

With a sinking feeling, she remembered the hatred Cyrus felt for his grandfather. Whatever else Cyrus was, he was not a man to waste his time and energy in groundless hate. Then there was her own instinctive mistrust. Add to that the words Geraldine had spoken long ago. 'Elmer Hansen is a very complicated man.' The words had been straightforward enough, but Geraldine's tone carried a warning. The prospect of dealing with Elmer Hansen from anything other than a position of strength was alarming. But she would do what she had to do. Cameron thought this with the passiveness of a patient who can no longer postpone the surgeon's knife. She would telephone Elmer Hansen the first thing tomorrow morning and insist on an immediate meeting.

28

As arranged earlier that morning, Cameron drove to Hansen corporate headquarters in New Jersey, and arrived well in time for her two o'clock appointment.

Elmer Hansen was on his feet, standing erect behind an old-fashioned, rolltop desk when she entered his office. 'Welcome, Cameron.' He strode briskly around the desk and held out his hand.

Cameron marvelled at the strength she felt in the old man's grip, because she realized that Elmer must be in his late eighties. But he didn't look it, he didn't sound his age, and he didn't move like an old man.

'Sit down,' Elmer gestured towards an oxblood leather chair, one of two in the office that were separated by a small Queen Anne table. The chairs faced the only window and overlooked the parking lot and lawn. She was certain that Elmer Hansen had been watching her from the moment she drove onto the Hansen property.

'How do you like my sanctum sanctorum?' Elmer asked.

Cameron scanned the room and was barely able to mask her surprise. Several worn, sagging bookshelves filled with out-of-date business books lined one wall. The telephone had no buttons. The brown carpet was old and threadbare in spots. The only pictures on the walls were black-and-white photographs of small buildings. One had the sign HANSEN & HANSEN over it, but the sign over the others said THE HANSEN COMPANY.

'Not exactly what you expected, is it?'

Cameron felt herself challenged in some strange way. 'No,' she answered truthfully. 'Not exactly.'

'I have another suite of offices. They're my "show offices". This is my "go office". Where I get things done.'

Cameron was not sure whether she should be flattered at being taken into Elmer's confidence or concerned that he did not think enough of her to put on the usual show. She glanced again at the one window in the office and thought about Elmer Hansen, Jr, and his plane crash. The girls at the Paddington School had repeated the gossip they'd overheard their parents whispering. Elmer, Jr, had tried to kill his father and failed. Although she hadn't put much stock in the story at the time, she now wondered if there was any truth to it. If he had crashed through the window out of which she was now staring, and if Elmer Hansen had been in this office at the time, there was no question that he would have died with his son.

'You mentioned on the phone you had something that we should talk about.' Elmer smiled at Cameron across the small table. 'You have my complete attention.'

This Elmer Hansen was not the man Cameron had braced herself to confront. He was not the ogre she had expected. Instead, he was gracious, charming, almost avuncular. The speech she'd carefully rehearsed did not fit this Elmer Hansen.

Noting her hesitation, Elmer stepped into the breach. 'Don't be concerned, Cameron. Whatever it is, rest assured, it will not come as a complete surprise to me. I've lived a long time and seen a lot of strange things. I doubt there is much in this world that would surprise me.'

'Well.' Cameron found herself struggling for words. 'It's about Byron Miller. I mean, Life Sciences and Byron Miller.'

'Aha! An interesting young man, Mr Miller. A fine business talent. He negotiated a tough deal.' Elmer chuckled.

'Usually I make the tough deals, but he had something I wanted, and he knew it. I have to admire that business instinct.'

Hearing Elmer's praise of Byron, Cameron was sorely tempted to say nothing more. Why fight the good luck of Elmer Hansen's overflowing goodwill? All she had to do was invent some reason for wanting this meeting, and let the Hansen Company accept delivery of the handmade Thermoscans. She would then talk to Byron and together they would work on redesigning the King Wheel while the Hansen Company tested the product. But if she did this, she would be part-and-parcel of the fraud.

She looked hard at Elmer Hansen. Beneath the gracious surface of his face, deep within his hooded and waiting eyes, lurked a menacing shadow. The conviction grew that this man could not be trusted. There must be no forfeit of honesty in dealing with him.

'Yes, Byron is unique,' she agreed 'A creative spirit. In fact, a little too creative for my taste.'

In as brief and neutral terms as possible, Cameron described what had happened. She watched carefully for any change of expression – surprise, outrage, disappointment, or dismay – to give her a clue as to Elmer's reaction to the information. But nothing changed, not his half smile or his relaxed posture. There was nothing to give her the slightest idea of what Elmer was thinking. When she finished talking, she sat tensely, waiting for his response.

When Elmer spoke, his tone remained friendly, actually more curious than anything else. 'You're quite sure the Thermoscans are being made by hand?'

'Absolutely! I saw it for myself. The only ones that aren't handmade come off the prototype machine,' Cameron said with vehemence.

Elmer chuckled. 'Very enterprising on young Miller's part.

And no one but you, Harry Horn, and I know of this? You haven't told anyone else?'

'No, I've spoken to no one.'

'What about Harry? You're sure you're the only person he's spoken to?'

'Yes. At least I'm as positive of that as I can be without actually asking him.' Cameron wondered what Elmer Hansen was driving at.

'What would you have me do, Cameron?'

They'd finally arrived at the reason why Cameron was in Elmer's office on a Saturday afternoon. She'd prepared what she hoped would be the best approach to persuade him to see things her way. But the difference between the benevolent surface Elmer Hansen presented and what her intuition told her lay behind that façade made her hesitate. Before she could respond, he continued for her.

'You would like me to reject the shipment but not cancel the contract.' This was made as a statement of fact.

The minute he said it, Cameron grasped that Elmer was ahead of her. 'Yes, that is what I would like.' She said it politely and then asked, because she knew he expected her to, 'How did you know?'

'Simple. If you didn't want me to reject the shipment, you wouldn't have driven all the way here to tell me the Thermoscans are being made by hand. And if you weren't concerned about my cancelling the contract, you also wouldn't be here. You could have told me the story on the telephone.'

Cameron's opinion of Elmer Hansen was reaffirmed. She must not relax her defences.

'Am I correct?' Elmer asked.

'You are.' Then, trying to keep her need from showing, Cameron asked, 'Will you do it?'

'Before I answer that, I have a few suggestions to make.'

She shrugged her shoulders. 'Please. Any help would be appreciated.'

'It seems to me that, given the circumstances, the wisest course for all concerned would be for the Hansen Company to accept delivery.'

'What!' Cameron erupted in surprise.

It was as though the one word Cameron spoke released Elmer Hansen's secret self, the real face behind the mask of urbane charm. Before her eyes, the genial, smiling Elmer Hansen disappeared, and was replaced by a harsh, domineering man who had no hesitation in imposing his will on the world, by any means at his disposal. Until now, he'd been humouring her.

'That's right, Cameron.' Elmer's voice was stronger. It would brook no argument. 'We will accept the shipment. And you will leave Byron Miller alone. At the right time, possibly four months from now – *I* will choose the right time – your Mr Miller will announce that the machine needs redesigning. And the Hansen Company will cooperate in the redesign.'

'But in the meantime, the stock will keep rising. Investors will be buying Life Sciences under a complete misconception ... at a highly inflated price,' Cameron sputtered. 'When you make the announcement, the stock will drop. People will lose thousands and thousands of dollars.'

'Spare me the pious platitudes about the fools who buy Life Sciences stock,' Elmer snapped. 'You have something more serious to concern you. Your investment-banking house, FitzGerald Associates.' Elmer's voice became low, beguiling, seductive; Cameron had to strain to make out his words. 'You own one hundred thousand shares of Life Sciences,' Elmer murmured. 'And you used the stock as collateral to borrow one hundred million dollars from a bank syndicate.'

'How did you know that?' The question burst from Cameron.

'I happen to be very good at my business. I foresee consequences. I do this by keeping abreast of everything concerning my interests. Life Sciences is one of my interests, and,' Elmer said with a note of arrogance, 'that includes its investment banker. So I know what will happen to FitzGerald Associates should Life Sciences' stock "fall out of bed," as they say. The investors will lose money, but you, Cameron, will lose everything. FitzGerald Associates will be bankrupt. The banks will see to that.'

The line holding the hook in Cameron's throat grew tighter. Elmer was reeling her in.

'As a salve to your conscience, I am prepared to lend FitzGerald Associates twelve million dollars' worth of Hansen stock which you can substitute at the banks for your Life Sciences stock. The banks will be quite happy to accept Hansen stock as collateral for the monies you owe them. My loan will be for a period of five years. At the end of that time, you should be able to repay me.' He smiled. 'It is my impression that twelve million dollars to save your company is enough to salve your conscience.'

Cameron said nothing.

'On the other hand, if you persist in the folly of making public Mr Miller's little deception, the Hansen Company will be properly outraged at the fraudulent shipment. We will immediately cancel the contract and see to it that the banks call your loan. Have I made my position clear?'

'You have,' Cameron said softly. 'Would you mind telling me why you're doing this?'

'I would mind very much. It's none of your business.'

Cameron made an effort to temporize. 'I have a partner as well as subordinated lenders. I must discuss your proposal with them.'

'You will not discuss Life Sciences or Byron Miller with anyone. If you do, I'll withdraw my generous offer to save your hide.'

It was fear that stopped Cameron from telling Elmer Hansen what she thought of him; fear of the disaster that she clearly saw waiting for her; for The Farm, for FitzGerald Associates, and above all for Gary, her son. But these recognitions brought with them another more astonishing realization: Elmer Hansen would not break the deal. He was not a man who offered help unless it was in his own best interests. For some reason, his best interests lay in keeping the lid on Byron's fraud. She had to take her chances that Hansen did not know how frightened she actually was.

'Mr Hansen,' she said coldly, 'unless I am free to discuss this matter with my associates, I will not accept your offer.'

'To how many people do you propose to speak?'

'Three trusted friends and associates.'

Elmer slapped the arm of his leather chair. 'So be it. Three, but no more. And I suggest you emphasize what is at risk. Their banking house, their money. And,' he added in a silken tone, 'your personal reputation.' He stood up. 'You have exactly one week to give me your answer.'

Driving back to Hightower Farm, Cameron gathered her courage. She was as frightened as she'd been when she was a child alone in St Croix. But there was no Geraldine waiting to help her; she had only herself to rely on and so much depended on what she did. If only Cyrus and she were on speaking terms – she dismissed the thought impatiently from her mind. Somehow she must find the way herself. She would talk to Jake. But all the talking in the world would only point to the choices she could already see. In the end, no matter what she decided, she must be strong enough to live with her own reality.

Elmer Hansen was brilliant, subtle, devious, and dangerous. However, he'd made one mistake. In his arrogance, he had told her how completely he kept himself informed. He knew everything there was to know about Life Sciences. He must have known all along that the King Wheel didn't work and that the Thermoscans were being made primarily by hand. Yet he planned to accept the fraudulent product. Why? That question led to another. Why was he willing to buy her silence? There had to be a reason. It had something to do with Life Sciences. Something he wanted to use the company for in the future, when he was ready. What did he have in mind? If she could answer that, it might help her to make the decision that faced her.

By Wednesday, Cameron had finished the unpleasant task of telling Jake and Lucia how much trouble they might be in. Jake, predictably, ranted; Lucia and her family were more tempered but similarly distressed.

Alone in her office, Cameron sat at her desk, fighting the despair that threatened to overwhelm her. She was damned if she did and damned if she didn't. Faced with the problem of making up her mind, the fact of her being alone returned with redoubled force. So much – too much – depended on her.

She was aimlessly sorting through her mail when Della buzzed on the intercom.

'Cyrus Hansen is here to see you.'

Cameron gasped.

'Send him in, Della,' she said immediately.

Although the office was warm, Cameron started to shiver. Only this past Saturday she'd again admitted to herself how much she needed Cyrus. She longed to talk over with him the whole unholy mess. Since the television show, she'd had the impression that his rage at her had subsided. What she particularly dreaded at this moment was not his anger but his tact. The tact of a former lover who had no wish to renew the intimacy, but who, for some reason, found it necessary to contact her. There was one truth that might alter his attitude. Their child. Even as she thought of it, Cameron dismissed the idea. Gary was not to be used as a pawn. She fixed her eyes on the window and stared blindly at the legendary street she loved. A faint current of air told her that Cyrus had entered the office.

Turning and seeing his large, quiet presence worked like a drug on her spirits, heightening her sense of the moment. She noticed that he had lost a little weight, which gave him an uncanny resemblance to a much younger Elmer. Also, unlike the Cyrus she knew, he was wearing a dark grey flannel suit with a white shirt and striped tie. Cameron had a sensation of shyness and an acute unwillingness to let him know how glad she was to see him.

'How pleasant that you dropped in, Cyrus,' Cameron said. She searched for words to cover her confusion and only succeeded in sounding inane. 'You must be very busy, and so am I. I don't mean to be ungracious, but since we're both pressed, what brings you here?'

Cyrus gave a slow, understanding nod. 'I appreciate your making the time to see me. It's important.'

'I know that. Or you wouldn't be here.' Cameron was ready to meet him halfway. 'Please, sit down.'

Cyrus moved to the chair next to her desk, and for an instant, they gazed at each other in silence across a gulf of memories. As Cyrus spoke, his blue eyes darkened.

'First,' he said as he seated himself, 'I owe you an apology.' He spoke impersonally, as if he were meeting a contractual obligation. Cyrus was a man doing what he believed must be done, like it or not. 'I'm apologizing for my abominable behaviour at the airport. My apology does not excuse it. All I can say is, I think I went temporarily insane at the idea of the Hansen Company contract with Life Sciences. I know now you had nothing to do with it.'

Holding his eyes, Cameron drew in a long breath of rich relief. 'Who told you?' she asked almost humbly.

'James Taylor, a vice president with the Hansen Company. For my purposes, I found it wise to develop lines into the company. Taylor finds it in his best interests to serve two masters, my grandfather and me. I have the advantage of knowing about Elmer, but Elmer is not aware that I know about him. If he did, Taylor would be fired. And he will be eventually. However, he has or had a relationship with Margo Bayless. Through Taylor, she introduced the product to my grandfather.'

'That's what Byron said.'

'So you told me.' A quiet enveloped them, and then, as though it were a matter of good taste that they drop any further mention of Byron, Cyrus asked, 'Have you seen today's *Wall Street Journal*? Or the *New York Times* business section?'

'No. Not yet.'

'That's the second reason I'm here. Look at page thirty-five in the *Journal*. It will explain part of what happened. You'll find an announcement by one Cyrus Hansen, who now owns some fourteen per cent of the Hansen Company. At the annual stockholders meeting, which takes place in sixty days, Cyrus Hansen is proposing to unseat the current board of directors. Cyrus Hansen is offering an impressive slate of his own candidates in their place. He is also soliciting proxies.'

Cameron gave him a tenderly appraising look. So that was it. She remembered Tim's words all those years ago. His guess about Cyrus had been absolutely right. Cyrus had been in training. 'You're going to fight your grandfather for control.' It was a statement.

495

'For control of the Hansen Company.' The words came easily, but the strain it caused him was almost physically painful.

'You waited a long time to make your move.'

'I waited until the time was right.'

'And then the Thermoscans happened,' she said wryly, closing her eyes for a second, her mind in a turmoil as she relived the past.

'Yes, they did.' Cyrus was unable to keep his pent-up bitterness from showing. 'Still, my grandfather is weaker now than he will be in a year. Though not as vulnerable as he has been.'

'The delivery of the Thermoscans has strengthened his position?' Cameron was careful to keep her voice neutral.

'It had to. It's been almost five years since the Hansen Company introduced a successful new product. That'll be the thrust of my attack.'

'And now he has one. A potentially very successful new product.' Her voice trembled slightly, but there was no failure in her logic. 'Or he's very close to having one.' She closed her eyes for a moment, running the tips of her fingers over her aching forehead. The nightmare was becoming more and more complex. 'That's why you insisted Life Sciences not do business with the Hansen Company. To keep your grandfather from getting his hands on the new technology.'

'Yes. It's an agreement I've insisted on with all the companies Acorn has invested in. And up until Byron' – an edge returned to Cyrus's voice – 'all the entrepreneurs have honoured the understanding. But as you explained, Byron didn't know.' Cyrus added drily, 'Neither you nor I thought to tell him.'

A number of thoughts flashed through Cameron's mind. Cyrus had the same extraordinary blue eyes as Elmer that saw everything. As she listened to his words and accepted their implications, she knew why everything had gone wrong between them. But her understanding had come too late.

'The proxy fight will take place at the next stockholders meeting?' she paused as if to let the words sink into her own ears.

'Yes.' He sounded half depressed, half boastful.

Cameron saw herself trapped in the middle. She was now able to answer the question she had asked herself on Saturday. Why would Elmer Hansen lie to the world and agree to put up $12 million to bribe her to support his lie? Why did he want to dupe the public into believing the Thermoscans were mass-produced? Because Elmer needed the time, needed those sixty days. He needed the Thermoscan, finished and ready to be test-marketed, to defeat Cyrus in the proxy fight. The Thermoscan and other products Life Sciences could produce would mean a revitalized Hansen Company. It was Elmer's trump card in his fight to remain in control.

She gave Cyrus an inquiring look but anticipated his answer. 'Do you believe your grandfather has always known of your plan to fight him?'

Cyrus laughed without humour. 'Of course. Always. I should have told you.'

'But you couldn't.' She glanced away. 'Anyway, I should have guessed,' she said wearily, knowing how completely she'd botched his plans.

'Why? Few did. Except, of course, for my grandfather.'

Cameron sighed gratefully. The way he accepted her failing him touched her. Then her long habit of self-control asserted itself and showed in the straightness of her question. 'Do you still have a chance to win?'

'I don't get into anything thinking I'll lose. As you know.'

It gave her an inward start, this reminder of their ancient

497

disagreement. They knew each other so well. She smiled and took a breath, gathering her strength. 'But it will be hard?'

'What isn't? One takes one's chances.'

Cameron said nothing, occupied as she was with weighing her choices and considering their consequences. What if she told Cyrus about the fraudulent delivery? If the maxim 'Knowledge is power' were true, she had both the knowledge and the power to devastate Elmer Hansen. But she couldn't use the power without wrecking FitzGerald Associates. Cyrus would make the fraud public. Life Sciences' stock would plunge. Her company would go bankrupt. She needed time to think.

'Can you win your fight now that Elmer has the Thermoscan?' she persisted anxiously.

'As I said, I don't get into anything – including proxy fights – to lose.'

Cameron became aware again of the impersonal pitch between Cyrus and herself. This meeting had run its course. Cyrus had done what he came to do.

'Thank you for the apology,' she said, standing up. 'And I am sorry for what happened.' It was the least she could say, and at this moment, the most she could say.

'Thank you. One always needs luck,' Cyrus said after staring at her for a long second. Then he left.

With Cyrus gone, the room seemed emptier than it had been before he arrived. Which leaves me Byron, Cameron thought. She'd lost her sense of proportion about him. From the beginning, he'd been a brash young man with prodigious gifts. He gravitated to visions. He had a dazzling way with the Street. He was frequently unorthodox and had a curious taste for the grand gesture. The real Byron was not a man who hired armed guards to keep the public from discovering he was committing a crime. But the fact was, he had done just that. She knew it and Elmer Hansen knew it. The more she

498

considered the possibility, the more certain she was that Elmer Hansen had known all along.

Why hadn't she told Cyrus about his grandfather? What did that say about her? Her sense of identity began a dangerous slide. What kind of a woman was she? She grappled to hold on to the self-image that she had lived with all these years. Until this disaster, she'd assumed she knew herself intimately; her strengths, her ethics, her limitations. This is who I am, she could tell herself. But now she was no longer so confident. She had taken her own honesty and integrity for granted. Were they truly ingrained in her nature?

The memory of Cyrus sitting across the desk from her sent a swift, keen pain running through her body. She was dazed by the recognition of how much she still loved him. How could she expect to escape the past when the mere sight of him triggered emotions she'd believed she no longer had?

Cameron studied the papers on her desk as if she really saw them, but in her mind was only Cyrus and their time together. He had been like a fever in her blood. How different her life might have been if only she'd known more. How simple to be wise after the fact. For an instant she was caught by a furious resentment of how life had played with them and caught them both. Then she shook her head as though to clear it. With her hours so numbered and the future upon her, she must take care. Any indulgence in regrets for the past was both frivolous and futile.

She weighed Elmer Hansen and Cyrus on the scale of power. If she said nothing and did nothing, Cyrus would be unable to use the Life Sciences fraud as a weapon. Without that – despite his brave words about not getting into a fight to lose – there wasn't a chance he could win the proxy fight. But if she made the fraud public, she would leave herself destitute. What then would she receive from Cyrus? His love or his pity?

499

Cameron felt bruised and beaten. Cyrus had only drawn her more deeply into the centre of the maelstrom. Now the possibility of accepting Elmer Hansen's bribe appalled her even more. But as a realist, she knew she might have to accept it. For her nothing had changed. She was not to be spared.

Tomorrow she must choose. She would go her own way, hellish though it might be. At least her choice would tell her, once and for all, who she really was.

29

'Mr Miller has arrived, sir.'

'Thank you, Harriet.' Elmer Hansen checked the time: eight o'clock. Miller was fifteen minutes early. He gave an involuntary, amused grunt. 'Tell him I'm busy and he should wait.'

'Yes, Mr Hansen.' Harriet Greene glanced up at the tall, lanky, nervous young man standing in front of her. She permitted herself a moment to feel sorry for him – but only a moment. She'd been Elmer Hansen's private secretary for a long time, and she knew that Mr Miller was in for a bad time. Making him wait was part of the Hansen technique for softening up people.

'Sit down, Mr Miller,' Harriet said in a commanding tone reminiscent of Elmer's. She used the forefinger of her left hand to point to the narrow, high-backed bench opposite her desk. 'Mr Hansen will see you when he's ready.'

'I know I'm early, but do you have any idea how long he'll be?' Byron asked in his most ingratiating voice.

'No.' Harriet repeated her order. 'Please wait over there.'

Byron hesitated and opened his mouth to suggest that this woman stop giving him orders; he then closed his mouth and walked slowly to the bench.

The minutes ticked by and Byron's nerves could barely sustain him. He asked himself why Elmer Hansen insisted that he come to the Hansen Company at eight o'clock on a Wednesday evening. His imagination began to run amok. He became convinced that despite his meticulous precautions, including the random sampling he'd done on the

Thermoscans before shipping them on Monday, Hansen had found something wrong with the devices. He had no idea what it might be, but that must be it. Why else was he here?

Byron sneaked a glance at his watch. He'd been waiting for almost half an hour. No wonder his ass hurt. No one could sit comfortably on this bench. He realized that a visitor to this room was not supposed to be comfortable.

At that moment the black phone on Harriet Greene's desk rang. She picked it up immediately. 'Yes, Mr Hansen. I'll send him in.' The secretary raised her eyes without moving her head. 'Mr Hansen's ready to see you.'

Byron hurried to the door and opened it without knocking.

'Sit down, Mr Miller,' Elmer said without removing the thick cigar from his mouth.

'Why did you want to see me?' Byron asked after settling himself in a straight-backed chair across from Hansen.

Elmer gave Byron a sideways glance. 'You don't seriously believe that the delivery of twenty thousand Thermoscans is sufficient to establish that you can actually mass-produce the product? That it would convince anyone but a moron?'

'I guess not,' Byron admitted.

'Therefore, you will continue to make regular shipments to us. You're here to settle on a production schedule agreeable to me.' Elmer Hansen was very satisfied with his demand, but Byron blanched at the prospect of additional fraudulent shipments.

'I thought this was a one-time thing,' he protested. 'We can't keep manufacturing them by hand. We can't!' Hearing his own words, he knew they were a useless plea for understanding.

Elmer shook his head slowly as though amazed at Byron's presumption and chuckled. He set the cigar on the rim of the ashtray. 'What reason do you have to think anything? You will do as I tell you to do, when I tell you to do it, and how I tell you to do it.'

'And you want me to continue to ship handmade Thermoscans?' Byron repeated Elmer's instructions as if he needed to say them in order to believe them.

'What choice do you have? Your machine – what's that silly name you call it. King Wheel? – does not work. It has never worked for more than fifteen minutes at a time.'

'How do you know that?'

'I told someone else several days ago that I consider it my business to know everything there is to know about Life Sciences' – Elmer's voice took on an ominous tone – 'and anyone connected with Life Sciences.'

'We can't continue to make deliveries.' Byron's words were charged with the electricity of fear. 'Someone will find out.' He braced himself. 'For my own reasons I did as you asked. It was a mistake, and I won't do it again.'

'"I won't do it again,"' Elmer Hansen mimicked Byron, the sarcasm dripping from his words. 'Byron Miller, stop fooling yourself. You didn't do anything for your own reasons. You made the delivery because I told you that if you didn't, I would cancel the Hansen Company contract.'

Byron said nothing.

'And you knew the price of the stock of Life Sciences would then have dropped at least one hundred points.'

Byron swallowed. It was true.

'If you refuse to make further deliveries, I will not only cancel the contract, but I'll tell the world your dirty little secret.'

Every instinct of pride and self-defence rose in Byron. 'What secret?'

'Exactly why the Hansen Company is killing the contract.'

Byron felt a terrible fright as to what Hansen might say

next. To hold him off, he said, almost by rote, 'Because we couldn't make delivery of the mass-produced product.'

'No!' Elmer's words crackeld. 'Because the chief executive officer of Life Sciences is a fraud! A con man. And the son of a con man!'

Byron suddenly appeared to age, to shrink, to sink deep into himself. His long body doubled over, his elbows were held close to his sides, his arms crossed and his hands trembled wildly. 'My father was a businessman,' he said in a constricted voice that contained an inner, private wail.

'Your father was a common thief!' Elmer roared.

Byron stared at Elmer. His eyes begged Elmer to spare him from having to listen to the truth about his father. The truth from which he'd spent his entire life trying to escape. But the truth had been searching for him for a long time, and now it had found him in the person of Elmer Hansen.

'He was a thief.' Elmer sounded almost sad. He had a fleeting regret for the young man's torment but dismissed it as wasteful. When it came to the Hansen Company, Elmer Hansen could and would do whatever he considered necessary. This human demolition was necessary.

He picked up a manila file folder from his desk. 'I'll read the record for you,' he said smoothly. 'Your father's record. Who he was and what he was.' Elmer opened the file and read from a cleanly typed report. 'Adam Miller. Born in Brooklyn, January 11, 1924. Died, May 20, 1982. Of a heart attack in a cheap motel in Lubbock, Texas. One jump ahead of the FBI. Married Sara Hauptmann, June 21, 1949. One child, Byron Miller. Born October 14, 1954.' Elmer Hansen looked up from the report. 'There's a lot of irrelevant items covering education, occasional legitimate employment, and the like. I'll skip all that and go directly to what concerns us.' He resumed reading from the report. 'Adam Miller was convicted of stock fraud in 1952. He received a suspended sentence as a first offender. Grand larceny 1954 – six months in Sing Sing.'

As Elmer recited the litany of Adam Miller's crimes and convictions, Byron began to mouth the words in unison with him. Byron didn't need the report. Every crime – each fraud, forgery, grand larceny, stock swindle – and each prison sentence, from the suspended sentence to the final five-to-ten-year sentence from which Adam Miller had been fleeing when he died, were indelibly etched in his memory. Sitting in Elmer Hansen's office and reciting his father's crimes, Byron accepted that there was no escape from being 'Adam's son'.

'I expect delivery of twenty thousand Thermoscans a month for the next two months.'

Byron made no sound, yet they both understood that he had agreed.

Once the matter was settled, Elmer felt an unexpected need to have a witness to his triumph. He regretted that he had not asked Harriet to sit in and take notes. She would have been the ideal audience to applaud his grand plan. Twenty years earlier, or ten years earlier, or even five years earlier, Elmer Hansen would never have considered the likes of Byron Miller as one in whom to confide. In those years, he had no need to seek the approval of anyone other than himself. But the last few years had been disappointing to Elmer because he had had no victories to preen over. Now, he demanded immediate bravos and Byron Miller was his only audience. So Miller would have to do.

'You'll be interested in the future I envision for Life Sciences,' Elmer said in a tone that commanded Byron's attention. 'In two months I will have disposed of a small but irritating business problem. You will then announce that there are some problems with the production machinery. I will threaten cancellation of the contract. The price of Life

Sciences' stock will collapse like a pricked balloon. When the price drops below ten dollars a share, I will offer the funds fifteen dollars a share. Universal Life, People's Trust, all the pension boys . . .' Elmer shook his head with thinly disguised scorn. 'The fastest guns on the Street. They'll climb all over themselves to get at my generous offer. I'll collect close to fifty per cent of the outstanding stock of Life Sciences from the club of fools. That, in addition to your ten per cent – which you will sell me for one dollar and other valuable considerations – will give me control of the company.' He cracked his knuckles in anticipation of his triumph. 'As for the general public, they'll sell for whatever I offer and thank their lucky stars for anything they get.'

Byron could almost hear the small, crunching sound a cat makes as it crushes the backbone of a mouse.

'In the end, the Hansen Company will own Life Sciences, lock, stock, and barrel. We will not only own the distribution rights to the Thermoscan, we will own the manufacturing rights and the patents as well. We will also control all the other products that will evolve from a liquid crystal technology. Of course, we'll have to develop a new piece of equipment to mass-produce the product – one that works. But having learned from your mistakes, that shouldn't be too difficult.' Elmer glanced at the still figure staring at him. 'Take heart, Miller. If you follow orders, there will be a job here for you, working on a new-product development.'

'What about Cameron Hightower?' Byron asked in a small voice.

'What about her?'

'She plans to visit the factory later this week to see the King Wheel in operation. I was going to tell her that the machine had broken down again. But if I have to continue making deliveries, how can I say that? She'll suspect there's something wrong.'

'What imagination you do have, you compensate for by gross negligence. Your security system was useless. Harry Horn warned her, and she was perched on the roof of your factory last Friday night. She saw everything. She knows everything.'

Cameron knew – and had said nothing! Byron was too numb with despair to do more than register this additional disaster.

Elmer studied Byron and made one of his few misjudgements of another man's character. He took the frozen expression on Byron's face for indifference to Cameron's knowing the truth. In a way, his mistake was logical. Except for the possibility that Cameron could cause trouble, whatever she thought or didn't think, did or didn't do, made no difference to him. Why then should it matter to Byron? So he added, 'I wouldn't be concerned about Cameron Hightower. She's a smart young woman who knows what's good for her. She'll keep quiet. I bought her silence. And given the stakes, she wasn't that expensive.'

Noting the continual lack of expression on Byron's face, Elmer detailed the financial difficulties facing Cameron. As he spoke, a fascinating idea crossed his fertile brain. 'It occurs to me that she may prove useful in other ways.' He did not say, especially with Cyrus. 'I think I'll change the terms of my loan and make it an investment. I'll take control of her company and keep her on a tight leash.' Elmer glanced at his watch. 'Go home, Miller. I'll let you know when I want the next delivery.'

Byron stumbled towards the door and stepped out into the cold night air. Even when he got away from Elmer, his brain remained paralysed. He could see no way to free himself from the human quagmire called Elmer Hansen. He drove back to the factory because the factory was the home he'd never had. He wanted to cry, but he couldn't. There were no tears to equal what he felt. Anyway, tears were a cheap way of getting rid of agony. And he'd learned it was better to keep certain agonies inside you; keep them always inside you so you'd never forget.

His concentration was not on the road, and he didn't notice the miles slipping away until he became aware that he'd arrived at the factory. He was surprised at being there so soon. There was only one car in the parking lot and a single light shone from the windows of his office. Harry Horn was still there, probably waiting for him. What would he say to Harry? Byron slumped in the seat, hating to move from the safety of his car. Poor old Harry was trapped in this lunatic shell game with the son of Adam Miller. There was a fear in his head like a steady, oppressive weight. All sense of purpose was gone.

Byron peered into the unforgiving night, trying to find the courage to move. He turned his head from side to side, stretching his neck to rid it of the cramped tension. As he looked to his right, he noticed *The Wall Street Journal* lying on the seat next to him. After Elmer Hansen's morning summons, he'd had no interest in looking at the paper, not even to check Life Sciences' bid and ask stock quotes. He'd automatically tossed the paper on the seat when he had left for the Hansen Company. Now the paper gave him something to do, something to postpone getting out of the car and telling Harry about their future.

Byron switched on the car light, picked up the paper, and started scanning, page by page. He found that Life Sciences had closed at 125½ bid – not bad. But once Elmer Hansen started shaking the bean stalk, that wouldn't last. Still, it was something to be proud of, to file forever in his memory. Maybe it took the son of Adam Miller to do the kind of promotion he'd done. He'd done a great job, so why be ashamed. It wasn't all hot air – the Thermoscan was real. It was that damned machine that had caused all the trouble.

Byron turned the pages rapidly. Then he stopped, stared, and blinked with disbelief. He let his breath out in a long, low whistle. Cyrus Hansen! Son of a bitch! Why hadn't he thought of it before? He'd been following the price of the Hansen Company stock almost as carefully as he tracked Life Sciences and had noticed months ago that the stock had stopped falling. He'd seen it but not seen it, had not wondered why. Now he knew why. Cyrus Hansen was accumulating Hansen stock. He was out for his grandfather. The pieces of the puzzle fell into place. That announcement was a declaration of war. No wonder Elmer wanted more deliveries of Thermoscans. To prove to the world and to each and every Hansen shareholder that he had a tiger by the tail – a great, new product and a technology that was the wave of the future. That would be enough to keep Elmer Hansen as chairman of the board. Cyrus didn't have a chance. Byron could truly appreciate Elmer's unrelenting need to keep control of the company he had built.

Byron's thoughts went around in a circle, a circle of the damned. Then he remembered Cameron and his internal temperature plunged. That she knew everything he'd done made his head ache as though from a blow. His heart gave a frightening leap, and he started to shake. Adam Miller's son had also tripped up Cameron. It was unthinkable Cameron Hightower should be forced to heel every time Elmer Hansen yanked on the leash. But how could he stop it?

Slowly, painfully, Byron realized there was one way to stop Elmer Hansen. What he could not do to save himself he could do to save Cameron. The great fear he felt for himself was wiped out by the greater fear he felt for her. He knew what he had to do.

Byron switched off the car light, folded up *The Wall Street Journal*, and dropped it on the seat beside him.

Harry Horn was seated in Byron's chair, dozing. At the sound of Byron's footsteps, he jumped to his feet.

'What happened? What did he want?'

'Elmer Hansen wants us to make more deliveries.' Byron grinned. 'That's the bad news. The good news is that we're not going to do it.' He took a deep breath. 'We are not going to deliver any more handmade Thermoscans.'

'You're telling me the truth?' Harry gasped.

'So help me God.'

Harry then did something uncharacteristic. Shy, little Harry Horn, who was basically a cerebrum and lived in his own version of a tree, threw his arms around Byron.

'I'm so glad,' he said.

'Good. Now go home and get a decent night's sleep.'

Stunned, Harry slipped out the door, and Byron turned back to his desk. For him the long night was only beginning. He asked himself, what would Adam Miller do under the circumstances? Adam Miller would have run for his life, as he always had. For Byron the running had stopped; the truth was that there was no place to run. And he no longer wanted to hide. He had finally understood that he was not Adam Miller, only his son.

30

Cameron had telephoned ahead so that Emma McCarthy, the nurse, would know she was coming. When she arrived at Hightower Farm, the nurse was in her room, wearing a flannel robe and dozing in front of the television set. Cameron let her be and tiptoed into the next room where Gary slept. She stood beside the crib for a long time, gazing at her child, his face clearly visible in the silver moonlight that filled the room. He looked so small and vulnerable that she was possessed by an emotion that was more savage and angry than tender.

As she straightened up, her eyes filled with tears. In a kind of primitive animal fashion, she wanted to protect her young. But how? How could she prevent the catastrophe that she faced from taking place unless she went along with the fraud?

Cameron lay awake for a long time that night, trapped in a prison of dread. Her fears hemmed her in as though they were stone walls and iron bars.

Towards dawn she slept a little and woke with an instant of lightheartedness, until she remembered. She bathed slowly and dressed to return to the city. She ached to be alone with her son, outside with him, under their sky.

Cameron held Gary's small hand as they walked slowly to the highest point on their farm. For a usually boisterous, energetic child he was now strangely quiet, seeming to sense that something important was happening. Cameron's eyes scanned the land, asleep under the late autumn chill.

Hightower Farm was all around them, with its lawns and gardens, the stands of oak and pine and blue spruce. All this was to have been Gary's.

Suddenly the small boy gave a cry of joy. 'Ma! Ma!' he shouted. 'Hi . . . Hi . . .'

It was the first time he had ever tried to say Hightower.

'Hightower, Gary,' Cameron said. 'High-tow-er.'

'Hitarow,' the small boy said.

Cameron gazed at her child, and the boy looked back at her confidently, then at the woodland world around him, and gave another shout of delight at the discovery of this wonderful universe.

Cameron turned back to the land, silent and serene, now mysteriously awake in the morning sun. A strong feeling resonated within her, and she felt as if she were being shaken by a giant hand. For generations the Hightowers had marked this land with their ideas and dreams. And had been marked by the land in return. The Hightowers took their strength from this land. She was one of them. So was her son.

Cameron collected her courage and came to a final decision.

Cameron stood for a moment outside the building at 65 Wall Street. Once she took the elevator to the thirtieth floor, there would be no going back. What she had to do would take all her courage – and more.

When Cameron reached the office, she was moving so fast that she barely heard Della call out to her, 'Mr Stern's waiting for you in there.'

Apparently, he'd been waiting for quite a while. His legs were stretched out and crossed at the ankles, and he was refolding *The Wall Street Journal* after having read it from cover to cover. Seeing her, he smiled, raised his right hand to his forehead, and saluted. The gaiety was contradicted by his weary movements, by the dark rings of exhaustion circling his eyes and the deep lines that ran from either side of his nose to the corners of his mouth.

'You look beat,' Cameron said.

'You don't look so hot yourself.'

'I didn't sleep much last night.'

'You and me and Rosemary makes three. We talked it out all last night, Rosemary and me. We talked ourselves deaf, dumb, and blind.'

Cameron interrupted him, to make her point before he took a position from which he couldn't back off. She spoke rapidly with great intensity. 'We can't do it. It's not simply a matter of accepting Elmer Hansen's money. As a partner, he smells to high heaven. But if it were only a matter of Hansen and his money, I'd hold my nose and grab it. It's the conditions. We'd be party to a fraud, just as guilty as Byron. And I can't – '

'You don't have to.' Jake held up his hand. 'You're flogging a dead horse. We came out in the same place. You see, Rosemary pointed out a few facts to me. For instance, when my late, lamented father fucked the duck, guess what happened?'

'The Jacob Stern Company went under.'

'That's not all.' Jake's smile had an odd quality of triumph, as though he'd finally won a terrible battle against a particularly tenacious foe. 'What happened was, nothing happened. Not one damned thing!'

Cameron spoke with extreme care. 'You mean no one went after you?'

'You got it. Not the SEC. Not even the Board of Govenors of the New York Stock Exchange. No one! They investigated every nook and cranny, looked in closets, under mattresses, and concluded I was an innocent victim. I fell into a tub of shit and came up smelling like the rose I really am. I was free

513

to walk the streets, to look for a job and get on with my life. Tim hired me two weeks later.' Jake sighed. 'You know, Cameron, I have a hunch the sky looks a lot bluer when you're not looking at it through prison bars. And with old Elmer's scheme there's always that possibility.'

Cameron reached impulsively across the desk and clasped Jake's hand. In all their years together, Cameron had never seen Jake so calm and resolute. Thanks to Rosemary, the crisis they were going through had enabled him to put the Jacob Stern Company behind him once and for all.

The intercom then buzzed. 'Margo Bayless is here,' Della said. 'She has a package for you from Byron Miller that she says is important. She insists on seeing you.'

'Show her in.' Cameron switched off the intercom.

There was a knock and Margo slipped past Della who was holding the door for her. She was wearing old, worn jeans, scuffed black leather boots, and a heavy woollen sweater that somehow managed to seem too tight. She had on no makeup, and her hair needed combing. She too looked as though she'd been up all night, and not celebrating. She was carrying a large manila envelope under her arm, the kind used by lawyers. When she spoke, her voice was subdued, even frightened.

'Byron asked me to deliver this to you. He said you'd understand.' Margo dropped the envelope on Cameron's desk and turned to leave.

'Wait a minute,' Cameron called out. 'Where's Byron?'

'In there,' Margo said, pointing at the envelope. Suddenly, she started to cry, then ran out of the office.

Cameron eyed the package as though it were a letter bomb that might explode at any minute. Cautiously, she slipped off the rubber band and dumped the contents on her desk. Two rectangles wrapped in tissue paper made a clunking sound as they landed. Cameron knew instantly what they were, but to satisfy Jake's curiosity, she unwrapped them. There were two pieces of clear Lucite. Buried in each was a print of one of the two Life Sciences tombstones. The first for $2 million and the second for $50 million. The only other items in the package were a brown envelope and a sealed white envelope. The white envelope was addressed to Miss Cameron Hightower and the words 'Personal' and 'Confidential' were printed in a bold handwriting. Cameron opened the brown envelope first and took out a stock certificate for 350,000 shares of Life Sciences made out to Byron Miller. Cameron turned the certificate over; Byron had endorsed it. She studied the signature thoughtfully before handing the certificate to Jake.

Jake took hold of the piece of paper with his thumb and forefinger, handling it gingerly. Jake had seen thousands of similar stock certificates, but he minutely examined the ornate green scroll on the face of this one. When he looked at the endorsement, his face was a study in confusion. With Byron's signature on the certificate, Cameron or he – or anyone for that matter – could write their name in the proper place and claim ownership of 350,000 shares of Life Sciences stock. Given the morning bid of $125 a share, that piece of paper was worth a large fortune.

'Jesus Christ!' he muttered. 'Forty-two million dollars on the hoof. Payable to anyone. What the hell is he pulling now?' But Jake's anger was diluted by a grudging respect, partially generated by the fact that Byron was worth over $40 million, on paper at least. It further impressed him that Byron was literally giving the money away.

'I don't know what he's doing.' Cameron picked up the sealed white envelope and looked at Jake, suddenly aware of an overwhelming need to be alone when she opened the envelope.

Jake saw her expression and glanced at the sealed envelope.

He'd also noted the words 'Personal' and 'Confidential'. The insecure Jake of an earlier time would have ridden roughshod over the instructions, lacking the confidence that Cameron would tell him what Byron had written. But this new Jake could wait. If Cameron considered it appropriate, she would reveal the contents of the envelope; if not, it was none of his business. He started to say something, then shook his head and left.

Cameron barely heard the door shut; her attention was riveted on the white envelope. Finally, she picked up the letter opener, inserted the blade with care at the edge of the flap, and made a clean cut. There were three smaller envelopes inside. Clumsily, with fumbling fingers, she fished out the envelopes one by one. She spread them on the desk in front of her, perplexed as to which to open first. Then she noticed that each envelope was plainly numbered: 1, 2, 3. Cameron opened the first one.

To the Board of Directors of Life Sciences: I hereby resign my position as Chairman of the Board of Life Sciences, Inc., to take effect immediately. I also resign my position as a member of the Board of Directors of Life Sciences, Inc., also to take effect immediately.

Very truly yours,
Byron Miller

Cameron was too shaken to do anything beyond placing Byron's resignation on top of the stock certificate. She looked at the second envelope, then slowly opened it and read the contents of the letter inside.

Dear Cameron,
As you know, I betrayed the trust you placed in me and perpetrated a fraud – pure and simple. For that reason, I've signed over my stock in blank so that you can use the shares as you see fit. Hopefully, they may be of some small help in undoing the disaster

I've caused. To this same end, I've resigned my position at Life Sciences. With the proper person running the company, Life Sciences will become the great success we both want it to be . . .

Byron went on to state vehemently – Cameron could almost hear his impassioned voice – that Life Sciences must end its association with the Hansen Company. He'd been coerced by Elmer Hansen into making the fraudulent delivery. The whole thing was a gigantic hoax intended to help Elmer Hansen win his proxy fight with Cyrus Hansen. Once that was accomplished, Elmer had a plan to take over Life Sciences.

As Cameron read on, a blush covered her face. Byron explained that Hansen told him of buying her silence. For this, more than anything else, Byron was full of guilt. He'd been a coward, but it had finally dawned on him that he wasn't the only one Elmer Hansen would ruin. When Elmer Hansen cancelled the contract – as he planned to do after the proxy fight – the collapse of Life Sciences' stock could lead to the collapse of FitzGerald Associates. Elmer merely intended to exploit her and discard her when he had no further use for her.

Byron concluded by asking her to read the contents of envelope number 3, which would help her to understand why the old man could muscle him. Should she need a scapegoat to throw to the wolves, he was reachable at his apartment. Since razors were painful, acid worse, guns could wound and nooses give way, he'd stick around. His signature was hurriedly scrawled at the bottom of the page.

Cameron added Byron's letter to the pile and slit open the third envelope. Inside was a single sheet of paper listing Adam Miller's criminal activities.

Now she understood everything, more than she wanted to understand. She tried to imagine what it would be like going through life with the ghost of Adam Miller pursuing her. Byron had as much in common with his family – Adam Miller – as she had with the current generation of Hightowers. The difference was that she'd been lucky. Geraldine had found and nurtured her. If there had been no Geraldine, the Hightower clan would have tossed her to whatever wolves were prowling.

But Byron had had only his mother, and Sara Miller was clearly not someone Byron could lean on for support.

Tentatively, Cameron reached for the phone. Once before she hadn't called Cyrus when she should have, and she'd lived the last two years with the results of those few days of cowardice. She must not make the same mistake again. Yet she hesitated. Even as Byron had feared the world's judgement, so she was afraid of Cyrus's judgement, once he learned that she had seriously considered accepting his grandfather's bribe. In precisely the way of the suspicious, the condemned, she felt demeaned and helpless. All the more so because Cyrus was Gary's father. How could she see him again and not mention Gary? The urge to tell Cyrus of his son was growing like a physical need. She forced herself to close her mind to that hunger. With a sudden, swift movement, she picked up the phone and punched the numbers of Cyrus's private line. The phone rang five times, and just as she was about to hang up, feeling a mixture of dismay and relief, the phone was picked up.

'Hansen here.'

'Cyrus, it's Cameron. Please listen to me. I have something to tell you.' She spoke rapidly, determined to get all the facts out in the open. She told him everything, starting with Harry Horn's call and ending with Elmer Hansen's offer of $12 million for her silence. When she finished, the only sounds that could be heard were the faint cracklings of telephone line noise.

Finally, Cyrus said, 'I had a feeling yesterday that you knew something I didn't. But not this.' He seemed to be thinking the matter through as he spoke. 'In other words, my grandfather tried to buy you.' He spoke so softly that Cameron pressed the receiver tightly to her ear. 'And you said, "Thanks, but no thanks." Or you will say it?'

'Yes. I'm rejecting his offer. I'm going to the SEC later this morning and tell them everything.'

'What about Miller's role in this mess?'

'Byron has written a full confession. He names Elmer Hansen as the moving force behind the fraud. He's resigned as chairman of the board and endorsed his Life Sciences stock over to me. The verdict is in. He's guilty, but with a twist. Byron the huckster never sold a single share of the stock in the company, never profited from any of his scam promotion. The only money he took out of Life Sciences was his salary.'

'Why did he let my grandfather push him around?' Cyrus asked.

'If one knows the right buttons, most people are pushable. Elmer knew how to push Byron.'

'Thank you for telling me all this,' he said. 'Now I'd like you to do me a favour.'

'If I can.'

'Do nothing until I see you. Above all, do not contact the SEC. I'll be there in thirty minutes.'

'I'll wait.'

Cameron was enveloped in a strange feeling of peace while she waited for Cyrus. She was a drowning person going down for the third time, choking and gasping for air, yet too tired to continue to struggle. She had done what she had to do. She could do no more. With the long fall of hope, she felt the exhausted peace that comes with an acceptance of failure.

FitzGerald Associates would sink into oblivion. The firm would become only a name, sometimes remembered on Wall Street when people gossiped about the great, old days.

She was still lost in her reverie when Cyrus arrived. Instead of accepting her automatic suggestion that he sit down, he paced about the room as though possessed. Then he stood before her and stared at her face, his hands resting on her desk. There occurred between them a mute exchange.

At last he said in a quiet voice, 'I'm glad about your decision.'

'I'm not glad and I'm not sad. I wish I could take a high moral tone, but I can't. I was tempted – really tempted.' Her face was excessively pale, her eyes half filled with tears, warning him of her wounds.

'We're all tempted sometimes.' With a gesture bordering on disgust, Cyrus flung himself into the chair opposite her. 'It's been very hard for us. Too hard. And I brought it all down on our heads.'

His saying this so unexpectedly forced Cameron to look at him differently. She saw something she had never seen before. Yes, he wanted her sexually, but that wasn't it. She knew her own merciless need for him. But it came as a shock to her that she might affect him the same way – as a compelling necessity.

'You did love me, didn't you?' she asked with some amazement, surrendering to a feeling both humble and stoic.

'I've always loved you. Since the day I saved your life.' He seemed to say this quite as much for his own relief as for her knowledge. 'Anyway, I've been punished sufficiently for my mistake.'

'*You* were punished?'

'You think you're the only one who suffered?'

'I only hoped you did. Forgive me,' Cameron said.

'There's nothing to forgive. More than anyone else, I

520

wanted to believe in you. So, of course, I looked for fatal flaws.' Cyrus smiled, and it appeared to Cameron that he had not smiled that way since they were very young and growing up in Princeton.

They were closer now and more complete than they had been when they were lovers. Cyrus leaned forward, his hand resting lightly on Cameron's desk. Slowly his fingers walked across the surface of the desk towards her. Almost like a ballet, Cameron's hand duplicated his movement until their hands met. First their fingertips touched, tentatively, seeking a deeper grasp. Then entwined. Their palms pressed together. It was as though their nerve endings were joined. Cyrus's rapid pulse stimulated Cameron's heart to beat faster. The longing in Cameron's body was intensified by the longing she could feel in Cyrus. Their eyes brushed.

Finally Cyrus said with a low, incredulous laugh, 'Yes, I loved you. I love you now. And I trust you. I never thought I could feel this way again.'

There was nothing for Cameron to say. All other feelings had to be communicated with their bodies . . . later. But now there were other matters to settle. With her free hand, she pushed a pile of papers towards Cyrus. This Cyrus could be trusted with Byron's secret. He looked at her questioningly, then glanced quickly at the history of Adam Miller. A low groan escaped from his lips. Of all men, Cyrus understood running away from one's family.

'No wonder he heeled.' Cyrus's fingers tightened around hers. 'We must deal with my grandfather first. When were you supposed to give him your answer?'

'By three o'clock Saturday.'

'Can you hold off notifying the SEC until Monday?'

'As long as FitzGerald Associates does no trading in the stock based on this inside information, I can wait.'

'Good. Call my grandfather and confirm the Saturday

521

meeting.' As Cyrus spoke, a design formed in his mind. 'Here's what we'll do.'

After Cyrus left, Cameron felt a mingling of relief, regret, and confusion that he'd made no suggestion they see each other before she picked him up at the Princeton Junction railroad station at 2:45 on Saturday. If he had, they undoubtedly would have ended up making love. She might have told him about Gary. But if she did that, suppose he misunderstood? Suppose he felt obligated? She didn't want a man who felt obligated. No! She was not prepared to tell Cyrus he had a son. Not yet. The idea gave her a queer pang. Maybe to dream is to hope? Could she influence the future by hope?

31

As she had a week earlier, Cameron stopped the car at the red brick guardhouse protecting the Hansen Company headquarters. This time Cyrus sat next to her in the front seat. The guard remembered her, and they were admitted to the parking lot.

As they got out of the car, Cameron carried her attaché case, holding Byron's papers and something more – something she had chosen not to mention to Cyrus.

When they exited from the small elevator at the top floor Cyrus looked around. Cameron saw his mouth tighten in a very private pain. 'Come on,' he said roughly. 'We don't want to keep him waiting. Knowing my grandfather, he's probably seen us arrive.'

Elmer Hansen's secretary was once again busy at her typewriter, but as soon as she saw them she picked up the phone.

'They're here, Mr Hansen . . . Yes, sir.' Harriet Greene managed a weak smile. 'You're expected. Go right in.'

'Cyrus!' Elmer said, standing up from behind his rolltop desk. 'What a pleasant surprise! Thank you for bringing me my grandson, Cameron.' Although he expressed surprise, Cameron had a sudden feeling of apprehension. She wondered to what extent he had factored Cyrus's presence into his plans? 'How long has it been? Twenty years at least?' There appeared to be a note of genuine pleasure in Elmer's greeting, and once again Cameron had the distinct impression that she'd acted exactly as Elmer Hansen had anticipated she would. Elmer continued, 'I'm forgetting my manners. Please sit down.' He gestured towards two chairs facing the window.

Cyrus looked long and soberly at the blue sky. 'No planes in the air today. It should be safe enough.'

Cameron winced and glanced at Elmer. He seemed not to have heard.

Elmer spoke first. 'I'm confused, Cameron. When we spoke Thursday, you indicated that you'd have your answer ready today. But judging from the presence of Cyrus, you have no need of my money.'

'No, I have great need of your money,' Cameron admitted. 'But there's the question of your terms.'

'You could have told me that on the phone.' Elmer's voice deepened. 'Why are you here?'

Cameron smiled. 'While I enjoy a good fight, Mr Hansen, I enjoy even more picking the winner.' She spoke with bubbling good humour. 'I think of this as a contest for my support. And may the best man win.'

'Let's dispense with the bad comedy, Cameron. I know where your loyalties lie, but I don't give a damn. You've served your purpose.'

By not so much as a flicker of her eyes or the slightest tightening of her easy smile did Cameron give any clue as to her thoughts. Elmer Hansen had confirmed her first impression. She was supposed to bring Cyrus to the meeting. The reason was obvious. He wanted to find out firsthand how strong a position Cyrus had in the fight for control of the company. It was interesting. For once, Elmer Hansen's wishes coincided with those of his grandson.

Elmer turned to Cyrus. 'I read your proxy solicitation with interest, Cyrus – and curiosity. What on earth makes you think that you – a man who inherited hundreds of millions of dollars and who has never really worked a day in his life – that you have either the ability, the knowledge, or the experience to run the Hansen Company? In the unlikely event that you do manage to win the proxy fight?'

Cyrus waited for the sound of his grandfather's strong voice to die down. The direct attack was in keeping with his grandfather's technique and in line with what he'd expected. When he answered, he spoke with a deliberate calm. 'I've spent years acquiring companies and funding start-up situations. There's little I don't know about managing a company.'

Elmer did not disguise his contempt. 'You compare those insignificant operations to the Hansen Company? One division of ours is larger than any company you've ever acquired. And having made your pitifully small acquisitions, what did you do? Have you ever sat in the chief executive's chair and made the countless daily decisions necessary to run a company? Is this product for us? Is this one ready for national distribution? Does that ad campaign work? Can that man handle the West Coast? Do we need a new division or can that new drug be folded into the US Operating Company? And what about bank lines of credit? Is this the time to float a new stock issue? Or a bond issue?'

Cameron heard all the pride in Elmer's voice as he recited only a few of the business questions with which he had dealt daily, and successfully, for over sixty years.

'No! Not you!' Elmer let himself go, enjoying himself to the fullest. 'You hired managers, got on your boat, and sailed off into the sunset. Leaving the managers behind to do the drudge work of running the company. Well, listen to me, young man, you can't do that with the Hansen Company. It's too large. We gross over ten *billion* dollars a year. You have to sit in this office and make all those decisions yourself. And you're not up to it. You have neither the experience nor the ability nor the stamina.'

Again, Cyrus waited for the echo of his grandfather's voice to subside. Then he laughed and applauded loudly. 'Well

525

done, old man. Well done. Practising your speech for the shareholders' meeting?'

'There'll be no speech. No need for one.' Elmer knew he had allowed himself to be carried away and had revealed too much of his plans. But if Cyrus responded in kind, it was worth it. 'You have something to say?'

Cyrus approached Elmer's desk and lowered his face until his eyes were on the same level as his grandfather's. Cameron stared at the two profiles, fascinated. They were so much alike. Elmer's showed some of the forty-odd years' difference between them but much less than one might expect. It took little imagination to envision Cyrus sitting in his grandfather's place.

'Listen to me, old man.' Cyrus's voice was soft, caressing, and lethal. He walked behind the chairs. 'This incompetent old man wants to hang on to power long after he should have retired. This incompetent old man will do anything to keep his power. Including committing fraud, a criminal fraud that will severely damage the Hansen Company. Your company!'

Elmer glanced at Cameron, who gave him her prettiest smile. 'Don't you agree, Mr Hansen, that his knowing the facts makes the fight more even?'

'In any case,' Cyrus continued, 'this incompetent old man . . .' Watching Elmer closely, Cameron sensed that Cyrus's continuous repetition of 'incompetent old man' was affecting Elmer as Cyrus intended it to. 'This incompetent old man permitted a false release to be put out that Life Sciences had finally delivered machine-made Thermoscans. Permitted it? Hell, no! Elmer Hansen ordered it. Elmer Hansen knew that the Thermoscans had been assembled by hand.'

Elmer left the protection of his desk. He stood toe-to-toe with his grandson. 'What you say is a lie,' he stated coolly. 'Only one thing is true. When I discovered that the shipment was actually handmade, I did not reject it as a fraud. The handmade Thermoscans will do very well for a small test market. And by the time we've finished testing them, that young man, Byron Miller, will have his production equipment operating.' He glanced at Cameron. 'Would you have preferred that I made a self-righteous, dramatic announcement?' Elmer's voice became stentorian. 'I have just discovered that Byron Miller is a fraud. The Hansen Company will sever its contract with Life Sciences immediately.' His voice dropped back to its normal baritone. 'Consider the damage such an announcement would have caused, not to the Hansen Company, but to Life Sciences.' He emphasized his next words, staring at Cameron. 'And to all the shareholders of Life Sciences!'

Cyrus spoke through his laughter. 'You pious old hypocrite. You did it all for the shareholders of Life Sciences? Do you really expect anyone to believe in your altruism?'

Elmer drew himself up to his full height. 'You call it altruism, but I call it good business. And the shareholders of the Hansen Company will agree because they believe in me. I built the Hansen Company. The company is mine and will remain mine. I see no point in continuing this useless argument. You know the way out.'

Cyrus leaned forward, bracing himself on Elmer's desk. 'I can prove that you not only knowingly accepted the handmade Thermoscans, but you were responsible for having them made in the first place.'

'Prove it? I doubt that very much '

Cyrus turned to Cameron, who carefully opened her attaché case. She handed Elmer a photocopy of Byron's letter to her. 'After our last meeting, I came to a few conclusions of my own. This letter confirms what I suspected.'

Elmer scanned Byron's letter and shrugged. 'This is your proof? I'm not impressed. A letter from a cheap promoter. The son of a con man and a swindler. The letter isn't worth a damn.' Elmer's icy blue eyes sought his grandson's face. 'No one will believe you. Not with Miller as your witness.'

'They'll believe me. Wait and see,' Cyrus replied.

In Cameron's ears Cyrus sounded unconvincing.

'You're mistaken,' Elmer said with satisfaction. Having estimated the total strength of Cyrus's accusations, he felt secure and free to shift his tactic to gain his next objective. 'I have held up my head in many a storm, against colder and harsher winds than you can stir up. I will deny everything. It will be my word against Miller's. And my years as chairman of the Hansen Company will carry the day.'

As Cameron listened, she came to realize how strong Elmer's position really was. Byron would make a poor witness. She'd been right to make special provisions for just that possibility.

'And to consolidate my position, I shall immediately cancel the Hansen Company contract with Life Sciences.'

'Old man, you disappoint me. You've missed my point completely.' There was strong rebuke in Cyrus's tone.

'I missed nothing.' Elmer studied Cyrus with grave attention. 'If you're referring to your proxy fight, you'll lose. Your case against me is fatally flawed by the bias of your two witnesses.'

'I won't lose. Before the meeting takes place, there will be releases to the media. Newspapers, television networks, the business magazines – they'll all pick up the story. Enough mud will stick to you to raise doubts in the shareholders' minds. Doubts about your age, your mental competence, your ability to continue to manage the company.' Cyrus's voice carried a warning like an animal baring its teeth.

Elmer concealed his impatience. All the bad publicity in the world would have little effect on the company. Rather than confront Cyrus with the truth, he chose a more devious course. He still had his real objective to win. He spoke thoughtfully. 'It would do that – and more – if you could make your charges stick. But you still lack the experience to run the Hansen Company.' Elmer paused, preparing to strike. 'So I have a suggestion. Consider it a compromise,' he added gently.

'I'm listening.'

From the moment Elmer had first made his offer to Cameron, he'd been aware of the possibility that she might go to Cyrus. In fact, if she hadn't, he planned to use his control of her company to force her to bring Cyrus to him. Everything he'd done up to this point was an attempt to soften up Cyrus and to prepare him for what he was about to say.

'Instead of fighting me, Cyrus, join me. It would be the way it began. Hansen and Hansen.'

Once Elmer had scornfully dismissed Byron Miller's testimony, the meeting should have ended. When it didn't Cyrus had puzzled over what was really in his grandfather's mind. Now he knew. He waited, sure that the old man had more to say.

'You join the company as president. As soon as you know enough, you'll become chief operating officer.'

'You'll remain chief executive officer?'

'Yes.'

'And you'll teach me?'

'Everything I know.'

'Including how you forced Byron into making that false delivery?' Cameron asked, joining the conversation.

Both men's heads swivelled towards her. Deeply involved with each other, they had momentarily forgotten about Cameron. Elmer laughed. 'It wasn't very hard. Everybody has a weak spot. Miller has more than most.'

'Then you did force Miller?' Cameron insisted.

Elmer was trying to read his grandson's face, but it told

him nothing. Impatiently he looked at Cameron. Her face was open and guileless. Anxious to end the interruption, Elmer shrugged. 'You care too much about why Miller made the delivery. But it makes no difference. Here, in this room, and only in this room, yes. Miller did exactly as I ordered him to do.' He turned back to Cyrus. 'About my offer?'

When he stared at Elmer now, it seemed as though Cyrus had released the restraining leash which he, himself, had fastened around his neck. 'You must think I'm a complete idiot,' he said. His voice was strained and barely audible. 'Come to the window, old man.' Despite himself, Elmer was drawn to stand next to Cyrus in front of the window. 'Look up there,' Cyrus said, pointing to the sky. The sun was low over the trees. 'Do you see anything?' Elmer shook his head. 'No? Do you hear anything?' A second negative motion from Elmer. 'Do you feel anything?'

Elmer exploded. 'What the hell are you talking about? There's nothing to see, nothing to hear, and nothing to feel.'

'There is. Look!' Cyrus gestured towards the sun. There's an old aeroplane – a Spad – circling in the sun. It's starting its dive towards us,' Cyrus whispered in Elmer's ear. 'Can't you hear the sound of the motor? The wind in the wings?' Elmer tried to turn away. 'Here it comes. Duck!' Cyrus's cry resounded through the room. 'Crash!' he screamed. 'Feel the heat of the fire, old man? The smell of the burning flesh? That was your son and my father who burned to death out there.' Cyrus pushed his grandfather into the vacant chair. 'He tried to kill you.'

The reminder of how his son had died might have shaken another man, but Elmer Hansen only glared at his grandson. 'He tried, all right. And like everything else he tried, he failed.'

'He lost his nerve, the poor bastard,' Cyrus murmured. 'If

I ever agreed to work with you, I'd end up trying to kill you. And I wouldn't fail.'

Elmer Hansen threw off Cyrus's restraining hand. He was barely able to contain his fury. 'I'll fight you every inch of the way, and I'll win.'

'And take the Hansen Company down with you. Having destroyed your only son in the sacred name of the Hansen Company, you're now perfectly willing to drag its name through the muck to save it from me. Just to keep yourself in power.'

'You have delusions, Cyrus. You started this fight. If the Hansen Company suffers any damage, it will be because you chose not to work with me.'

Cyrus exhaled sharply. 'I'll see you at the shareholders' meeting.' He held out his hand to Cameron. 'Are you ready to leave?'

'Not quite, Cyrus,' Cameron said. She stood up and stepped between the two men. 'I never believed your grandfather would listen to you – or, for that matter, to anyone. Or that you would listen to him. So I made my own arrangements for this meeting.' Her voice, her posture, everything about her carried authority.

Cyrus looked at Cameron in bewilderment, and Elmer stared at her with angry suspicion. This was a Cameron neither of them had seen before. The Cameron who had survived the year alone on St Croix, who had surmounted the tragic death of Tim FitzGerald, who had taken over a penniless company and built it into a successful Wall Street house. She'd given Cyrus his chance, put every weapon she possessed at his disposal, and he'd lost. Now the meeting belonged to her.

She opened her attaché case and produced a small tape recorder. She pressed the stop button and then the rewind. After a few seconds, she stopped the tape again and pushed the play button. She'd estimated correctly. The first sound was Elmer laughing. The quality of the tape was thin but perfectly recognizable. Elmer was saying, 'It wasn't very hard. Everybody has a weak spot. Miller has more than most.' Cameron's voice followed. 'Then you did force Miller?' Elmer said, 'You care too much about why Miller made the delivery. But it makes no difference. Here, in this room, and only in this room, yes. Miller did exactly as I ordered him to do.' Cameron stopped the tape and replaced the recorder in her attaché case.

'I imagine, Mr Hansen, having a tape recording of you admitting you conspired to commit fraud alters the odds on how the shareholders will vote. I've just placed my bet on Cyrus Hansen.'

'That evidence is not admissible in court,' Elmer stated.

'Court!' Cameron laughed. 'Who said anything about court? Add this to Byron's letter, and the media will have a field day.' Cameron did not exult in what she'd done. She despised the tactic. But she'd learned that one does not survive as an innocent. Having dealt with Elmer Hansen once before, she'd counted on his concentration on his grandson to trap him into admitting privately what he would convincingly deny in public. She had waited patiently for the precise moment to make her move. Now she looked at Cyrus, but not for his approval. If she lost FitzGerald Associates and The Farm, if she lost her son's inheritance, she intended to make damn sure that Elmer Hansen lost the Hansen Company. All she wanted from Cyrus was his understanding of the power she'd given him.

Cyrus's face was a mixture of surprise, approval, and chagrin. He did understand and appreciate what she'd handed him. He only wished he'd done as well.

Elmer sat very still. The stockholders' meeting would have been a dirty fight, but he'd have won it. Now everything was changed. That tape recording made the difference. Although his face revealed nothing, he accepted that he had lost. He'd lost in private, and he'd lost in public. Yet, in the final analysis, he drew some small satisfaction from the knowledge that Cyrus had not beaten him. He'd beaten himself. His compulsion to convince Cyrus to work with him, to provide the Hansen Company with another Hansen to run it, had trapped him into a foolish blunder with regard to Cameron. His need for Cyrus had betrayed him.

'You expect me to resign?' he asked in a neutral voice.

'I don't give a damn what you do,' Cameron seethed. 'Resign or get thrown out.'

'And you, Cyrus? What do you want?'

'Resign,' Cyrus said. 'Plead ill health or old age. It makes no difference to me what reason you give. The next board meeting is in ten days. Resign then and have your puppets elect me in your place. And vote your stock for my board at the next election.'

Cameron studied Elmer. He appeared a beaten man. But was he? There was a glitter in his eye.

'If I do this,' Elmer asked, 'will that end it?'

'That will end it,' Cyrus answered. 'You retire with your reputation intact. And the Hansen Company remains clean.'

'You sound like my own father. A cut-rate preacher praying over a corpse he never knew. My reputation!' Elmer said scornfully. 'What the hell do I care about my reputation? I'm eighty-nine years old and worth over a billion dollars. If I do this – and I said *if* – I'll do it because I *am* the Hansen Company. That tape has done what neither you nor all the Millers in the world could do, it's made me a liability to my own company.'

Cyrus gave him a stony look. 'In that case, you can do something quite valuable for your company, something I intended to do. Make a tender offer for Life Sciences.'

Elmer placed his two hands on the arms of his chair. He stared at his grandson. 'You want me to buy that company?'

'Yes. I want the Hansen Company to own the manufacturing as well as the distribution rights to the Thermoscan. And to all the other products that company is working on.'

Elmer's chest heaved in silent laughter. 'That's what I had in mind.'

'I know. Offer $130 a share.'

'No!' Elmer said sharply.

'Yes!' Cyrus insisted.

'That's more than it's currently selling for.'

'That's how we make sure we get it. I've watched you for years, old man. We're very much alike, but we also have our differences. I won't steal the company. I'll buy it. Thanks to the financial strength of the Hansen Company, we can afford to pay top dollar for the company.'

Cameron said nothing. At $130 a share for her stock, she'd be covered at the banks.

Elmer stood up, walked about the office, and stopped, facing Cyrus. Slowly, he nodded.

'I'd like to be alone now, if you don't mind?' he said then.

After Cameron and Cyrus left, Elmer felt a curious sadness. Cyrus was the son he had wanted Ellie to be; someone who cared as much as he did about the Hansen name, who stood to lose as much as he did if the Hansen Company was damaged. Oh, yes! Cyrus would manage the company properly; he would build on what he'd created. That was as it should be. When all was said and done, losing wasn't so bad. Cyrus was coming home, ready to be the Hansen of the Hansen Company.

Elmer settled himself again in his chair and looked over the lawn. The glow of the setting sun washed the office in pink and gold, and a strange cold began to creep into Elmer's bones. It had been a long and arduous life. He was tired, very tired. He should go home, but he needed more time to collect himself. And at that, wasn't this office really his home? In a drowsy way he thought that if he had only one final wish, he would wish that the time remaining to him on earth be brief.

32

The invisible network that carries corporate gossip is a mysterious phenomenon, but never more remarkable than when one is the focus of the news. As Cameron and Cyrus drove past the Hansen Company guardhouse, she was given a respectful salute. It was as though something in the air told the guard that a major change had taken place that afternoon at the Hansen Company. The old order had given way to the new.

When Cameron reached Route 1, she turned left in the direction of Princeton. Cyrus was resting against the black leather headrest, his eyes half closed. They swung around the traffic circle at the junction of Route 1 and Washington Street, and Cameron pulled onto the dirt shoulder. It was dusk, but she would have done the same thing in the daylight. She put her arms around Cyrus, held him close to her for long minutes. She felt the tension in his rigid body begin to seep away.

'It's all right,' she whispered.

'I know. Thanks to you, it's all right.'

'I did what I could.' Cameron started the car again. Neither of them spoke for a while. 'I know how hard it was for you,' Cameron said at last.

When they drove past Hansen Hall, Cyrus's eyes were riveted on the house where he'd grown up. He murmured half to himself and half to Cameron, 'Some victories are defeats.'

'I know,' Cameron said softly. She remembered all her gains that had come from grievous losses. Victories that

536

weren't victories – there should be a special name for them – because they were battles that should never have had to be fought.

'Listen, if you don't feel up to it, we can do it tomorrow,' she said casually.

'It was my idea. I want to do it now.'

'Why now?' she could see, under the surface of his resolution, how troubled he was.

'Because I owe it to him. Not as much as I owe to you. But I still owe it.'

Cyrus was prouder than most men, and because of his pride, also more vulnerable to shame than most men. Cameron watched him accept his own humiliation and pass beyond it.

'I thought I was a better man than he. I'm not.'

Cameron made no further protests. She stopped the car in front of Hightower Farm. The servants had been alerted to the possibility that she might be arriving with Cyrus Hansen. They were to keep themselves out of the way. And under no circumstances was Miss McCarthy, his nurse, to permit Gary to leave his room. Cameron unlocked the front door and led the way to her study. She opened a file cabinet and took out the envelope containing Byron's resignation, Byron's stock certificate, Byron's letter to her, and the one-page history of Byron's father. One by one she placed the documents on her desk. There was almost no colour in Cyrus's face as he concentrated on the papers. Watching him, she realized there was more than Byron's life spread out on the desk. Cyrus was seeing his own life. Although the circumstances were vastly different, Byron and he had much in common. Neither was exempt from the claims of the past.

Cyrus reached for the document containing Adam Miller's history. 'I'm going to tear this up,' he said. Cameron nodded. Meticulously, Cyrus tore the paper into shreds and dropped the pieces into the wastepaper basket. 'That leaves Byron's resignation and his stock certificate.' Cyrus hesitated. 'Are we still in agreement as to what to do about Byron?'

Cameron nodded.

'This should never have happened. But my grandfather has his own way of doing things. Will you call Byron, please?'

Cameron pressed each button carefully. When the call was answered, she came alive.

'Byron! It's Cameron. Cyrus is with me. I'm going to put you on the squawk box. That way we can all talk.' She switched the connection.

'I've been waiting for your call, Cameron.' Byron's voice sounded hollow, his exhaustion flowed through the telephone lines.

'Byron, this is Cyrus Hansen.' Cyrus briefly described the meeting with his grandfather and explained that he was taking over the Hansen Company.

'Congratulations!' Byron said. There was genuine enthusiasm in his voice.

'Byron.' Cameron spoke with scrupulous care. 'As far as we're concerned, Adam Miller is dead and buried. But there are two things. Your resignation and your stock. Because of what has happened, I must accept your resignation, and I can't return the stock.' She paused and looked at Cyrus.

Cyrus picked up the conversation, telling Byron what Cameron and he had decided. 'But there is a place for you at Life Sciences. Working with Harry Horn on new-product development. At the same salary.'

It was impossible to tell whether Byron was laughing or crying. Cameron caught the words, 'Generous . . . very generous . . .' Finally Byron managed to speak coherently. 'I feel too many things right now to make any sense . . .' He coughed and cleared his throat. 'I appreciate your offer, but I can't take it.'

'You don't want the job?' Cameron was surprised.

'If it were only a question of wanting . . .'

'You're upset. You've been under a lot of stress and strain.'

'Oh, sure. Everybody needs a little stress and strain now and then. It gets the adrenaline going and I think I read in *Science* magazine that adrenaline is an anticarcinogen.' It was the old Byron trying his best to sound loose and whippy. 'Anyway, I'd make a lousy corporate employee. I don't wear the right clothes. And I still don't like cafeteria food.'

'Please accept Cyrus's offer. It won't be the same without you. I'd miss you badly.'

Cameron's plea gave Byron an extraordinary moment. 'And I you . . . But, you see, somewhere there's a man with a Bunsen burner and a test tube. He's praying over a miracle of some kind. A miracle that he invented that no one else believes in. He needs me. I need him. And when I find him – '

'But you're needed here. What about Life Sciences?' She almost said, what about us? Our friendship?

'Life Sciences is launched,' Byron continued, making his voice cheerful. 'It'll be a division of the Hansen Company. It doesn't need me.' He paused, his voice getting softer. 'Anyway, I can't. Because of you, Cameron. Because of how I failed you. No. Scratch that. Because of how I failed myself. I have to find my own way back. Alone.' He thought for a moment. 'Well, not quite alone. Margo is coming with me.'

'Byron,' Cyrus said, 'when you find that guy with the Bunsen burner and the miracle, remember Acorn Ventures.'

'Thanks, Cyrus. We'll see. Good-bye, Cameron.'

'Good luck, Byron.'

Byron hung up, and Cameron shut off the speaker. She gave Cyrus a searching look. 'Are you glad he didn't accept?'

'It's better this way. He's too quirky for corporate life. But I have a hunch he'll be back. Sooner than we expect.'

'I think so, too.' Cameron accepted this as a hopeful promise. 'And if the invention works, you'd like the Hansen Company to see it first?'

'Of course. He is what he is. But he has imagination, guts, and an eye for new products.' Cyrus's eyes met hers. He inclined his head and smiled. He was so proud of her, and he wanted her as intensely as he ever had. 'There's still the last item on the agenda to settle. It's time we talked about the future.'

'The future?' Cameron returned his smile. 'It looks like fair weather ahead. You'll be running the Hansen Company. That's a big change for the better. And I'll be at my desk at FitzGerald Associates, no longer dreading the prospect of bankruptcy. What a wonderful change for me.'

'I wasn't thinking about business. I was thinking about us. It might be a good idea if we started seeing each other again.'

'We owe ourselves that at least,' Cameron said breathlessly. 'A second chance, you might say.'

'We owe ourselves more than that. Remember the blueprints for the *Acorn II*?'

Cameron's eyes grew wary. She guessed what might be in his mind, and she sought to head him off. 'Oh . . . Yes. Of course I remember. The plans. The blueprints. They were wonderful. But we were smart to table them. We barely knew each other. Or ourselves.'

'But we do now. I think it's time to revive them.'

'Isn't it a bit premature? I mean . . .' She felt unexpectedly shy seeing all the possibilities for embarrassment that could follow. If he persisted, she might have to tell him about Gary, and she wasn't prepared for that. Not yet. 'I mean . . . Unless I misunderstand you . . .'

'Why are you mumbling?'

'Am I mumbling?'

540

'Yes. And I'm trying to propose.' Somehow he'd managed to get the words out.

Cameron could only stare, hardly daring to believe what she'd heard.

'Did you hear what I said? I'm proposing. I'm asking you to marry me.'

For a long moment, Cameron couldn't trust herself to speak. 'Marry you?' she said at last.

'Marry me. I mean it.' It would have been difficult for Cyrus to look more defenceless.

Cameron sat motionless with lowered lids.

Her stillness prompted a curious reaction in Cyrus. 'What's the matter? You said you love me. We love each other.'

'I do. But I can't marry you.' Cameron started to tremble.

'Why not?'

'I can't!' They stared at each other, and Cameron grew pale. She had no idea how a ready-made family would strike Cyrus. Instant fatherhood could be an unpleasant shock. But she knew she must make up her mind now. If she continued to evade, the newly formed ties between them would snap. When she spoke, she sounded faintly giddy. 'You see, I'm not a free woman.'

'Not free? You're married?'

'Not exactly. But I am committed to someone else.'

Cyrus's imagination spun around, grasping at straws. 'Are you in love with him?'

'I'm not in love with him, but I love him very much.'

Her tone had grown so natural that he felt more at a loss than ever. 'Do I know him?'

'No, but I can introduce you.'

'Some other time, thank you,' Cyrus said in a strangled voice as he stood up to leave.

'No! Now! I've been avoiding it. It might as well be now.'

She came around the desk and stood facing him. 'You can meet him in a few minutes. He's upstairs.'

'Upstairs? He lives with you? I don't understand.'

'I know you don't,' she said softly. 'So come with me.'

Herbert and Greta Coz were having dinner on the terrace of their Central Park South apartment when Gloria Coz Loomis telephoned. She ignored the fact that she might be interrupting her brother's dinner. When Coz came to the phone, she told him she was tired of using Eric Hefflin as her broker. He'd been wrong about National Rec and doubly wrong about Life Sciences. Her friends had made fortunes in the stock, and he had talked her out of buying it. She wondered if her brother would handle her portfolio? And coyly asked if Greta and he would come to Sunday brunch tomorrow? When Coz answered, his voice carried no clue as to his opinion of his sister. He said he'd think about her portfolio. But, 'No. Greta and I can't come to Sunday brunch tomorrow. We're going to a wedding. Cameron Hightower is marrying Cyrus Hansen.'

He hung up, almost smiling.